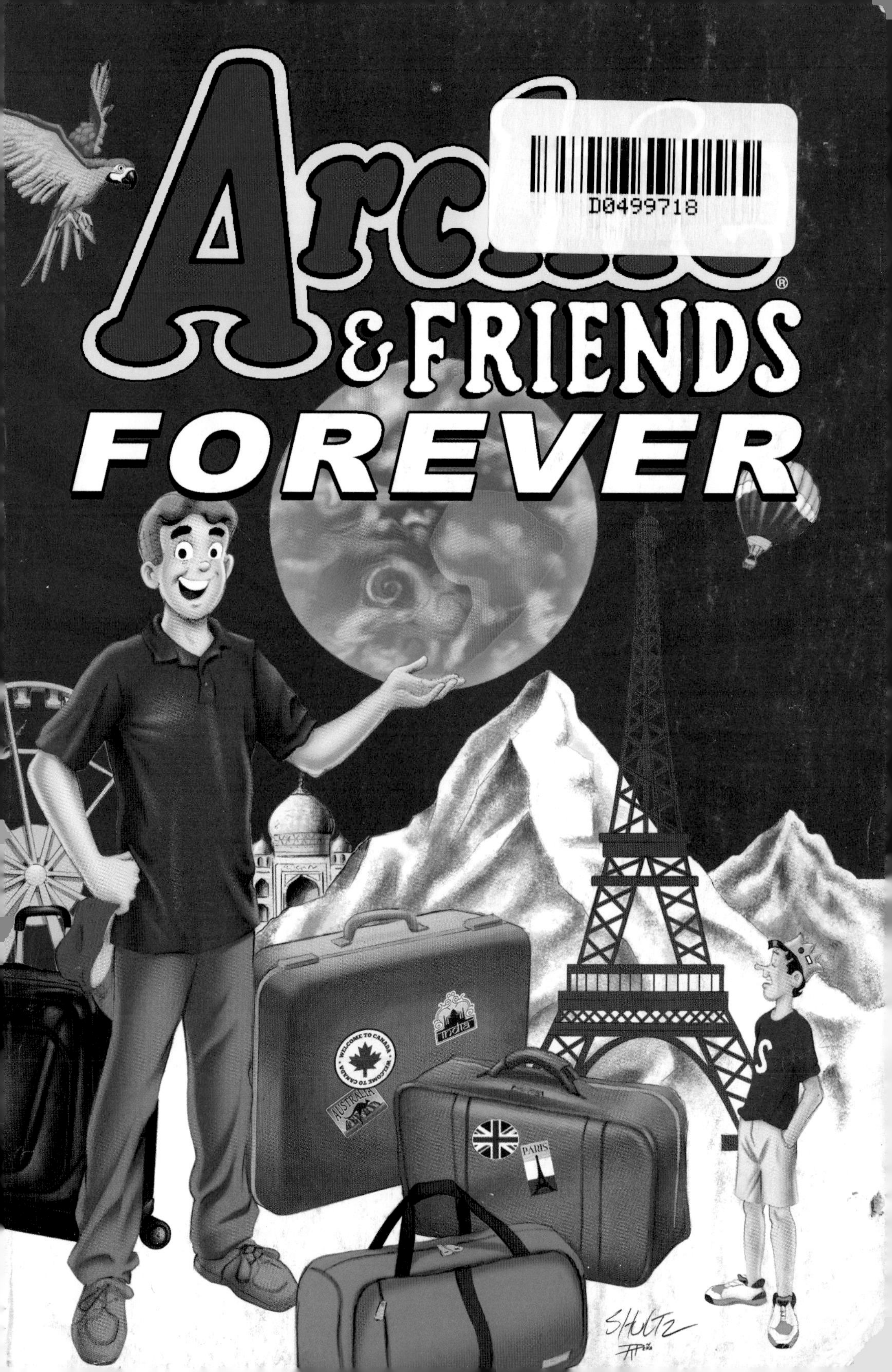

Archie®
& FRIENDS
FOREVER
WELCOME TO CANADA
India
AUSTRALIA
PARIS
SHULTZ

Publisher / Co-CEO: Jon Goldwater

Co-President / Editor-In-Chief: Victor Gorelick

Co-President: Mike Pellerito

Co-President: Alex Segura

Chief Creative Officer: Roberto Aguirre-Sacasa

Chief Operating Officer: William Mooar

Chief Financial Officer: Robert Wintle

Director: Jonathan Betancourt

Production Manager: Stephen Oswald

Art Director: Vincent Lovallo

Lead Designer: Kari McLachlan

Editor: Jamie Lee Rotante

Co-CEO: Nancy Silberkleit

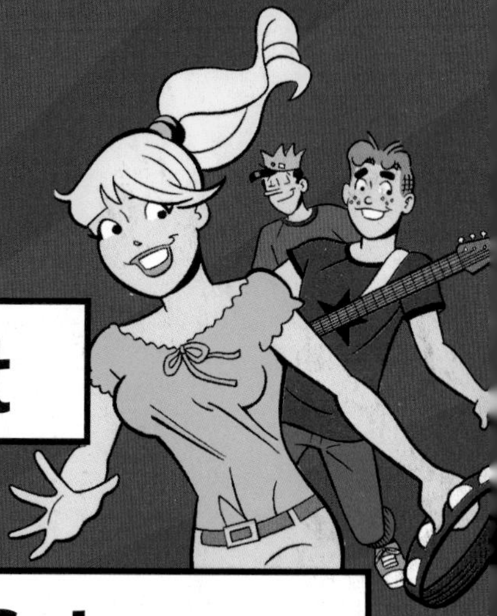

STORIES
Dan Parent

PENCILS
Dan Parent, Bill Galvan, Bill Golliher, Jeff Shultz, Pat & Tim Kennedy

INKS
Jim Amash & Bob Smith

COLORS
Glenn Whitmore

LETTERS
Jack Morelli

Archie® & FRIENDS INTRODUCTION

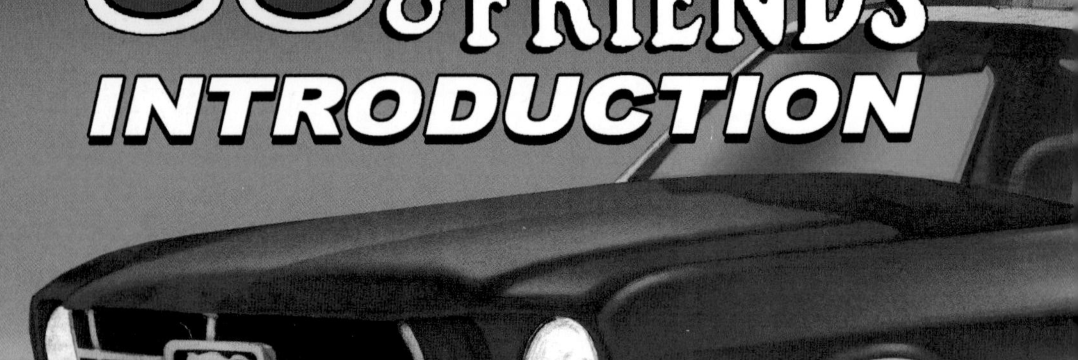

Archie Andrews and all his pals 'n' gals in Riverdale have been providing entertainment for decades—and that's not stopping any time soon! This collection of modern stories told in the classic-style emphasize what everyone loves best about Archie—music, adventure and excitement! From the musical aspirations of The Archies—be it in the recording studio or at the music awards—to fun in the sun

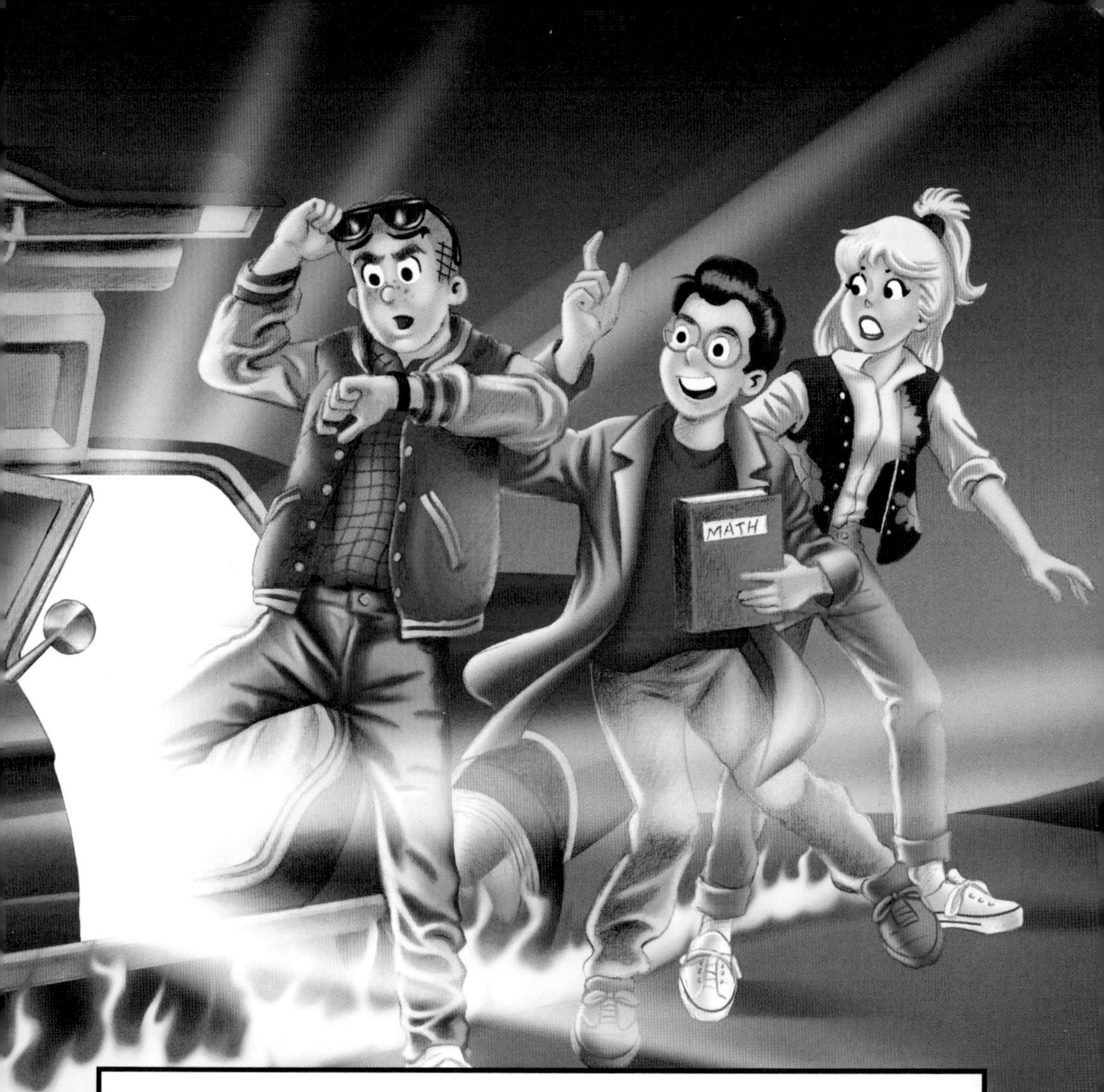
MATH

beach parties; and the amusement doesn't end there—travel along with Archie from his hometown of Riverdale with some high school hijinks, like lab experiments gone awry, to traveling around the globe, from a music tour in the Philippines to a documentary in India, and everywhere in between.

When it comes to Archie, the fun never ends!

Archie & Friends

TABLE OF CONTENTS

8   MUSIC JAM

9   THE FILL-IN!
14   BRIGITTE'S JINGLE JANGLE!
19   AND THE WINNER IS...
24   VIVA LA VINYL!

30   BEACH PARTY

31   BEACH PARTY BLOSSOM
36   WHAT A BREAK!
41   VACATION VEXATION!
46   BEACHWATCH!

52 BACK TO SCHOOL

53 THE FRESHMAN'S GUIDE TO
    RIVERDALE HIGH
58 HOW SHOCKING!
63 DON'T TEST MY PATIENCE
68 IT'S ALL RELATIVE!

74 TRAVEL

75 ON THE ROAD AGAIN!
80 FROM INDIA WITH LOVE!
85 OH, CANADA!
90 WHEN IN ROME...

96 WINTER WONDERLAND

97   BABY IT'S COLD OUTSIDE
102 GIRLS ON TOUR
107 SOMETING FISHY
112 READY, SET, GO!

118 SPECIAL FEATURES

Archie® & FRIENDS
MUSIC JAM

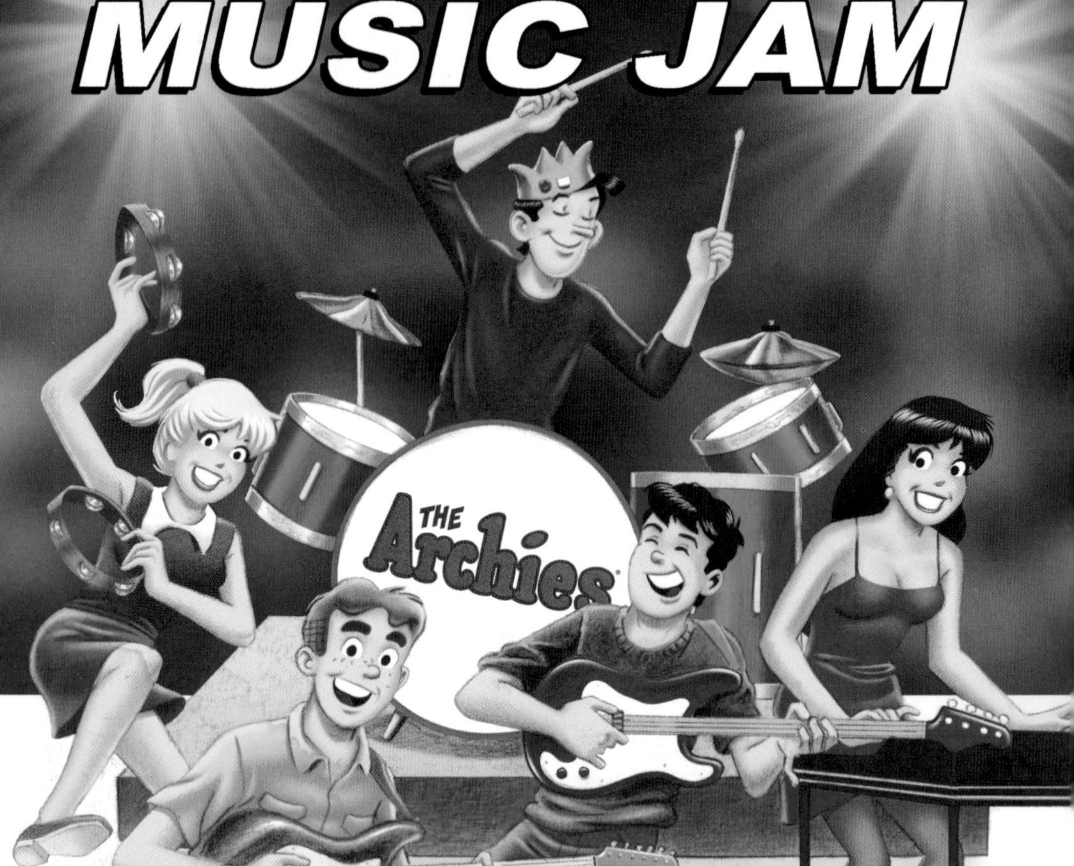
THE
Archies

ART BY JEFF SHULTZ AND ROSARIO "TITO" PEÑA

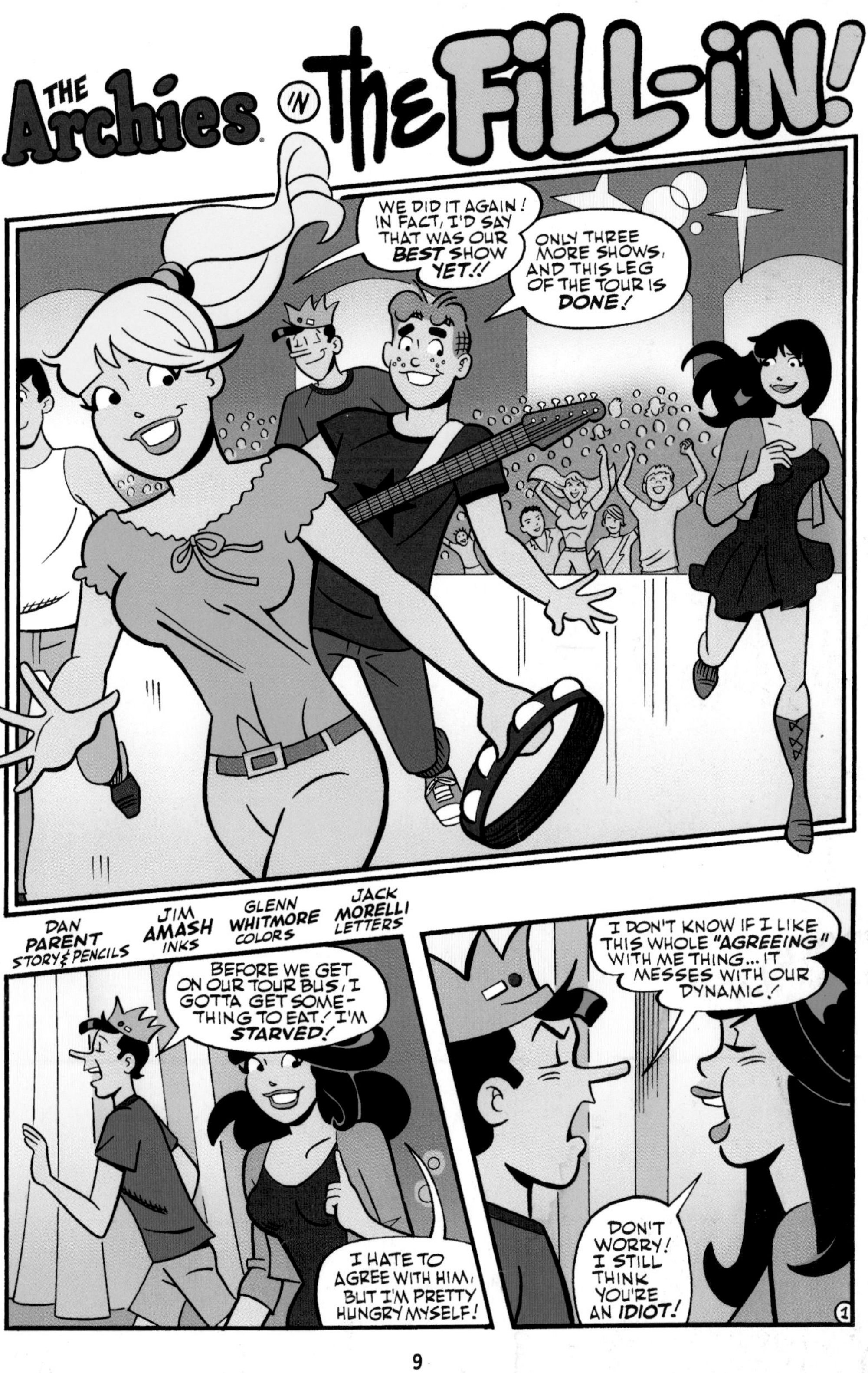
THE Archies IN The FiLL-iN!
WE DID IT AGAIN! IN FACT, I'D SAY THAT WAS OUR BEST SHOW YET!!
ONLY THREE MORE SHOWS, AND THIS LEG OF THE TOUR IS DONE!
DAN PARENT STORY & PENCILS
JIM AMASH INKS
GLENN WHITMORE COLORS
JACK MORELLI LETTERS
BEFORE WE GET ON OUR TOUR BUS, I GOTTA GET SOMETHING TO EAT! I'M STARVED!
I HATE TO AGREE WITH HIM, BUT I'M PRETTY HUNGRY MYSELF!
I DON'T KNOW IF I LIKE THIS WHOLE "AGREEING" WITH ME THING... IT MESSES WITH OUR DYNAMIC!
DON'T WORRY! I STILL THINK YOU'RE AN IDIOT!
1

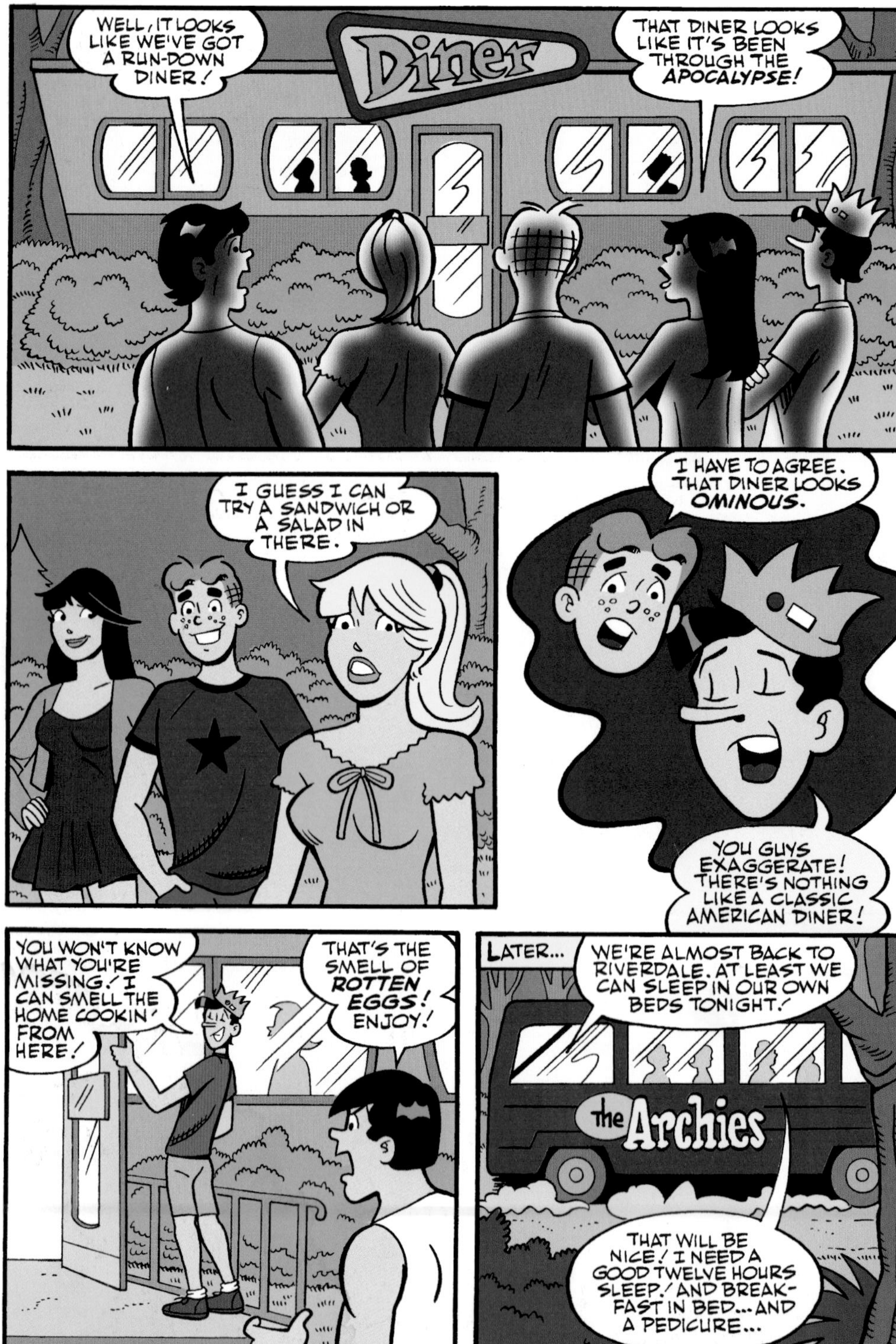
WELL, IT LOOKS LIKE WE'VE GOT A RUN-DOWN DINER!
Diner
THAT DINER LOOKS LIKE IT'S BEEN THROUGH THE APOCALYPSE!
I GUESS I CAN TRY A SANDWICH OR A SALAD IN THERE.
I HAVE TO AGREE. THAT DINER LOOKS OMINOUS.
YOU GUYS EXAGGERATE! THERE'S NOTHING LIKE A CLASSIC AMERICAN DINER!
YOU WON'T KNOW WHAT YOU'RE MISSING! I CAN SMELL THE HOME COOKIN' FROM HERE!
THAT'S THE SMELL OF ROTTEN EGGS! ENJOY!
LATER...
WE'RE ALMOST BACK TO RIVERDALE. AT LEAST WE CAN SLEEP IN OUR OWN BEDS TONIGHT!
the Archies
THAT WILL BE NICE! I NEED A GOOD TWELVE HOURS SLEEP! AND BREAK-FAST IN BED... AND A PEDICURE...
2

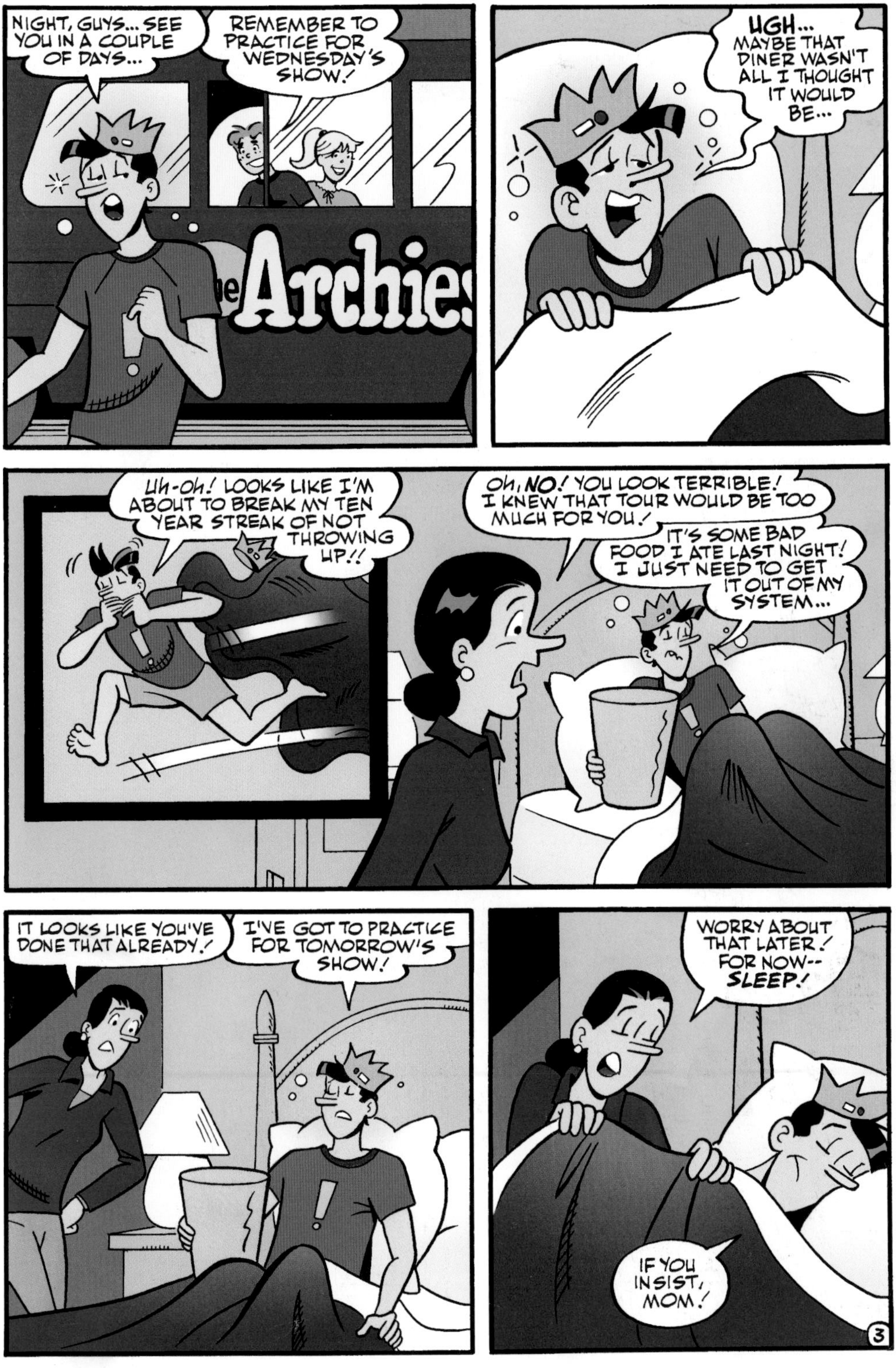
NIGHT, GUYS... SEE YOU IN A COUPLE OF DAYS...
REMEMBER TO PRACTICE FOR WEDNESDAY'S SHOW!
The Archies
UGH... MAYBE THAT DINER WASN'T ALL I THOUGHT IT WOULD BE...
UH-OH! LOOKS LIKE I'M ABOUT TO BREAK MY TEN YEAR STREAK OF NOT THROWING UP!!
OH, NO! YOU LOOK TERRIBLE! I KNEW THAT TOUR WOULD BE TOO MUCH FOR YOU!
IT'S SOME BAD FOOD I ATE LAST NIGHT! I JUST NEED TO GET IT OUT OF MY SYSTEM...
IT LOOKS LIKE YOU'VE DONE THAT ALREADY!
I'VE GOT TO PRACTICE FOR TOMORROW'S SHOW!
WORRY ABOUT THAT LATER! FOR NOW-- SLEEP!
IF YOU INSIST, MOM!
3

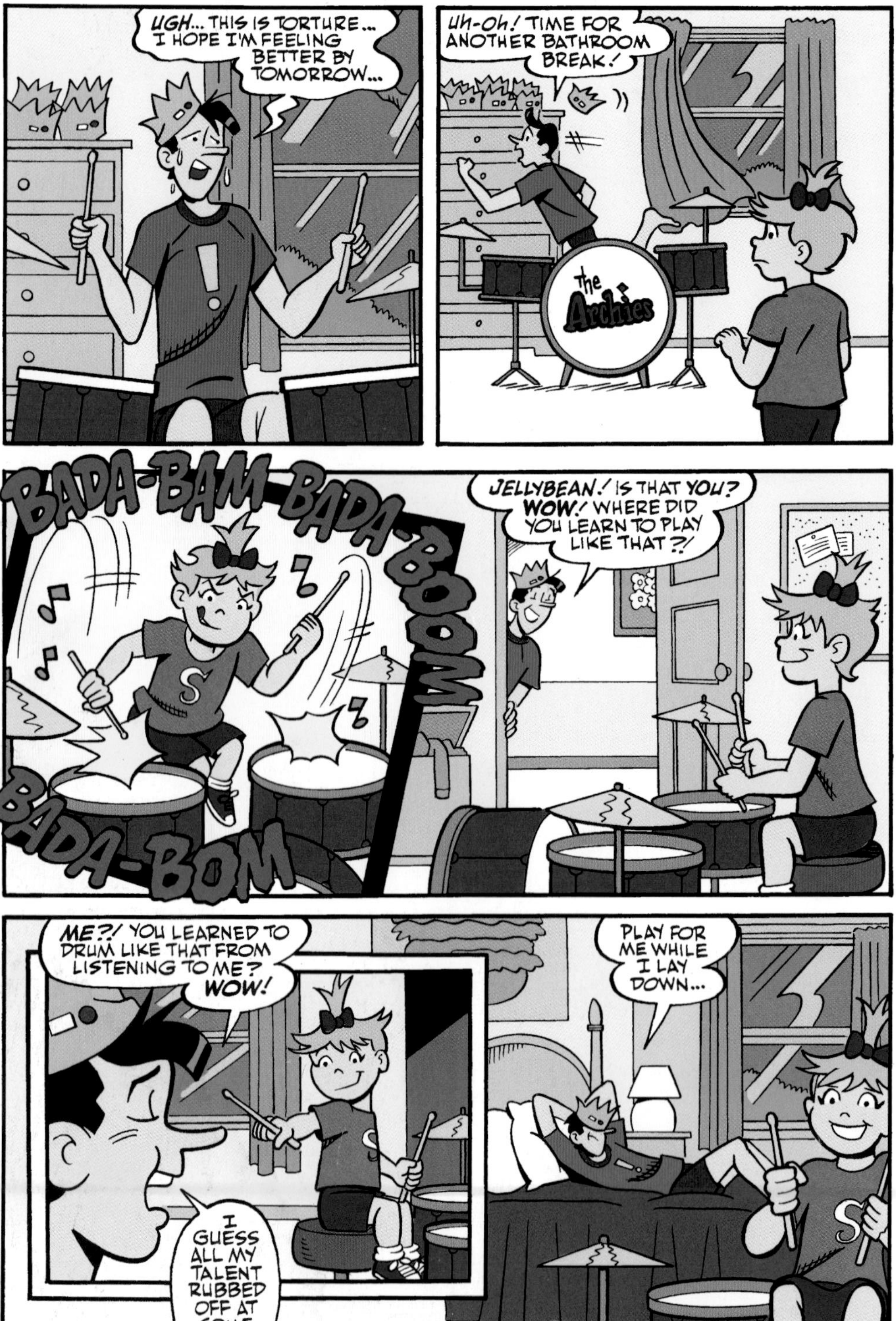
UGH... THIS IS TORTURE... I HOPE I'M FEELING BETTER BY TOMORROW...
UH-OH! TIME FOR ANOTHER BATHROOM BREAK!
The Archies
BADA-BAM BADA-BOOM
BADA-BOM
JELLYBEAN! IS THAT YOU? WOW! WHERE DID YOU LEARN TO PLAY LIKE THAT?!
ME?! YOU LEARNED TO DRUM LIKE THAT FROM LISTENING TO ME? WOW!
I GUESS ALL MY TALENT RUBBED OFF AT SOME POINT!
PLAY FOR ME WHILE I LAY DOWN...
4

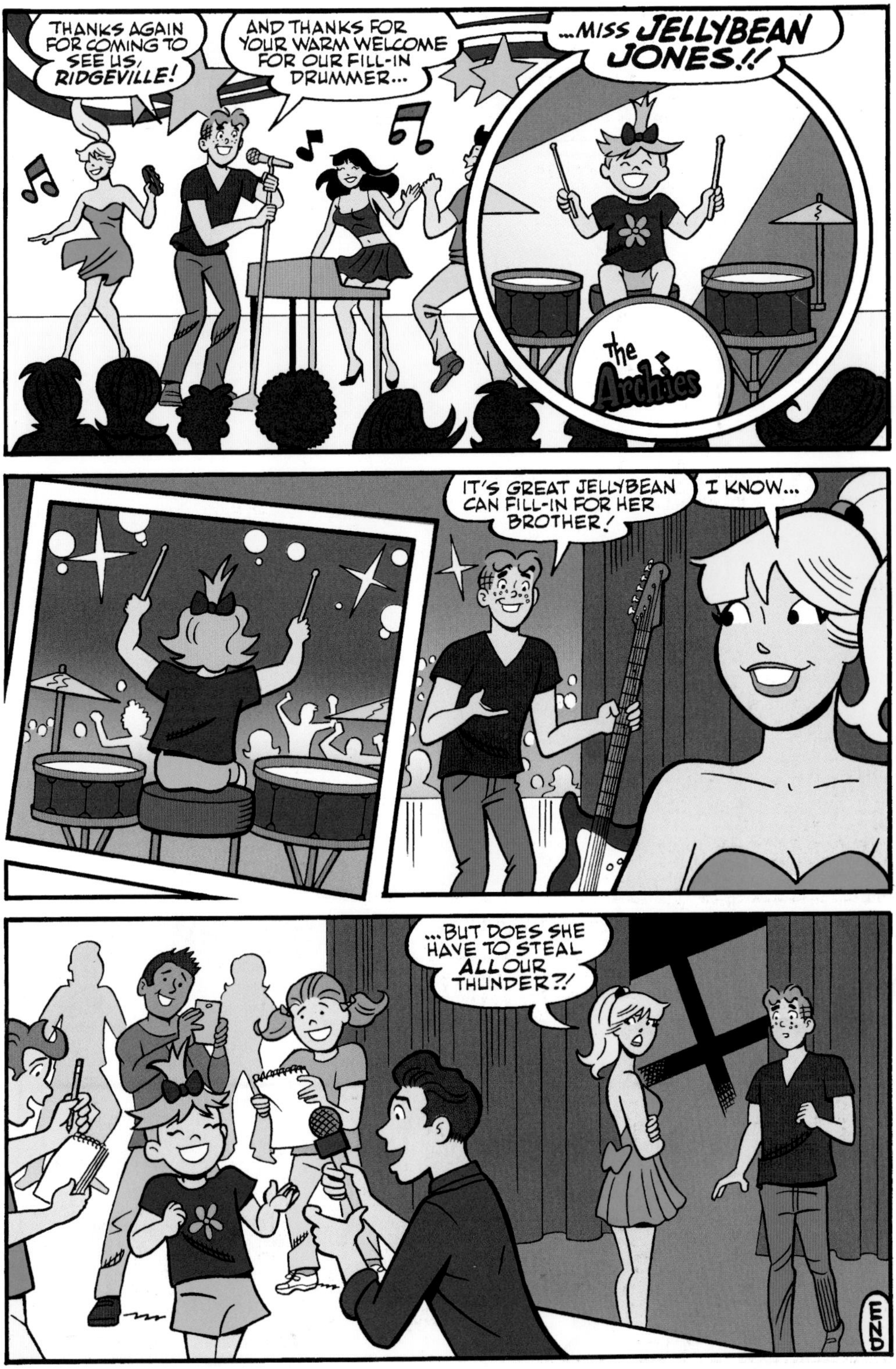
THANKS AGAIN FOR COMING TO SEE US, RIDGEVILLE!
AND THANKS FOR YOUR WARM WELCOME FOR OUR FILL-IN DRUMMER...
...MISS JELLYBEAN JONES!!
The Archies
IT'S GREAT JELLYBEAN CAN FILL-IN FOR HER BROTHER!
I KNOW...
...BUT DOES SHE HAVE TO STEAL ALL OUR THUNDER?!
END

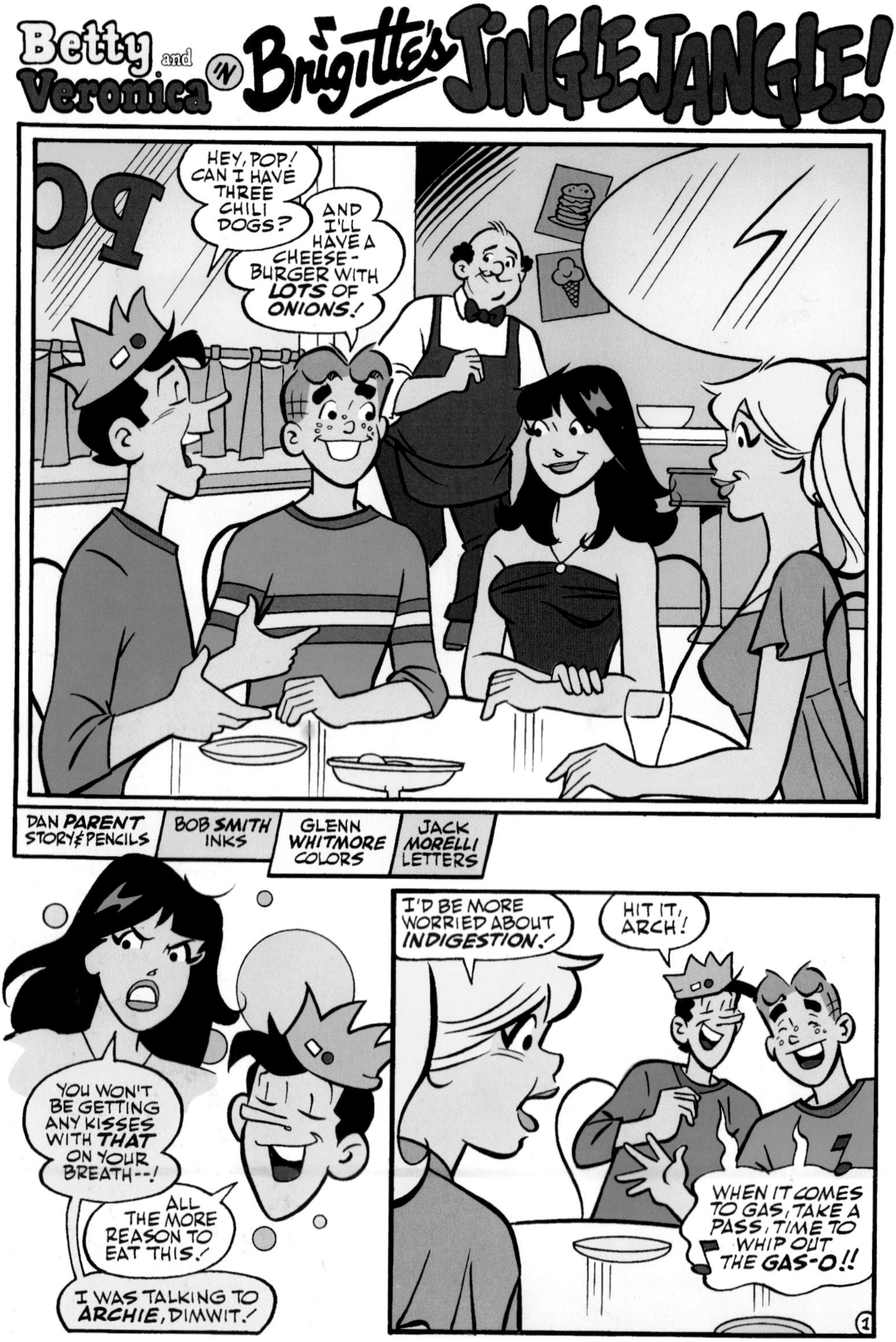
Betty and Veronica in Brigitte's JINGLE JANGLE!
HEY, POP! CAN I HAVE THREE CHILI DOGS?
AND I'LL HAVE A CHEESE-BURGER WITH LOTS OF ONIONS!
DAN PARENT STORY & PENCILS
BOB SMITH INKS
GLENN WHITMORE COLORS
JACK MORELLI LETTERS
YOU WON'T BE GETTING ANY KISSES WITH THAT ON YOUR BREATH--!
ALL THE MORE REASON TO EAT THIS!
I WAS TALKING TO ARCHIE, DIMWIT!
I'D BE MORE WORRIED ABOUT INDIGESTION!
HIT IT, ARCH!
WHEN IT COMES TO GAS, TAKE A PASS, TIME TO WHIP OUT THE GAS-O!!
1

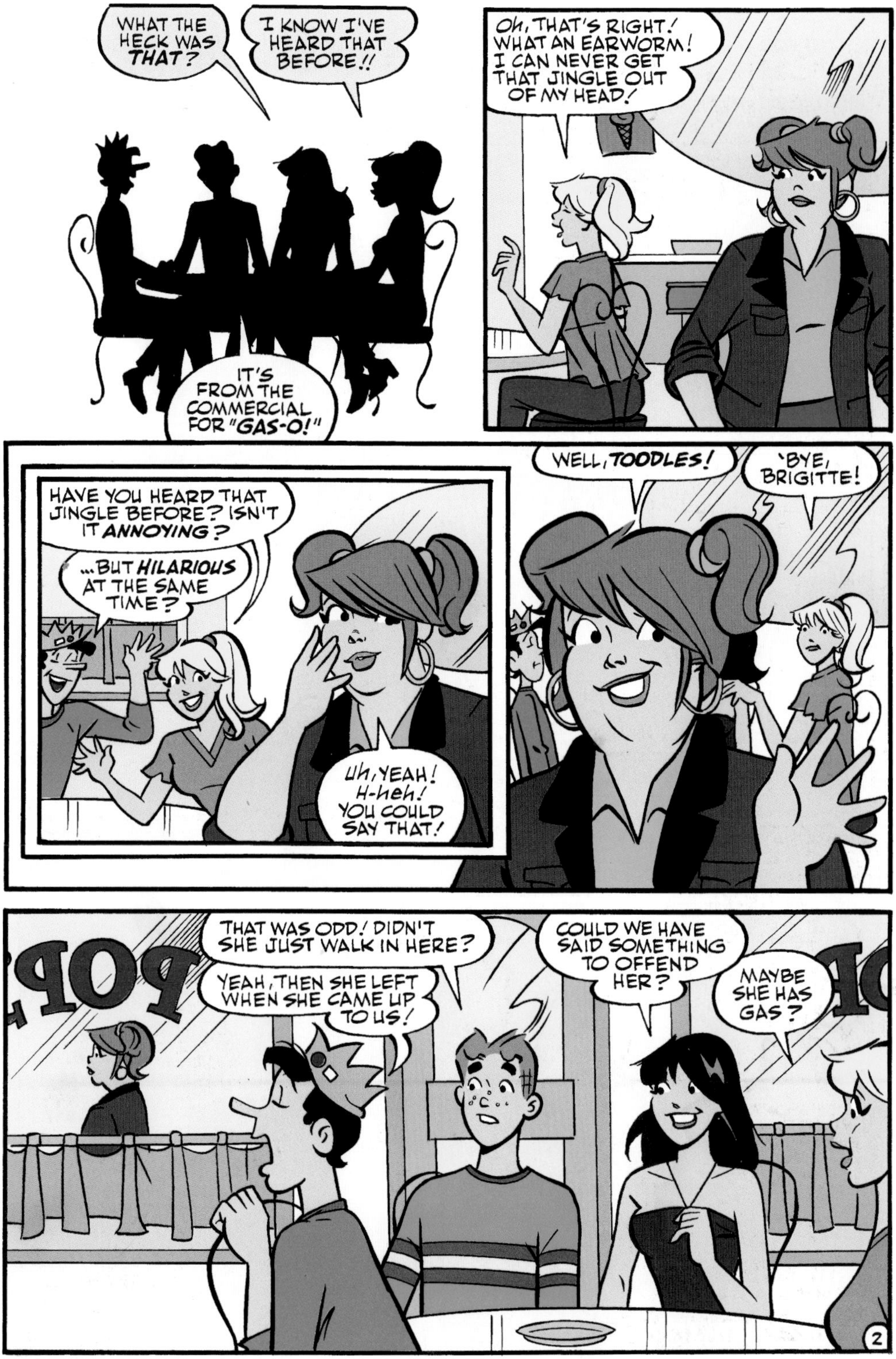
WHAT THE HECK WAS THAT?
I KNOW I'VE HEARD THAT BEFORE!!
IT'S FROM THE COMMERCIAL FOR "GAS-O!"
OH, THAT'S RIGHT! WHAT AN EARWORM! I CAN NEVER GET THAT JINGLE OUT OF MY HEAD!
HAVE YOU HEARD THAT JINGLE BEFORE? ISN'T IT ANNOYING?
...BUT HILARIOUS AT THE SAME TIME?
UH, YEAH! H-HEH! YOU COULD SAY THAT!
WELL, TOODLES!
'BYE, BRIGITTE!
THAT WAS ODD! DIDN'T SHE JUST WALK IN HERE?
YEAH, THEN SHE LEFT WHEN SHE CAME UP TO US!
COULD WE HAVE SAID SOMETHING TO OFFEND HER?
MAYBE SHE HAS GAS?
2

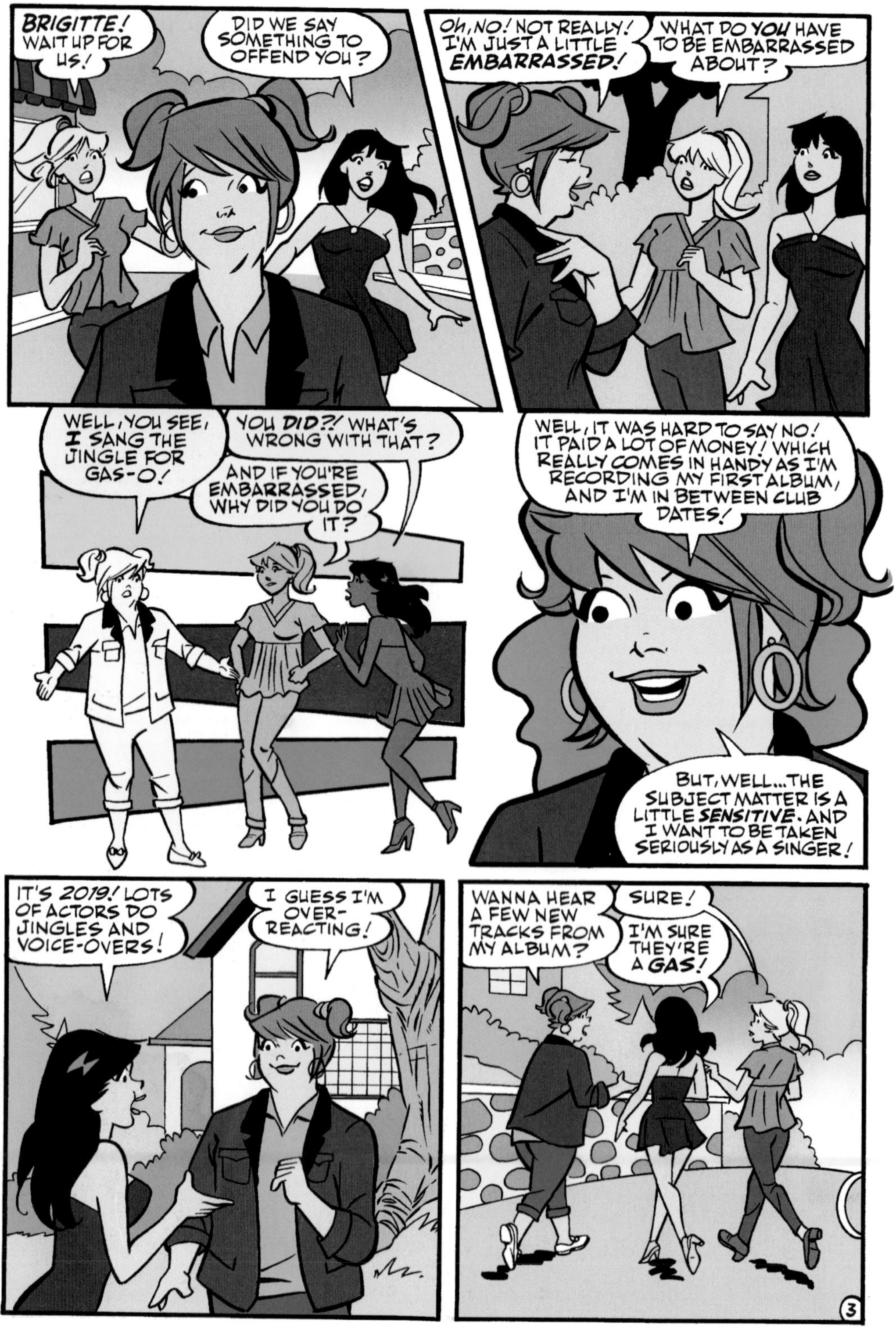
BRIGITTE! WAIT UP FOR US!
DID WE SAY SOMETHING TO OFFEND YOU?
OH, NO! NOT REALLY! I'M JUST A LITTLE EMBARRASSED!
WHAT DO YOU HAVE TO BE EMBARRASSED ABOUT?
WELL, YOU SEE, I SANG THE JINGLE FOR GAS-O!
YOU DID?! WHAT'S WRONG WITH THAT?
AND IF YOU'RE EMBARRASSED, WHY DID YOU DO IT?
WELL, IT WAS HARD TO SAY NO! IT PAID A LOT OF MONEY! WHICH REALLY COMES IN HANDY AS I'M RECORDING MY FIRST ALBUM, AND I'M IN BETWEEN CLUB DATES!
BUT, WELL... THE SUBJECT MATTER IS A LITTLE SENSITIVE. AND I WANT TO BE TAKEN SERIOUSLY AS A SINGER!
IT'S 2019! LOTS OF ACTORS DO JINGLES AND VOICE-OVERS!
I GUESS I'M OVER-REACTING!
WANNA HEAR A FEW NEW TRACKS FROM MY ALBUM?
SURE!
I'M SURE THEY'RE A GAS!
3

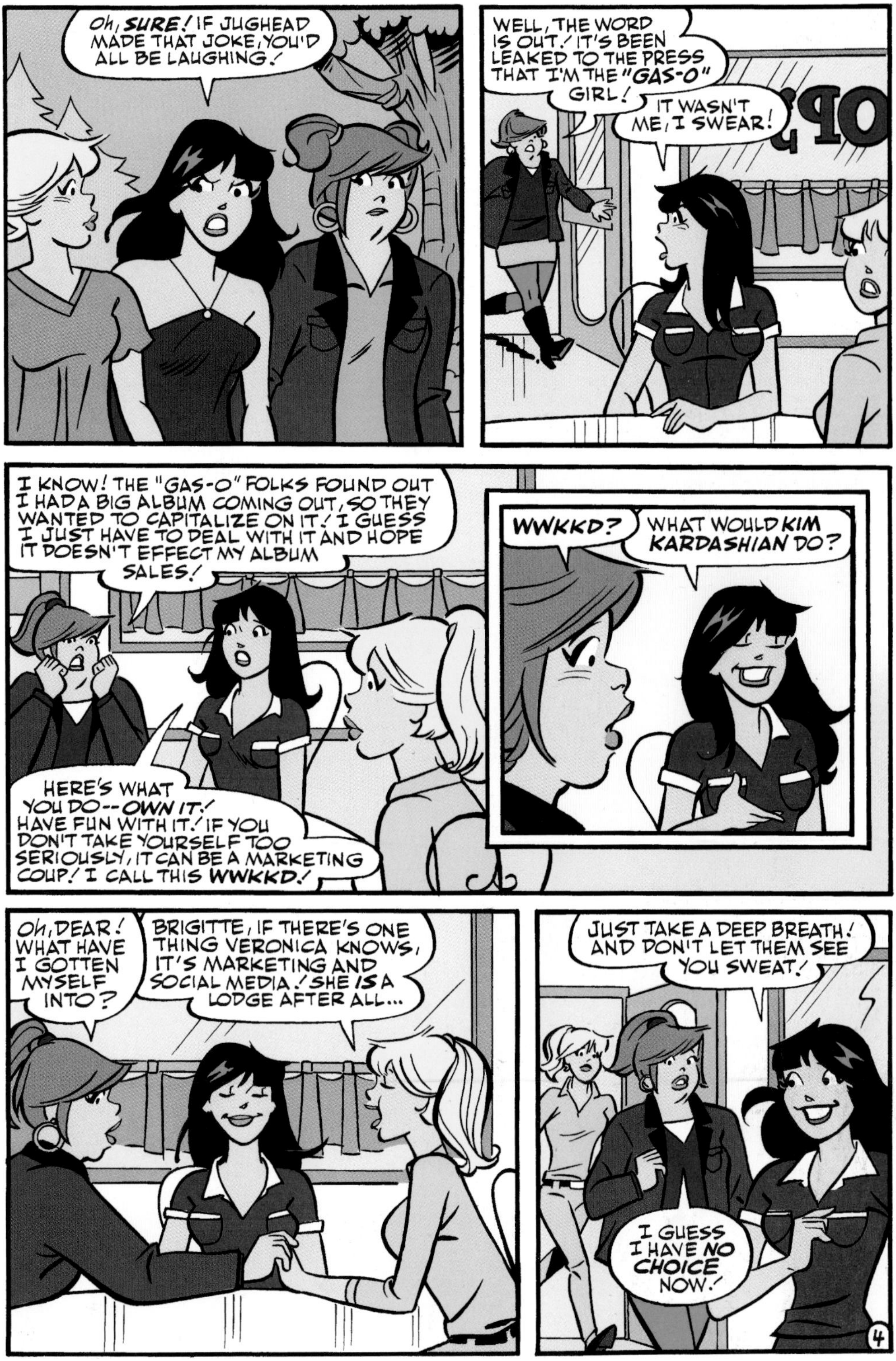
Oh, SURE! IF JUGHEAD MADE THAT JOKE, YOU'D ALL BE LAUGHING!
WELL, THE WORD IS OUT! IT'S BEEN LEAKED TO THE PRESS THAT I'M THE "GAS-O" GIRL!
IT WASN'T ME, I SWEAR!
OP
I KNOW! THE "GAS-O" FOLKS FOUND OUT I HAD A BIG ALBUM COMING OUT, SO THEY WANTED TO CAPITALIZE ON IT! I GUESS I JUST HAVE TO DEAL WITH IT AND HOPE IT DOESN'T EFFECT MY ALBUM SALES!
HERE'S WHAT YOU DO--OWN IT! HAVE FUN WITH IT! IF YOU DON'T TAKE YOURSELF TOO SERIOUSLY, IT CAN BE A MARKETING COUP! I CALL THIS WWKKD!
WWKKD?
WHAT WOULD KIM KARDASHIAN DO?
Oh, DEAR! WHAT HAVE I GOTTEN MYSELF INTO?
BRIGITTE, IF THERE'S ONE THING VERONICA KNOWS, IT'S MARKETING AND SOCIAL MEDIA! SHE IS A LODGE AFTER ALL...
JUST TAKE A DEEP BREATH! AND DON'T LET THEM SEE YOU SWEAT!
I GUESS I HAVE NO CHOICE NOW!
4

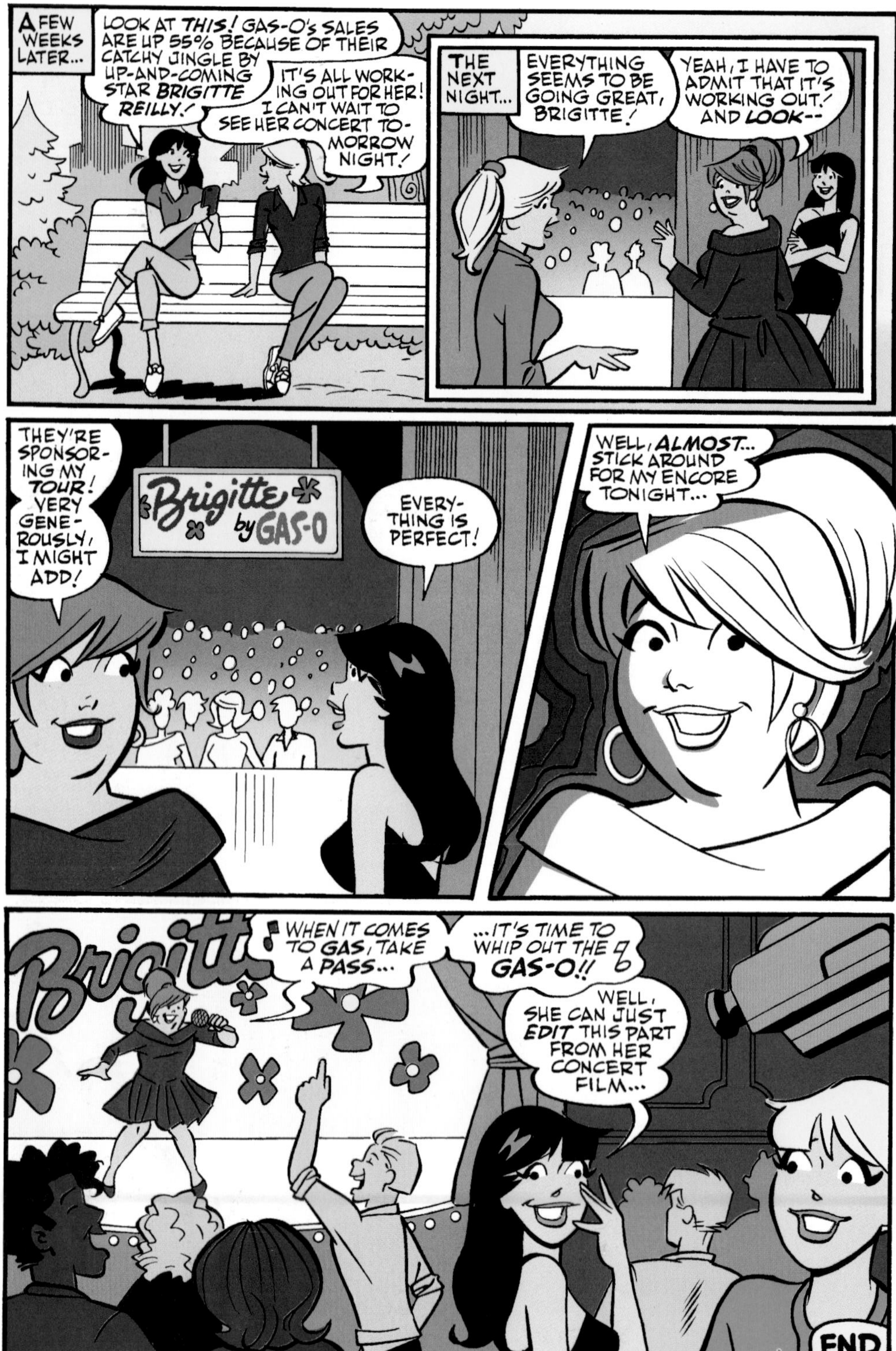
A FEW WEEKS LATER...
LOOK AT THIS! GAS-O's SALES ARE UP 55% BECAUSE OF THEIR CATCHY JINGLE BY UP-AND-COMING STAR BRIGITTE REILLY!
IT'S ALL WORKING OUT FOR HER! I CAN'T WAIT TO SEE HER CONCERT TOMORROW NIGHT!
THE NEXT NIGHT...
EVERYTHING SEEMS TO BE GOING GREAT, BRIGITTE!
YEAH, I HAVE TO ADMIT THAT IT'S WORKING OUT! AND LOOK--
THEY'RE SPONSORING MY TOUR! VERY GENEROUSLY, I MIGHT ADD!
Brigitte by GAS-O
EVERYTHING IS PERFECT!
WELL, ALMOST... STICK AROUND FOR MY ENCORE TONIGHT...
WHEN IT COMES TO GAS, TAKE A PASS...
...IT'S TIME TO WHIP OUT THE GAS-O!!
WELL, SHE CAN JUST EDIT THIS PART FROM HER CONCERT FILM...
END

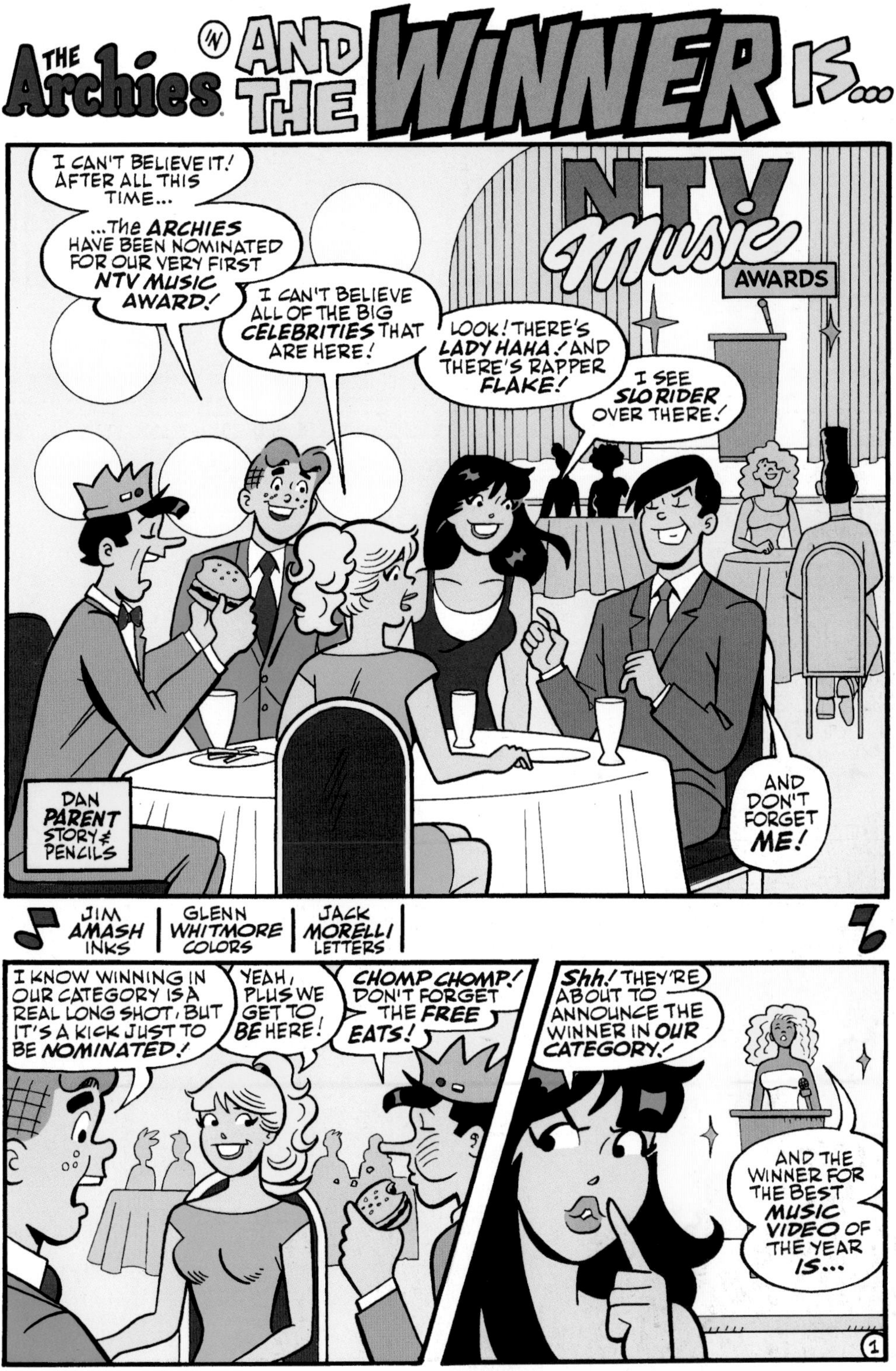
THE Archies IN AND THE WINNER IS...
I CAN'T BELIEVE IT! AFTER ALL THIS TIME...
...The ARCHIES HAVE BEEN NOMINATED FOR OUR VERY FIRST NTV MUSIC AWARD!
I CAN'T BELIEVE ALL OF THE BIG CELEBRITIES THAT ARE HERE!
NTV Music AWARDS
LOOK! THERE'S LADY HAHA! AND THERE'S RAPPER FLAKE!
I SEE SLO RIDER OVER THERE!
AND DON'T FORGET ME!
DAN PARENT STORY & PENCILS
JIM AMASH INKS
GLENN WHITMORE COLORS
JACK MORELLI LETTERS
I KNOW WINNING IN OUR CATEGORY IS A REAL LONG SHOT, BUT IT'S A KICK JUST TO BE NOMINATED!
YEAH, PLUS WE GET TO BE HERE!
CHOMP CHOMP! DON'T FORGET THE FREE EATS!
Shh! THEY'RE ABOUT TO ANNOUNCE THE WINNER IN OUR CATEGORY!
AND THE WINNER FOR THE BEST MUSIC VIDEO OF THE YEAR IS...
1

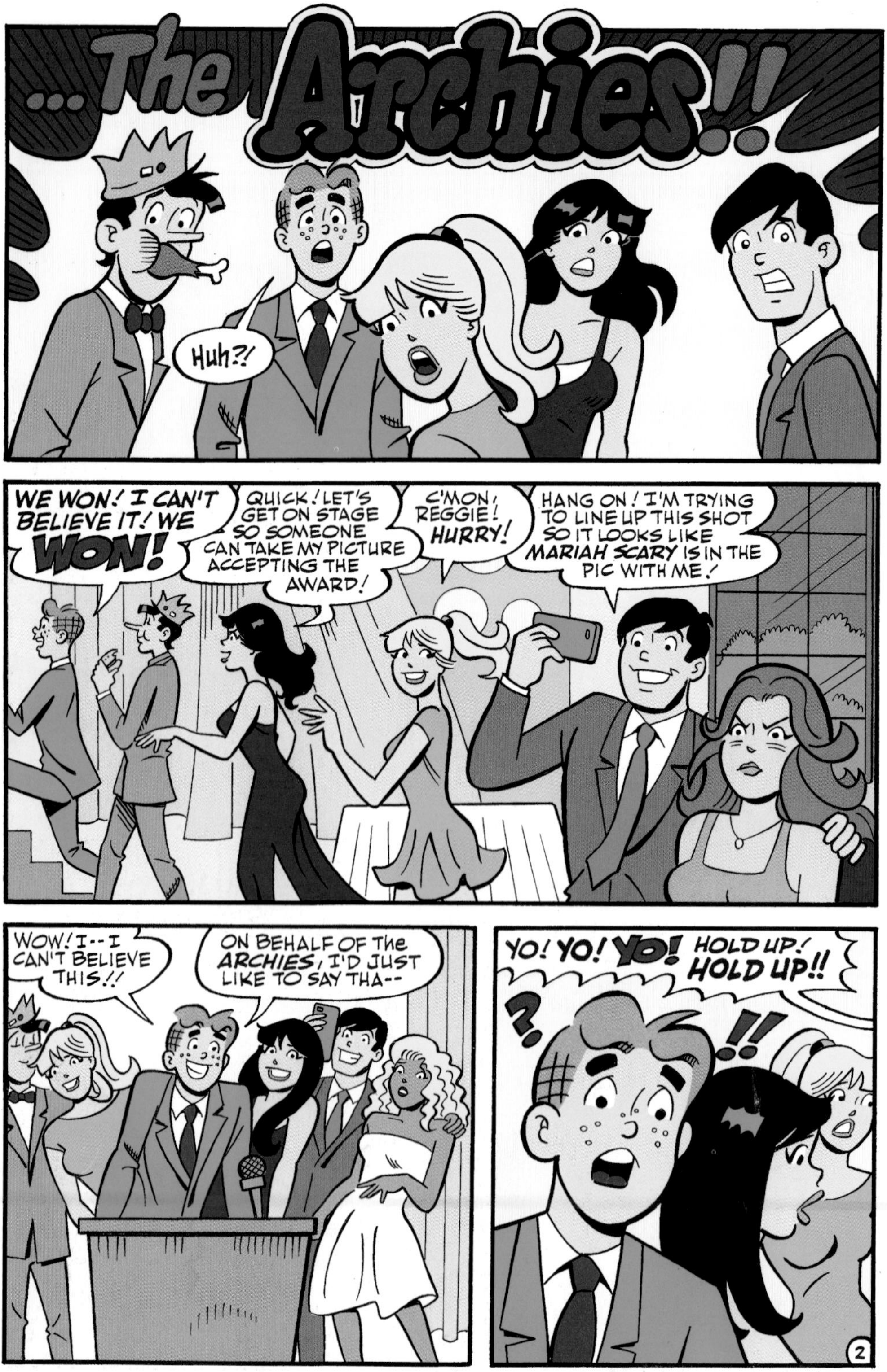
...The Archies!!
Huh?!
WE WON! I CAN'T BELIEVE IT! WE WON!
QUICK! LET'S GET ON STAGE SO SOMEONE CAN TAKE MY PICTURE ACCEPTING THE AWARD!
C'MON, REGGIE! HURRY!
HANG ON! I'M TRYING TO LINE UP THIS SHOT SO IT LOOKS LIKE MARIAH SCARY IS IN THE PIC WITH ME!
WOW! I-- I CAN'T BELIEVE THIS!!
ON BEHALF OF THE ARCHIES, I'D JUST LIKE TO SAY THA--
YO! YO! YO! HOLD UP! HOLD UP!!
?
!!
2

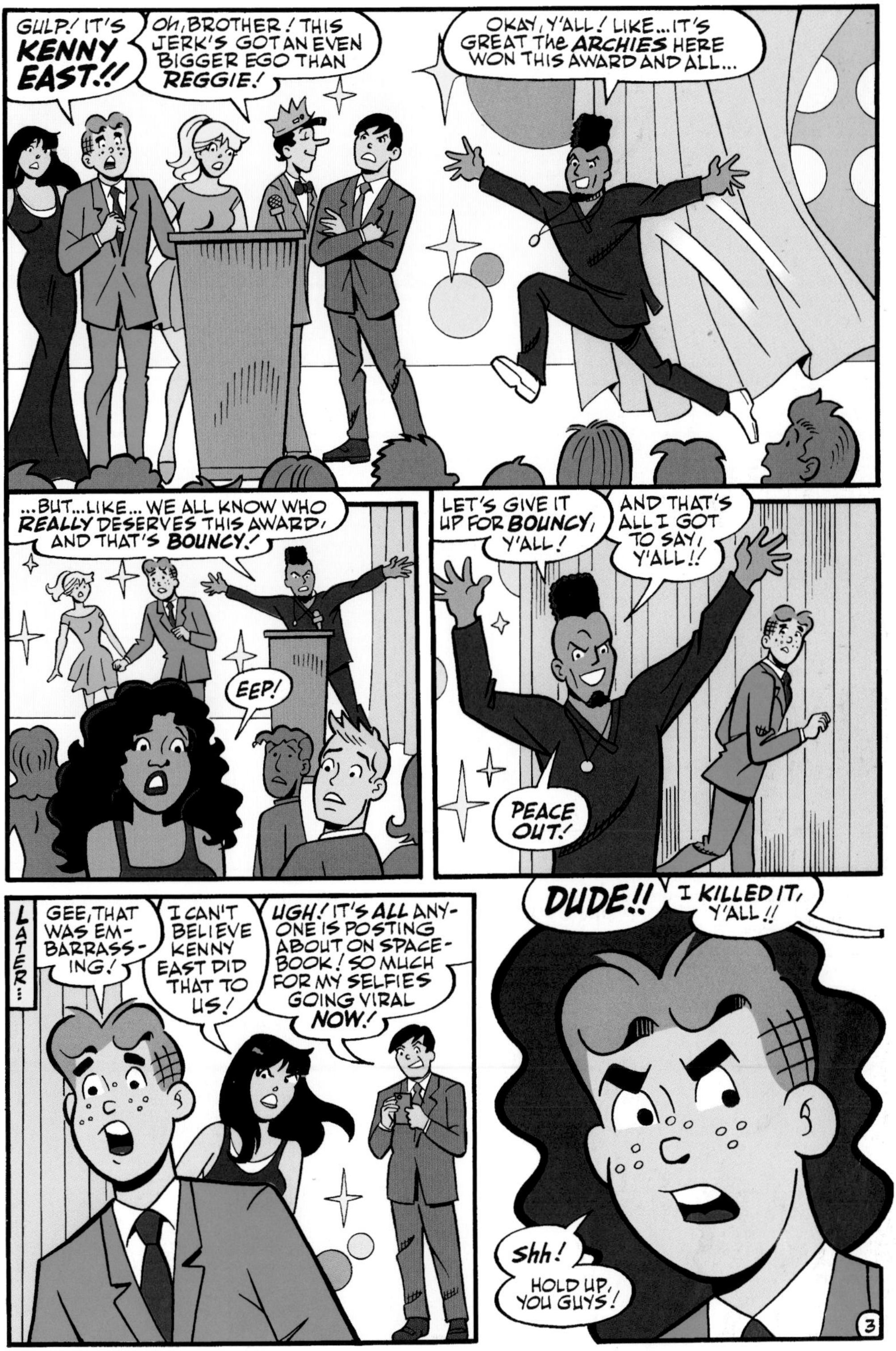
GULP! IT'S KENNY EAST!!
Oh, BROTHER! THIS JERK'S GOT AN EVEN BIGGER EGO THAN REGGIE!
OKAY, Y'ALL! LIKE... IT'S GREAT the ARCHIES HERE WON THIS AWARD AND ALL...
...BUT... LIKE... WE ALL KNOW WHO REALLY DESERVES THIS AWARD, AND THAT'S BOUNCY!
EEP!
LET'S GIVE IT UP FOR BOUNCY, Y'ALL!
AND THAT'S ALL I GOT TO SAY, Y'ALL!!
PEACE OUT!
LATER...
GEE, THAT WAS EM-BARRASS-ING!
I CAN'T BELIEVE KENNY EAST DID THAT TO US!
UGH! IT'S ALL ANY-ONE IS POSTING ABOUT ON SPACE-BOOK! SO MUCH FOR MY SELFIES GOING VIRAL NOW!
DUDE!!
I KILLED IT, Y'ALL!!
Shh!
HOLD UP, YOU GUYS!
3

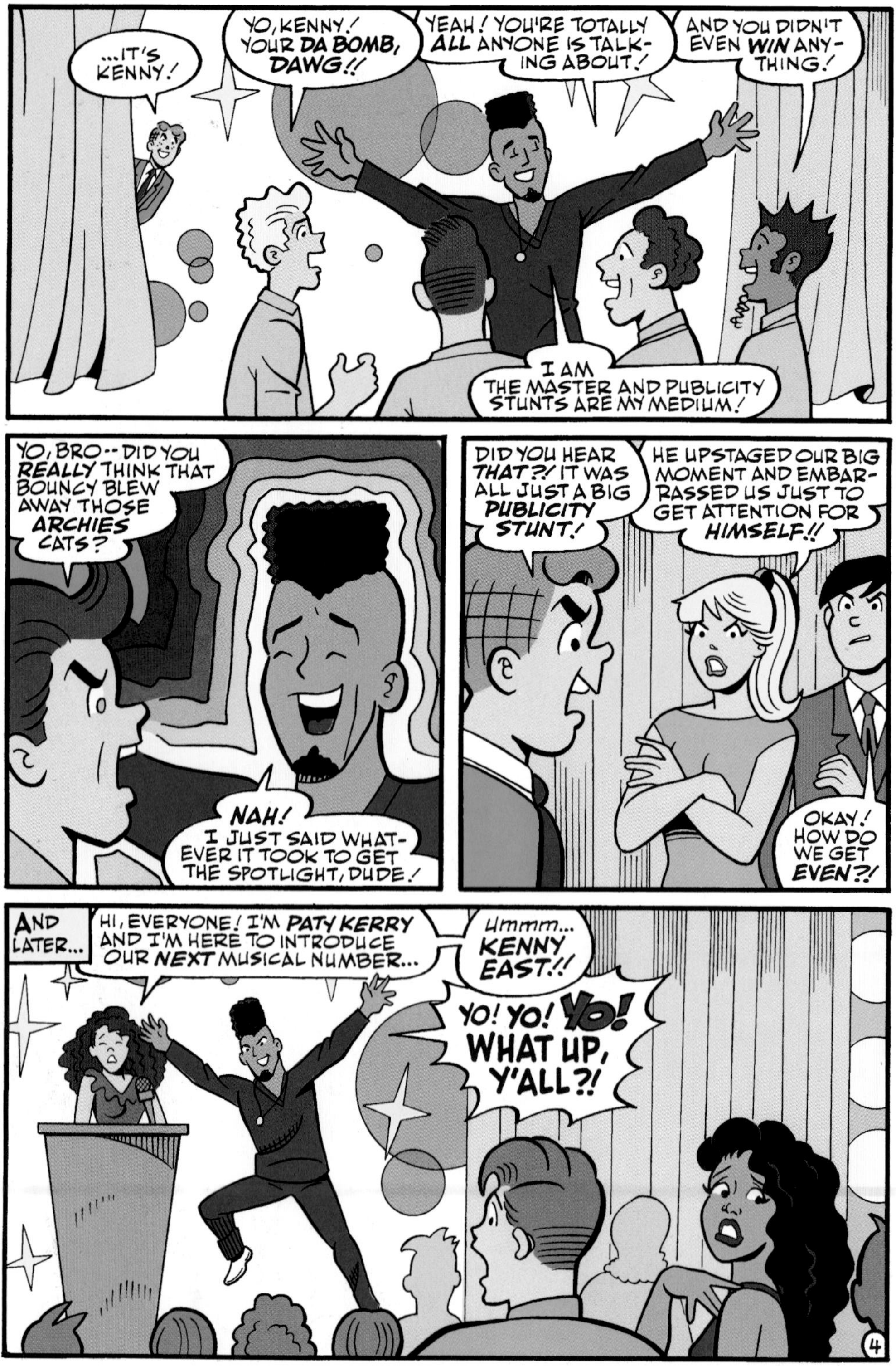
...IT'S KENNY!
YO, KENNY! YOUR DA BOMB, DAWG!!
YEAH! YOU'RE TOTALLY ALL ANYONE IS TALKING ABOUT!
AND YOU DIDN'T EVEN WIN ANYTHING!
I AM THE MASTER AND PUBLICITY STUNTS ARE MY MEDIUM!
YO, BRO-- DID YOU REALLY THINK THAT BOUNCY BLEW AWAY THOSE ARCHIES CATS?
NAH! I JUST SAID WHATEVER IT TOOK TO GET THE SPOTLIGHT, DUDE!
DID YOU HEAR THAT?! IT WAS ALL JUST A BIG PUBLICITY STUNT!
HE UPSTAGED OUR BIG MOMENT AND EMBARRASSED US JUST TO GET ATTENTION FOR HIMSELF!!
OKAY! HOW DO WE GET EVEN?!
AND LATER...
HI, EVERYONE! I'M PATY KERRY AND I'M HERE TO INTRODUCE OUR NEXT MUSICAL NUMBER...
Ummm... KENNY EAST!!
YO! YO! YO! WHAT UP, Y'ALL?!
4

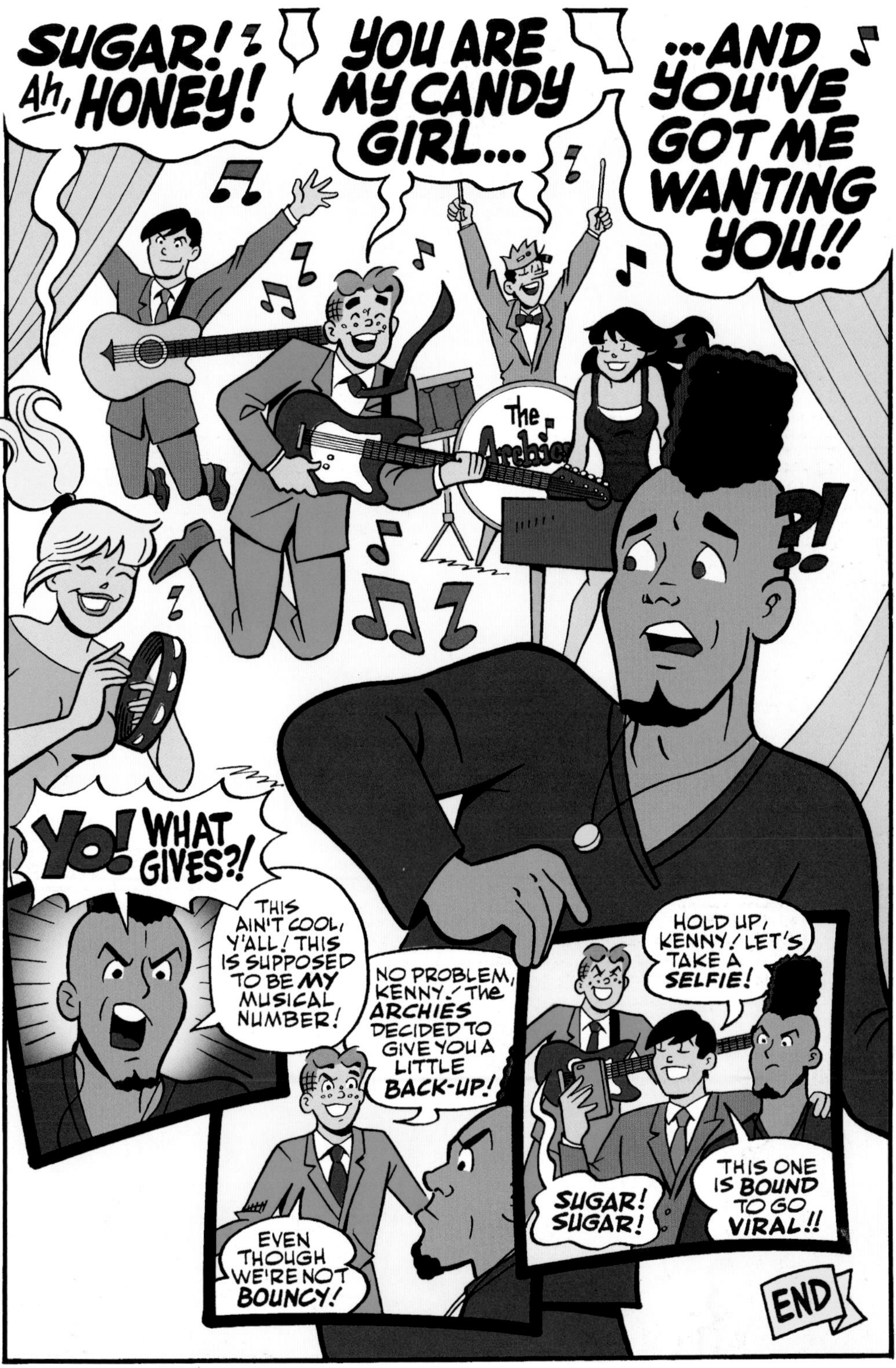
SUGAR! Ah, HONEY!
YOU ARE MY CANDY GIRL...
...AND YOU'VE GOT ME WANTING YOU!!
The Archies
?!
YO! WHAT GIVES?!
THIS AIN'T COOL, Y'ALL! THIS IS SUPPOSED TO BE MY MUSICAL NUMBER!
NO PROBLEM, KENNY! THE ARCHIES DECIDED TO GIVE YOU A LITTLE BACK-UP!
EVEN THOUGH WE'RE NOT BOUNCY!
HOLD UP, KENNY! LET'S TAKE A SELFIE!
SUGAR! SUGAR!
THIS ONE IS BOUND TO GO VIRAL!!
END

Archie in VIVA La VINYL!

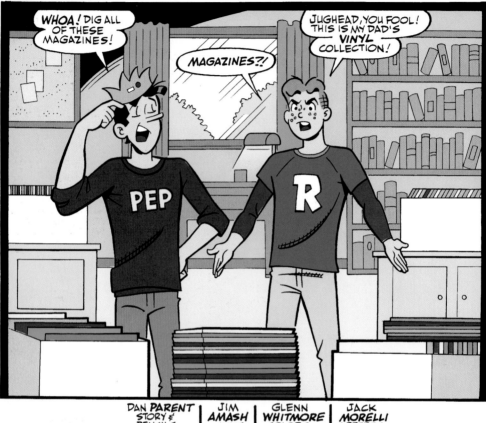

WHOA! DIG ALL OF THESE MAGAZINES!

MAGAZINES?!

JUGHEAD, YOU FOOL! THIS IS MY DAD'S **VINYL** COLLECTION!

DAN **PARENT** STORY & PENCILS | JIM **AMASH** INKS | GLENN **WHITMORE** COLORS | JACK **MORELLI** LETTERS

YOUR DAD COLLECTS VINYL SIDING?!

NO, YOU DOLT! THESE ARE **RECORDS!** THIS IS MY DAD'S ALBUM COLLECTION! HE'S HAD THESE SINCE HE WAS A KID!

SINCE **HE** WAS A KID?!

HOW HAVE THEY NOT TURNED TO **DUST?**

THIS IS THE CROWN JEWEL OF HIS ENTIRE COLLECTION...

...HIS FIRST **ELTON PRETZLEY** ALBUM!

①

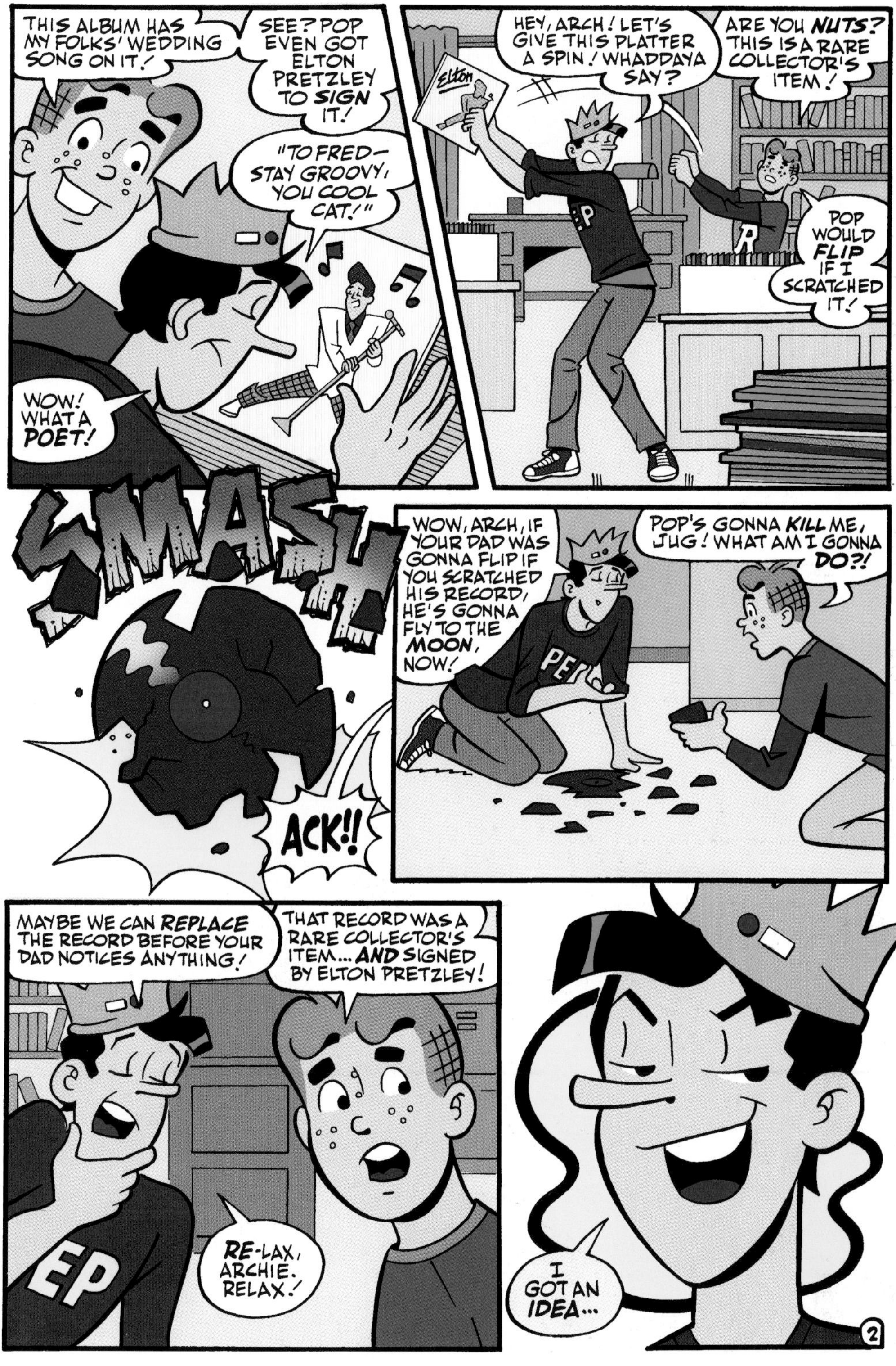
THIS ALBUM HAS MY FOLKS' WEDDING SONG ON IT!
SEE? POP EVEN GOT ELTON PRETZLEY TO SIGN IT!
"TO FRED— STAY GROOVY, YOU COOL CAT!"
WOW! WHAT A POET!
Elton
HEY, ARCH! LET'S GIVE THIS PLATTER A SPIN! WHADDAYA SAY?
ARE YOU NUTS? THIS IS A RARE COLLECTOR'S ITEM!
POP WOULD FLIP IF I SCRATCHED IT!
SMASH
ACK!!
WOW, ARCH, IF YOUR DAD WAS GONNA FLIP IF YOU SCRATCHED HIS RECORD, HE'S GONNA FLY TO THE MOON, NOW!
POP'S GONNA KILL ME, JUG! WHAT AM I GONNA DO?!
MAYBE WE CAN REPLACE THE RECORD BEFORE YOUR DAD NOTICES ANYTHING!
THAT RECORD WAS A RARE COLLECTOR'S ITEM... AND SIGNED BY ELTON PRETZLEY!
RE-LAX, ARCHIE. RELAX!
I GOT AN IDEA...
2

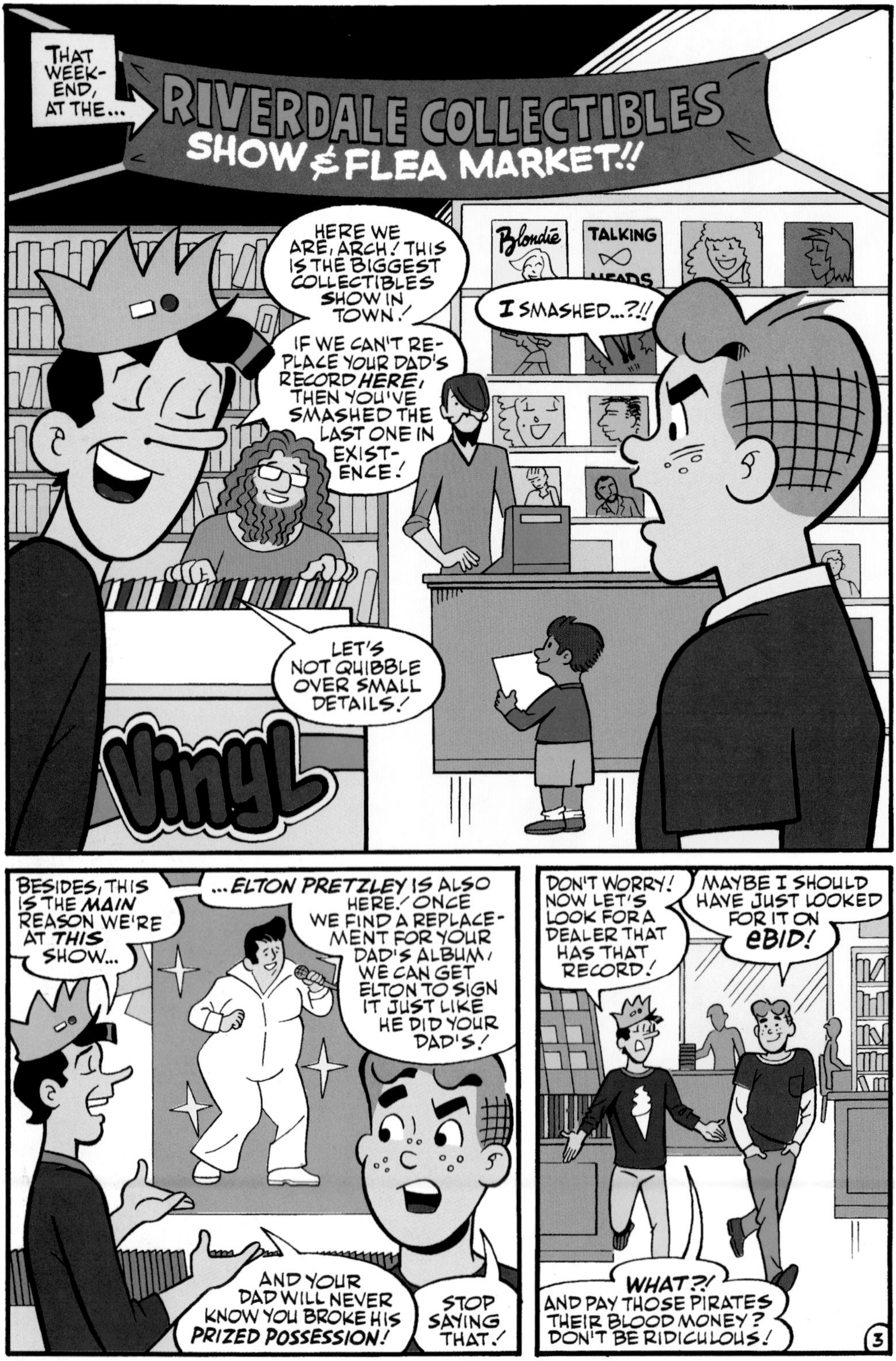
THAT WEEK-END, AT THE...
RIVERDALE COLLECTIBLES SHOW & FLEA MARKET!!
HERE WE ARE, ARCH! THIS IS THE BIGGEST COLLECTIBLES SHOW IN TOWN!
IF WE CAN'T RE-PLACE YOUR DAD'S RECORD HERE, THEN YOU'VE SMASHED THE LAST ONE IN EXIST-ENCE!
I SMASHED...?!!
LET'S NOT QUIBBLE OVER SMALL DETAILS!
Blondie
TALKING HEADS
VinyL
BESIDES, THIS IS THE MAIN REASON WE'RE AT THIS SHOW...
...ELTON PRETZLEY IS ALSO HERE! ONCE WE FIND A REPLACE-MENT FOR YOUR DAD'S ALBUM, WE CAN GET ELTON TO SIGN IT JUST LIKE HE DID YOUR DAD'S!
AND YOUR DAD WILL NEVER KNOW YOU BROKE HIS PRIZED POSSESSION!
STOP SAYING THAT!
DON'T WORRY! NOW LET'S LOOK FOR A DEALER THAT HAS THAT RECORD!
MAYBE I SHOULD HAVE JUST LOOKED FOR IT ON eBID!
WHAT?! AND PAY THOSE PIRATES THEIR BLOOD MONEY? DON'T BE RIDICULOUS!
3

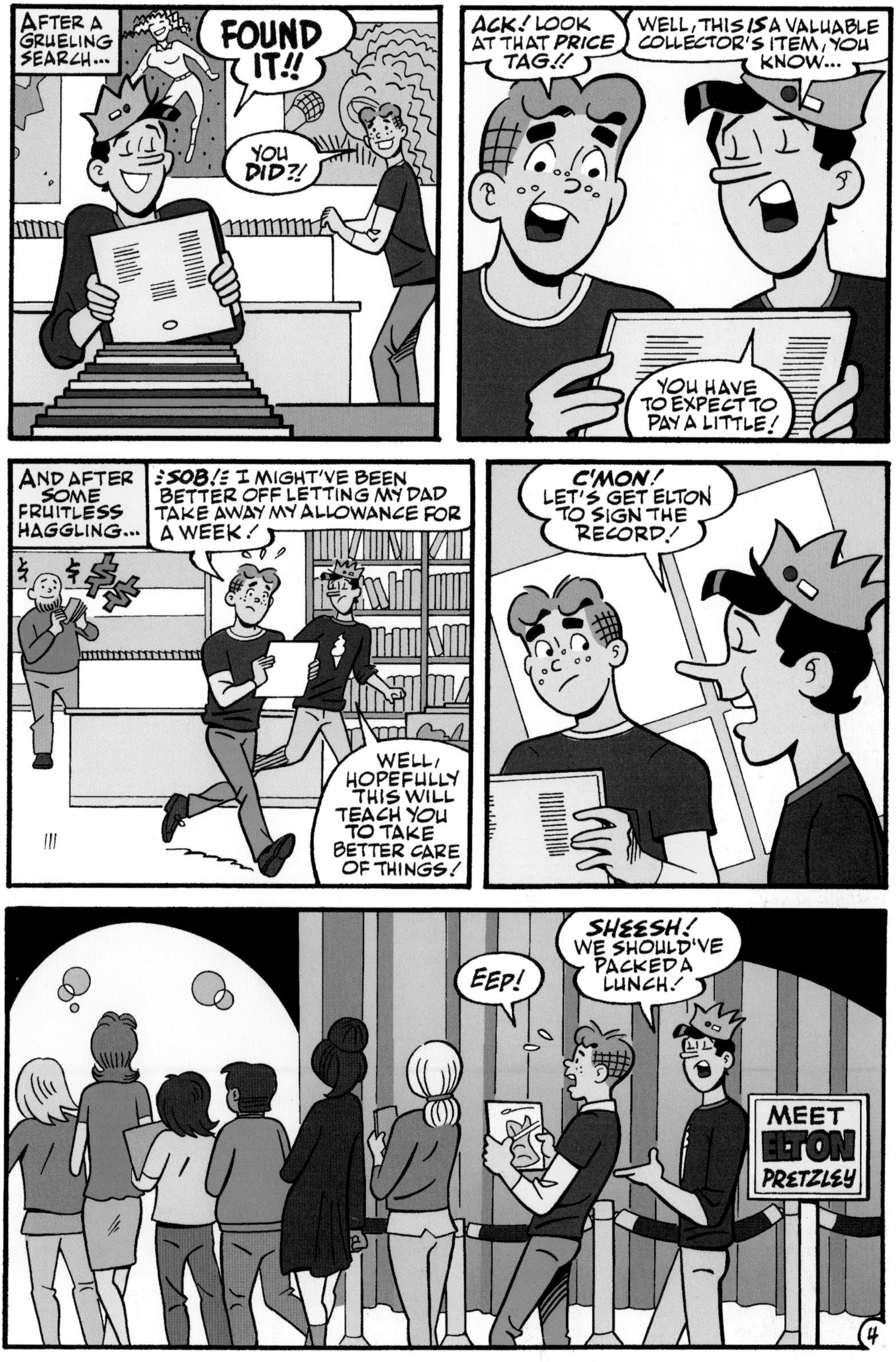
AFTER A GRUELING SEARCH...
FOUND IT!!
YOU DID?!
ACK! LOOK AT THAT PRICE TAG!!
WELL, THIS IS A VALUABLE COLLECTOR'S ITEM, YOU KNOW...
YOU HAVE TO EXPECT TO PAY A LITTLE!
AND AFTER SOME FRUITLESS HAGGLING...
SOB! I MIGHT'VE BEEN BETTER OFF LETTING MY DAD TAKE AWAY MY ALLOWANCE FOR A WEEK!
WELL, HOPEFULLY THIS WILL TEACH YOU TO TAKE BETTER CARE OF THINGS!
C'MON! LET'S GET ELTON TO SIGN THE RECORD!
EEP!
SHEESH! WE SHOULD'VE PACKED A LUNCH!
MEET ELTON PRETZLEY
4

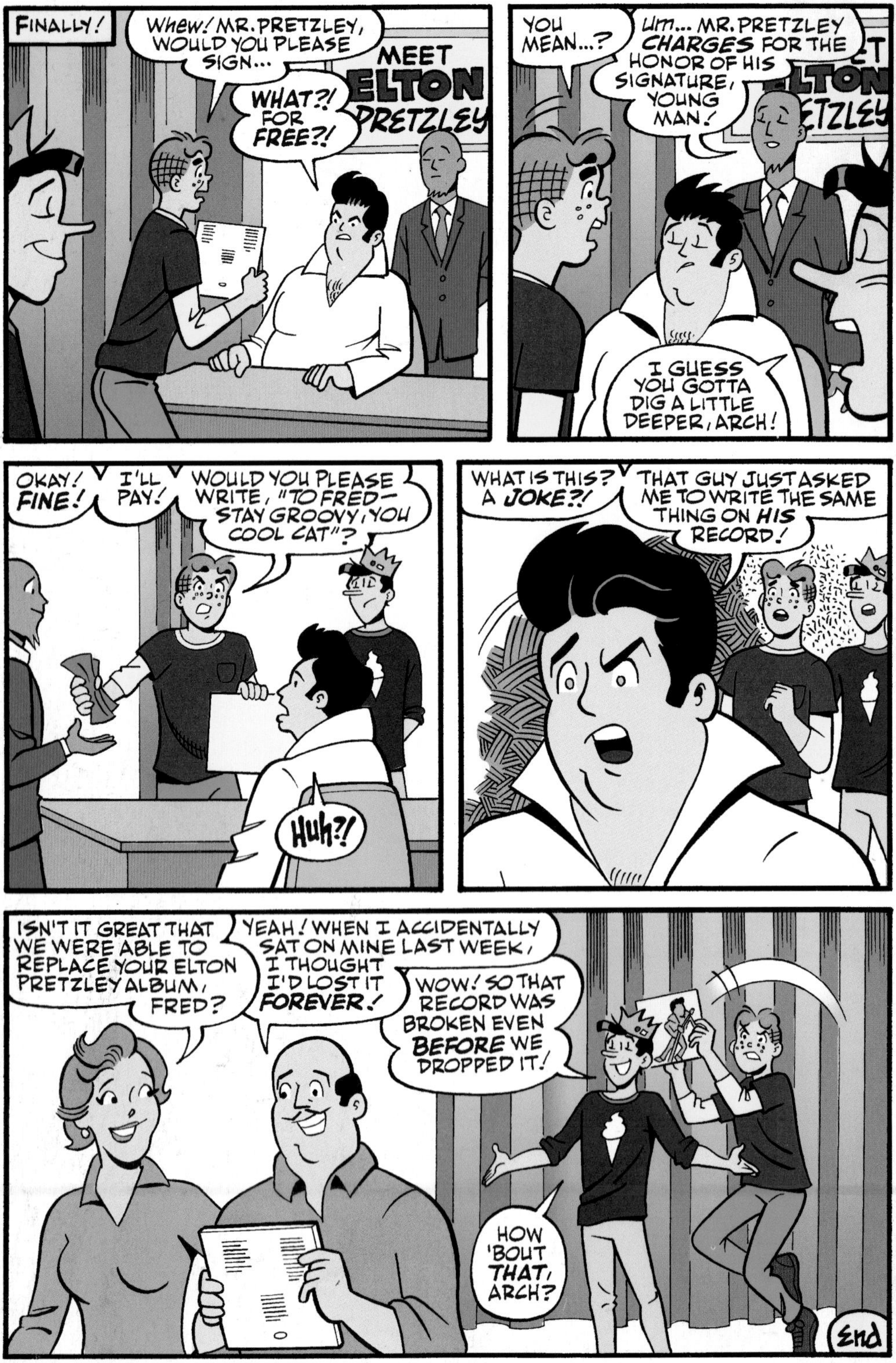
FINALLY!
WHEW! MR. PRETZLEY, WOULD YOU PLEASE SIGN...
MEET ELTON PRETZLEY
WHAT?! FOR FREE?!
YOU MEAN...?
UM... MR. PRETZLEY CHARGES FOR THE HONOR OF HIS SIGNATURE, YOUNG MAN!
I GUESS YOU GOTTA DIG A LITTLE DEEPER, ARCH!
OKAY! FINE!
I'LL PAY!
WOULD YOU PLEASE WRITE, "TO FRED—STAY GROOVY, YOU COOL CAT"?
HUH?!
WHAT IS THIS? A JOKE?!
THAT GUY JUST ASKED ME TO WRITE THE SAME THING ON HIS RECORD!
ISN'T IT GREAT THAT WE WERE ABLE TO REPLACE YOUR ELTON PRETZLEY ALBUM, FRED?
YEAH! WHEN I ACCIDENTALLY SAT ON MINE LAST WEEK, I THOUGHT I'D LOST IT FOREVER!
WOW! SO THAT RECORD WAS BROKEN EVEN BEFORE WE DROPPED IT!
HOW 'BOUT THAT, ARCH?
END

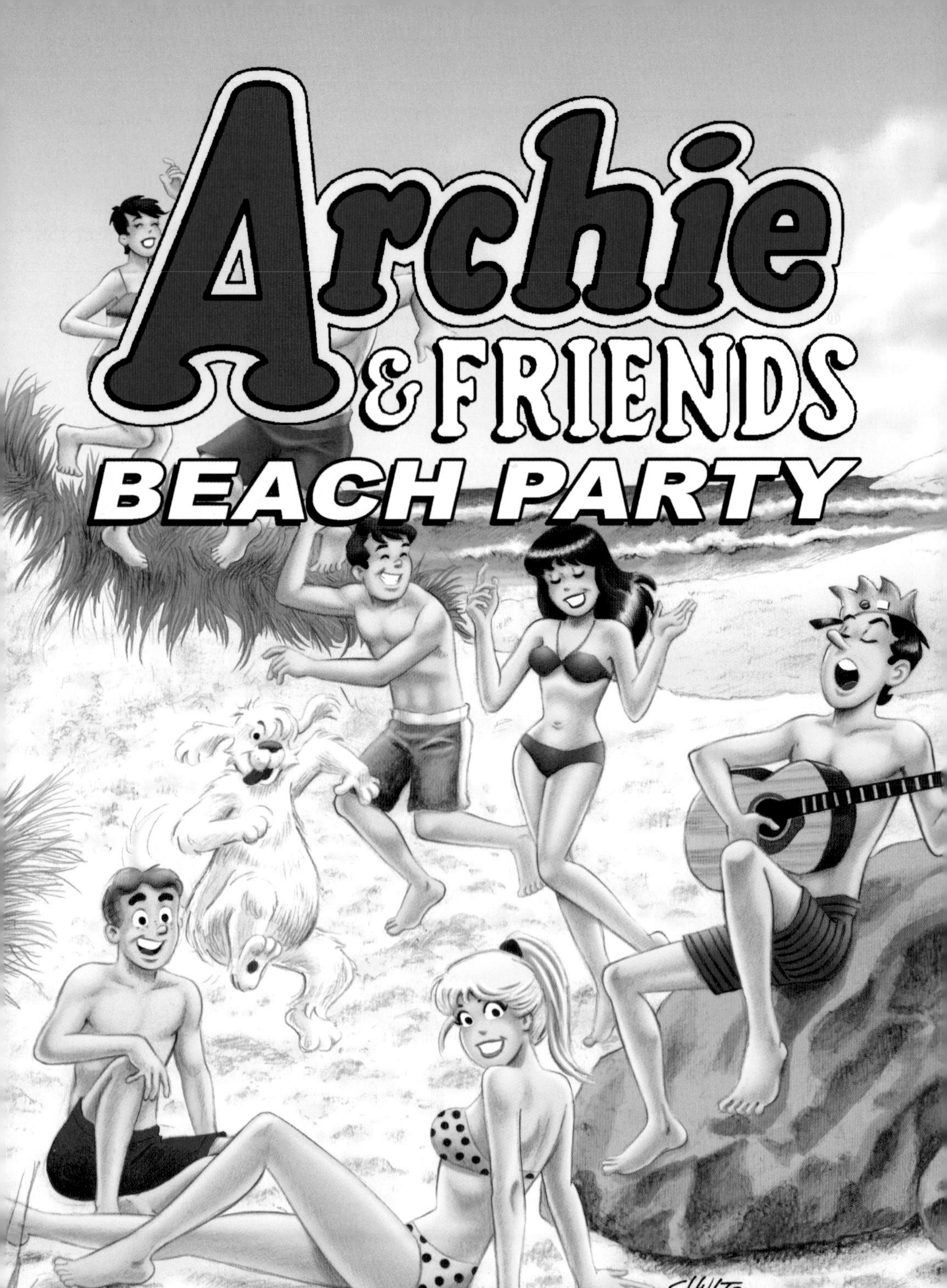
Archie
& FRIENDS
BEACH PARTY
SHULTZ

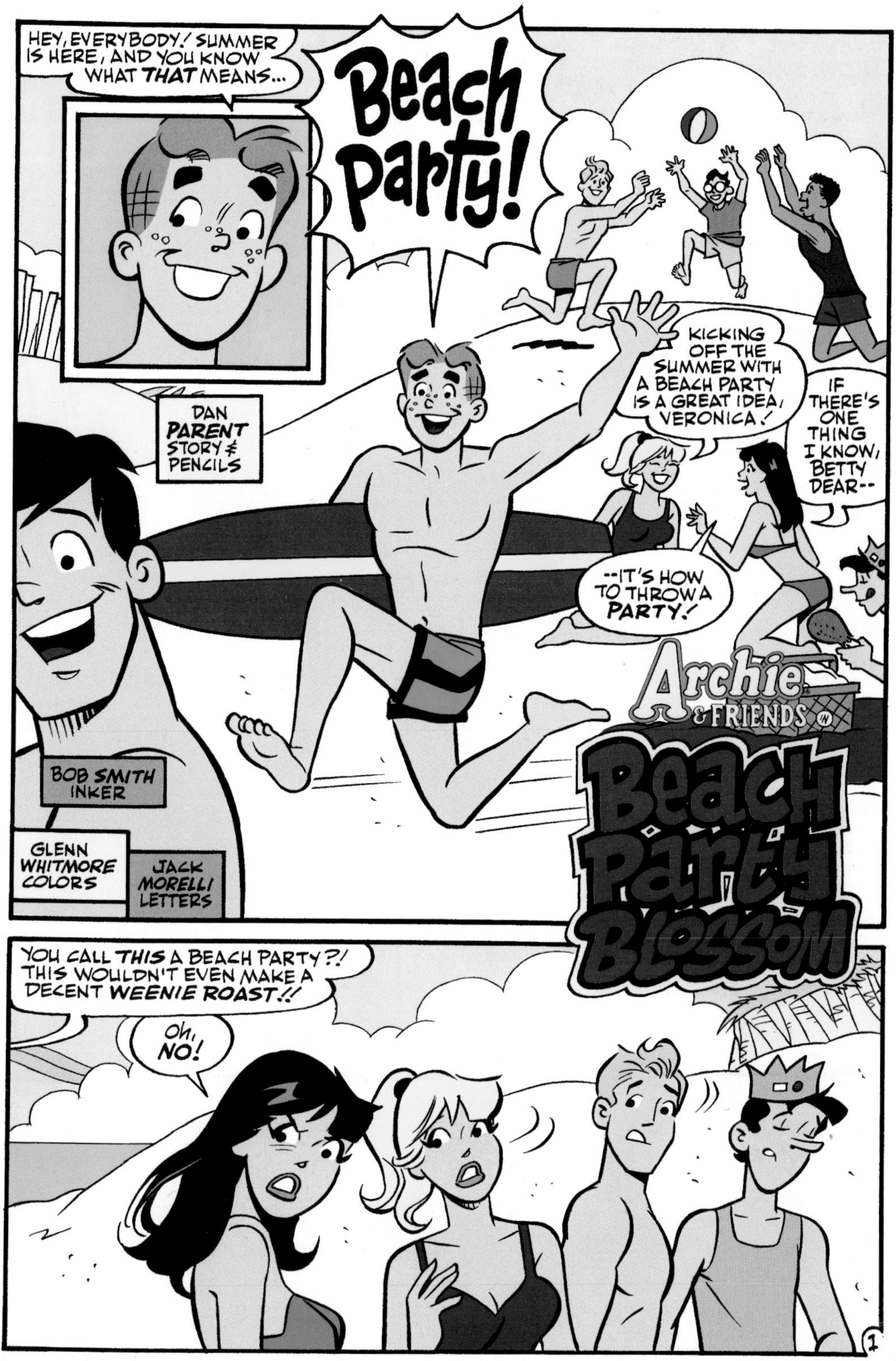
HEY, EVERYBODY! SUMMER IS HERE, AND YOU KNOW WHAT THAT MEANS...
Beach Party!
KICKING OFF THE SUMMER WITH A BEACH PARTY IS A GREAT IDEA, VERONICA!
IF THERE'S ONE THING I KNOW, BETTY DEAR--
--IT'S HOW TO THROW A PARTY!
DAN PARENT STORY & PENCILS
BOB SMITH INKER
GLENN WHITMORE COLORS
JACK MORELLI LETTERS
Archie & FRIENDS in
Beach Party Blossom
YOU CALL THIS A BEACH PARTY?! THIS WOULDN'T EVEN MAKE A DECENT WEENIE ROAST!!
Oh, NO!
1

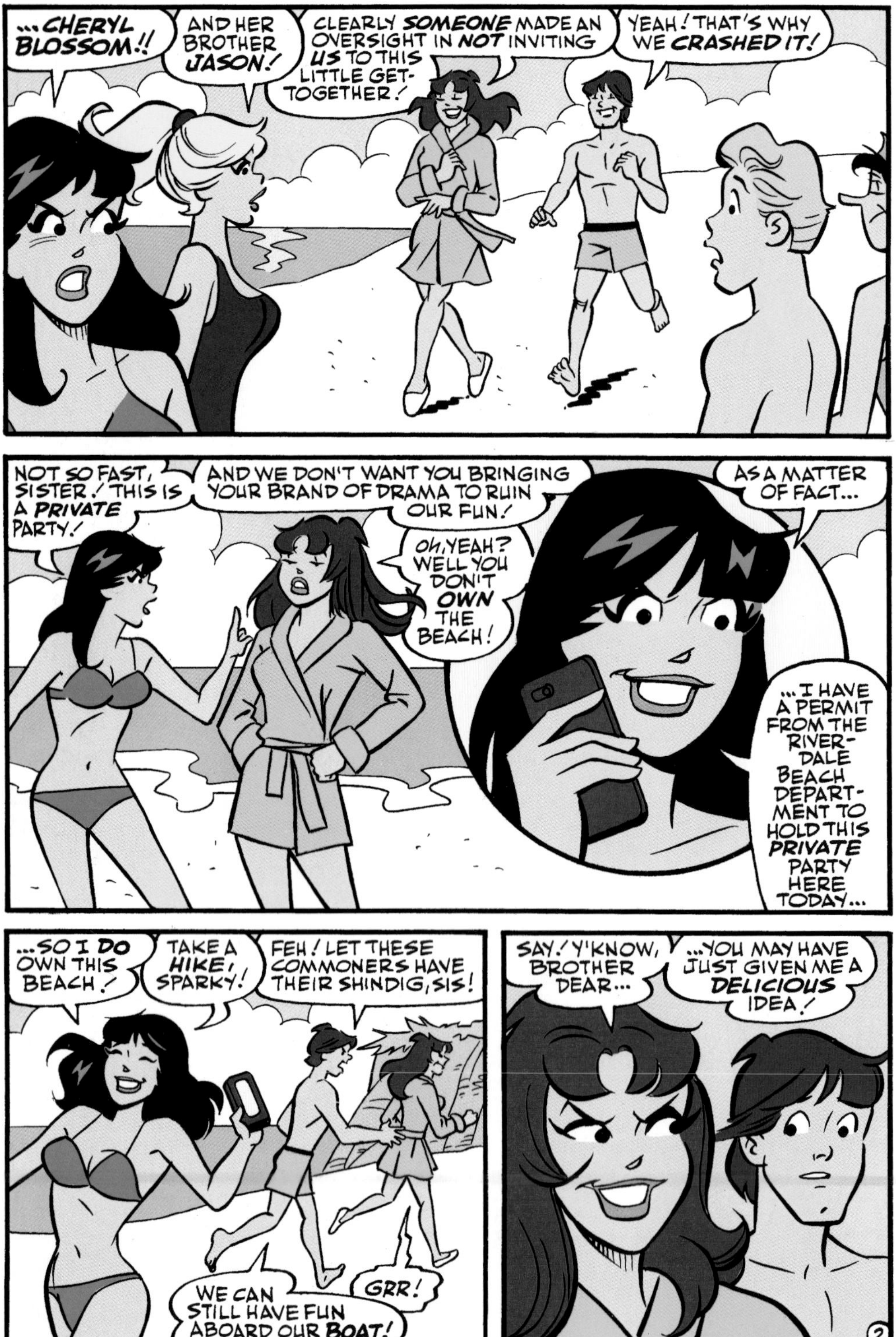
...CHERYL BLOSSOM!!
AND HER BROTHER JASON!
CLEARLY SOMEONE MADE AN OVERSIGHT IN NOT INVITING US TO THIS LITTLE GET-TOGETHER!
YEAH! THAT'S WHY WE CRASHED IT!
NOT SO FAST, SISTER! THIS IS A PRIVATE PARTY!
AND WE DON'T WANT YOU BRINGING YOUR BRAND OF DRAMA TO RUIN OUR FUN!
OH, YEAH? WELL YOU DON'T OWN THE BEACH!
AS A MATTER OF FACT...
...I HAVE A PERMIT FROM THE RIVER-DALE BEACH DEPART-MENT TO HOLD THIS PRIVATE PARTY HERE TODAY...
...SO I DO OWN THIS BEACH!
TAKE A HIKE, SPARKY!
FEH! LET THESE COMMONERS HAVE THEIR SHINDIG, SIS!
WE CAN STILL HAVE FUN ABOARD OUR BOAT!
GRR!
SAY! Y'KNOW, BROTHER DEAR...
...YOU MAY HAVE JUST GIVEN ME A DELICIOUS IDEA!
2

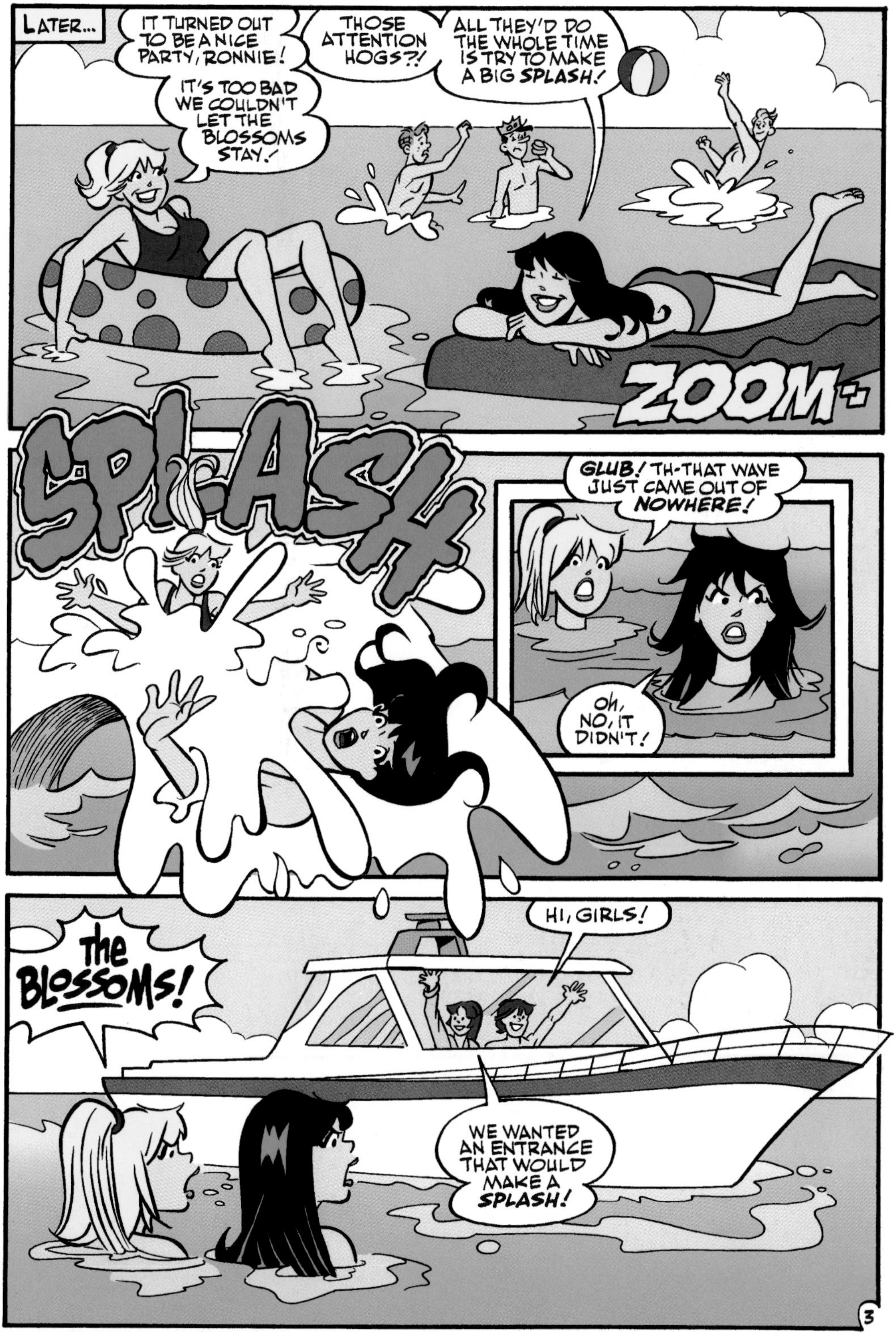
LATER...
IT TURNED OUT TO BE A NICE PARTY, RONNIE!
IT'S TOO BAD WE COULDN'T LET THE BLOSSOMS STAY!
THOSE ATTENTION HOGS?!
ALL THEY'D DO THE WHOLE TIME IS TRY TO MAKE A BIG SPLASH!
ZOOM-
SPLASH
GLUB! TH-THAT WAVE JUST CAME OUT OF NOWHERE!
OH, NO, IT DIDN'T!
the BLOSSOMS!
HI, GIRLS!
WE WANTED AN ENTRANCE THAT WOULD MAKE A SPLASH!
3

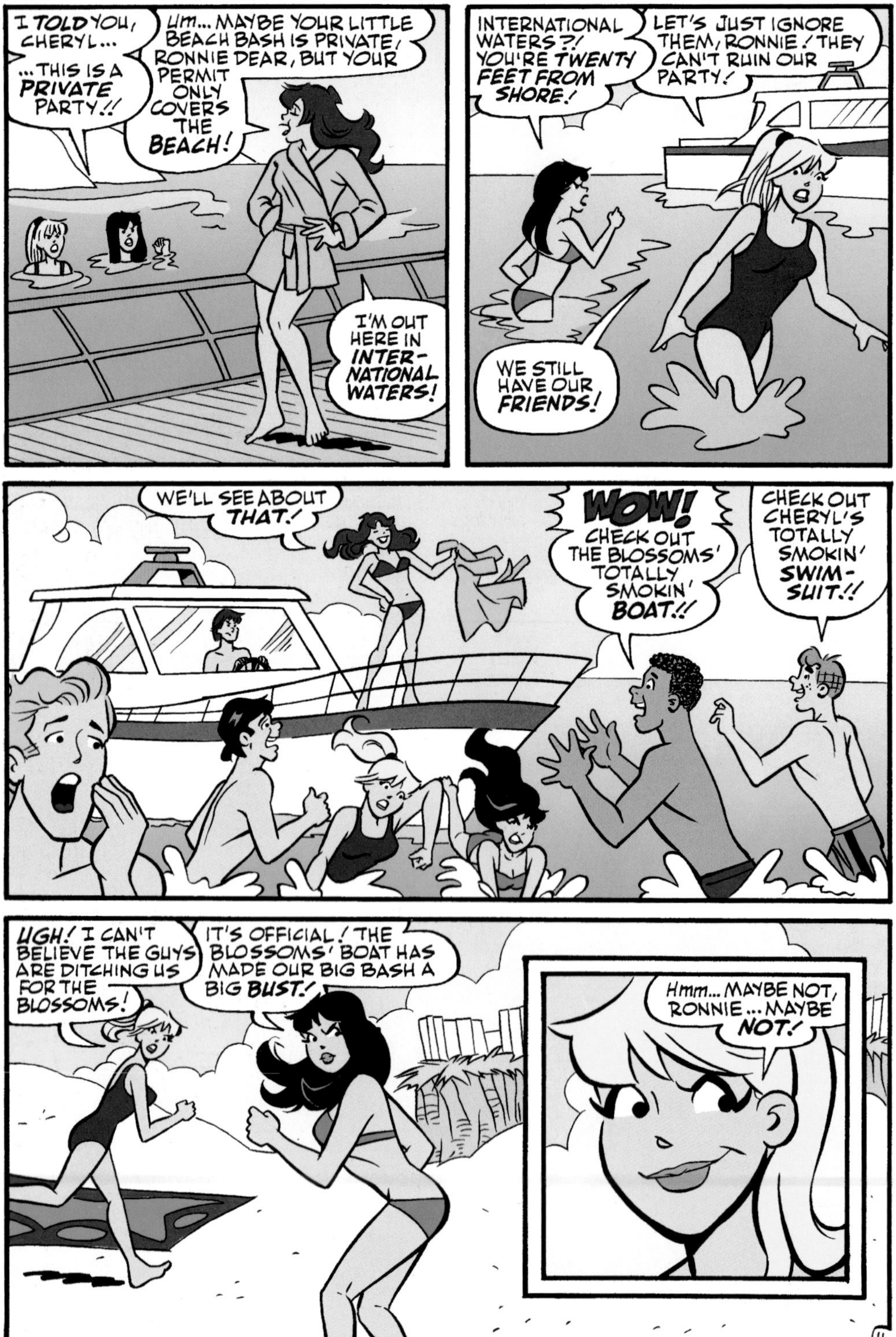
I TOLD YOU, CHERYL...
...THIS IS A PRIVATE PARTY!!
UM... MAYBE YOUR LITTLE BEACH BASH IS PRIVATE, RONNIE DEAR, BUT YOUR PERMIT ONLY COVERS THE BEACH!
I'M OUT HERE IN INTERNATIONAL WATERS!
INTERNATIONAL WATERS?! YOU'RE TWENTY FEET FROM SHORE!
LET'S JUST IGNORE THEM, RONNIE! THEY CAN'T RUIN OUR PARTY!
WE STILL HAVE OUR FRIENDS!
WE'LL SEE ABOUT THAT!
WOW! CHECK OUT THE BLOSSOMS' TOTALLY SMOKIN' BOAT!!
CHECK OUT CHERYL'S TOTALLY SMOKIN' SWIM-SUIT!!
UGH! I CAN'T BELIEVE THE GUYS ARE DITCHING US FOR THE BLOSSOMS!
IT'S OFFICIAL! THE BLOSSOMS' BOAT HAS MADE OUR BIG BASH A BIG BUST!
Hmm... MAYBE NOT, RONNIE... MAYBE NOT!
4

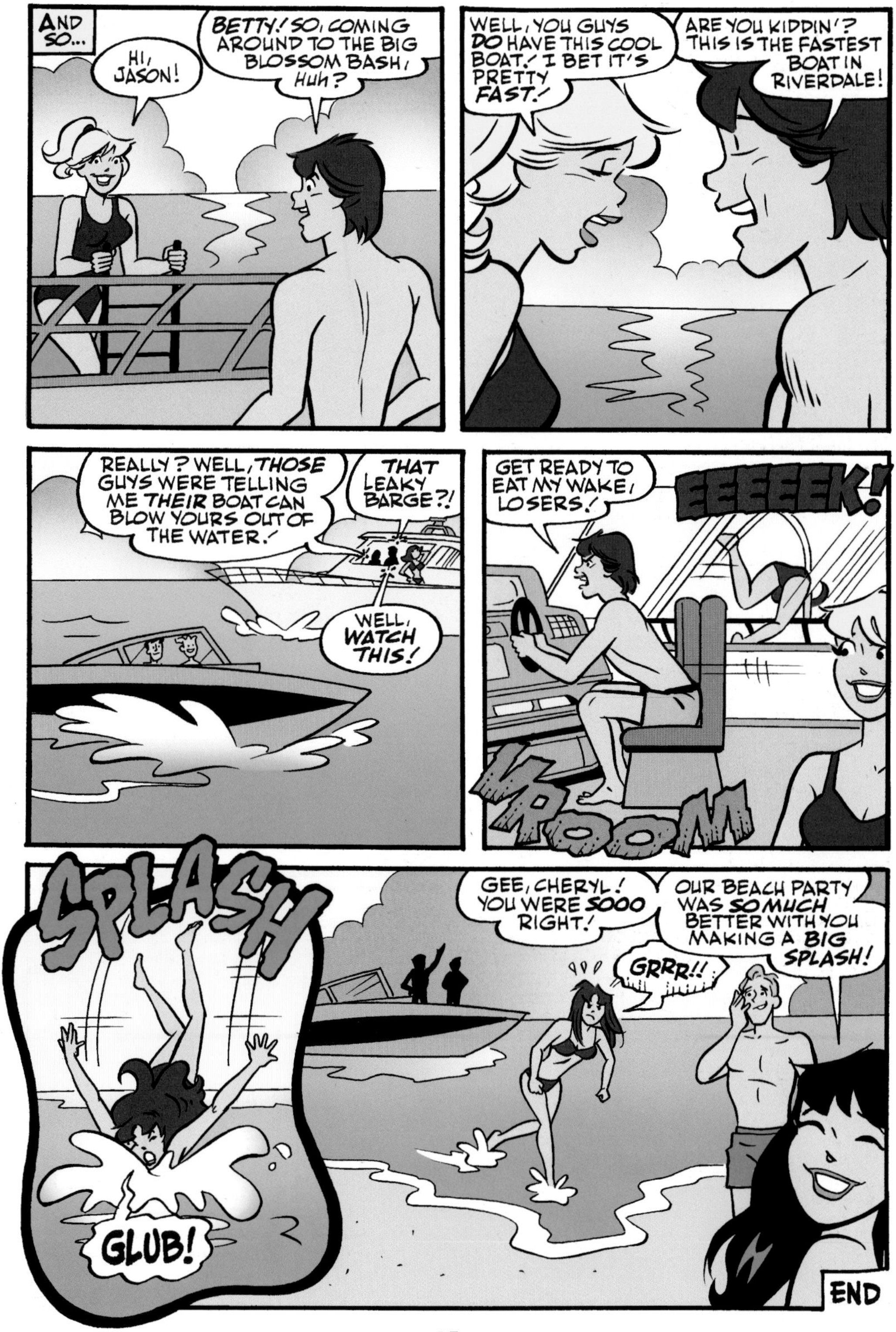
AND SO...
HI, JASON!
BETTY! SO, COMING AROUND TO THE BIG BLOSSOM BASH, HUH?
WELL, YOU GUYS DO HAVE THIS COOL BOAT! I BET IT'S PRETTY FAST!
ARE YOU KIDDIN'? THIS IS THE FASTEST BOAT IN RIVERDALE!
REALLY? WELL, THOSE GUYS WERE TELLING ME THEIR BOAT CAN BLOW YOURS OUT OF THE WATER!
THAT LEAKY BARGE?!
WELL, WATCH THIS!
GET READY TO EAT MY WAKE, LOSERS!
EEEEEK!
VROOOM
SPLASH
GLUB!
GEE, CHERYL! YOU WERE SOOO RIGHT!
OUR BEACH PARTY WAS SO MUCH BETTER WITH YOU MAKING A BIG SPLASH!
GRRR!!
END

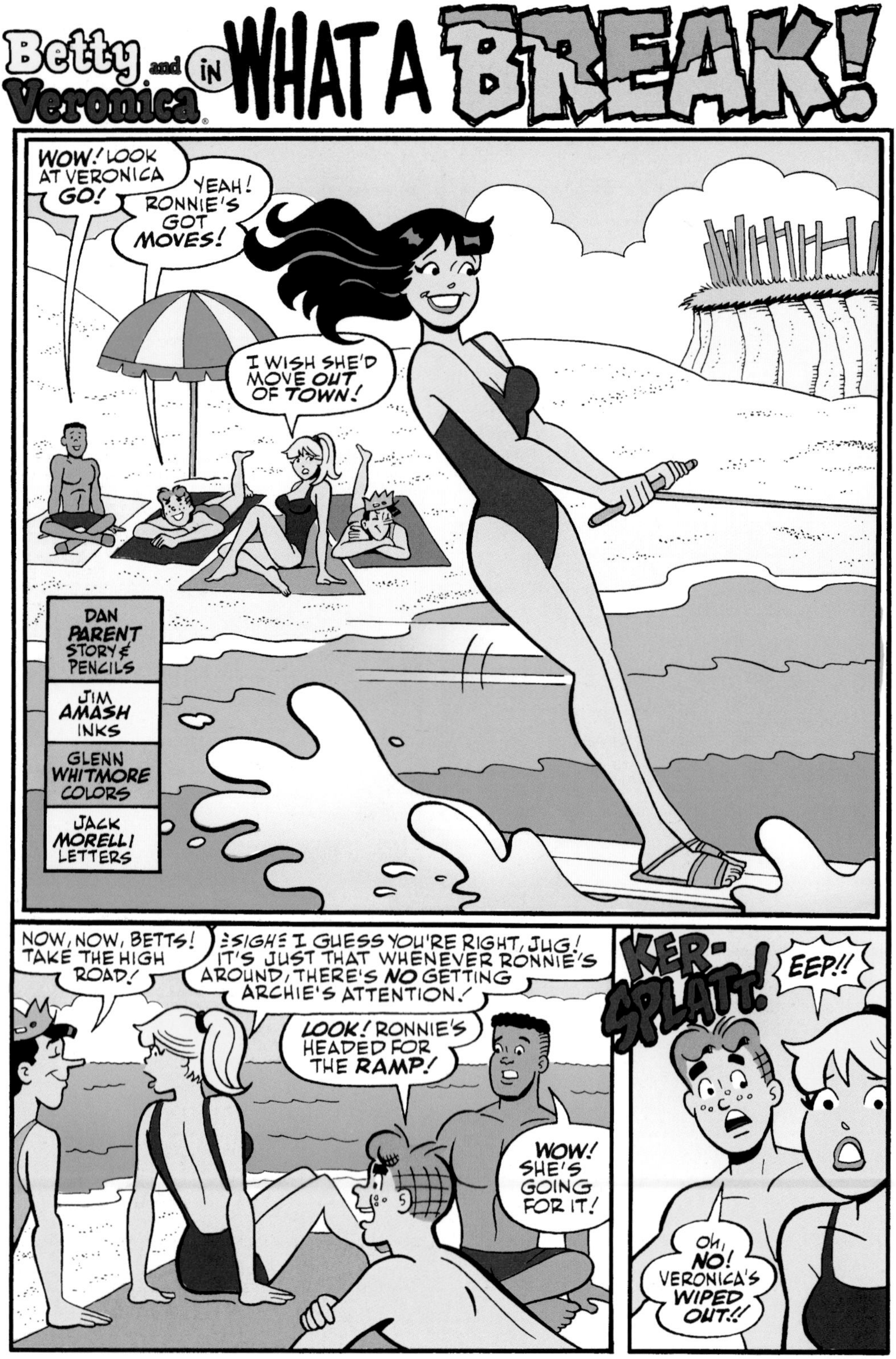
Betty and Veronica in WHAT A BREAK!
WOW! LOOK AT VERONICA GO!
YEAH! RONNIE'S GOT MOVES!
I WISH SHE'D MOVE OUT OF TOWN!
DAN PARENT STORY & PENCILS
JIM AMASH INKS
GLENN WHITMORE COLORS
JACK MORELLI LETTERS
NOW, NOW, BETTS! TAKE THE HIGH ROAD!
SIGH I GUESS YOU'RE RIGHT, JUG! IT'S JUST THAT WHENEVER RONNIE'S AROUND, THERE'S NO GETTING ARCHIE'S ATTENTION!
LOOK! RONNIE'S HEADED FOR THE RAMP!
WOW! SHE'S GOING FOR IT!
KER-SPLATT!
EEP!!
OH, NO! VERONICA'S WIPED OUT!!

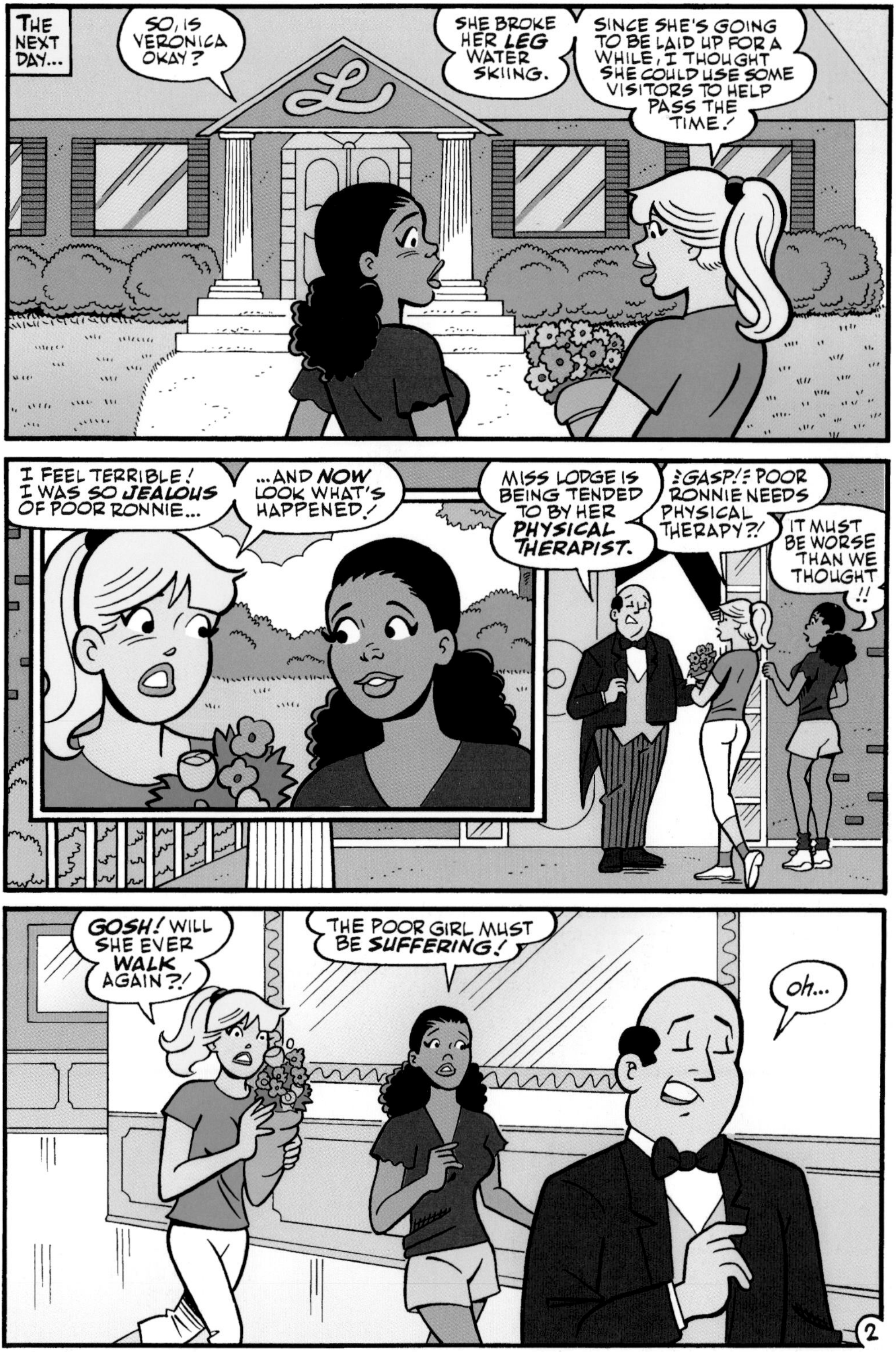
THE NEXT DAY...
SO, IS VERONICA OKAY?
SHE BROKE HER LEG WATER SKIING.
SINCE SHE'S GOING TO BE LAID UP FOR A WHILE, I THOUGHT SHE COULD USE SOME VISITORS TO HELP PASS THE TIME!
I FEEL TERRIBLE! I WAS SO JEALOUS OF POOR RONNIE...
...AND NOW LOOK WHAT'S HAPPENED!
MISS LODGE IS BEING TENDED TO BY HER PHYSICAL THERAPIST.
GASP! POOR RONNIE NEEDS PHYSICAL THERAPY?!
IT MUST BE WORSE THAN WE THOUGHT!!
GOSH! WILL SHE EVER WALK AGAIN?!
THE POOR GIRL MUST BE SUFFERING!
oh...
2

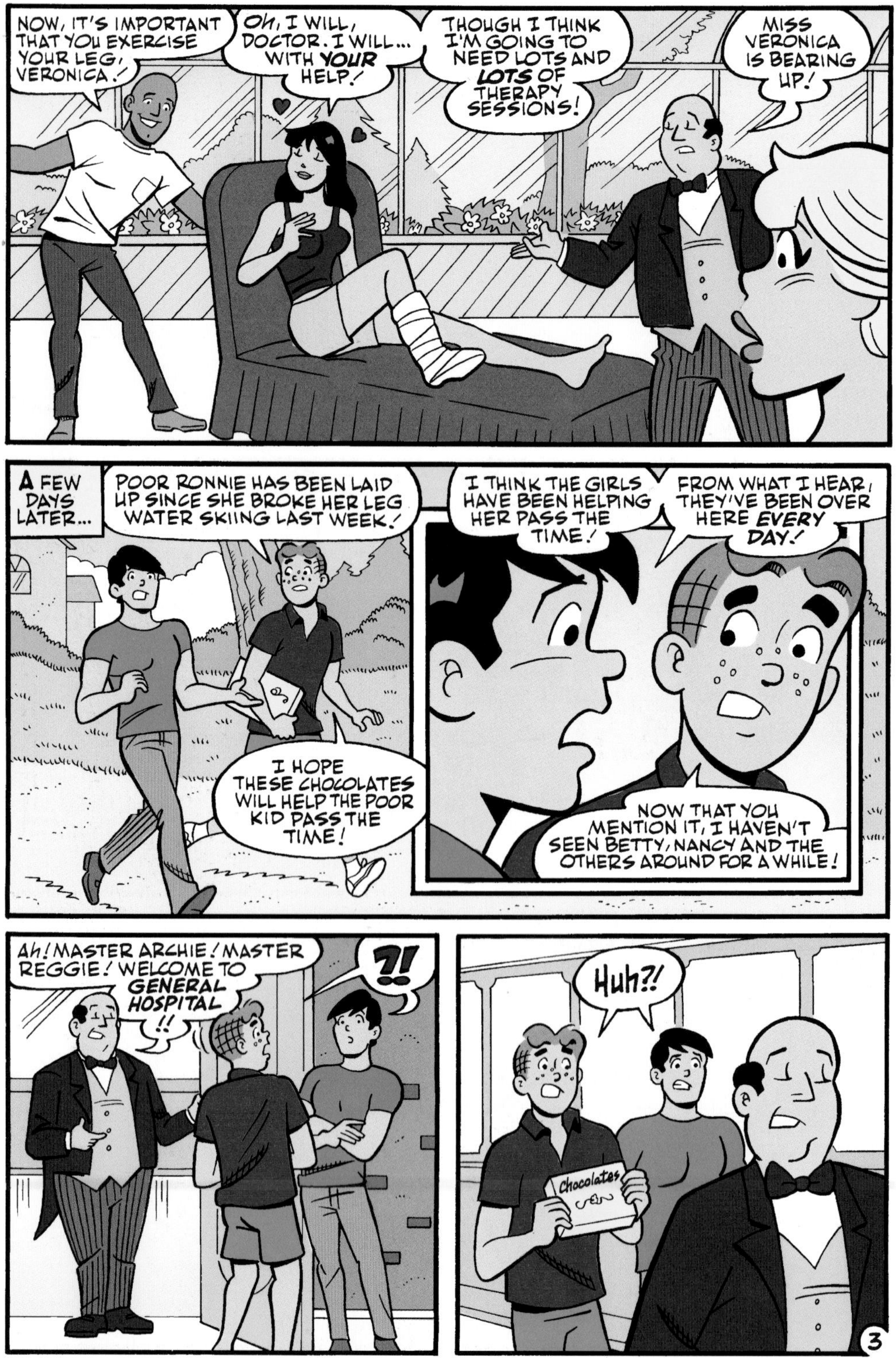
NOW, IT'S IMPORTANT THAT YOU EXERCISE YOUR LEG, VERONICA!
OH, I WILL, DOCTOR. I WILL... WITH YOUR HELP!
THOUGH I THINK I'M GOING TO NEED LOTS AND LOTS OF THERAPY SESSIONS!
MISS VERONICA IS BEARING UP!
A FEW DAYS LATER...
POOR RONNIE HAS BEEN LAID UP SINCE SHE BROKE HER LEG WATER SKIING LAST WEEK!
I HOPE THESE CHOCOLATES WILL HELP THE POOR KID PASS THE TIME!
I THINK THE GIRLS HAVE BEEN HELPING HER PASS THE TIME!
FROM WHAT I HEAR, THEY'VE BEEN OVER HERE EVERY DAY!
NOW THAT YOU MENTION IT, I HAVEN'T SEEN BETTY, NANCY AND THE OTHERS AROUND FOR A WHILE!
AH! MASTER ARCHIE! MASTER REGGIE! WELCOME TO GENERAL HOSPITAL
!!
?!
Huh?!
Chocolates
3

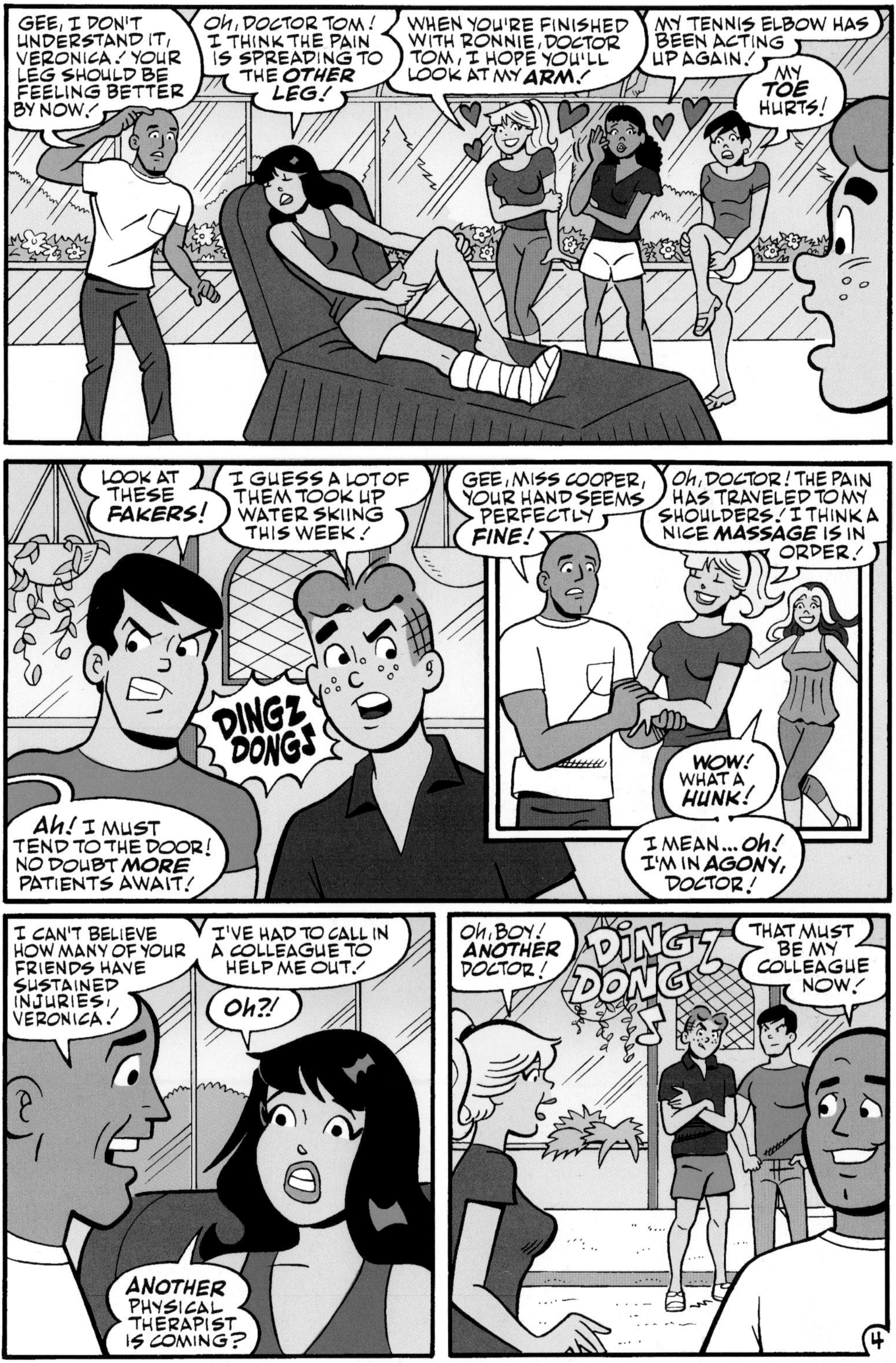
GEE, I DON'T UNDERSTAND IT, VERONICA! YOUR LEG SHOULD BE FEELING BETTER BY NOW!
OH, DOCTOR TOM! I THINK THE PAIN IS SPREADING TO THE OTHER LEG!
WHEN YOU'RE FINISHED WITH RONNIE, DOCTOR TOM, I HOPE YOU'LL LOOK AT MY ARM!
MY TENNIS ELBOW HAS BEEN ACTING UP AGAIN!
MY TOE HURTS!
LOOK AT THESE FAKERS!
I GUESS A LOT OF THEM TOOK UP WATER SKIING THIS WEEK!
DING DONG
AH! I MUST TEND TO THE DOOR! NO DOUBT MORE PATIENTS AWAIT!
GEE, MISS COOPER, YOUR HAND SEEMS PERFECTLY FINE!
OH, DOCTOR! THE PAIN HAS TRAVELED TO MY SHOULDERS! I THINK A NICE MASSAGE IS IN ORDER!
WOW! WHAT A HUNK!
I MEAN... OH! I'M IN AGONY, DOCTOR!
I CAN'T BELIEVE HOW MANY OF YOUR FRIENDS HAVE SUSTAINED INJURIES, VERONICA!
I'VE HAD TO CALL IN A COLLEAGUE TO HELP ME OUT!
OH?!
ANOTHER PHYSICAL THERAPIST IS COMING?
OH, BOY! ANOTHER DOCTOR!
DING DONG
THAT MUST BE MY COLLEAGUE NOW!
4

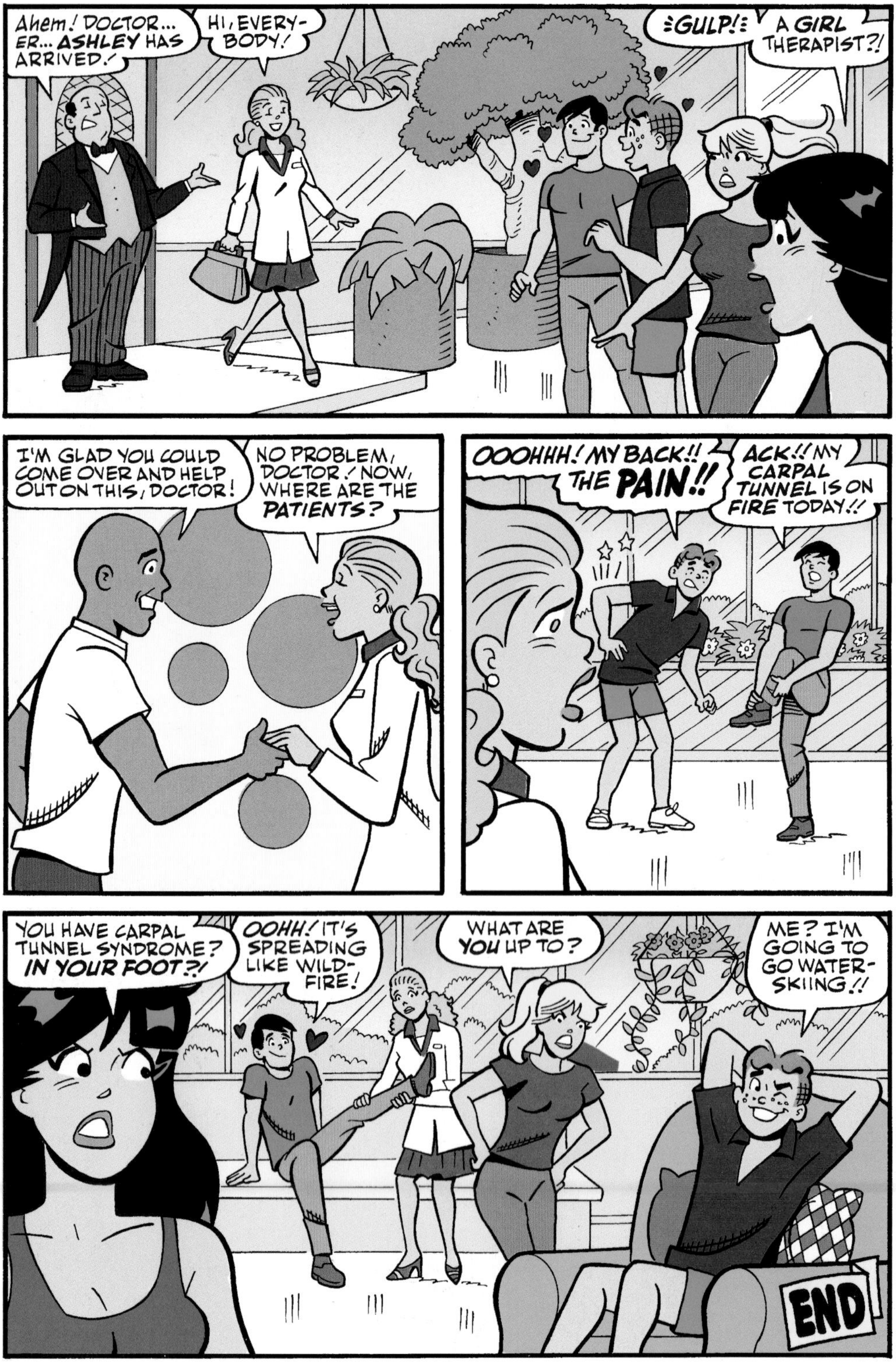
Ahem! DOCTOR... ER... ASHLEY HAS ARRIVED!
HI, EVERY-BODY!
GULP!
A GIRL THERAPIST?!
I'M GLAD YOU COULD COME OVER AND HELP OUT ON THIS, DOCTOR!
NO PROBLEM, DOCTOR! NOW, WHERE ARE THE PATIENTS?
OOOHHH! MY BACK!! THE PAIN!!
ACK!! MY CARPAL TUNNEL IS ON FIRE TODAY!!
YOU HAVE CARPAL TUNNEL SYNDROME? IN YOUR FOOT?!
OOHH! IT'S SPREADING LIKE WILD-FIRE!
WHAT ARE YOU UP TO?
ME? I'M GOING TO GO WATER-SKIING!!
END

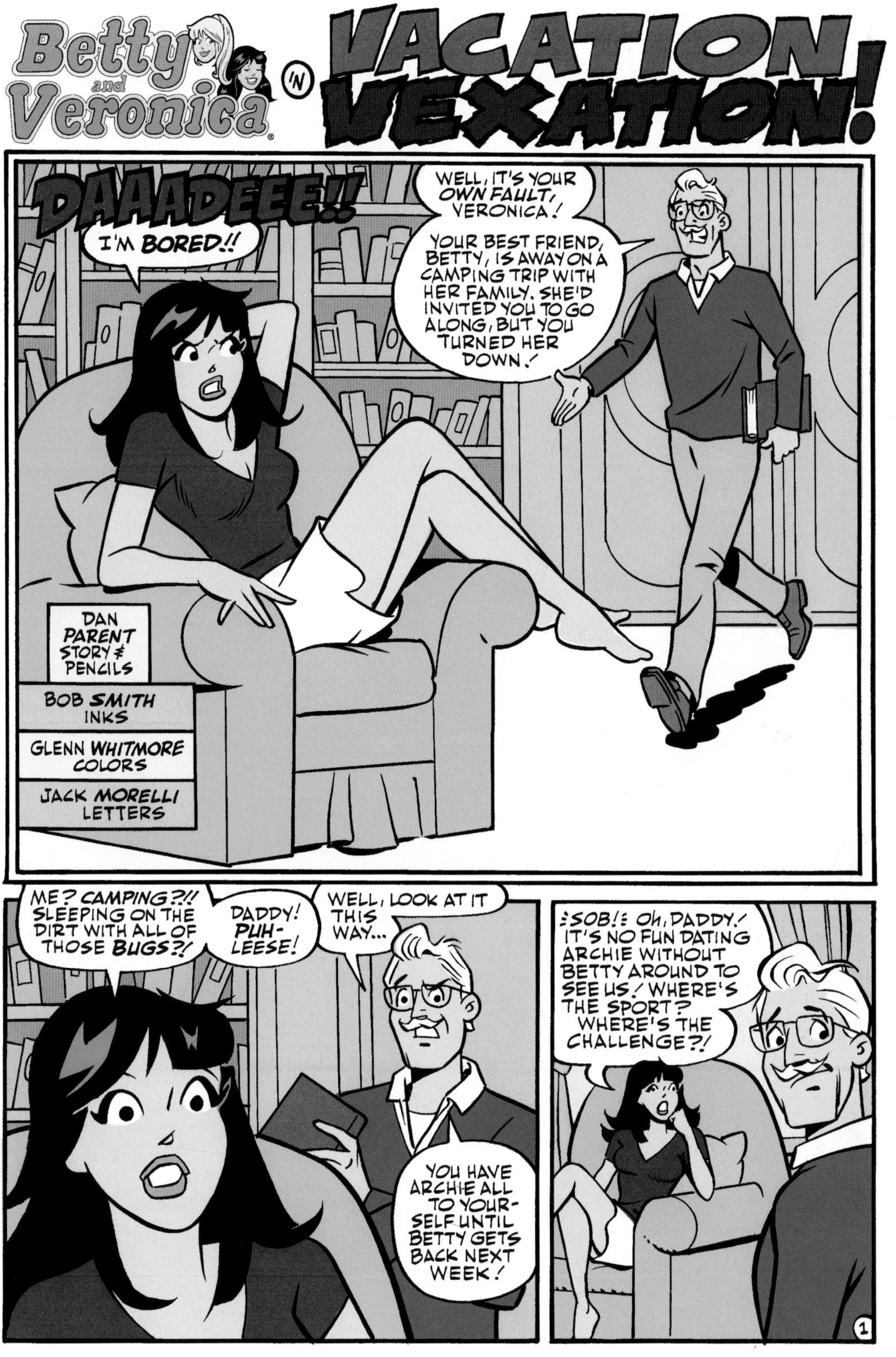
Betty and Veronica
IN
VACATION VEXATION!
DAAADEEE!!
I'M BORED!!
WELL, IT'S YOUR OWN FAULT, VERONICA!
YOUR BEST FRIEND, BETTY, IS AWAY ON A CAMPING TRIP WITH HER FAMILY. SHE'D INVITED YOU TO GO ALONG, BUT YOU TURNED HER DOWN!
DAN PARENT STORY & PENCILS
BOB SMITH INKS
GLENN WHITMORE COLORS
JACK MORELLI LETTERS
ME? CAMPING?!! SLEEPING ON THE DIRT WITH ALL OF THOSE BUGS?!
DADDY! PUH-LEESE!
WELL, LOOK AT IT THIS WAY...
YOU HAVE ARCHIE ALL TO YOURSELF UNTIL BETTY GETS BACK NEXT WEEK!
:SOB!: Oh, DADDY! IT'S NO FUN DATING ARCHIE WITHOUT BETTY AROUND TO SEE US! WHERE'S THE SPORT? WHERE'S THE CHALLENGE?!
1

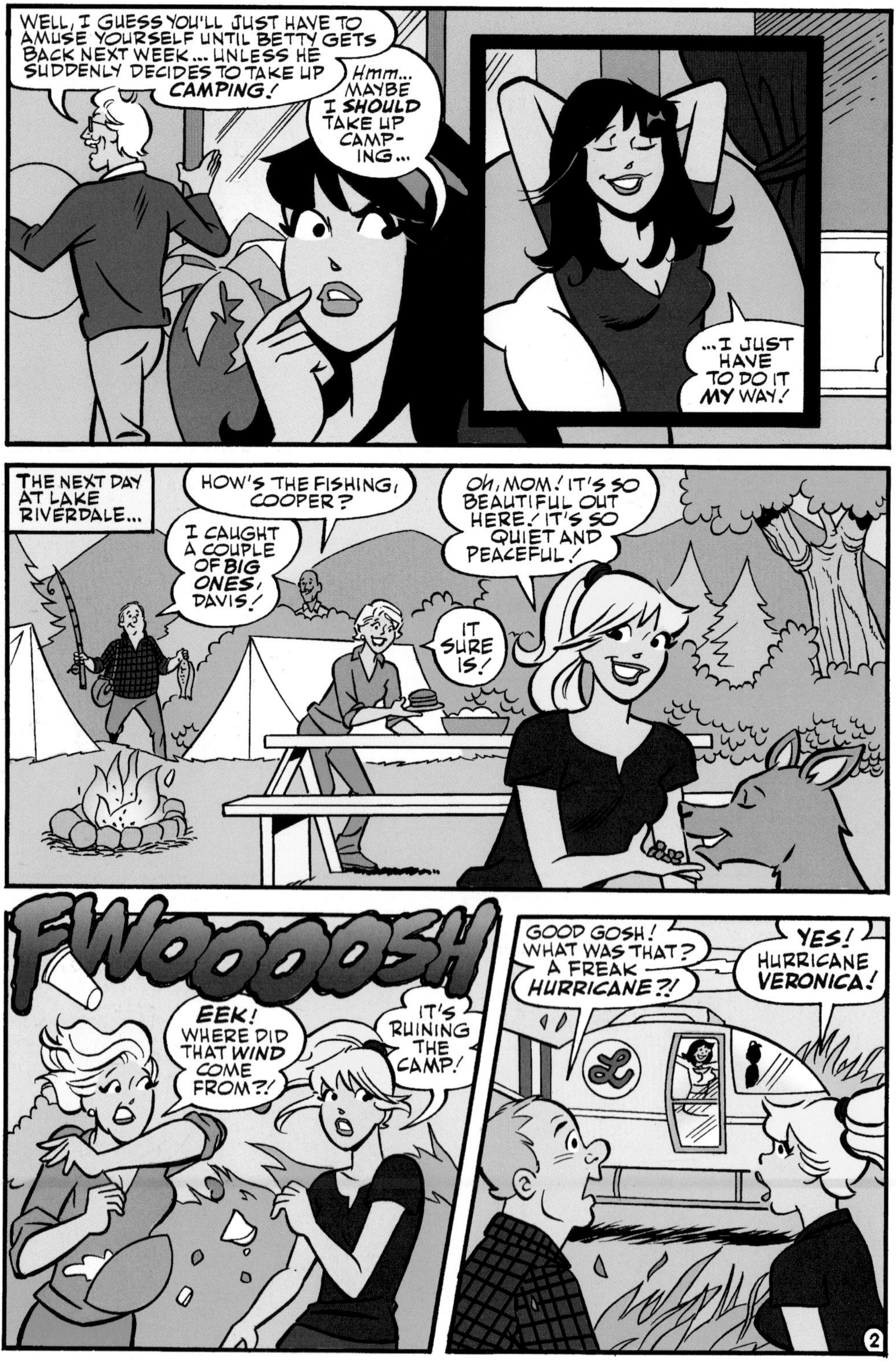
WELL, I GUESS YOU'LL JUST HAVE TO AMUSE YOURSELF UNTIL BETTY GETS BACK NEXT WEEK... UNLESS HE SUDDENLY DECIDES TO TAKE UP CAMPING!
Hmm... MAYBE I SHOULD TAKE UP CAMP-ING...
...I JUST HAVE TO DO IT MY WAY!
THE NEXT DAY AT LAKE RIVERDALE...
HOW'S THE FISHING, COOPER?
I CAUGHT A COUPLE OF BIG ONES, DAVIS!
Oh, MOM! IT'S SO BEAUTIFUL OUT HERE! IT'S SO QUIET AND PEACEFUL!
IT SURE IS!
FWOOOOSH
EEK! WHERE DID THAT WIND COME FROM?!
IT'S RUINING THE CAMP!
GOOD GOSH! WHAT WAS THAT? A FREAK HURRICANE?!
YES! HURRICANE VERONICA!
2

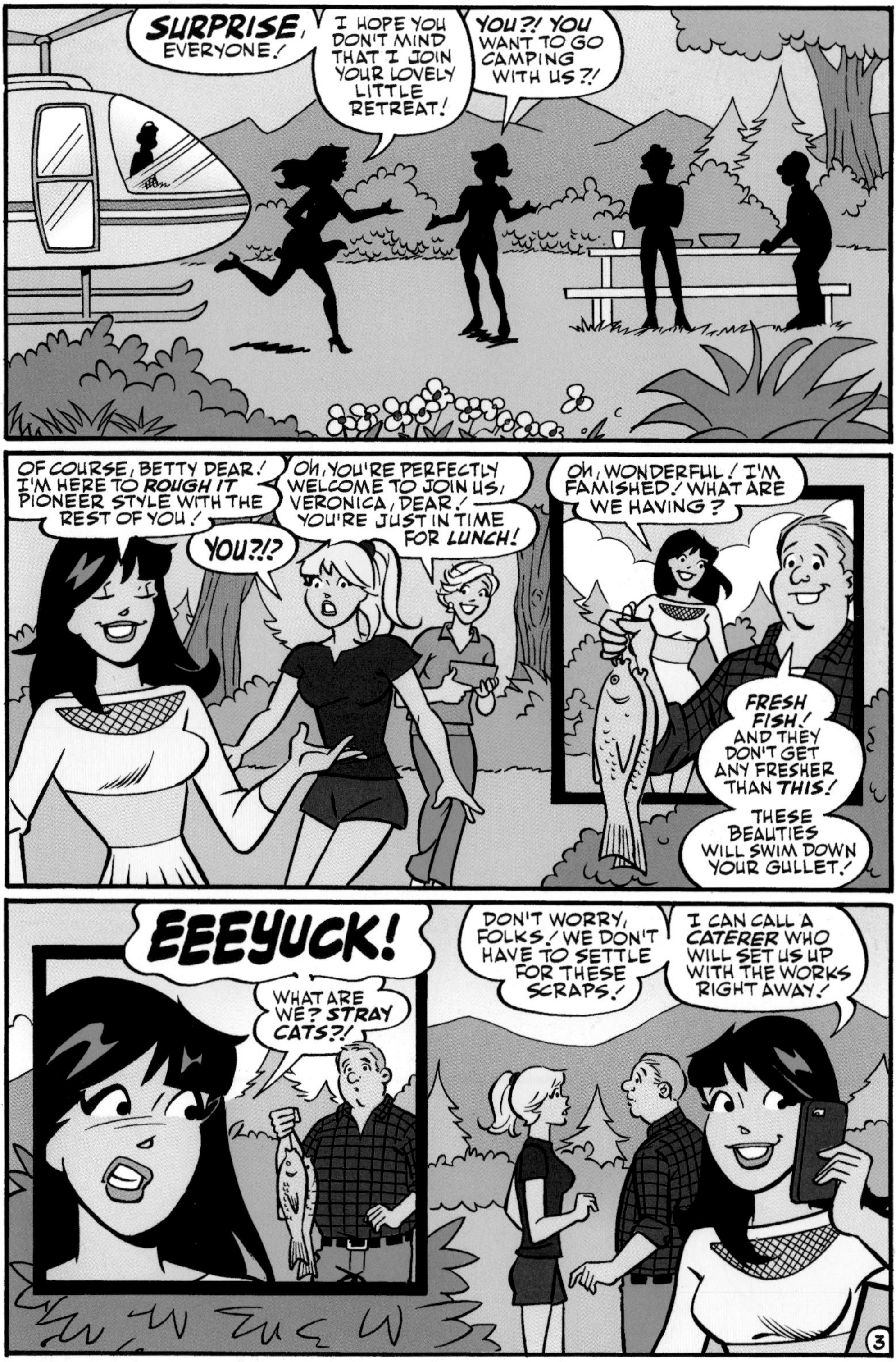
SURPRISE, EVERYONE!
I HOPE YOU DON'T MIND THAT I JOIN YOUR LOVELY LITTLE RETREAT!
YOU?! YOU WANT TO GO CAMPING WITH US?!
OF COURSE, BETTY DEAR! I'M HERE TO ROUGH IT PIONEER STYLE WITH THE REST OF YOU!
YOU?!?
OH, YOU'RE PERFECTLY WELCOME TO JOIN US, VERONICA, DEAR! YOU'RE JUST IN TIME FOR LUNCH!
OH, WONDERFUL! I'M FAMISHED! WHAT ARE WE HAVING?
FRESH FISH! AND THEY DON'T GET ANY FRESHER THAN THIS!
THESE BEAUTIES WILL SWIM DOWN YOUR GULLET!
EEEYUCK!
WHAT ARE WE? STRAY CATS?!
DON'T WORRY, FOLKS! WE DON'T HAVE TO SETTLE FOR THESE SCRAPS!
I CAN CALL A CATERER WHO WILL SET US UP WITH THE WORKS RIGHT AWAY!
3

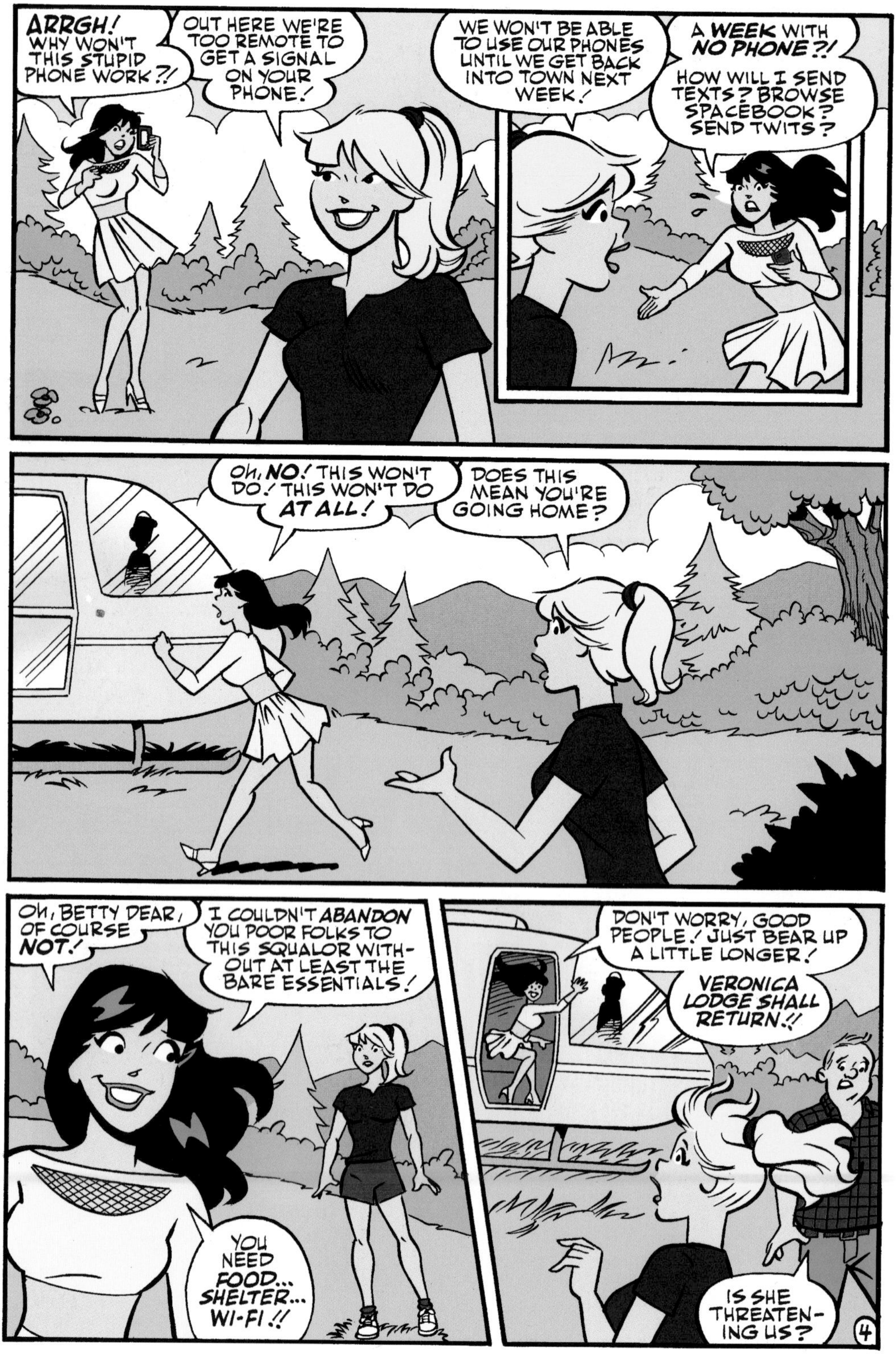
ARRGH! WHY WON'T THIS STUPID PHONE WORK?!
OUT HERE WE'RE TOO REMOTE TO GET A SIGNAL ON YOUR PHONE!
WE WON'T BE ABLE TO USE OUR PHONES UNTIL WE GET BACK INTO TOWN NEXT WEEK!
A WEEK WITH NO PHONE?!
HOW WILL I SEND TEXTS? BROWSE SPACEBOOK? SEND TWITS?
Oh, NO! THIS WON'T DO! THIS WON'T DO AT ALL!
DOES THIS MEAN YOU'RE GOING HOME?
Oh, BETTY DEAR, OF COURSE NOT!
I COULDN'T ABANDON YOU POOR FOLKS TO THIS SQUALOR WITHOUT AT LEAST THE BARE ESSENTIALS!
YOU NEED FOOD... SHELTER... WI-FI!!
DON'T WORRY, GOOD PEOPLE! JUST BEAR UP A LITTLE LONGER!
VERONICA LODGE SHALL RETURN!!
IS SHE THREATENING US?
4

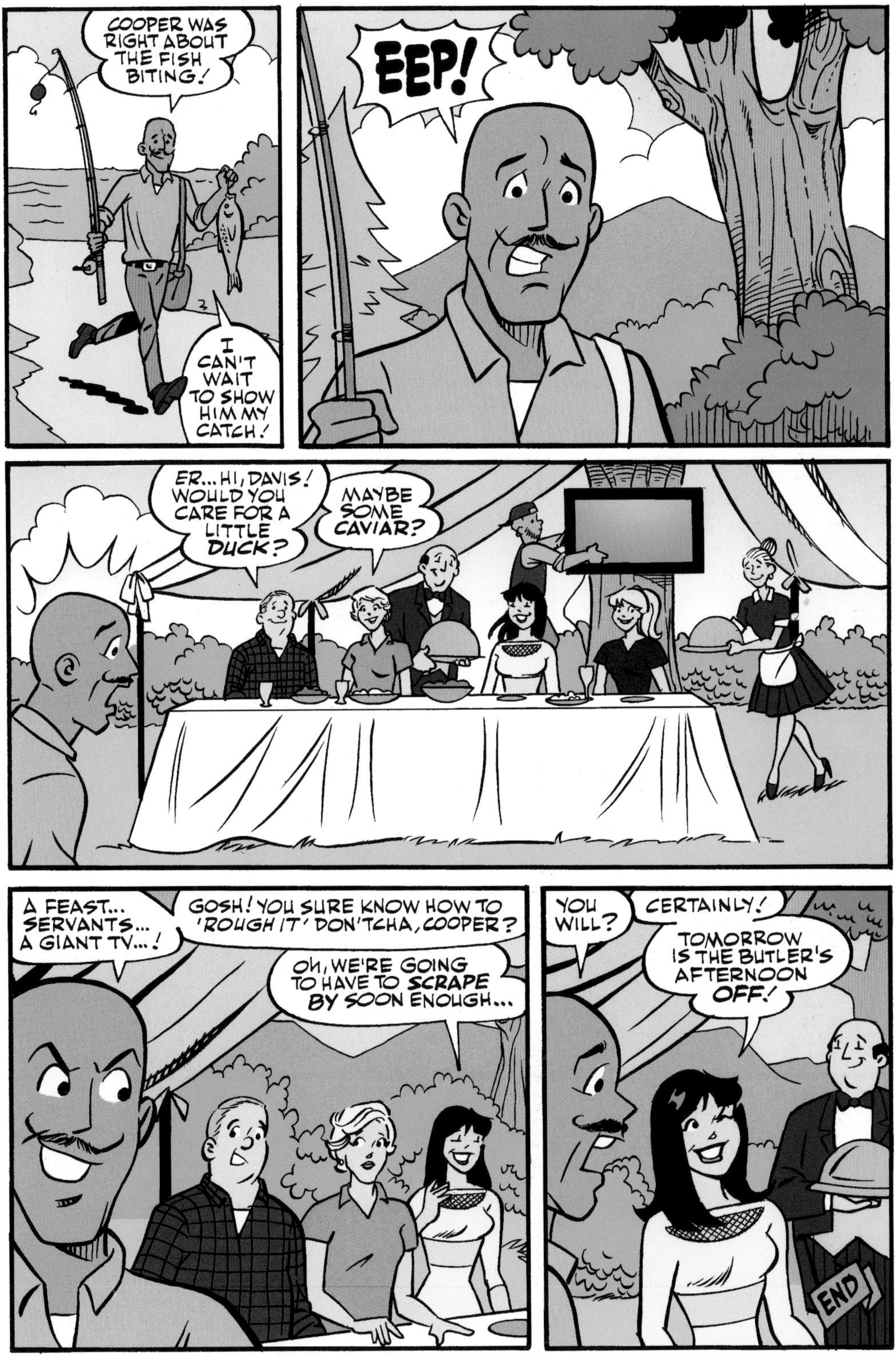
COOPER WAS RIGHT ABOUT THE FISH BITING!
I CAN'T WAIT TO SHOW HIM MY CATCH!
EEP!
ER...HI, DAVIS! WOULD YOU CARE FOR A LITTLE DUCK?
MAYBE SOME CAVIAR?
A FEAST... SERVANTS... A GIANT TV...!
GOSH! YOU SURE KNOW HOW TO 'ROUGH IT' DON'TCHA, COOPER?
OH, WE'RE GOING TO HAVE TO SCRAPE BY SOON ENOUGH...
YOU WILL?
CERTAINLY!
TOMORROW IS THE BUTLER'S AFTERNOON OFF!
END

Archie in BEACHWATCH!

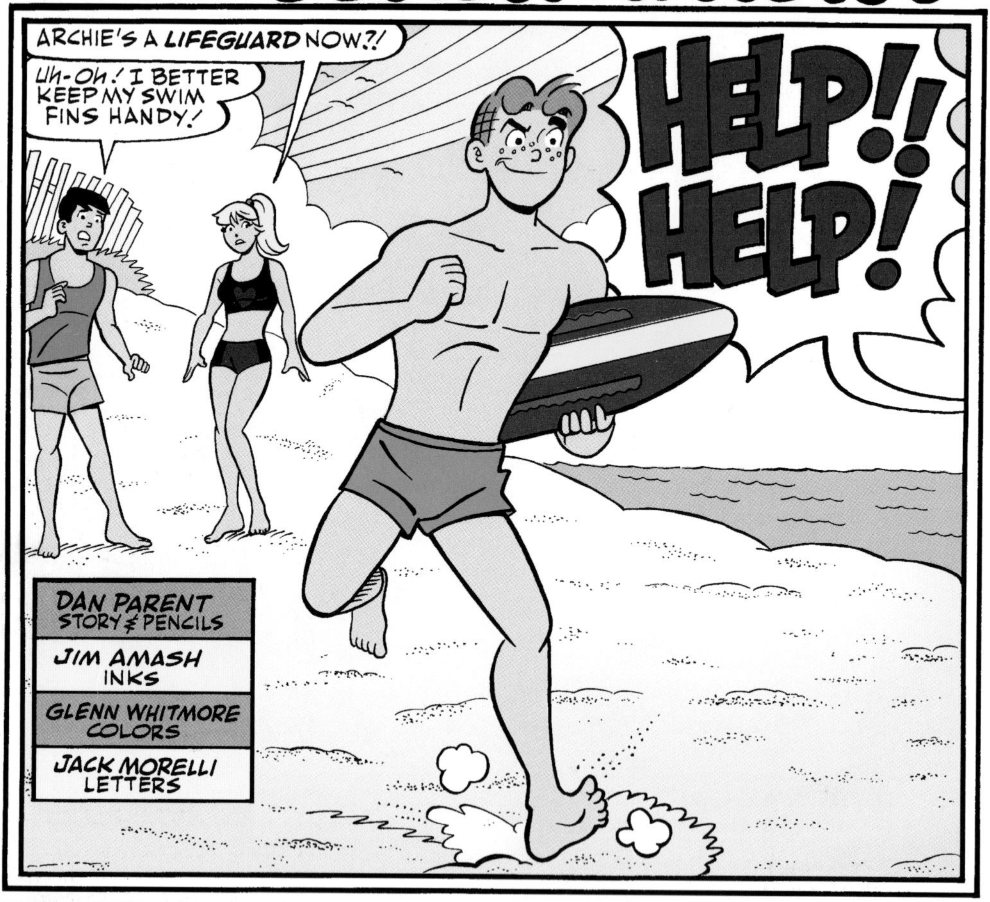
ARCHIE'S A LIFEGUARD NOW?!
UH-OH! I BETTER KEEP MY SWIM FINS HANDY!
HELP!! HELP!
DAN PARENT STORY & PENCILS
JIM AMASH INKS
GLENN WHITMORE COLORS
JACK MORELLI LETTERS

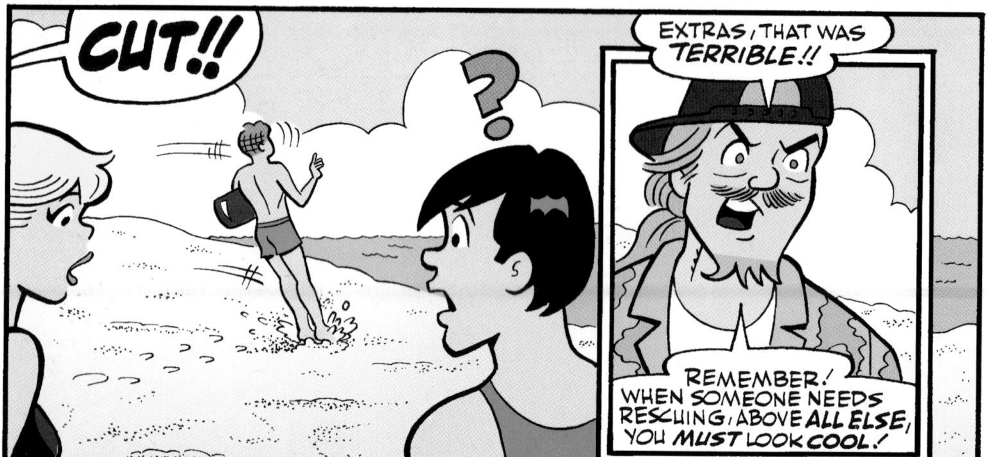
CUT!!
?
EXTRAS, THAT WAS TERRIBLE!!
REMEMBER! WHEN SOMEONE NEEDS RESCUING, ABOVE ALL ELSE, YOU MUST LOOK COOL!

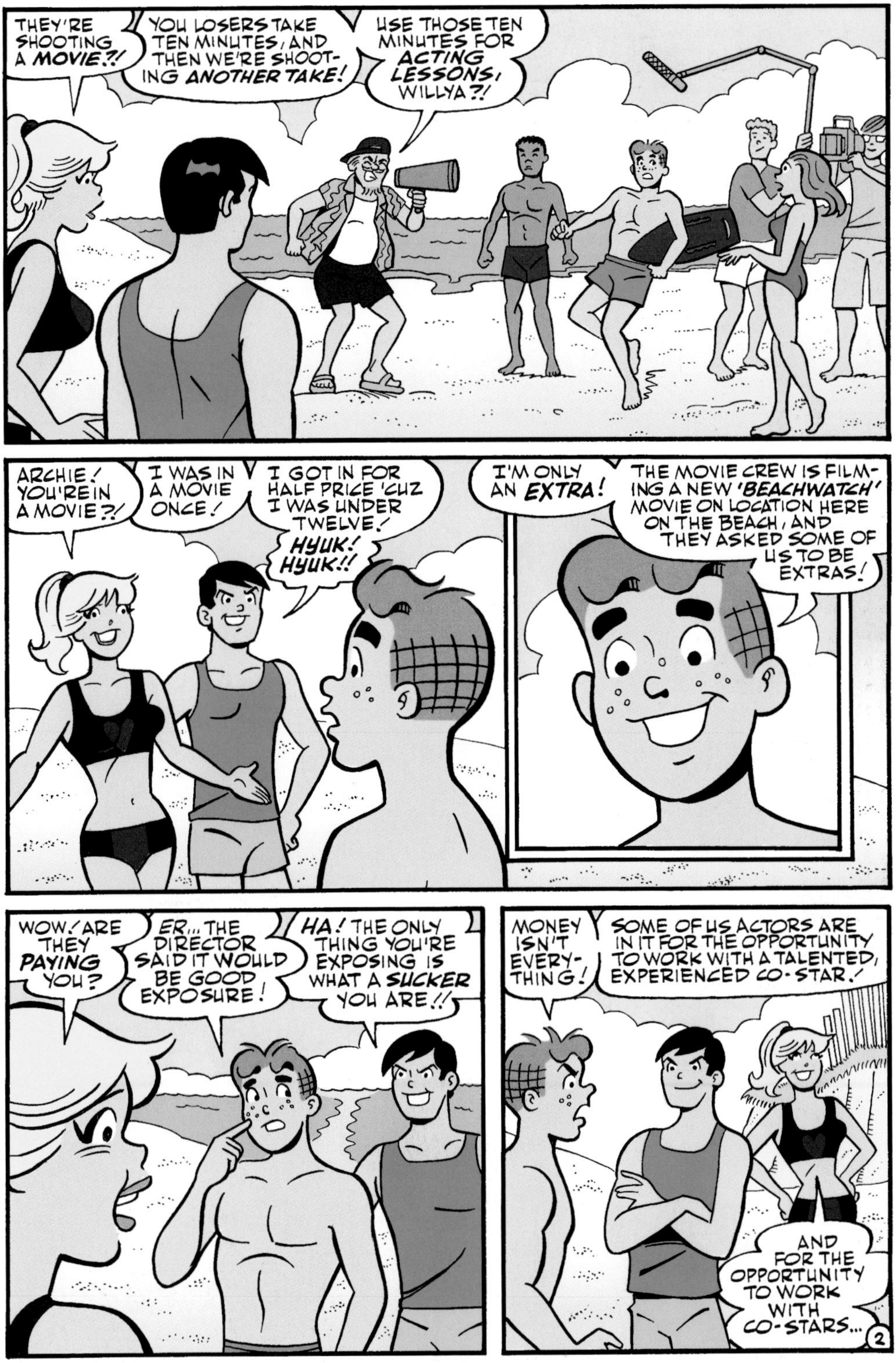
THEY'RE SHOOTING A MOVIE?!
YOU LOSERS TAKE TEN MINUTES, AND THEN WE'RE SHOOTING ANOTHER TAKE!
USE THOSE TEN MINUTES FOR ACTING LESSONS, WILLYA?!
ARCHIE! YOU'RE IN A MOVIE?!
I WAS IN A MOVIE ONCE!
I GOT IN FOR HALF PRICE 'CUZ I WAS UNDER TWELVE! HYUK! HYUK!!
I'M ONLY AN EXTRA!
THE MOVIE CREW IS FILMING A NEW 'BEACHWATCH' MOVIE ON LOCATION HERE ON THE BEACH, AND THEY ASKED SOME OF US TO BE EXTRAS!
WOW! ARE THEY PAYING YOU?
ER... THE DIRECTOR SAID IT WOULD BE GOOD EXPOSURE!
HA! THE ONLY THING YOU'RE EXPOSING IS WHAT A SUCKER YOU ARE!!
MONEY ISN'T EVERYTHING!
SOME OF US ACTORS ARE IN IT FOR THE OPPORTUNITY TO WORK WITH A TALENTED, EXPERIENCED CO-STAR!
AND FOR THE OPPORTUNITY TO WORK WITH CO-STARS...
2

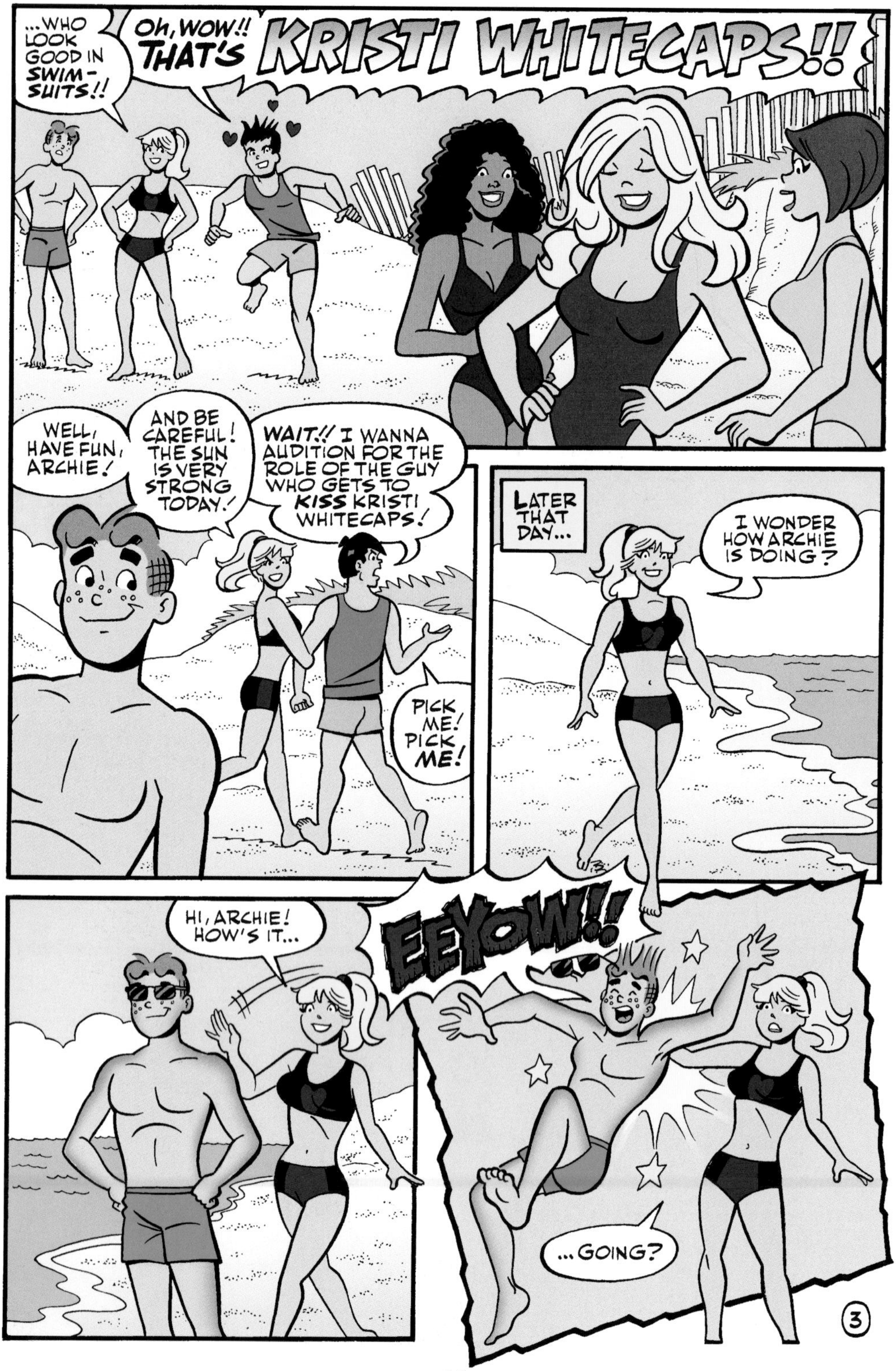
...WHO LOOK GOOD IN SWIM-SUITS!!
Oh, WOW!! THAT'S KRISTI WHITECAPS!!
WELL, HAVE FUN, ARCHIE!
AND BE CAREFUL! THE SUN IS VERY STRONG TODAY!
WAIT!! I WANNA AUDITION FOR THE ROLE OF THE GUY WHO GETS TO KISS KRISTI WHITECAPS!
PICK ME! PICK ME!
LATER THAT DAY...
I WONDER HOW ARCHIE IS DOING?
HI, ARCHIE! HOW'S IT...
EEYOW!!
...GOING?
3

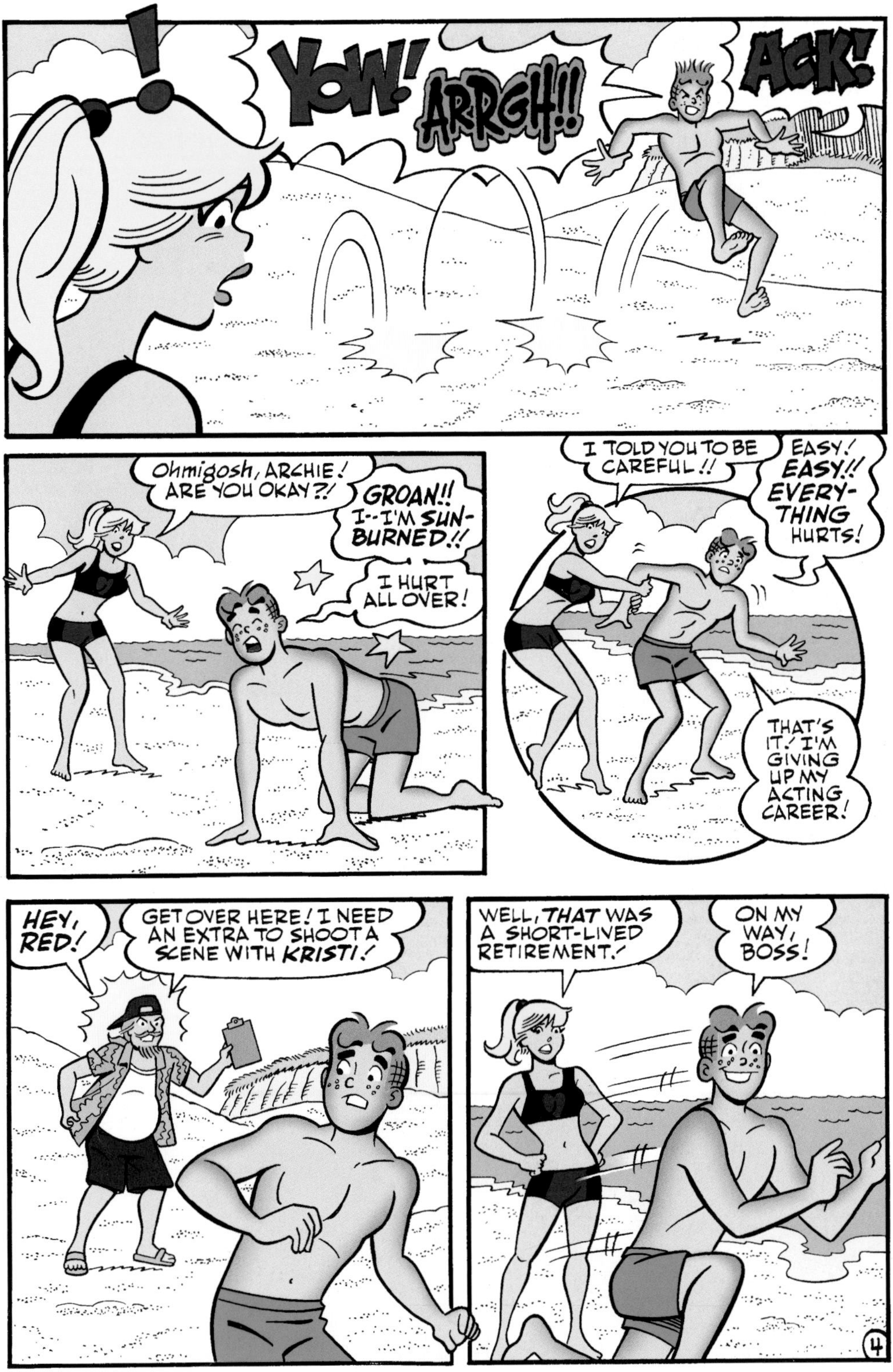
!
YOW!
ARRGH!!
ACK!
Ohmigosh, ARCHIE! ARE YOU OKAY?!
GROAN!! I--I'M SUN-BURNED!!
I HURT ALL OVER!
I TOLD YOU TO BE CAREFUL!!
EASY! EASY!! EVERY-THING HURTS!
THAT'S IT! I'M GIVING UP MY ACTING CAREER!
HEY, RED!
GET OVER HERE! I NEED AN EXTRA TO SHOOT A SCENE WITH KRISTI!
WELL, THAT WAS A SHORT-LIVED RETIREMENT!
ON MY WAY, BOSS!
4

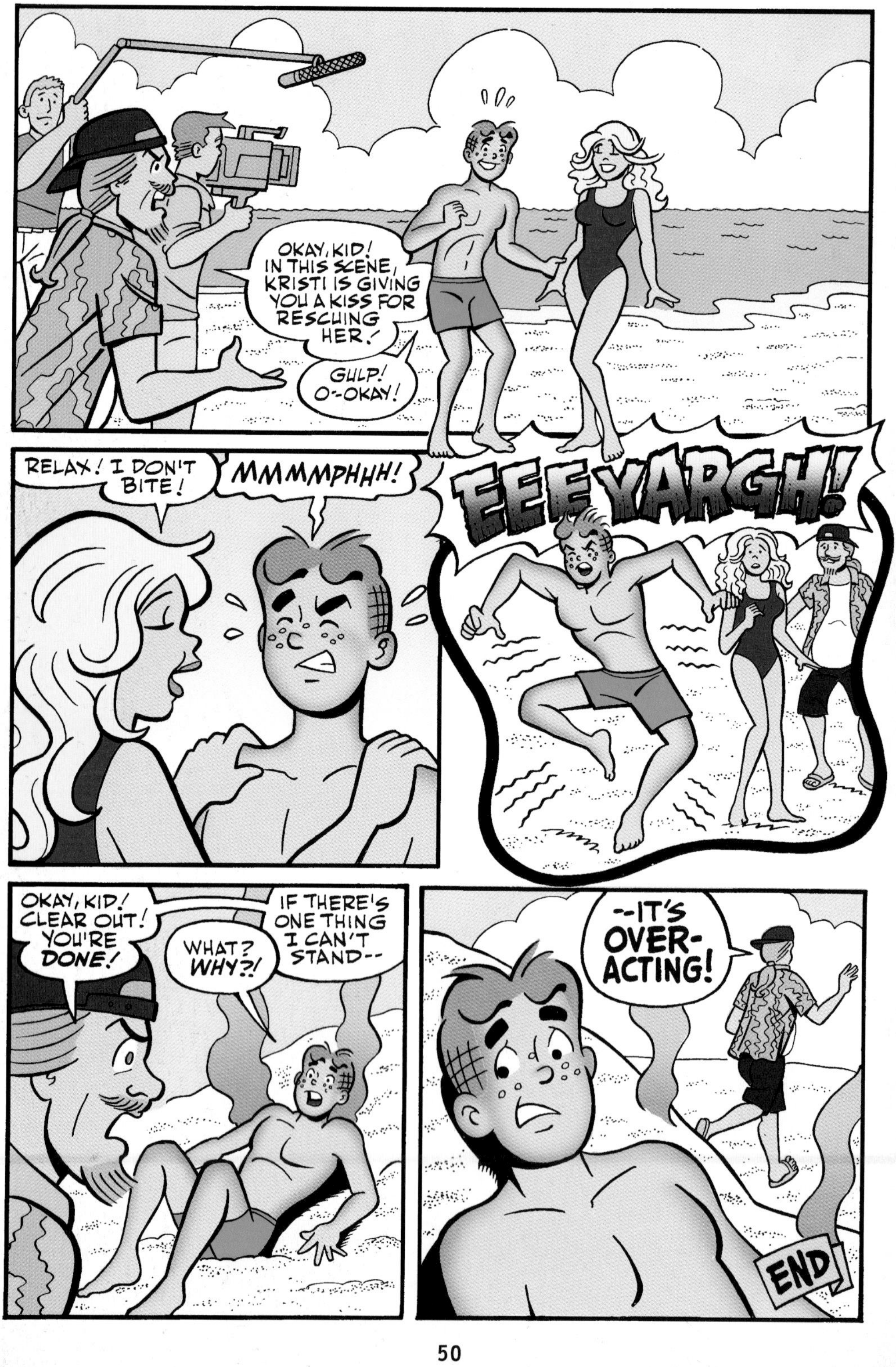
OKAY, KID! IN THIS SCENE, KRISTI IS GIVING YOU A KISS FOR RESCUING HER!
GULP! O-OKAY!
RELAX! I DON'T BITE!
MMMMPHHH!
EEEYARGH!
OKAY, KID! CLEAR OUT! YOU'RE DONE!
WHAT? WHY?!
IF THERE'S ONE THING I CAN'T STAND--
--IT'S OVER-ACTING!
END

Archie® & FRIENDS
BACK TO SCHOOL

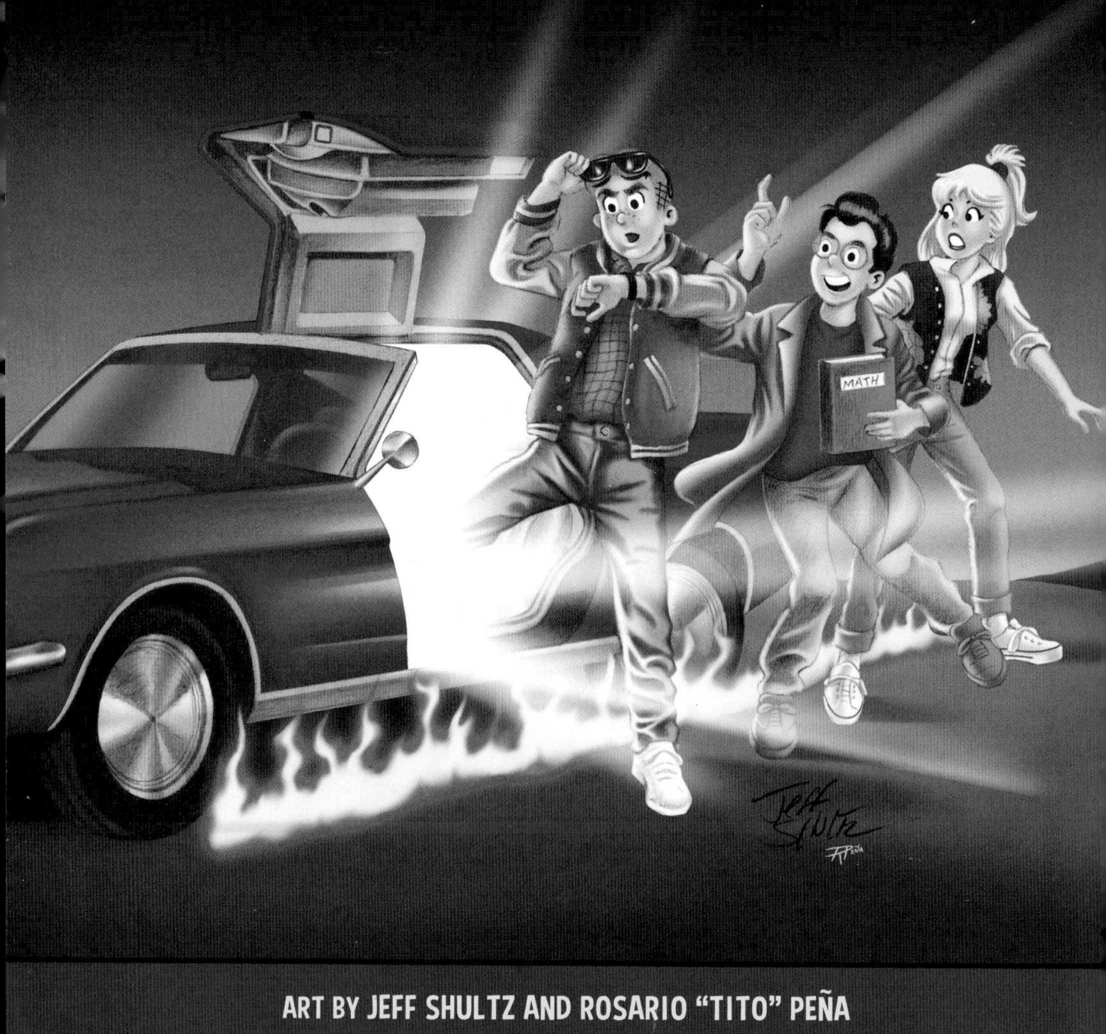
MATH

ART BY JEFF SHULTZ AND ROSARIO "TITO" PEÑA

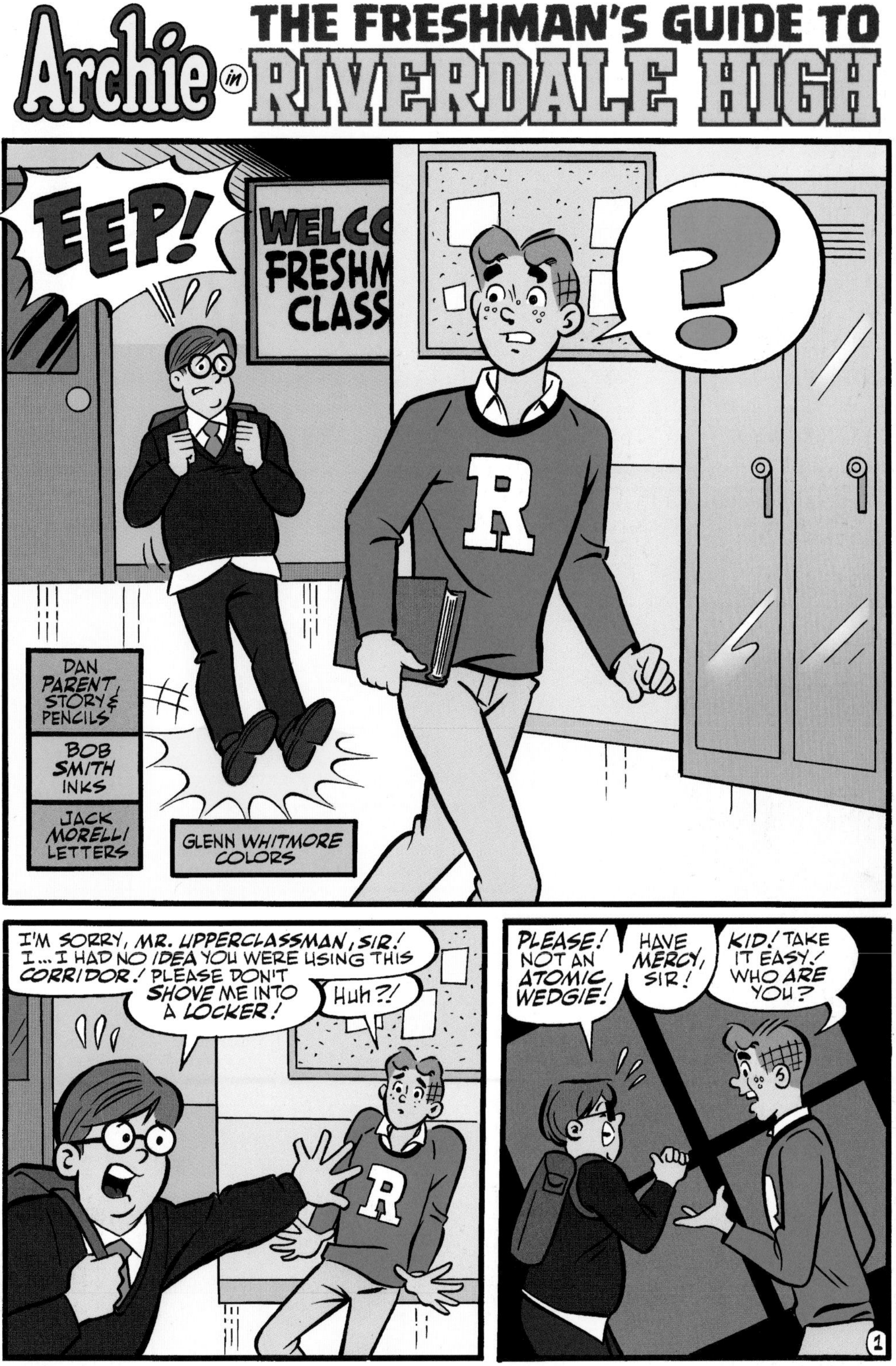
Archie in
THE FRESHMAN'S GUIDE TO
RIVERDALE HIGH
EEP!
WELCO
FRESHM
CLASS
?
DAN PARENT/ STORY & PENCILS
BOB SMITH INKS
JACK MORELLI/ LETTERS
GLENN WHITMORE COLORS
I'M SORRY, MR. UPPERCLASSMAN, SIR! I... I HAD NO IDEA YOU WERE USING THIS CORRIDOR! PLEASE DON'T SHOVE ME INTO A LOCKER!
Huh?!
PLEASE! NOT AN ATOMIC WEDGIE!
HAVE MERCY, SIR!
KID! TAKE IT EASY! WHO ARE YOU?
1

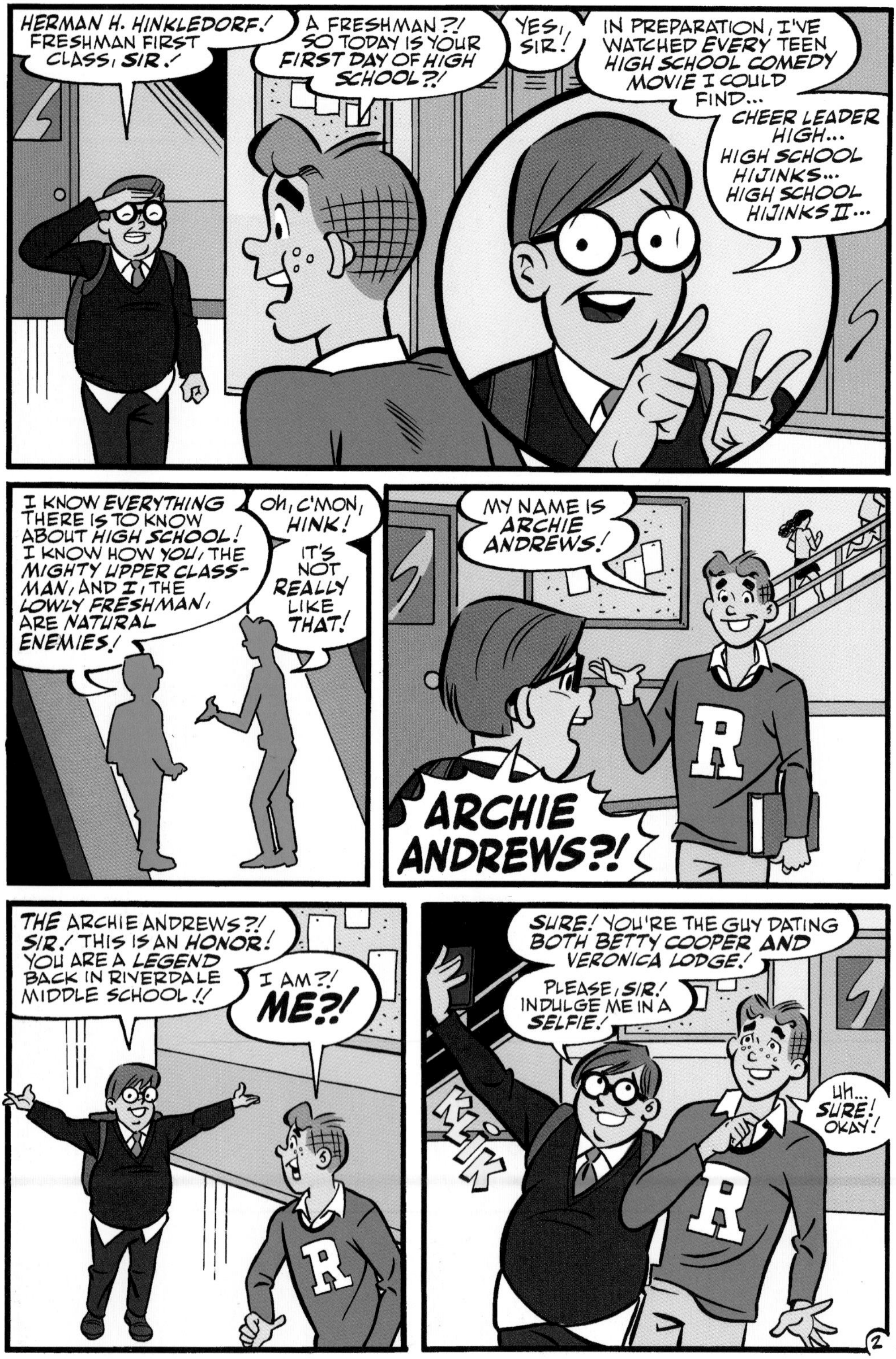
HERMAN H. HINKLEDORF! FRESHMAN FIRST CLASS, SIR!
A FRESHMAN?! SO TODAY IS YOUR FIRST DAY OF HIGH SCHOOL?!
YES, SIR!
IN PREPARATION, I'VE WATCHED EVERY TEEN HIGH SCHOOL COMEDY MOVIE I COULD FIND...
CHEER LEADER HIGH... HIGH SCHOOL HIJINKS... HIGH SCHOOL HIJINKS II...
I KNOW EVERYTHING THERE IS TO KNOW ABOUT HIGH SCHOOL! I KNOW HOW YOU, THE MIGHTY UPPER CLASSMAN, AND I, THE LOWLY FRESHMAN, ARE NATURAL ENEMIES!
OH, C'MON, HINK!
IT'S NOT REALLY LIKE THAT!
MY NAME IS ARCHIE ANDREWS!
ARCHIE ANDREWS?!
THE ARCHIE ANDREWS?! SIR! THIS IS AN HONOR! YOU ARE A LEGEND BACK IN RIVERDALE MIDDLE SCHOOL!!
I AM?! ME?!
SURE! YOU'RE THE GUY DATING BOTH BETTY COOPER AND VERONICA LODGE!
PLEASE, SIR! INDULGE ME IN A SELFIE!
KLIK
UH... SURE! OKAY!
2

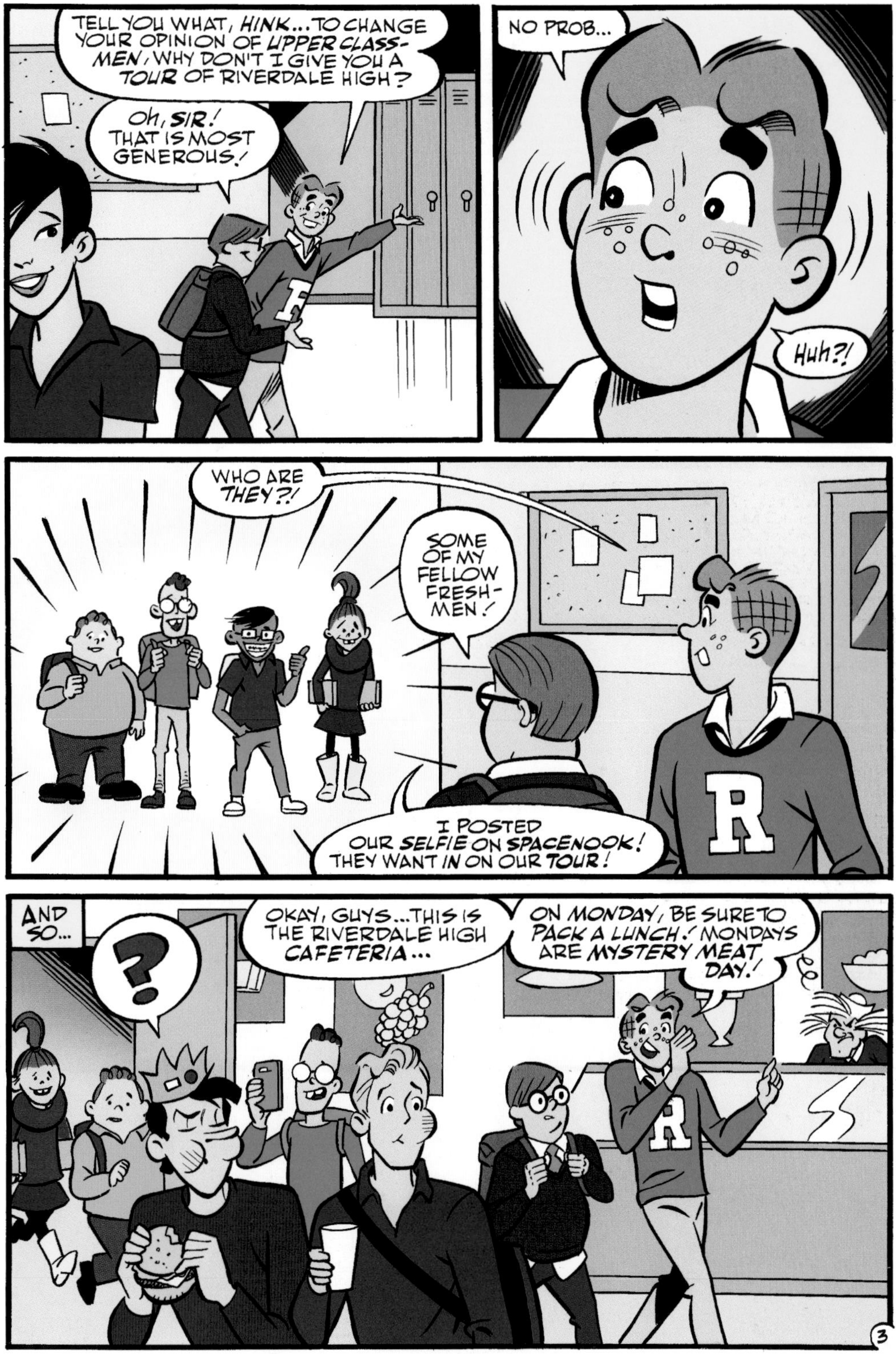
TELL YOU WHAT, HINK...TO CHANGE YOUR OPINION OF UPPER CLASSMEN, WHY DON'T I GIVE YOU A TOUR OF RIVERDALE HIGH?
OH, SIR! THAT IS MOST GENEROUS!
NO PROB...
HUH?!
WHO ARE THEY?!
SOME OF MY FELLOW FRESHMEN!
I POSTED OUR SELFIE ON SPACENOOK! THEY WANT IN ON OUR TOUR!
AND SO...
?
OKAY, GUYS...THIS IS THE RIVERDALE HIGH CAFETERIA...
ON MONDAY, BE SURE TO PACK A LUNCH! MONDAYS ARE MYSTERY MEAT DAY!
3

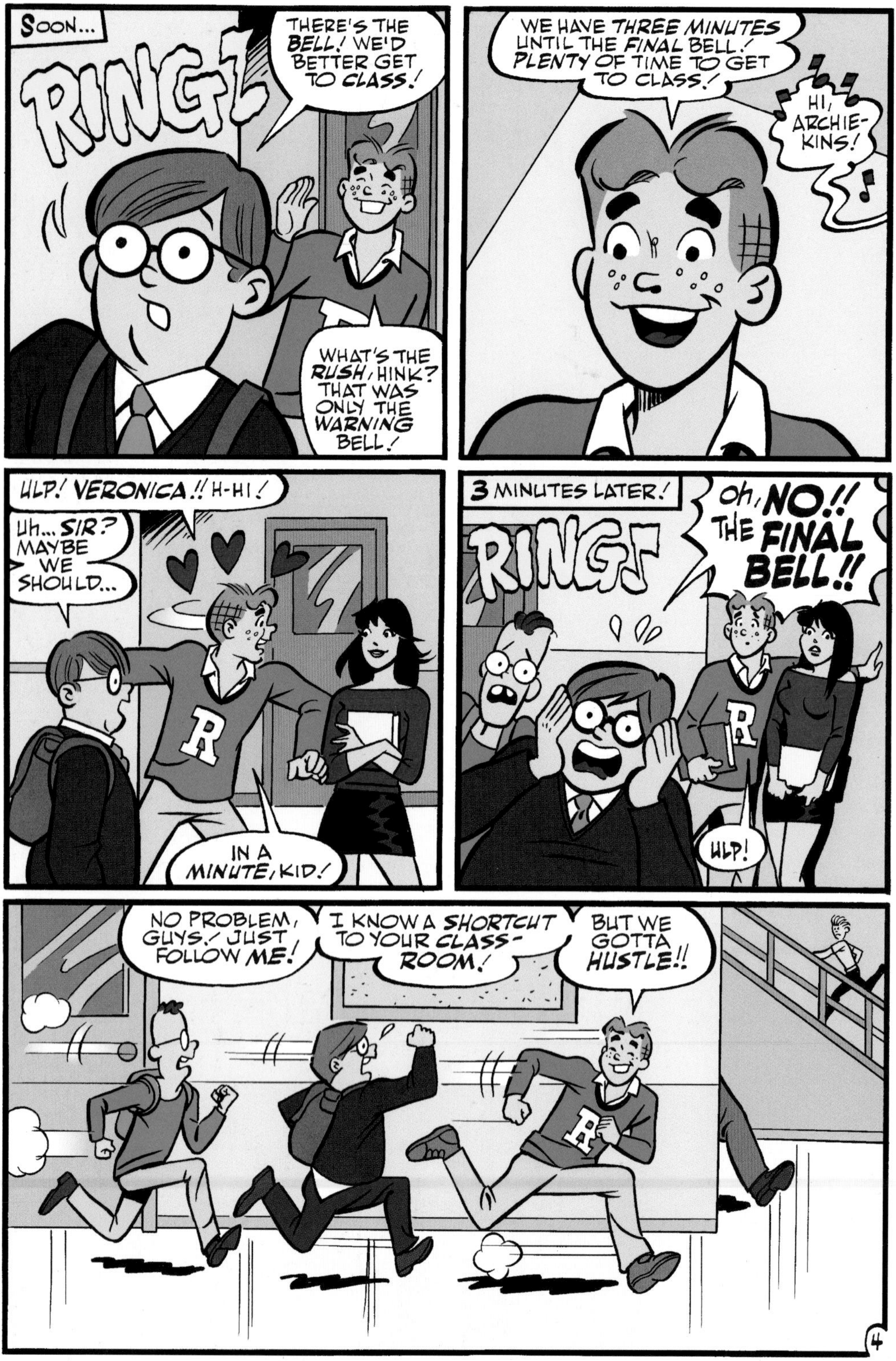
SOON...
RING!
THERE'S THE BELL! WE'D BETTER GET TO CLASS!
WHAT'S THE RUSH, HINK? THAT WAS ONLY THE WARNING BELL!
WE HAVE THREE MINUTES UNTIL THE FINAL BELL! PLENTY OF TIME TO GET TO CLASS!
HI, ARCHIE-KINS!
ULP! VERONICA!! H-HI!
UH... SIR? MAYBE WE SHOULD...
IN A MINUTE, KID!
3 MINUTES LATER!
RING!
OH, NO!! THE FINAL BELL!!
ULP!
NO PROBLEM, GUYS! JUST FOLLOW ME!
I KNOW A SHORTCUT TO YOUR CLASS-ROOM!
BUT WE GOTTA HUSTLE!!
4

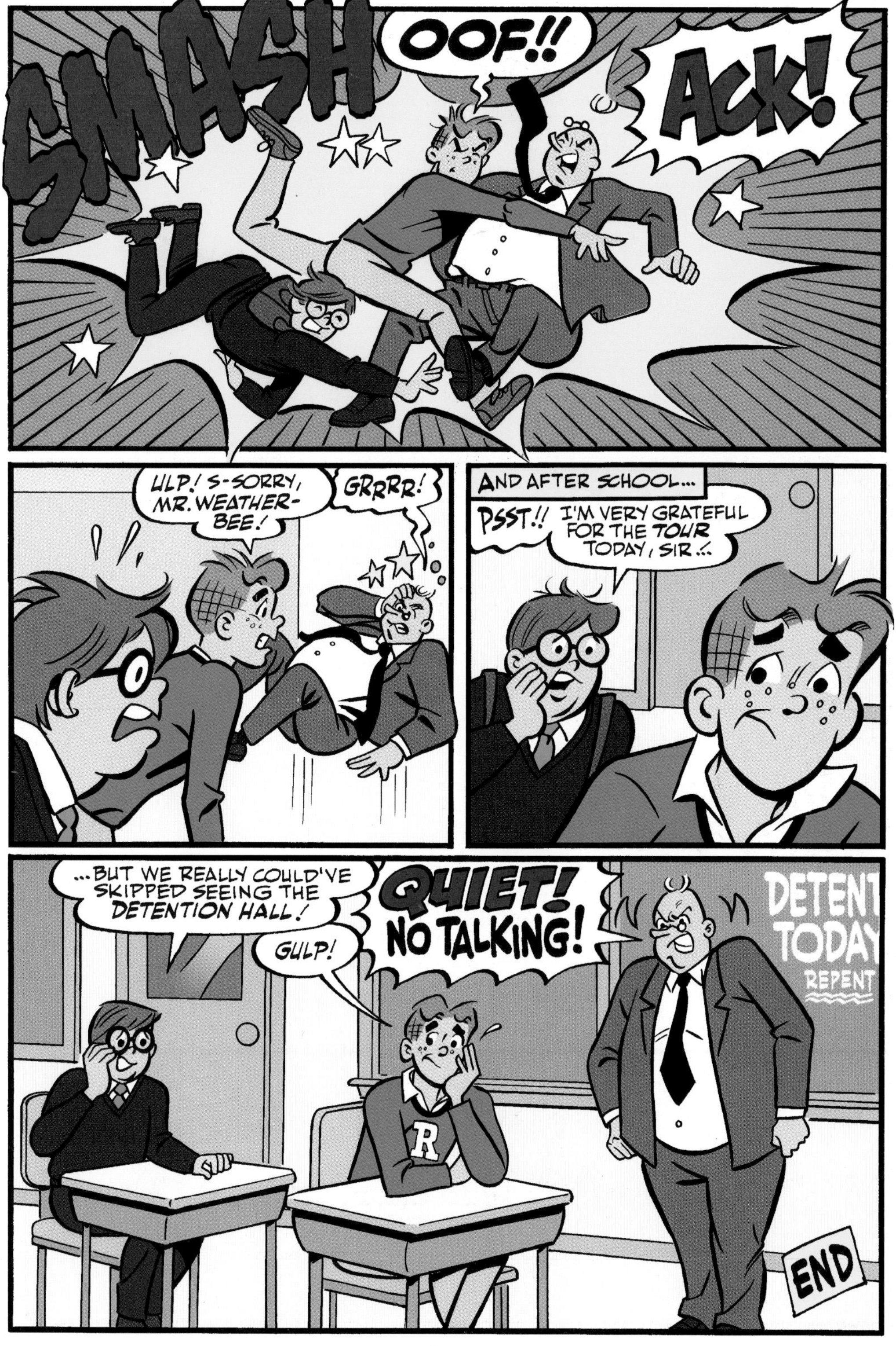
SMASH
OOF!!
ACK!
ULP! S-SORRY, MR. WEATHER-BEE!
GRRRR!
AND AFTER SCHOOL...
PSST.!! I'M VERY GRATEFUL FOR THE TOUR TODAY, SIR...
...BUT WE REALLY COULD'VE SKIPPED SEEING THE DETENTION HALL!
GULP!
QUIET! NO TALKING!
DETENT
TODAY
REPENT
END

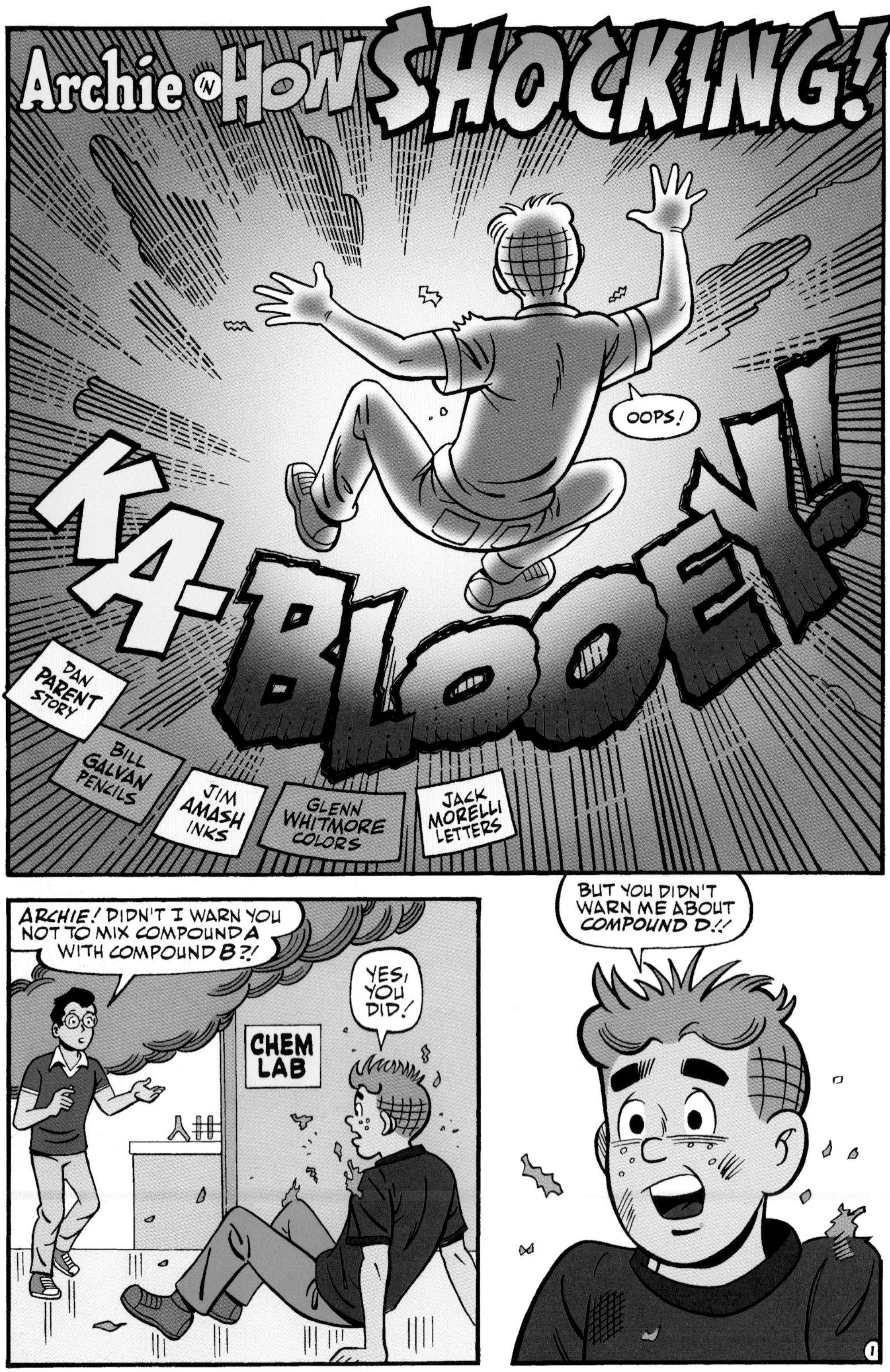
Archie in HOW SHOCKING!
OOPS!
KA-BLOOEY!
DAN PARENT STORY
BILL GALVAN PENCILS
JIM AMASH INKS
GLENN WHITMORE COLORS
JACK MORELLI LETTERS
ARCHIE! DIDN'T I WARN YOU NOT TO MIX COMPOUND A WITH COMPOUND B?!
YES, YOU DID!
CHEM LAB
BUT YOU DIDN'T WARN ME ABOUT COMPOUND D!!
1

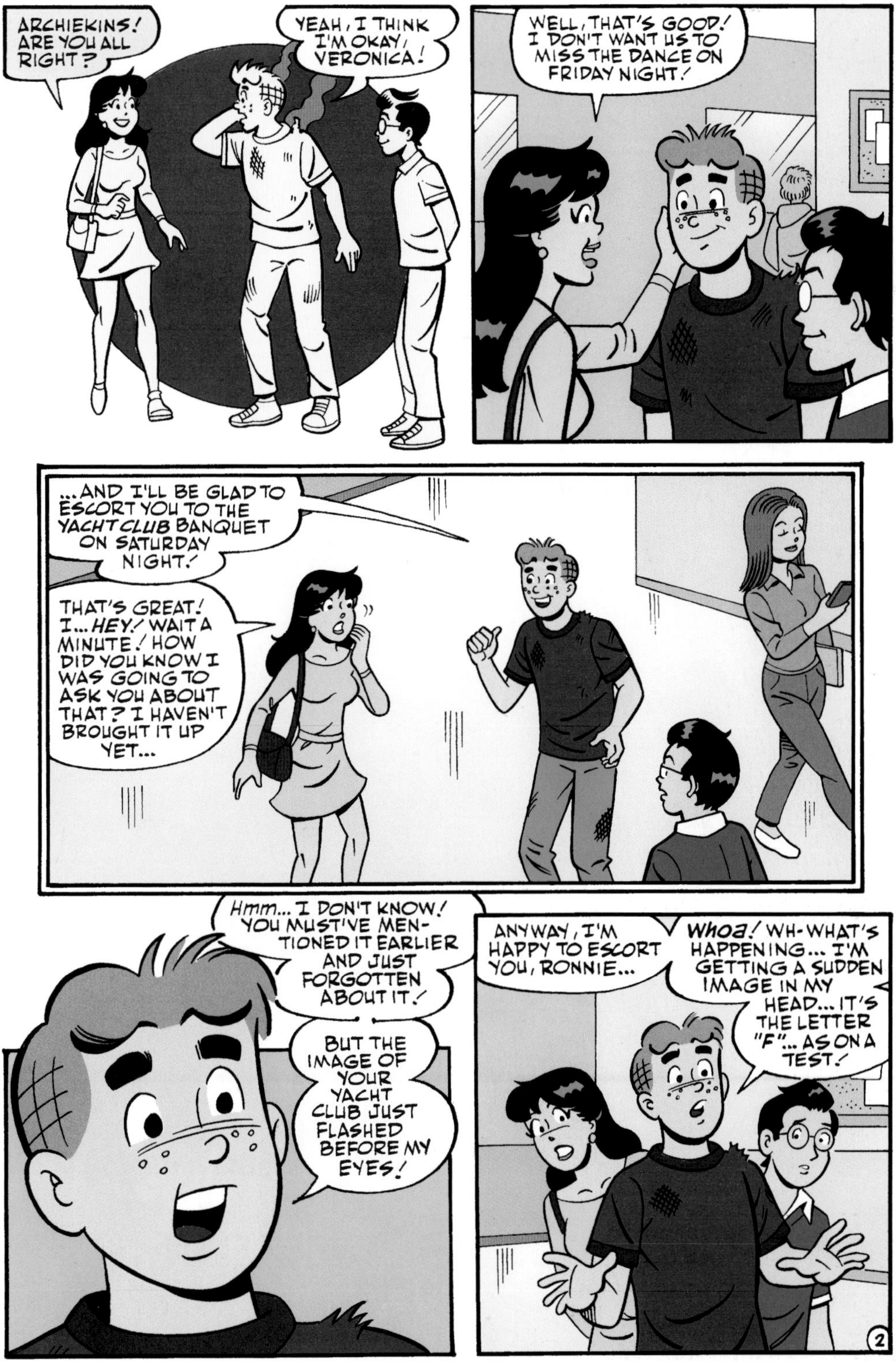
ARCHIEKINS! ARE YOU ALL RIGHT?
YEAH, I THINK I'M OKAY, VERONICA!
WELL, THAT'S GOOD! I DON'T WANT US TO MISS THE DANCE ON FRIDAY NIGHT!
...AND I'LL BE GLAD TO ESCORT YOU TO THE YACHT CLUB BANQUET ON SATURDAY NIGHT!
THAT'S GREAT! I... HEY! WAIT A MINUTE! HOW DID YOU KNOW I WAS GOING TO ASK YOU ABOUT THAT? I HAVEN'T BROUGHT IT UP YET...
Hmm... I DON'T KNOW! YOU MUST'VE MENTIONED IT EARLIER AND JUST FORGOTTEN ABOUT IT!
BUT THE IMAGE OF YOUR YACHT CLUB JUST FLASHED BEFORE MY EYES!
ANYWAY, I'M HAPPY TO ESCORT YOU, RONNIE...
Whoa! WH-WHAT'S HAPPENING... I'M GETTING A SUDDEN IMAGE IN MY HEAD... IT'S THE LETTER "F"... AS ON A TEST!
2

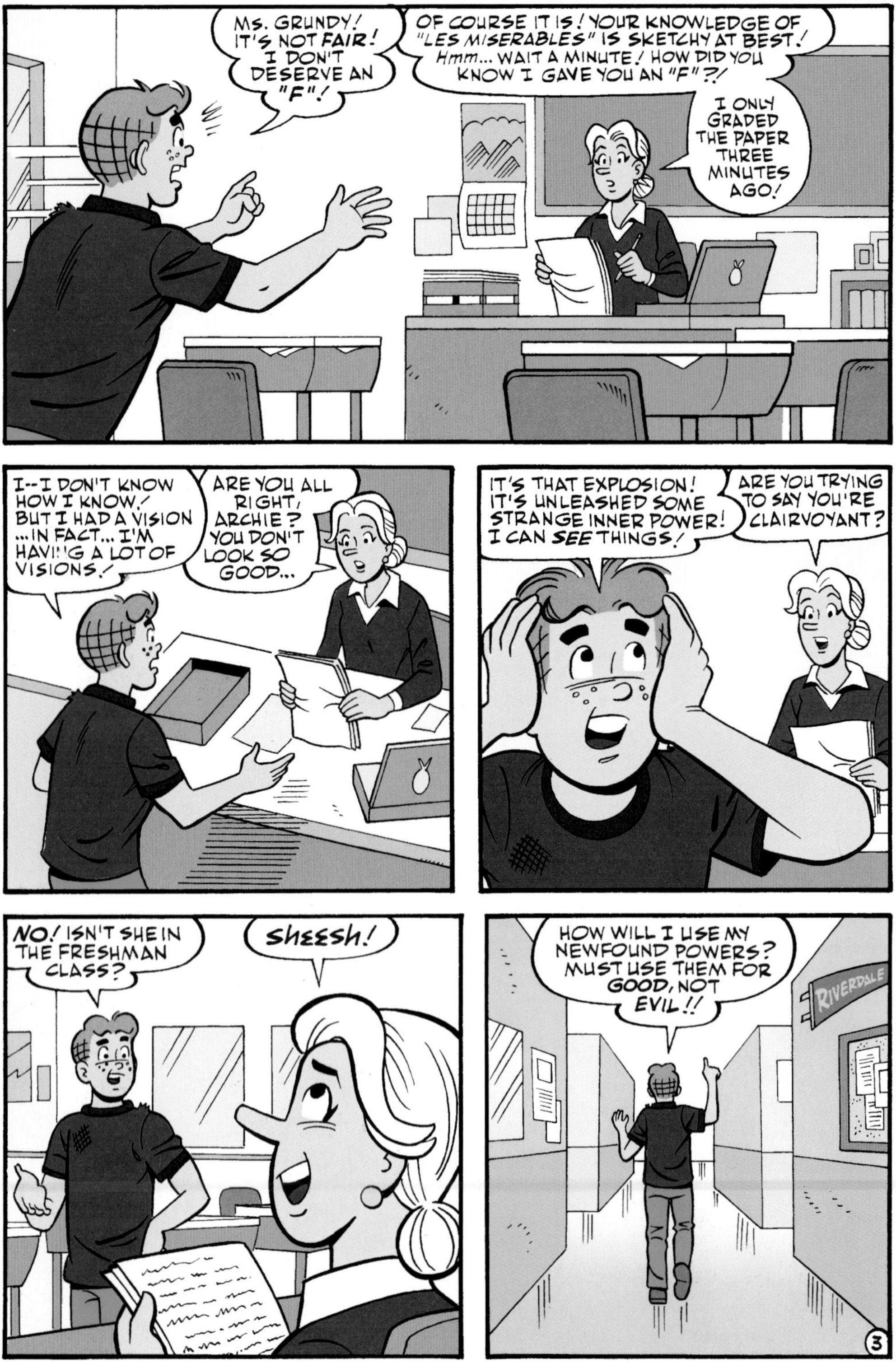
MS. GRUNDY! IT'S NOT FAIR! I DON'T DESERVE AN "F"!
OF COURSE IT IS! YOUR KNOWLEDGE OF "LES MISERABLES" IS SKETCHY AT BEST! Hmm... WAIT A MINUTE! HOW DID YOU KNOW I GAVE YOU AN "F"?!
I ONLY GRADED THE PAPER THREE MINUTES AGO!
I--I DON'T KNOW HOW I KNOW! BUT I HAD A VISION ...IN FACT... I'M HAVING A LOT OF VISIONS!
ARE YOU ALL RIGHT, ARCHIE? YOU DON'T LOOK SO GOOD...
IT'S THAT EXPLOSION! IT'S UNLEASHED SOME STRANGE INNER POWER! I CAN SEE THINGS!
ARE YOU TRYING TO SAY YOU'RE CLAIRVOYANT?
NO! ISN'T SHE IN THE FRESHMAN CLASS?
SHEESH!
HOW WILL I USE MY NEWFOUND POWERS? MUST USE THEM FOR GOOD, NOT EVIL!!
RIVERDALE
3

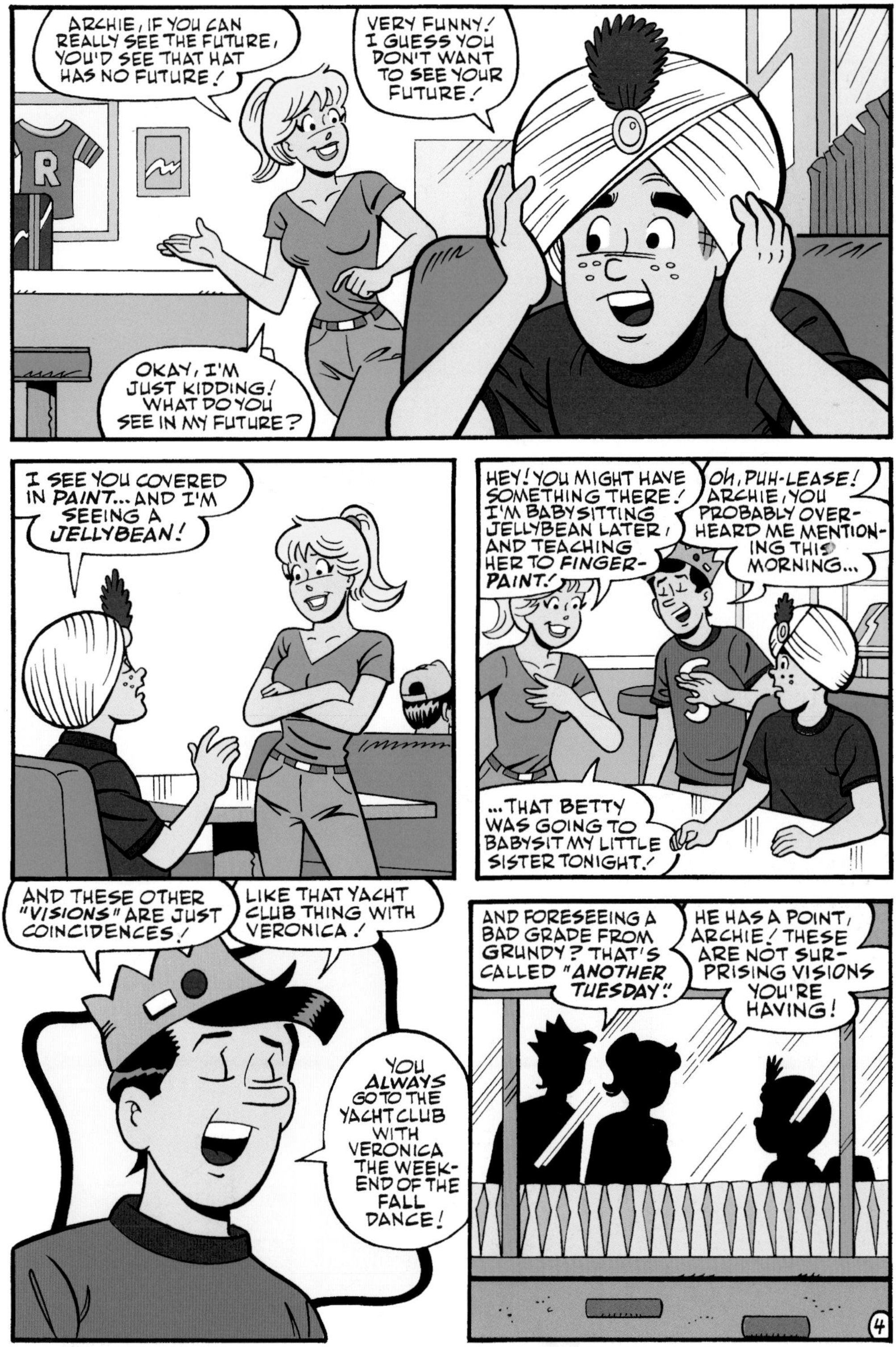
ARCHIE, IF YOU CAN REALLY SEE THE FUTURE, YOU'D SEE THAT HAT HAS NO FUTURE!
VERY FUNNY! I GUESS YOU DON'T WANT TO SEE YOUR FUTURE!
OKAY, I'M JUST KIDDING! WHAT DO YOU SEE IN MY FUTURE?
I SEE YOU COVERED IN PAINT... AND I'M SEEING A JELLYBEAN!
HEY! YOU MIGHT HAVE SOMETHING THERE! I'M BABYSITTING JELLYBEAN LATER, AND TEACHING HER TO FINGER-PAINT!
OH, PUH-LEASE! ARCHIE, YOU PROBABLY OVER-HEARD ME MENTION-ING THIS MORNING...
...THAT BETTY WAS GOING TO BABYSIT MY LITTLE SISTER TONIGHT!
AND THESE OTHER "VISIONS" ARE JUST COINCIDENCES!
LIKE THAT YACHT CLUB THING WITH VERONICA!
YOU ALWAYS GO TO THE YACHT CLUB WITH VERONICA THE WEEK-END OF THE FALL DANCE!
AND FORESEEING A BAD GRADE FROM GRUNDY? THAT'S CALLED "ANOTHER TUESDAY"!
HE HAS A POINT, ARCHIE! THESE ARE NOT SUR-PRISING VISIONS YOU'RE HAVING!
4

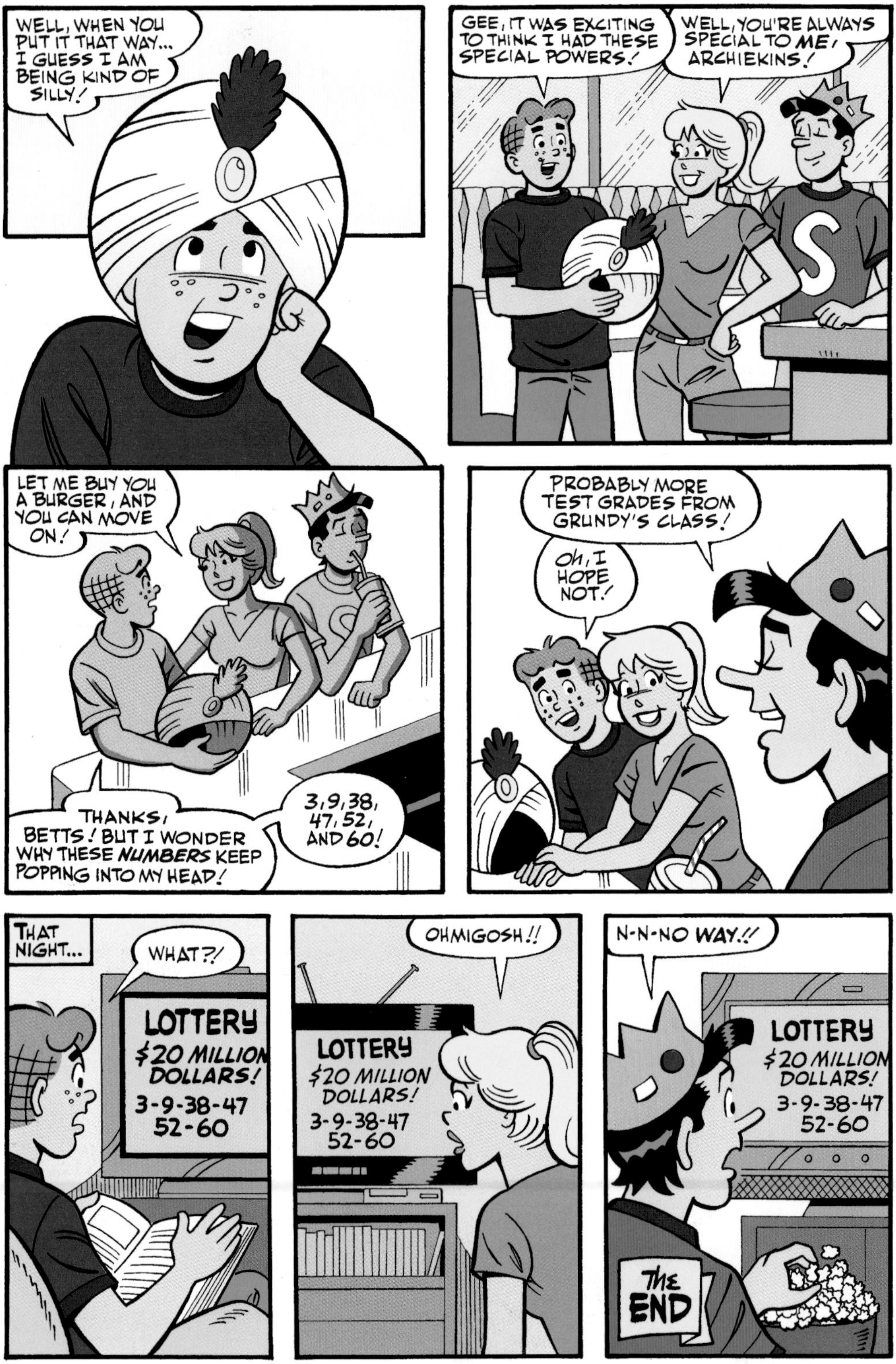
WELL, WHEN YOU PUT IT THAT WAY... I GUESS I AM BEING KIND OF SILLY!
GEE, IT WAS EXCITING TO THINK I HAD THESE SPECIAL POWERS!
WELL, YOU'RE ALWAYS SPECIAL TO ME, ARCHIEKINS!
LET ME BUY YOU A BURGER, AND YOU CAN MOVE ON!
THANKS, BETTS! BUT I WONDER WHY THESE NUMBERS KEEP POPPING INTO MY HEAD!
3, 9, 38, 47, 52, AND 60!
PROBABLY MORE TEST GRADES FROM GRUNDY'S CLASS!
Oh, I HOPE NOT!
THAT NIGHT...
WHAT?!
LOTTERY
$20 MILLION DOLLARS!
3-9-38-47
52-60
OHMIGOSH!!
LOTTERY
$20 MILLION DOLLARS!
3-9-38-47
52-60
N-N-NO WAY!!
LOTTERY
$20 MILLION DOLLARS!
3-9-38-47
52-60
THE END

Betty and Veronica in DON'T TEST my PATIENCE

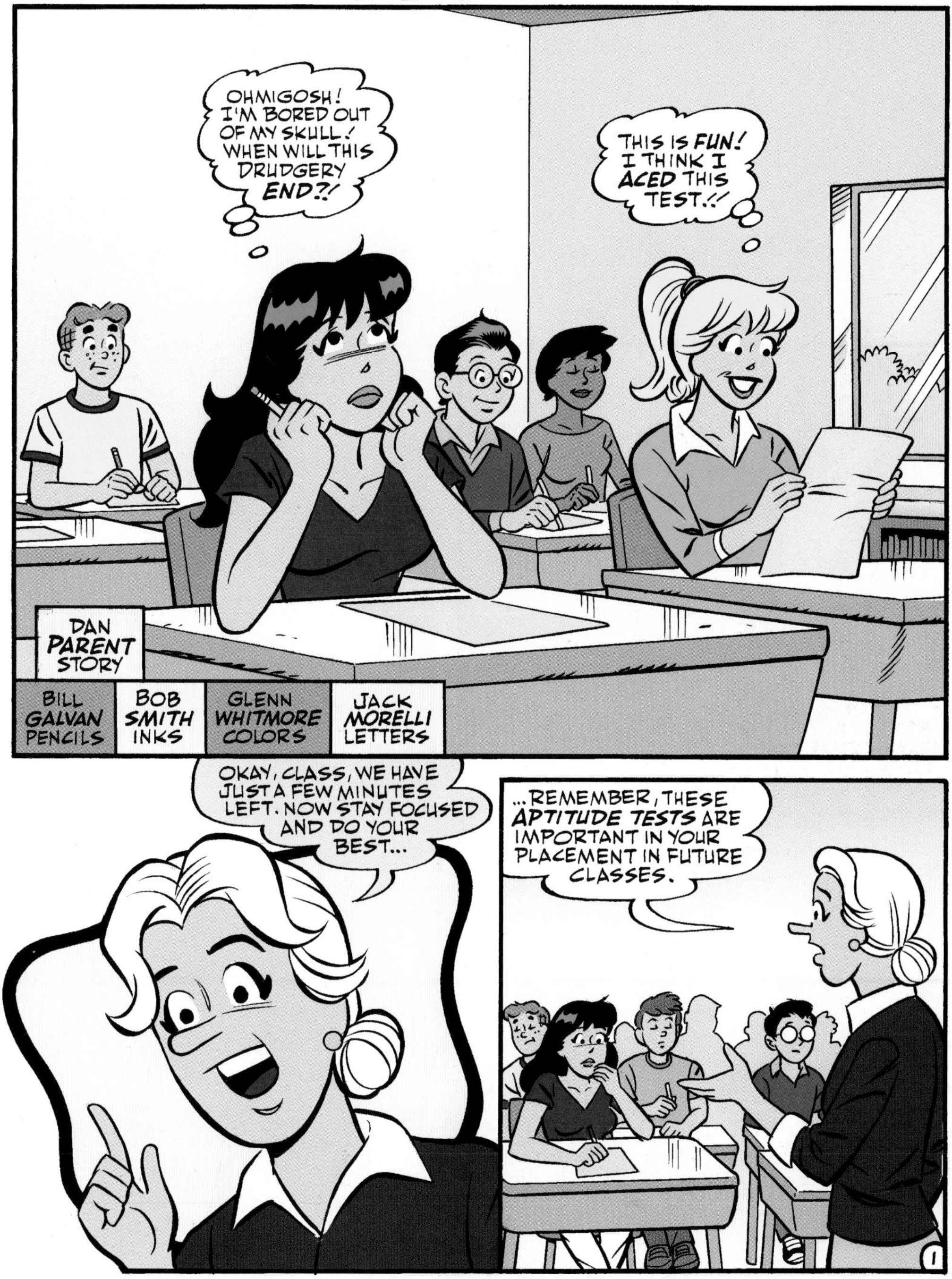
OHMIGOSH! I'M BORED OUT OF MY SKULL! WHEN WILL THIS DRUDGERY END?!
THIS IS FUN! I THINK I ACED THIS TEST!!
DAN PARENT STORY
BILL GALVAN PENCILS
BOB SMITH INKS
GLENN WHITMORE COLORS
JACK MORELLI LETTERS
OKAY, CLASS, WE HAVE JUST A FEW MINUTES LEFT. NOW STAY FOCUSED AND DO YOUR BEST...
...REMEMBER, THESE APTITUDE TESTS ARE IMPORTANT IN YOUR PLACEMENT IN FUTURE CLASSES.
1

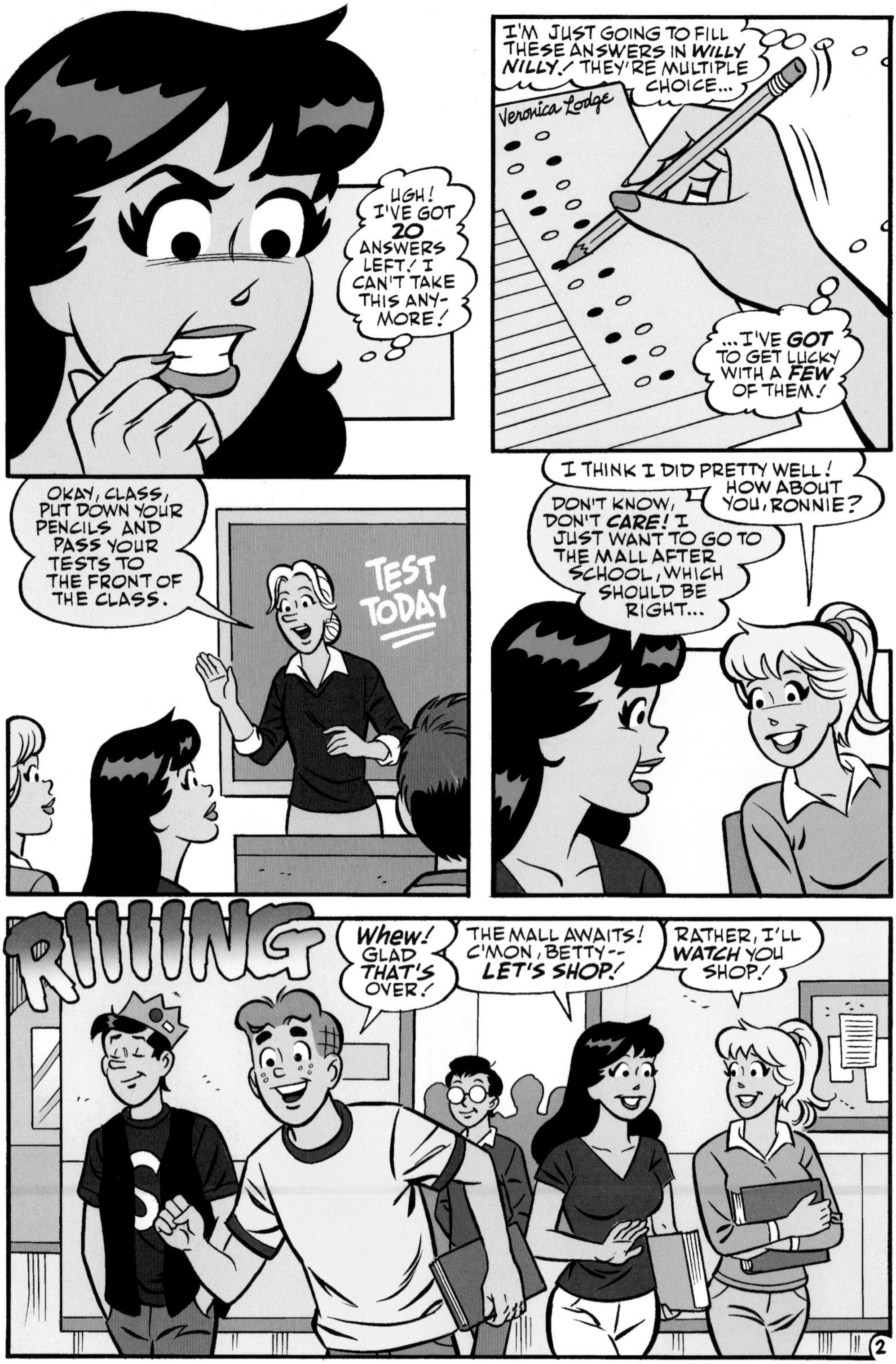
UGH! I'VE GOT 20 ANSWERS LEFT! I CAN'T TAKE THIS ANY-MORE!
I'M JUST GOING TO FILL THESE ANSWERS IN WILLY NILLY! THEY'RE MULTIPLE CHOICE...
Veronica Lodge
...I'VE GOT TO GET LUCKY WITH A FEW OF THEM!
OKAY, CLASS, PUT DOWN YOUR PENCILS AND PASS YOUR TESTS TO THE FRONT OF THE CLASS.
TEST TODAY
I THINK I DID PRETTY WELL! HOW ABOUT YOU, RONNIE?
DON'T KNOW, DON'T CARE! I JUST WANT TO GO TO THE MALL AFTER SCHOOL, WHICH SHOULD BE RIGHT...
RIIIING
Whew! GLAD THAT'S OVER!
THE MALL AWAITS! C'MON, BETTY-- LET'S SHOP!
RATHER, I'LL WATCH YOU SHOP!
2

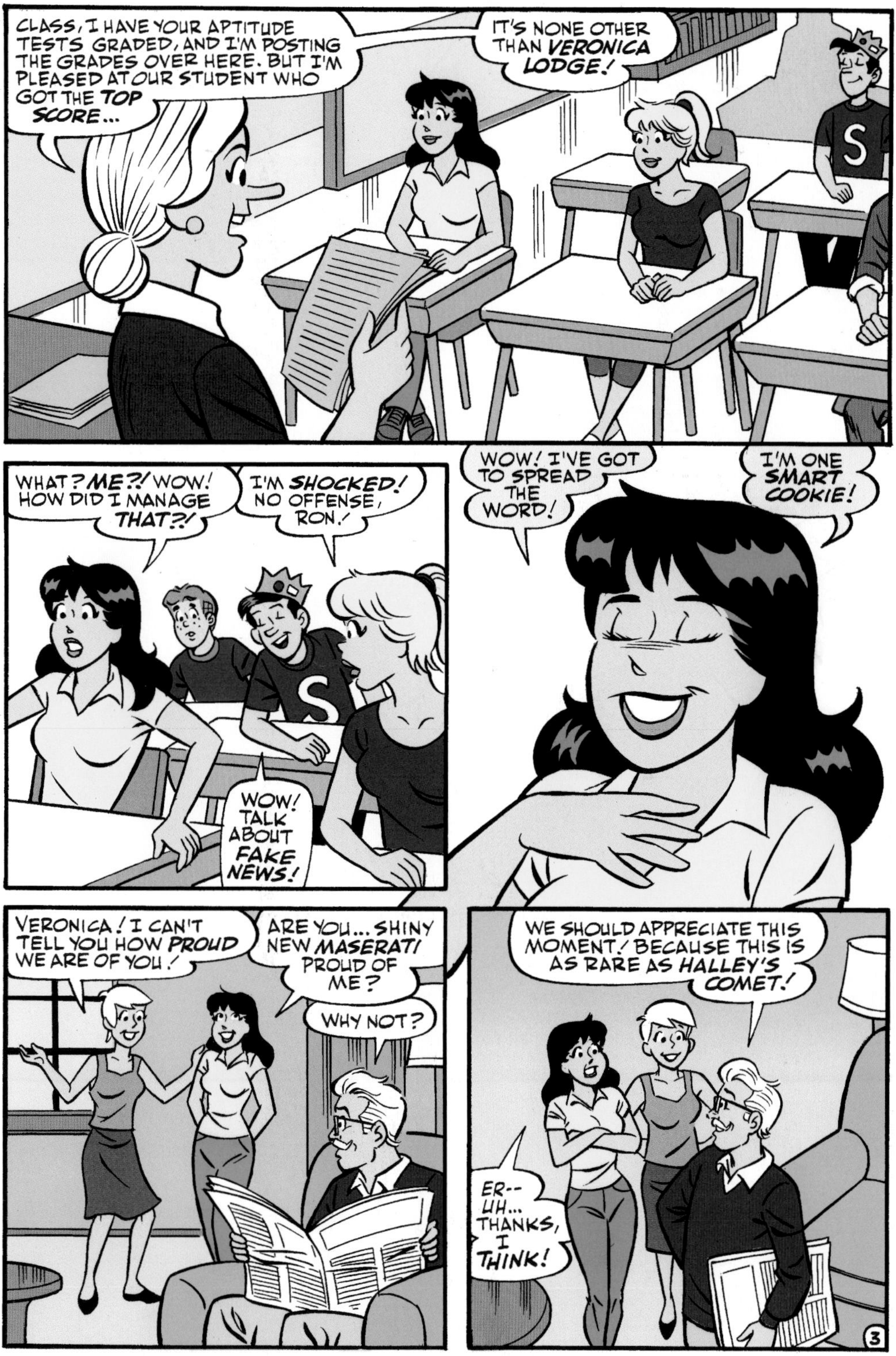
CLASS, I HAVE YOUR APTITUDE TESTS GRADED, AND I'M POSTING THE GRADES OVER HERE. BUT I'M PLEASED AT OUR STUDENT WHO GOT THE TOP SCORE...
IT'S NONE OTHER THAN VERONICA LODGE!
WHAT? ME?! WOW! HOW DID I MANAGE THAT?!
I'M SHOCKED! NO OFFENSE, RON.!
WOW! TALK ABOUT FAKE NEWS!
WOW! I'VE GOT TO SPREAD THE WORD!
I'M ONE SMART COOKIE!
VERONICA! I CAN'T TELL YOU HOW PROUD WE ARE OF YOU!
ARE YOU... SHINY NEW MASERATI PROUD OF ME?
WHY NOT?
WE SHOULD APPRECIATE THIS MOMENT! BECAUSE THIS IS AS RARE AS HALLEY'S COMET!
ER-- UH... THANKS, I THINK!
3

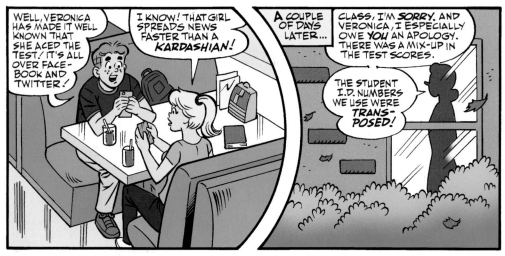

WELL, VERONICA HAS MADE IT WELL KNOWN THAT SHE ACED THE TEST! IT'S ALL OVER FACE-BOOK AND TWITTER!

I KNOW! THAT GIRL SPREADS NEWS FASTER THAN A *KARDASHIAN!*

A COUPLE OF DAYS LATER...

CLASS, I'M *SORRY*. AND VERONICA, I ESPECIALLY OWE *YOU* AN APOLOGY. THERE WAS A MIX-UP IN THE TEST SCORES.

THE STUDENT I.D. NUMBERS WE USE WERE *TRANS-POSED!*

VERONICA'S TEST WAS MIXED UP WITH A TEST FROM *ANOTHER CLASS.* SO *DILTON DOILEY* ACTUALLY RECEIVED THE HIGHEST GRADE IN THE CLASS!

AND WHAT DID *I* GET?

YOUR SCORE, VERONICA, WAS *57!*

GULP!

AND THINGS ARE NORMAL AGAIN IN THE UNI-VERSE!

MS. GRUNDY

THIS IS UNACCEPTABLE! YOU'LL HEAR FROM MY *LAWYERS!*

VERONICA! YOU'RE OVERREACTING! CALM *DOWN!*

WHAT DO YOU THINK SHE'LL DO?

I DON'T THINK SHE'LL GO DOWN QUIETLY!

4

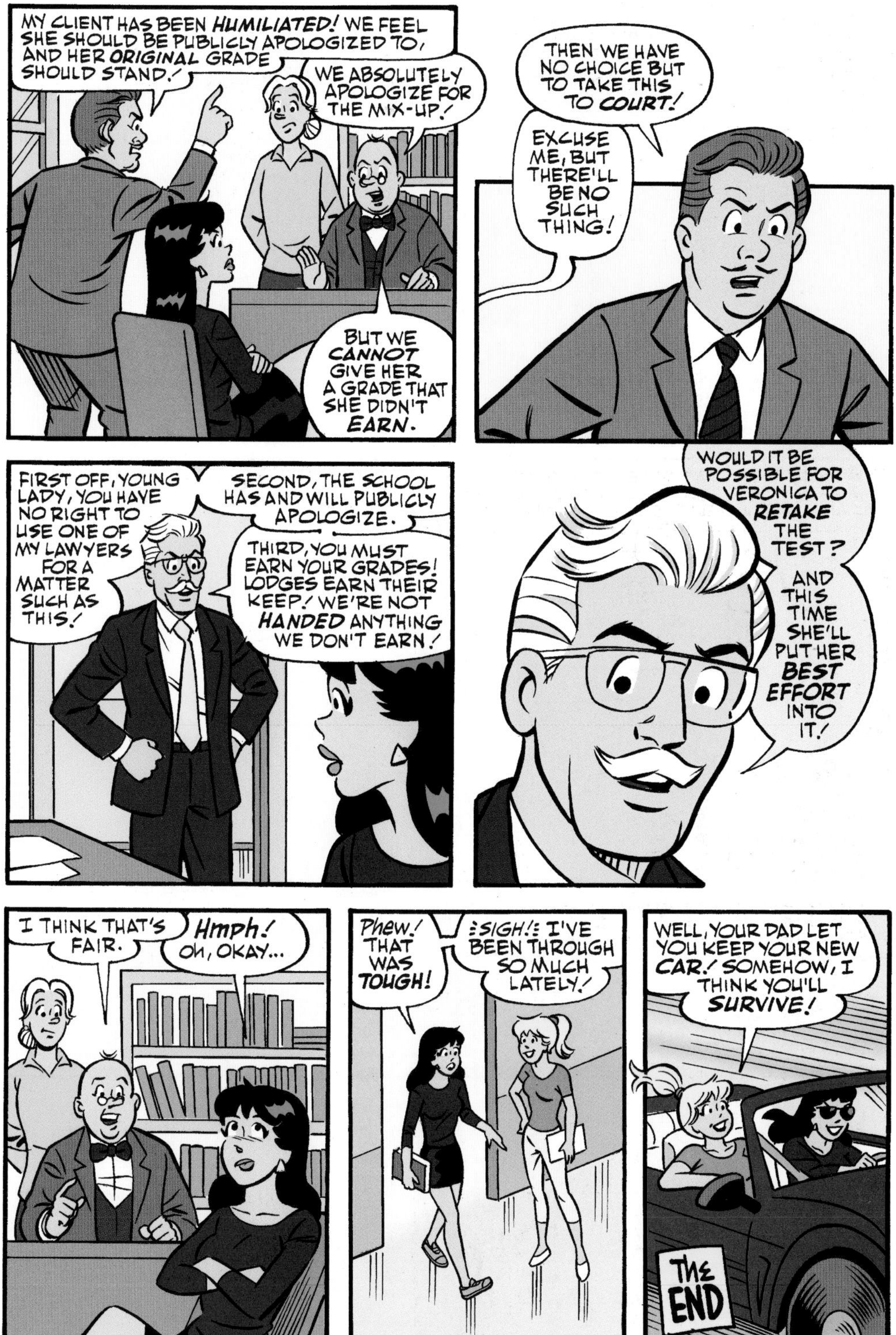
MY CLIENT HAS BEEN HUMILIATED! WE FEEL SHE SHOULD BE PUBLICLY APOLOGIZED TO, AND HER ORIGINAL GRADE SHOULD STAND.!
WE ABSOLUTELY APOLOGIZE FOR THE MIX-UP!
BUT WE CANNOT GIVE HER A GRADE THAT SHE DIDN'T EARN.
THEN WE HAVE NO CHOICE BUT TO TAKE THIS TO COURT!
EXCUSE ME, BUT THERE'LL BE NO SUCH THING!
FIRST OFF, YOUNG LADY, YOU HAVE NO RIGHT TO USE ONE OF MY LAWYERS FOR A MATTER SUCH AS THIS!
SECOND, THE SCHOOL HAS AND WILL PUBLICLY APOLOGIZE.
THIRD, YOU MUST EARN YOUR GRADES! LODGES EARN THEIR KEEP! WE'RE NOT HANDED ANYTHING WE DON'T EARN!
WOULD IT BE POSSIBLE FOR VERONICA TO RETAKE THE TEST?
AND THIS TIME SHE'LL PUT HER BEST EFFORT INTO IT!
I THINK THAT'S FAIR.
Hmph! Oh, OKAY...
Phew! THAT WAS TOUGH!
SIGH! I'VE BEEN THROUGH SO MUCH LATELY!
WELL, YOUR DAD LET YOU KEEP YOUR NEW CAR! SOMEHOW, I THINK YOU'LL SURVIVE!
THE END

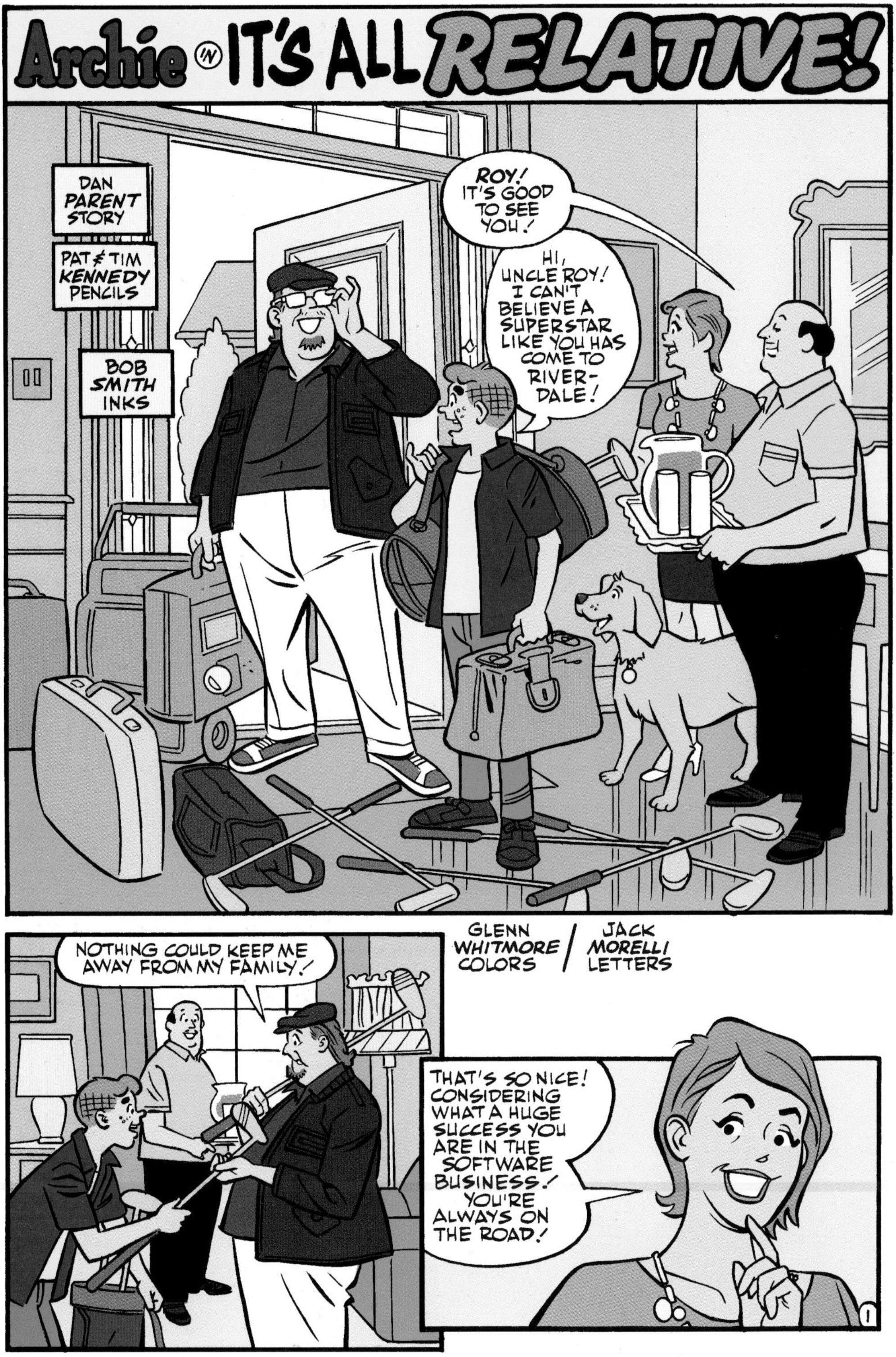
Archie in IT'S ALL RELATIVE!
DAN PARENT STORY
PAT & TIM KENNEDY PENCILS
BOB SMITH INKS
ROY! IT'S GOOD TO SEE YOU!
HI, UNCLE ROY! I CAN'T BELIEVE A SUPERSTAR LIKE YOU HAS COME TO RIVER-DALE!
GLENN WHITMORE COLORS / JACK MORELLI LETTERS
NOTHING COULD KEEP ME AWAY FROM MY FAMILY!
THAT'S SO NICE! CONSIDERING WHAT A HUGE SUCCESS YOU ARE IN THE SOFTWARE BUSINESS! YOU'RE ALWAYS ON THE ROAD!
1

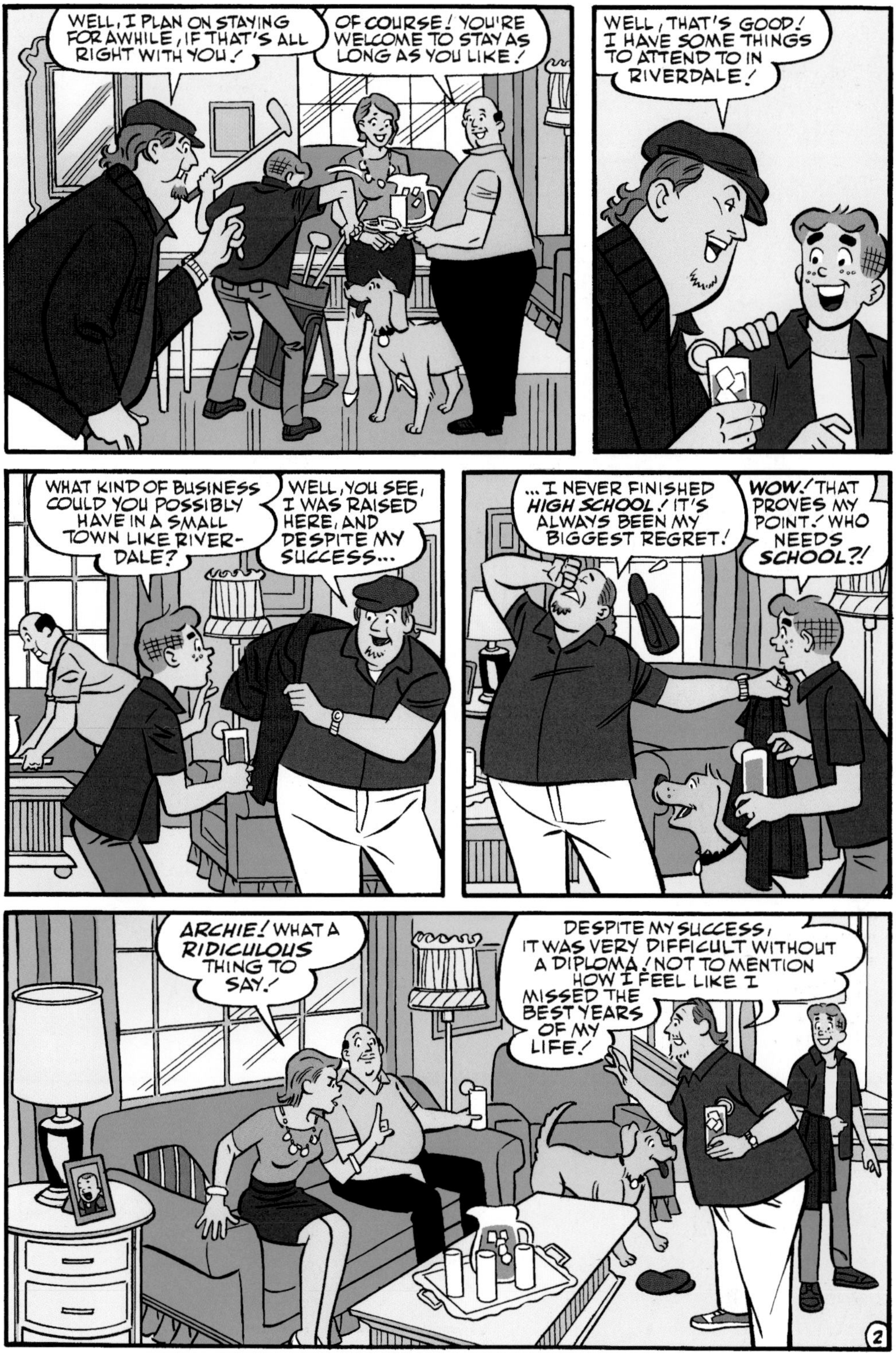
WELL, I PLAN ON STAYING FOR AWHILE, IF THAT'S ALL RIGHT WITH YOU!
OF COURSE! YOU'RE WELCOME TO STAY AS LONG AS YOU LIKE!
WELL, THAT'S GOOD! I HAVE SOME THINGS TO ATTEND TO IN RIVERDALE!
WHAT KIND OF BUSINESS COULD YOU POSSIBLY HAVE IN A SMALL TOWN LIKE RIVER-DALE?
WELL, YOU SEE, I WAS RAISED HERE, AND DESPITE MY SUCCESS...
...I NEVER FINISHED HIGH SCHOOL! IT'S ALWAYS BEEN MY BIGGEST REGRET!
WOW! THAT PROVES MY POINT! WHO NEEDS SCHOOL?!
ARCHIE! WHAT A RIDICULOUS THING TO SAY!
DESPITE MY SUCCESS, IT WAS VERY DIFFICULT WITHOUT A DIPLOMA! NOT TO MENTION HOW I FEEL LIKE I MISSED THE BEST YEARS OF MY LIFE!
2

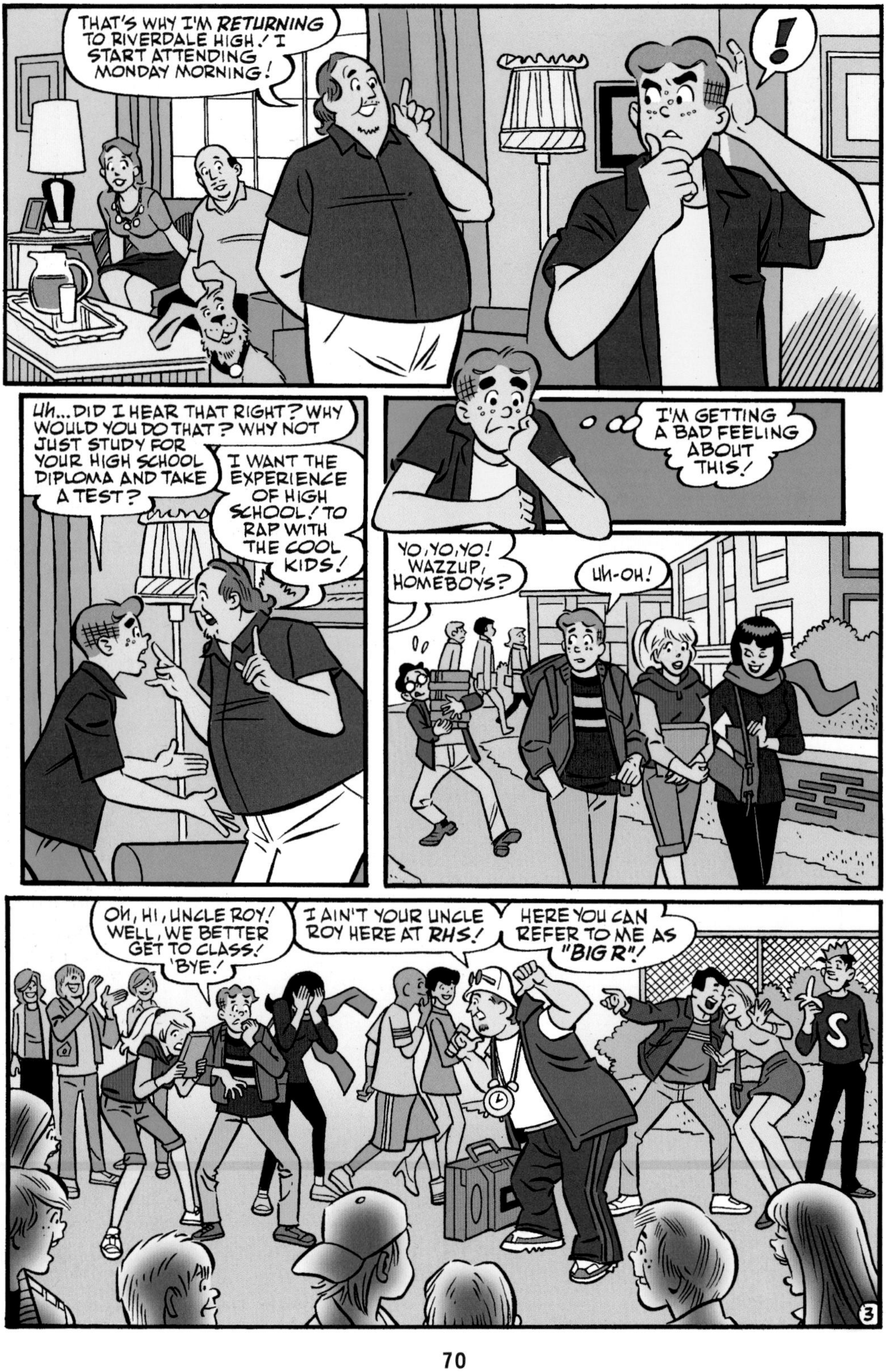
THAT'S WHY I'M RETURNING TO RIVERDALE HIGH! I START ATTENDING MONDAY MORNING!
!
UH...DID I HEAR THAT RIGHT? WHY WOULD YOU DO THAT? WHY NOT JUST STUDY FOR YOUR HIGH SCHOOL DIPLOMA AND TAKE A TEST?
I WANT THE EXPERIENCE OF HIGH SCHOOL! TO RAP WITH THE COOL KIDS!
I'M GETTING A BAD FEELING ABOUT THIS!
YO, YO, YO! WAZZUP, HOMEBOYS?
UH-OH!
OH, HI, UNCLE ROY! WELL, WE BETTER GET TO CLASS! 'BYE!
I AIN'T YOUR UNCLE ROY HERE AT RHS!
HERE YOU CAN REFER TO ME AS "BIG R"!
3

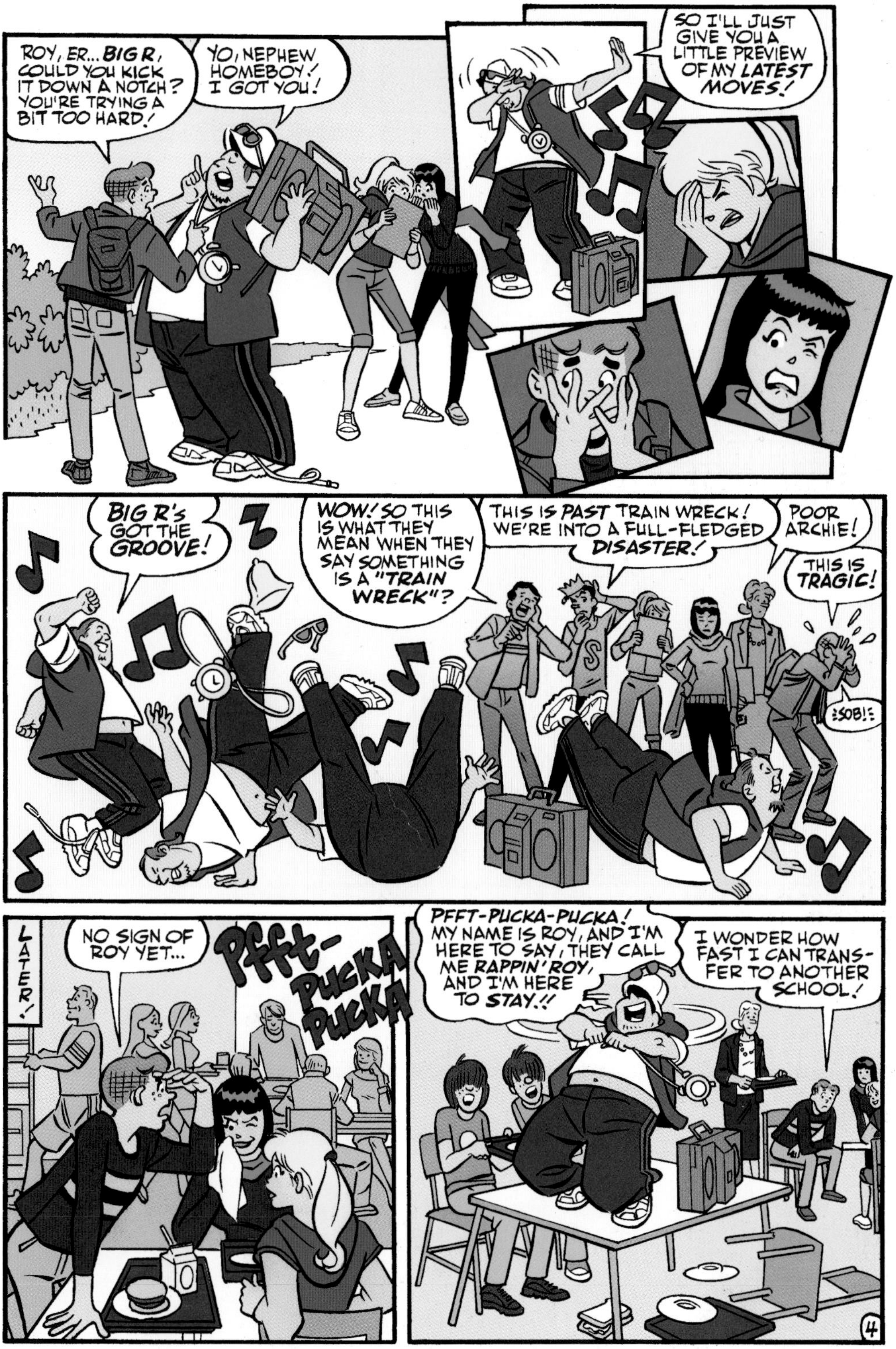
ROY, ER... BIG R, COULD YOU KICK IT DOWN A NOTCH? YOU'RE TRYING A BIT TOO HARD!
YO, NEPHEW HOMEBOY! I GOT YOU!
SO I'LL JUST GIVE YOU A LITTLE PREVIEW OF MY LATEST MOVES!
BIG R's GOT THE GROOVE!
WOW! SO THIS IS WHAT THEY MEAN WHEN THEY SAY SOMETHING IS A "TRAIN WRECK"?
THIS IS PAST TRAIN WRECK! WE'RE INTO A FULL-FLEDGED DISASTER!
POOR ARCHIE!
THIS IS TRAGIC!
SOB!
LATER!
NO SIGN OF ROY YET...
Pfft-PUCKA PUCKA
PFFT-PUCKA-PUCKA! MY NAME IS ROY, AND I'M HERE TO SAY, THEY CALL ME RAPPIN' ROY, AND I'M HERE TO STAY!!
I WONDER HOW FAST I CAN TRANS-FER TO ANOTHER SCHOOL!
4

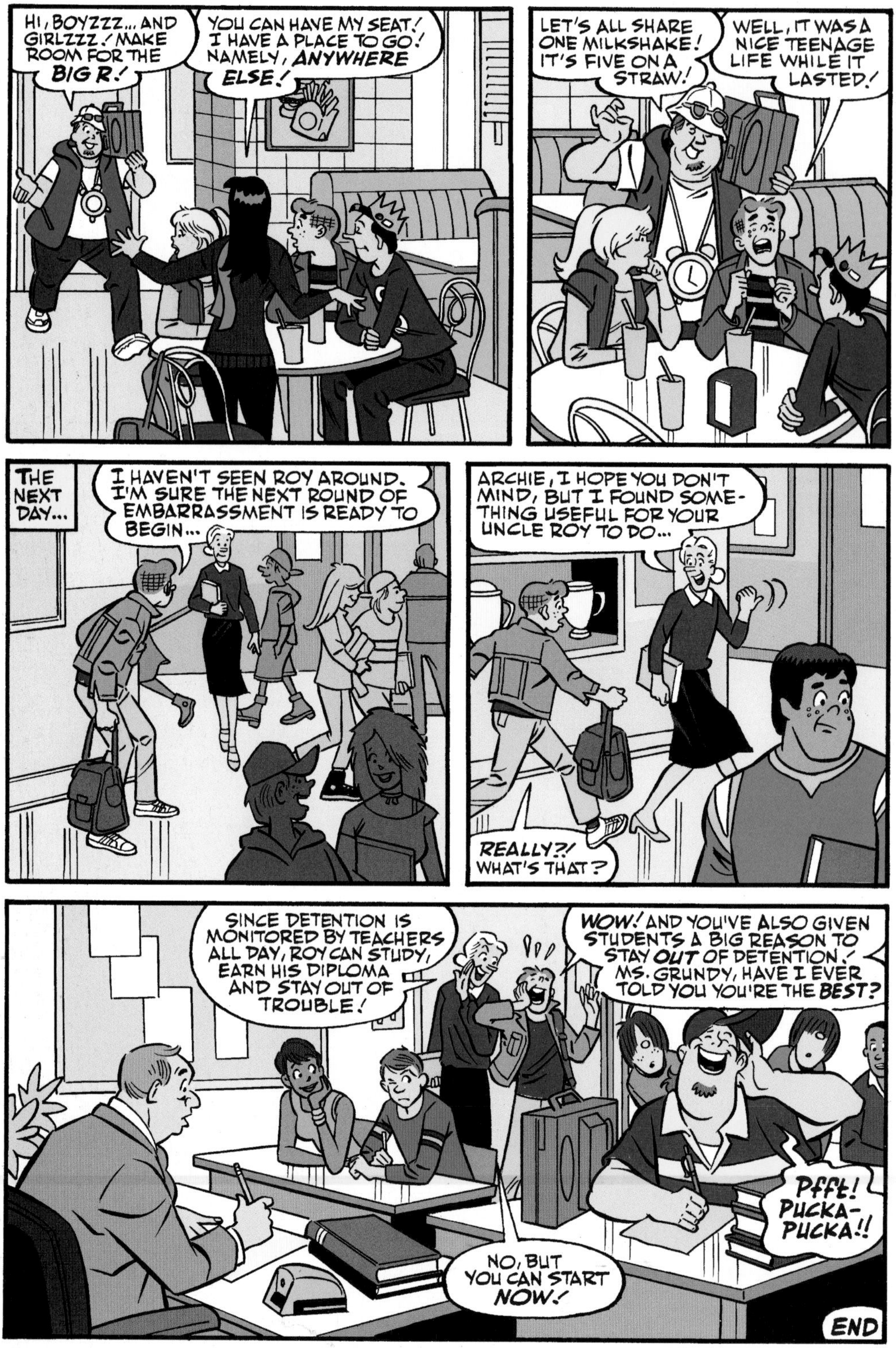
HI, BOYZZZ... AND GIRLZZZ! MAKE ROOM FOR THE BIG R!
YOU CAN HAVE MY SEAT! I HAVE A PLACE TO GO! NAMELY, ANYWHERE ELSE!
LET'S ALL SHARE ONE MILKSHAKE! IT'S FIVE ON A STRAW!
WELL, IT WAS A NICE TEENAGE LIFE WHILE IT LASTED!
THE NEXT DAY...
I HAVEN'T SEEN ROY AROUND. I'M SURE THE NEXT ROUND OF EMBARRASSMENT IS READY TO BEGIN...
ARCHIE, I HOPE YOU DON'T MIND, BUT I FOUND SOMETHING USEFUL FOR YOUR UNCLE ROY TO DO...
REALLY?! WHAT'S THAT?
SINCE DETENTION IS MONITORED BY TEACHERS ALL DAY, ROY CAN STUDY, EARN HIS DIPLOMA AND STAY OUT OF TROUBLE!
WOW! AND YOU'VE ALSO GIVEN STUDENTS A BIG REASON TO STAY OUT OF DETENTION! MS. GRUNDY, HAVE I EVER TOLD YOU YOU'RE THE BEST?
NO, BUT YOU CAN START NOW!
Pfft! PUCKA-PUCKA!!
END

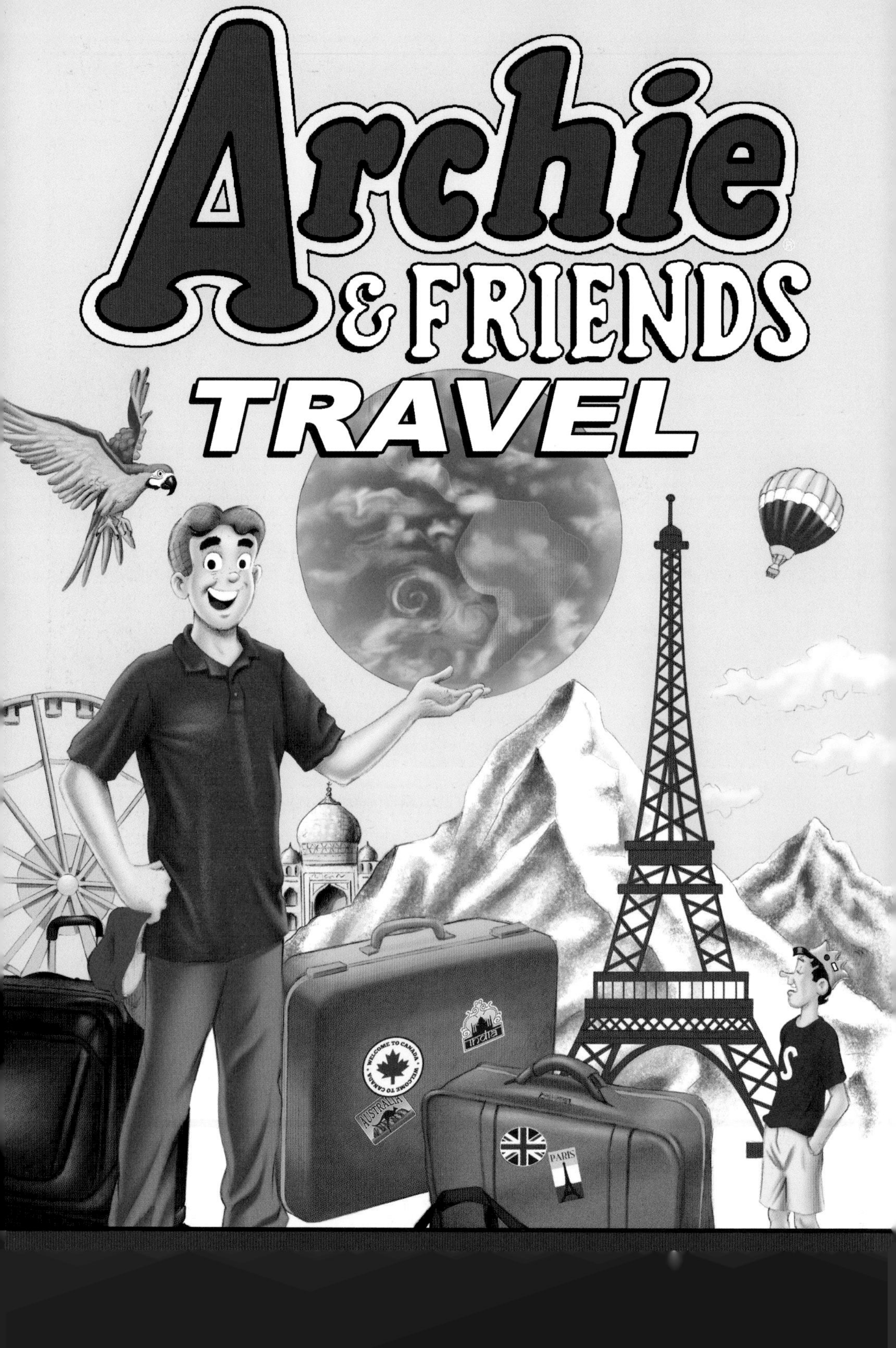
Archie®
& FRIENDS
TRAVEL
WELCOME TO CANADA
AUSTRALIA
India
PARIS

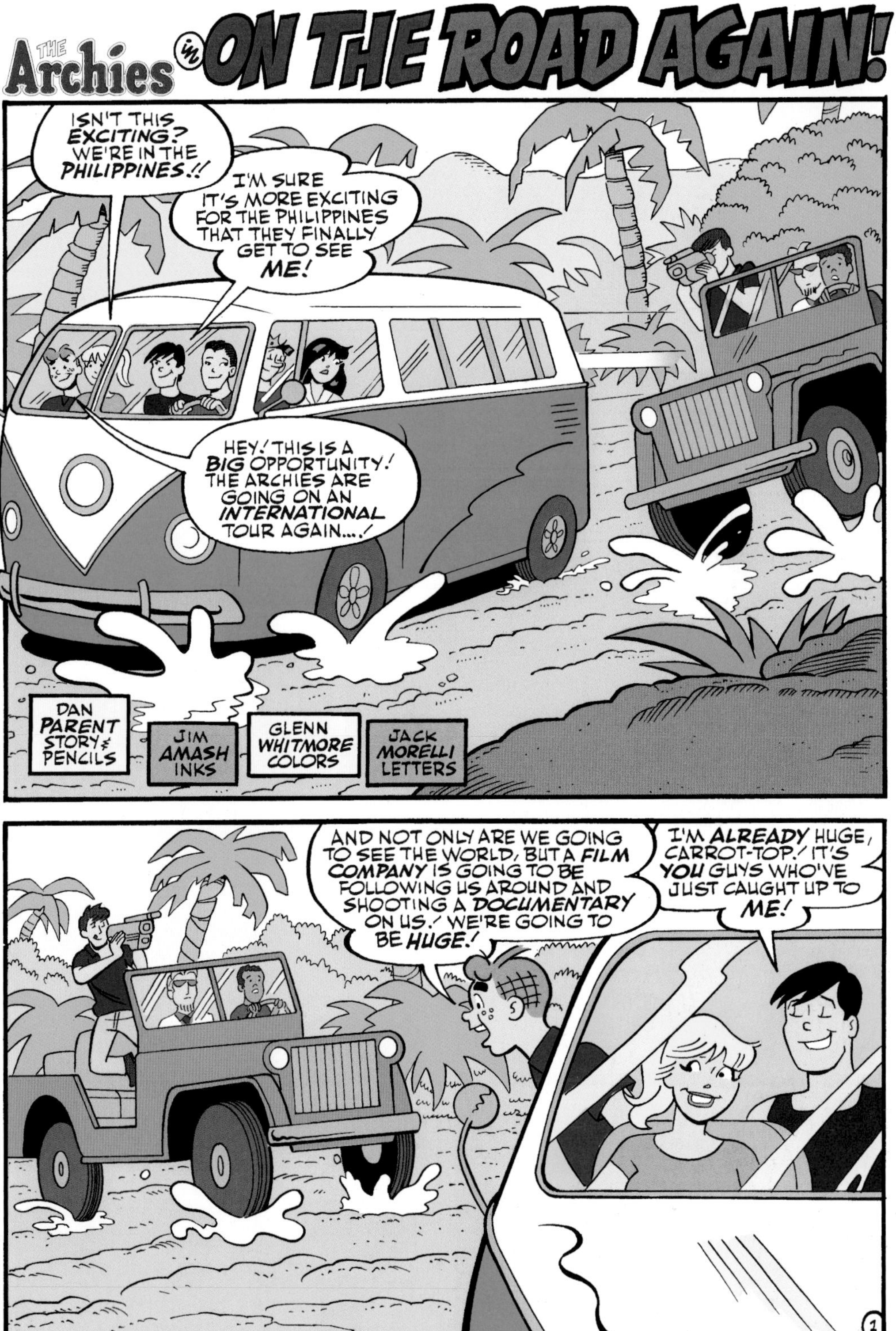
THE Archies in ON THE ROAD AGAIN!
ISN'T THIS EXCITING? WE'RE IN THE PHILIPPINES!!
I'M SURE IT'S MORE EXCITING FOR THE PHILIPPINES THAT THEY FINALLY GET TO SEE ME!
HEY! THIS IS A BIG OPPORTUNITY! THE ARCHIES ARE GOING ON AN INTERNATIONAL TOUR AGAIN...!
DAN PARENT STORY & PENCILS
JIM AMASH INKS
GLENN WHITMORE COLORS
JACK MORELLI LETTERS
AND NOT ONLY ARE WE GOING TO SEE THE WORLD, BUT A FILM COMPANY IS GOING TO BE FOLLOWING US AROUND AND SHOOTING A DOCUMENTARY ON US! WE'RE GOING TO BE HUGE!
I'M ALREADY HUGE, CARROT-TOP! IT'S YOU GUYS WHO'VE JUST CAUGHT UP TO ME!
1

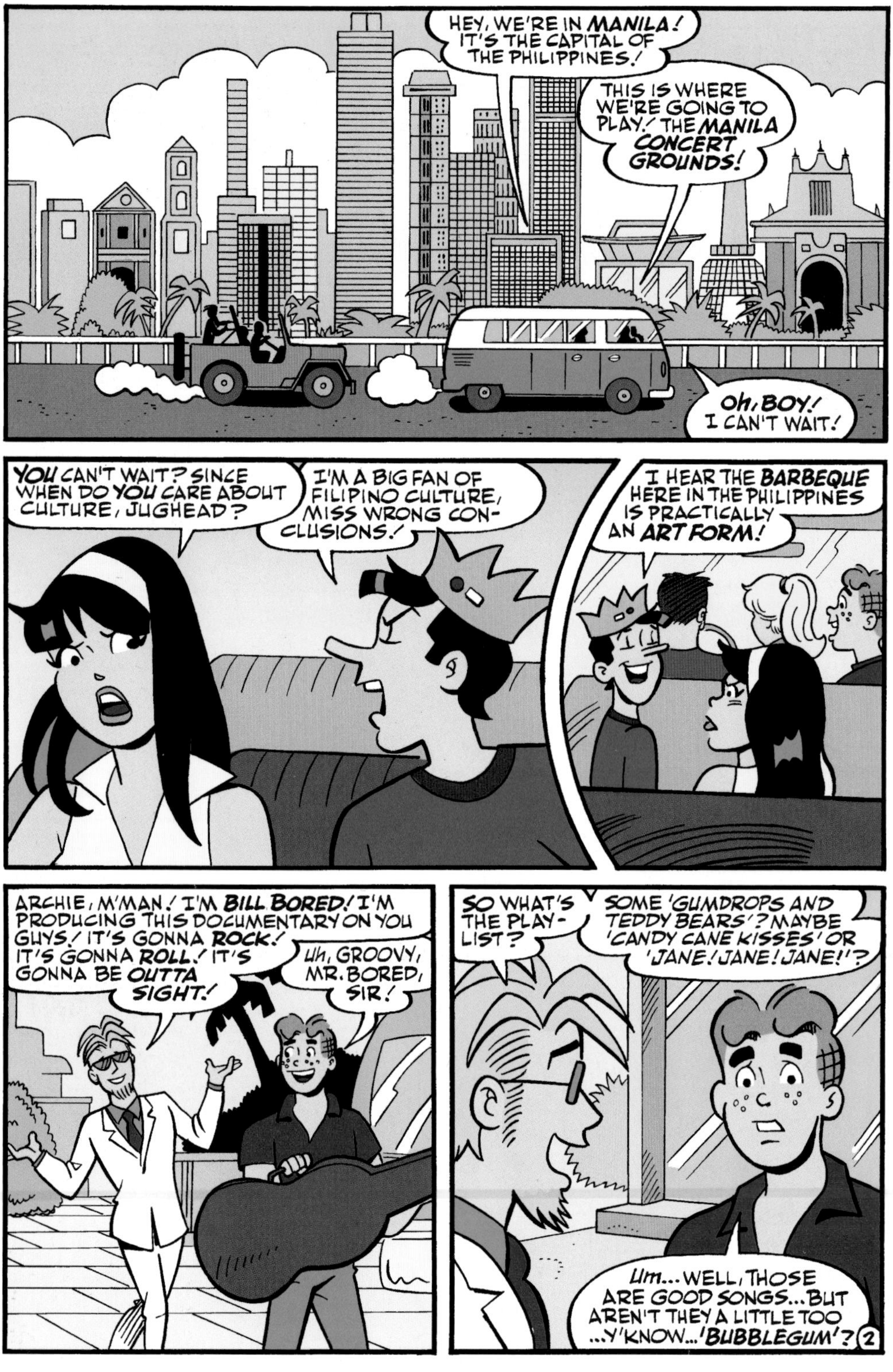
HEY, WE'RE IN MANILA! IT'S THE CAPITAL OF THE PHILIPPINES!
THIS IS WHERE WE'RE GOING TO PLAY! THE MANILA CONCERT GROUNDS!
OH, BOY! I CAN'T WAIT!
YOU CAN'T WAIT? SINCE WHEN DO YOU CARE ABOUT CULTURE, JUGHEAD?
I'M A BIG FAN OF FILIPINO CULTURE, MISS WRONG CON-CLUSIONS!
I HEAR THE BARBEQUE HERE IN THE PHILIPPINES IS PRACTICALLY AN ART FORM!
ARCHIE, M'MAN! I'M BILL BORED! I'M PRODUCING THIS DOCUMENTARY ON YOU GUYS! IT'S GONNA ROCK! IT'S GONNA ROLL! IT'S GONNA BE OUTTA SIGHT!
UH, GROOVY, MR. BORED, SIR!
SO WHAT'S THE PLAY-LIST?
SOME 'GUMDROPS AND TEDDY BEARS'? MAYBE 'CANDY CANE KISSES' OR 'JANE! JANE! JANE!'?
UM... WELL, THOSE ARE GOOD SONGS... BUT AREN'T THEY A LITTLE TOO ...Y'KNOW... 'BUBBLEGUM'?
2

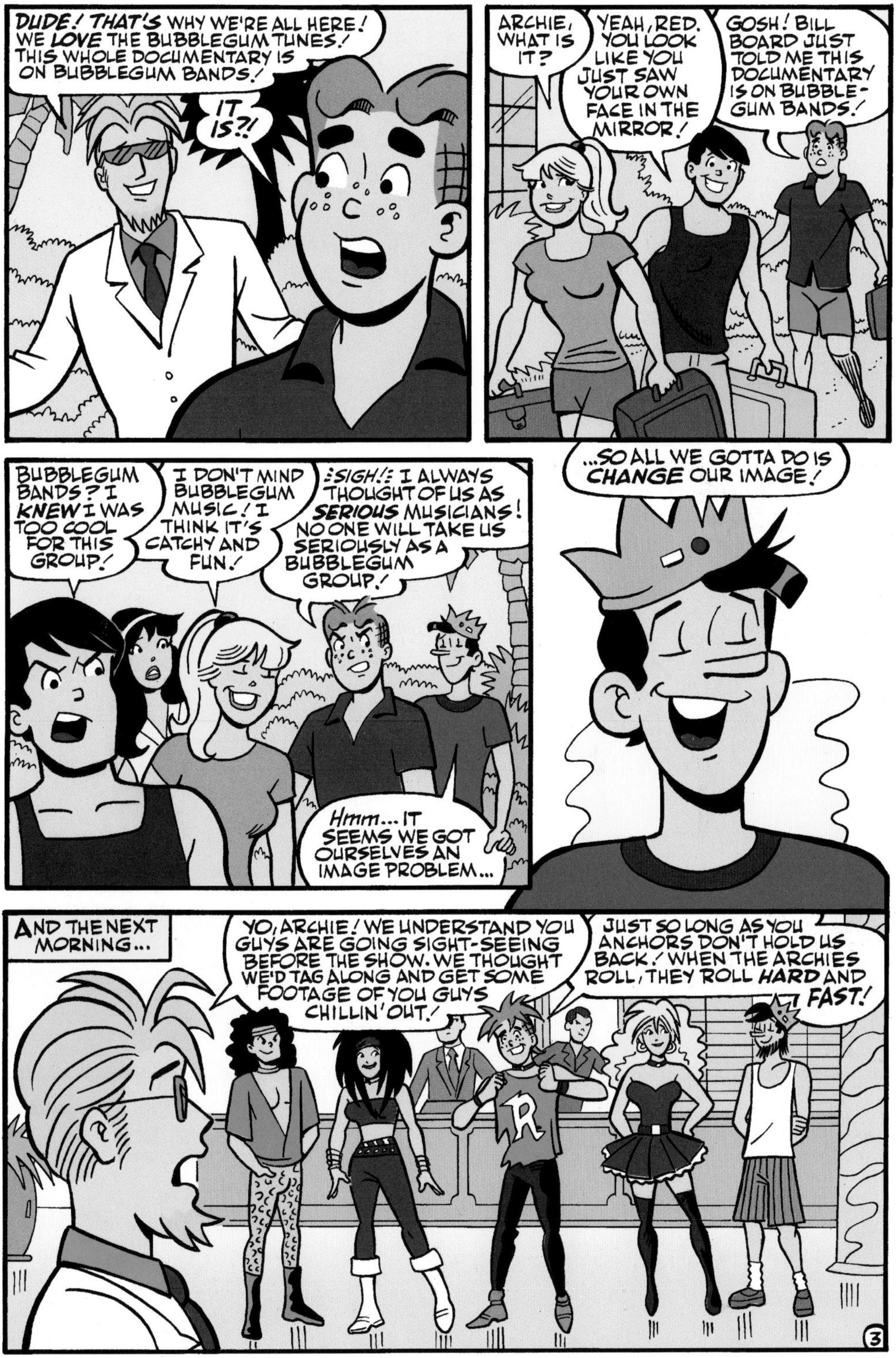
DUDE! THAT'S WHY WE'RE ALL HERE! WE LOVE THE BUBBLEGUM TUNES! THIS WHOLE DOCUMENTARY IS ON BUBBLEGUM BANDS!
IT IS?!
ARCHIE, WHAT IS IT?
YEAH, RED. YOU LOOK LIKE YOU JUST SAW YOUR OWN FACE IN THE MIRROR!
GOSH! BILL BOARD JUST TOLD ME THIS DOCUMENTARY IS ON BUBBLE-GUM BANDS!
BUBBLEGUM BANDS? I KNEW I WAS TOO COOL FOR THIS GROUP!
I DON'T MIND BUBBLEGUM MUSIC! I THINK IT'S CATCHY AND FUN!
SIGH! I ALWAYS THOUGHT OF US AS SERIOUS MUSICIANS! NO ONE WILL TAKE US SERIOUSLY AS A BUBBLEGUM GROUP!
Hmm... IT SEEMS WE GOT OURSELVES AN IMAGE PROBLEM...
...SO ALL WE GOTTA DO IS CHANGE OUR IMAGE!
AND THE NEXT MORNING...
YO, ARCHIE! WE UNDERSTAND YOU GUYS ARE GOING SIGHT-SEEING BEFORE THE SHOW. WE THOUGHT WE'D TAG ALONG AND GET SOME FOOTAGE OF YOU GUYS CHILLIN' OUT!
JUST SO LONG AS YOU ANCHORS DON'T HOLD US BACK! WHEN THE ARCHIES ROLL, THEY ROLL HARD AND FAST!
R
3

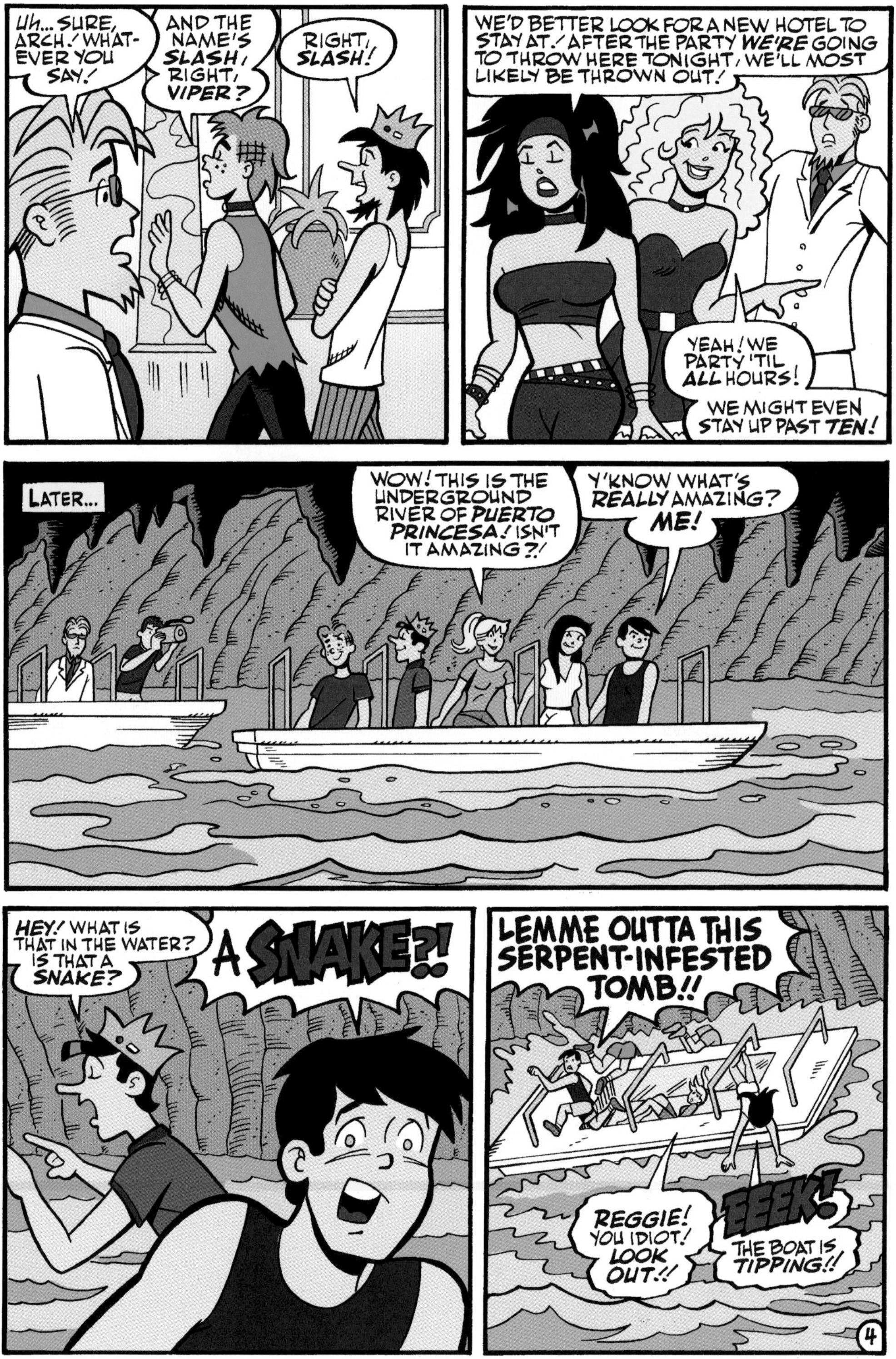
UH... SURE, ARCH.! WHATEVER YOU SAY.!
AND THE NAME'S SLASH, RIGHT, VIPER?
RIGHT, SLASH!
WE'D BETTER LOOK FOR A NEW HOTEL TO STAY AT.! AFTER THE PARTY WE'RE GOING TO THROW HERE TONIGHT, WE'LL MOST LIKELY BE THROWN OUT.!
YEAH! WE PARTY 'TIL ALL HOURS!
WE MIGHT EVEN STAY UP PAST TEN!
LATER...
WOW! THIS IS THE UNDERGROUND RIVER OF PUERTO PRINCESA! ISN'T IT AMAZING?!
Y'KNOW WHAT'S REALLY AMAZING? ME!
HEY! WHAT IS THAT IN THE WATER? IS THAT A SNAKE?
A SNAKE?!
LEMME OUTTA THIS SERPENT-INFESTED TOMB!!
REGGIE! YOU IDIOT! LOOK OUT!!
EEEK!
THE BOAT IS TIPPING!!
4

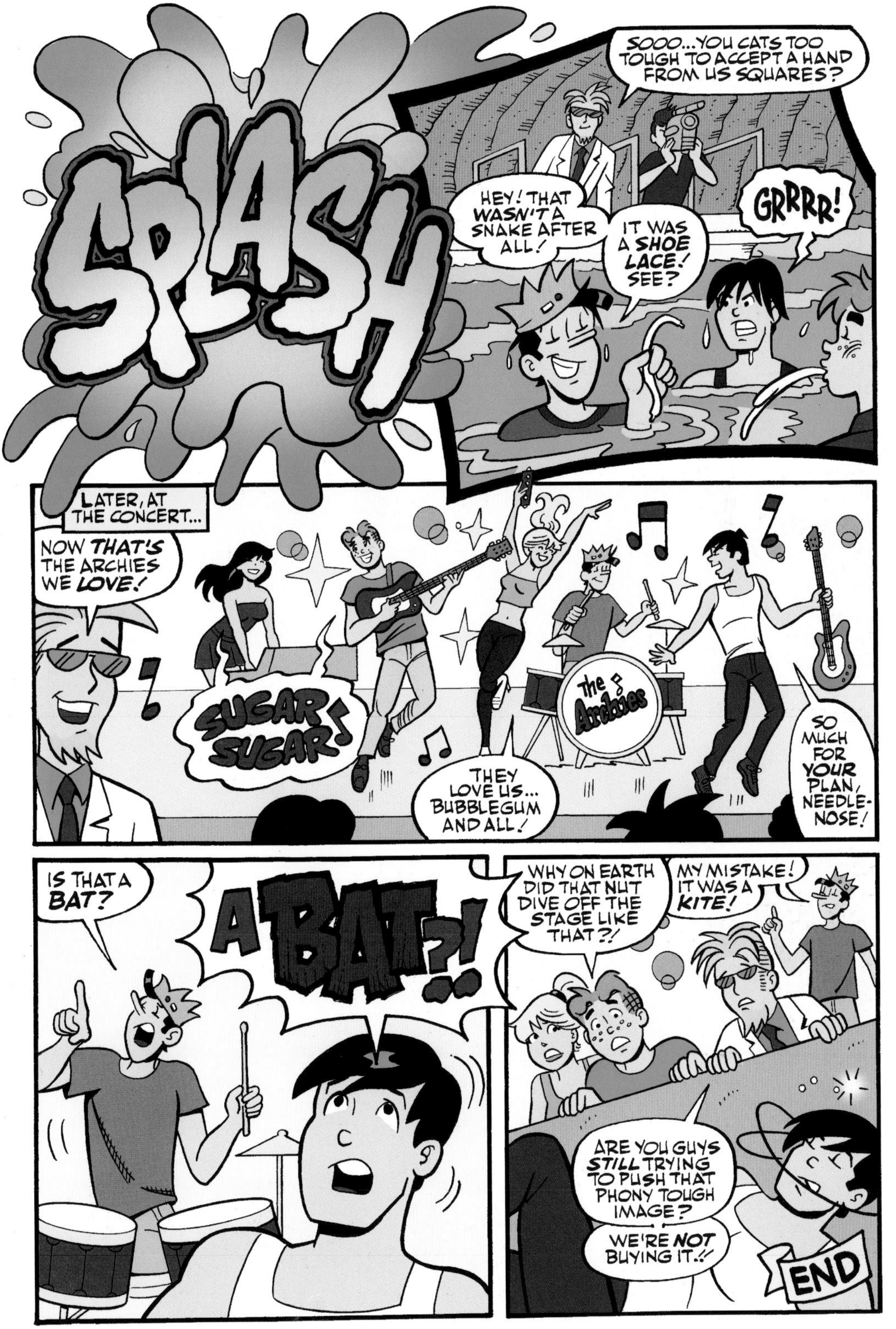
SPLASH
SOOO... YOU CATS TOO TOUGH TO ACCEPT A HAND FROM US SQUARES?
HEY! THAT WASN'T A SNAKE AFTER ALL!
IT WAS A SHOE LACE! SEE?
GRRRR!
LATER, AT THE CONCERT...
NOW THAT'S THE ARCHIES WE LOVE!
SUGAR SUGAR
The Archies
THEY LOVE US... BUBBLEGUM AND ALL!
SO MUCH FOR YOUR PLAN, NEEDLE-NOSE!
IS THAT A BAT?
A BAT?!
WHY ON EARTH DID THAT NUT DIVE OFF THE STAGE LIKE THAT?!
MY MISTAKE! IT WAS A KITE!
ARE YOU GUYS STILL TRYING TO PUSH THAT PHONY TOUGH IMAGE?
WE'RE NOT BUYING IT.!!
END

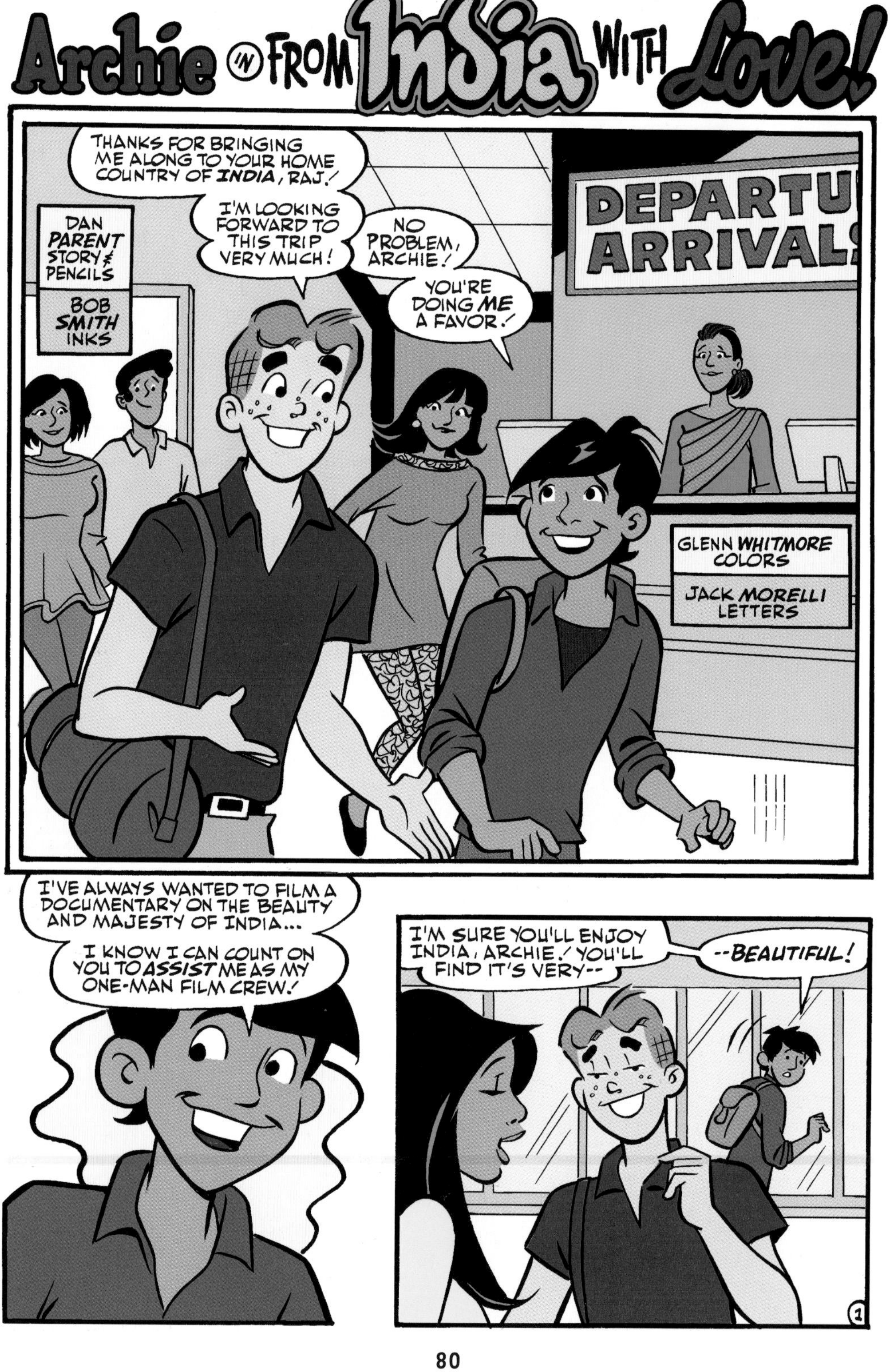
Archie in FROM India WITH Love!
THANKS FOR BRINGING ME ALONG TO YOUR HOME COUNTRY OF INDIA, RAJ!
I'M LOOKING FORWARD TO THIS TRIP VERY MUCH!
NO PROBLEM, ARCHIE!
YOU'RE DOING ME A FAVOR!
DAN PARENT STORY & PENCILS
BOB SMITH INKS
DEPARTU
ARRIVAL
GLENN WHITMORE COLORS
JACK MORELLI LETTERS
I'VE ALWAYS WANTED TO FILM A DOCUMENTARY ON THE BEAUTY AND MAJESTY OF INDIA...
I KNOW I CAN COUNT ON YOU TO ASSIST ME AS MY ONE-MAN FILM CREW!
I'M SURE YOU'LL ENJOY INDIA, ARCHIE! YOU'LL FIND IT'S VERY--
--BEAUTIFUL!
1

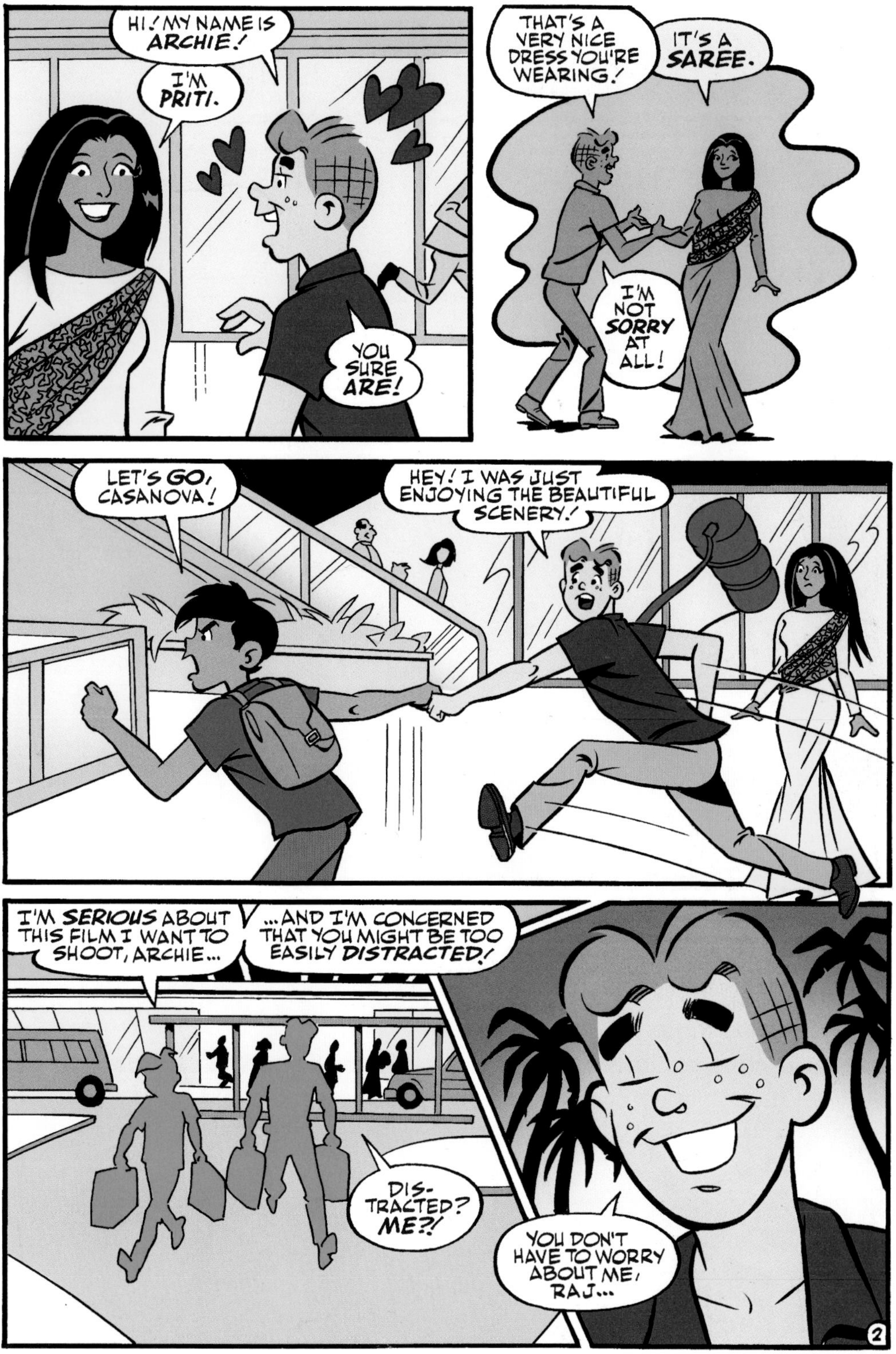
HI! MY NAME IS ARCHIE!
I'M PRITI.
YOU SURE ARE!
THAT'S A VERY NICE DRESS YOU'RE WEARING!
IT'S A SAREE.
I'M NOT SORRY AT ALL!
LET'S GO, CASANOVA!
HEY! I WAS JUST ENJOYING THE BEAUTIFUL SCENERY!
I'M SERIOUS ABOUT THIS FILM I WANT TO SHOOT, ARCHIE...
...AND I'M CONCERNED THAT YOU MIGHT BE TOO EASILY DISTRACTED!
DIS-TRACTED? ME?!
YOU DON'T HAVE TO WORRY ABOUT ME, RAJ...
2

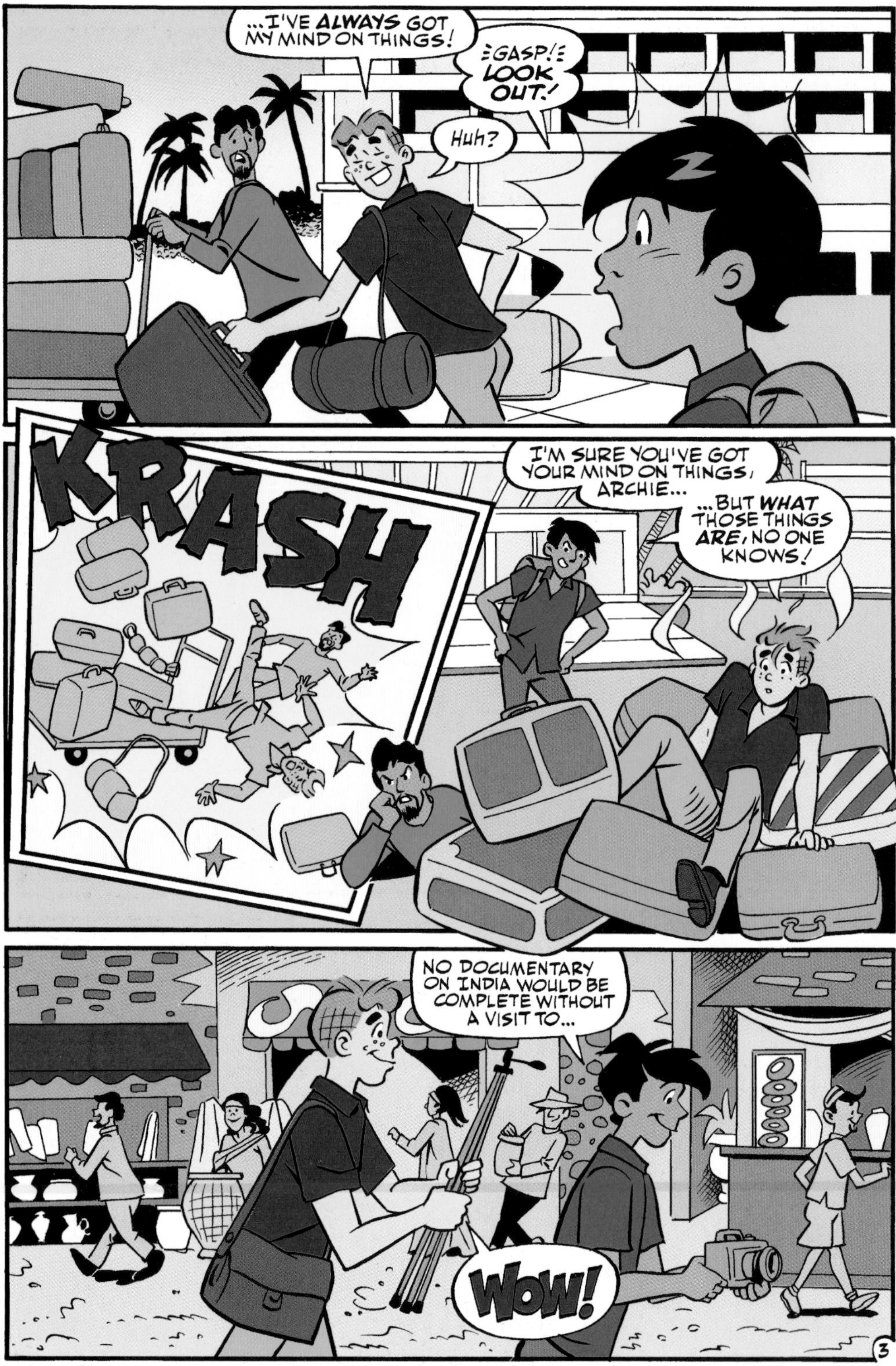
...I'VE ALWAYS GOT MY MIND ON THINGS!
GASP! LOOK OUT!
Huh?
KRASH
I'M SURE YOU'VE GOT YOUR MIND ON THINGS, ARCHIE...
...BUT WHAT THOSE THINGS ARE, NO ONE KNOWS!
NO DOCUMENTARY ON INDIA WOULD BE COMPLETE WITHOUT A VISIT TO...
WOW!
3

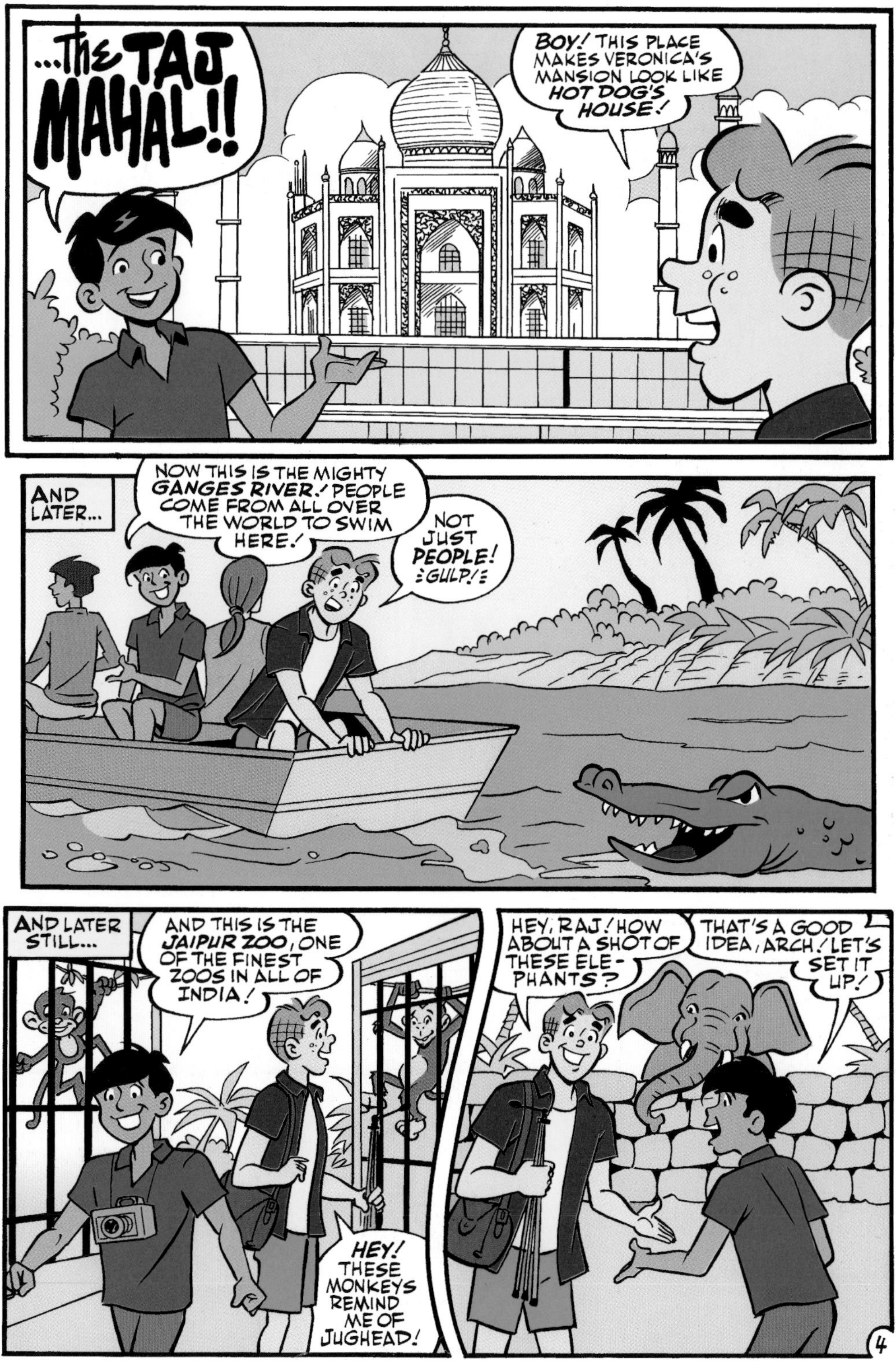

...The TAJ MAHAL!!
BOY! THIS PLACE MAKES VERONICA'S MANSION LOOK LIKE HOT DOG'S HOUSE!
AND LATER...
NOW THIS IS THE MIGHTY GANGES RIVER! PEOPLE COME FROM ALL OVER THE WORLD TO SWIM HERE!
NOT JUST PEOPLE! GULP!
AND LATER STILL...
AND THIS IS THE JAIPUR ZOO, ONE OF THE FINEST ZOOS IN ALL OF INDIA!
HEY! THESE MONKEYS REMIND ME OF JUGHEAD!
HEY, RAJ! HOW ABOUT A SHOT OF THESE ELE-PHANTS?
THAT'S A GOOD IDEA, ARCH! LET'S SET IT UP!
4

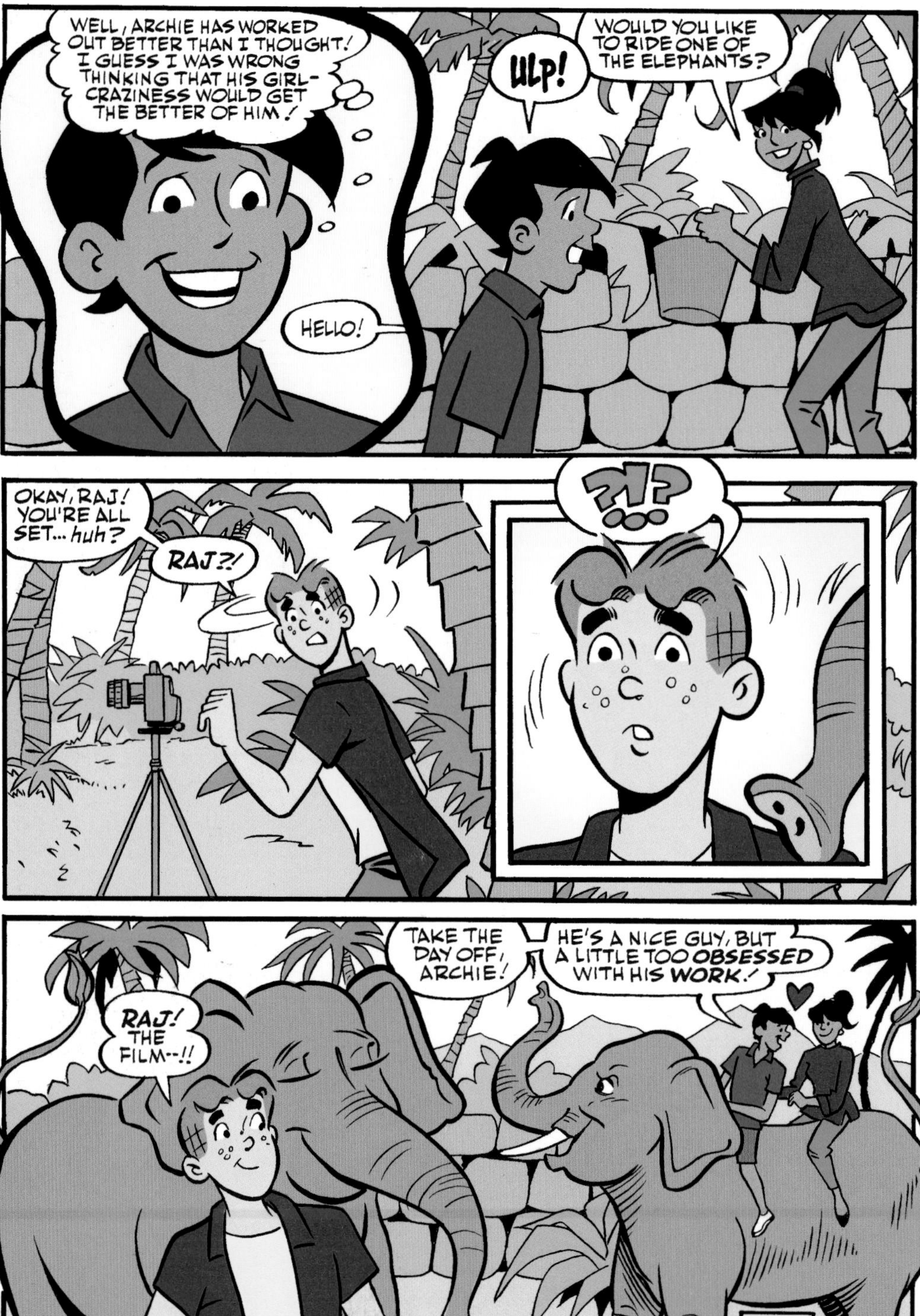
WELL, ARCHIE HAS WORKED OUT BETTER THAN I THOUGHT! I GUESS I WAS WRONG THINKING THAT HIS GIRL-CRAZINESS WOULD GET THE BETTER OF HIM!
HELLO!
ULP!
WOULD YOU LIKE TO RIDE ONE OF THE ELEPHANTS?
OKAY, RAJ! YOU'RE ALL SET... huh?
RAJ?!
?!?...
RAJ! THE FILM--!!
TAKE THE DAY OFF, ARCHIE!
HE'S A NICE GUY, BUT A LITTLE TOO OBSESSED WITH HIS WORK!
THE END

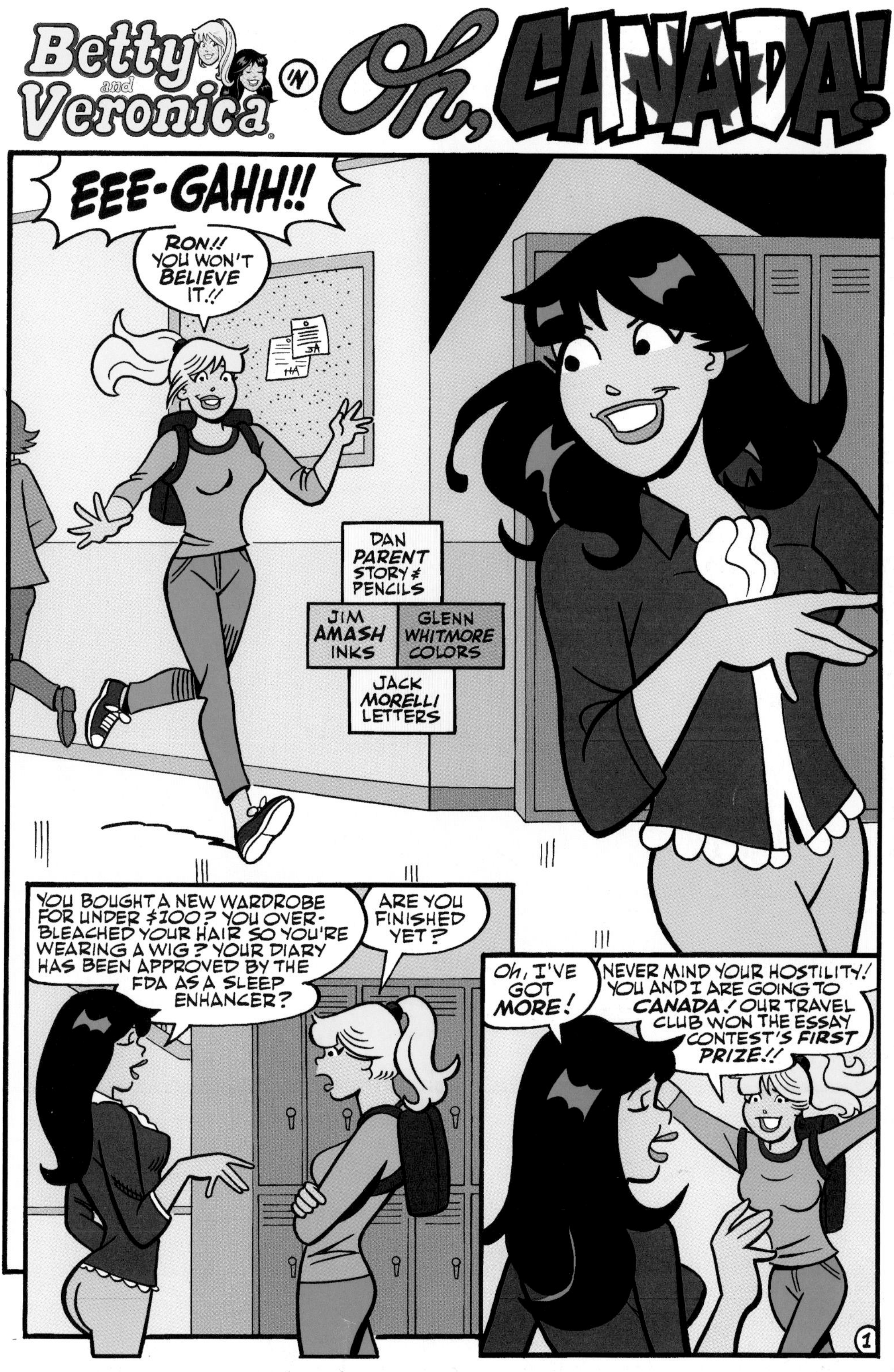
Betty and Veronica
IN
Oh, CANADA!
EEE-GAHH!!
RON!! YOU WON'T BELIEVE IT!!
DAN PARENT STORY & PENCILS
JIM AMASH INKS
GLENN WHITMORE COLORS
JACK MORELLI LETTERS
YOU BOUGHT A NEW WARDROBE FOR UNDER $100? YOU OVER-BLEACHED YOUR HAIR SO YOU'RE WEARING A WIG? YOUR DIARY HAS BEEN APPROVED BY THE FDA AS A SLEEP ENHANCER?
ARE YOU FINISHED YET?
Oh, I'VE GOT MORE!
NEVER MIND YOUR HOSTILITY! YOU AND I ARE GOING TO CANADA! OUR TRAVEL CLUB WON THE ESSAY CONTEST'S FIRST PRIZE!!
1

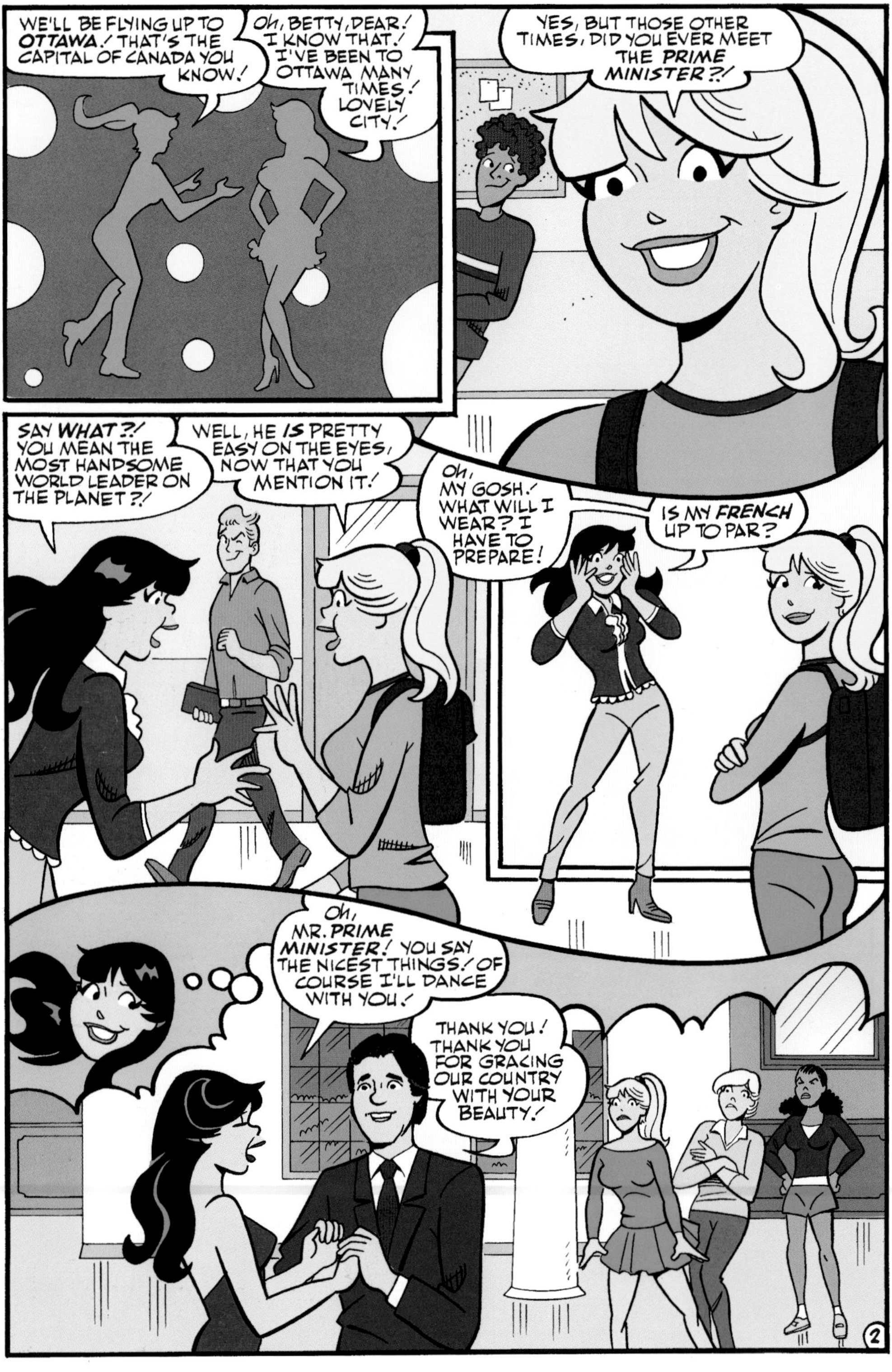
WE'LL BE FLYING UP TO OTTAWA! THAT'S THE CAPITAL OF CANADA YOU KNOW!
OH, BETTY, DEAR! I KNOW THAT! I'VE BEEN TO OTTAWA MANY TIMES! LOVELY CITY!
YES, BUT THOSE OTHER TIMES, DID YOU EVER MEET THE PRIME MINISTER?!
SAY WHAT?! YOU MEAN THE MOST HANDSOME WORLD LEADER ON THE PLANET?!
WELL, HE IS PRETTY EASY ON THE EYES, NOW THAT YOU MENTION IT!
OH, MY GOSH! WHAT WILL I WEAR? I HAVE TO PREPARE!
IS MY FRENCH UP TO PAR?
OH, MR. PRIME MINISTER! YOU SAY THE NICEST THINGS! OF COURSE I'LL DANCE WITH YOU!
THANK YOU! THANK YOU FOR GRACING OUR COUNTRY WITH YOUR BEAUTY!
2

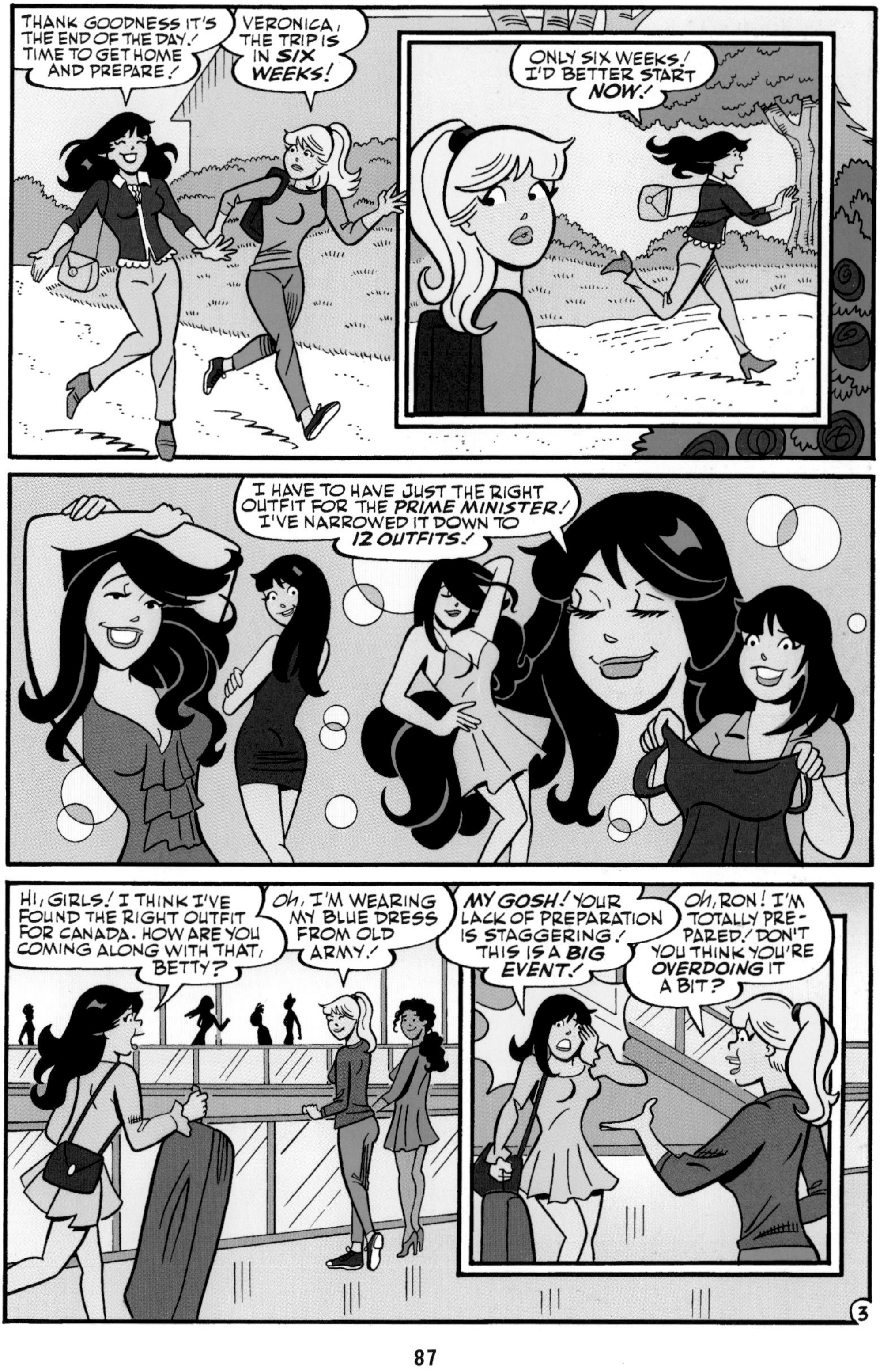
THANK GOODNESS IT'S THE END OF THE DAY! TIME TO GET HOME AND PREPARE!
VERONICA, THE TRIP IS IN SIX WEEKS!
ONLY SIX WEEKS! I'D BETTER START NOW!
I HAVE TO HAVE JUST THE RIGHT OUTFIT FOR THE PRIME MINISTER! I'VE NARROWED IT DOWN TO 12 OUTFITS!
HI, GIRLS! I THINK I'VE FOUND THE RIGHT OUTFIT FOR CANADA. HOW ARE YOU COMING ALONG WITH THAT, BETTY?
OH, I'M WEARING MY BLUE DRESS FROM OLD ARMY!
MY GOSH! YOUR LACK OF PREPARATION IS STAGGERING! THIS IS A BIG EVENT!
OH, RON! I'M TOTALLY PRE-PARED! DON'T YOU THINK YOU'RE OVERDOING IT A BIT?
3

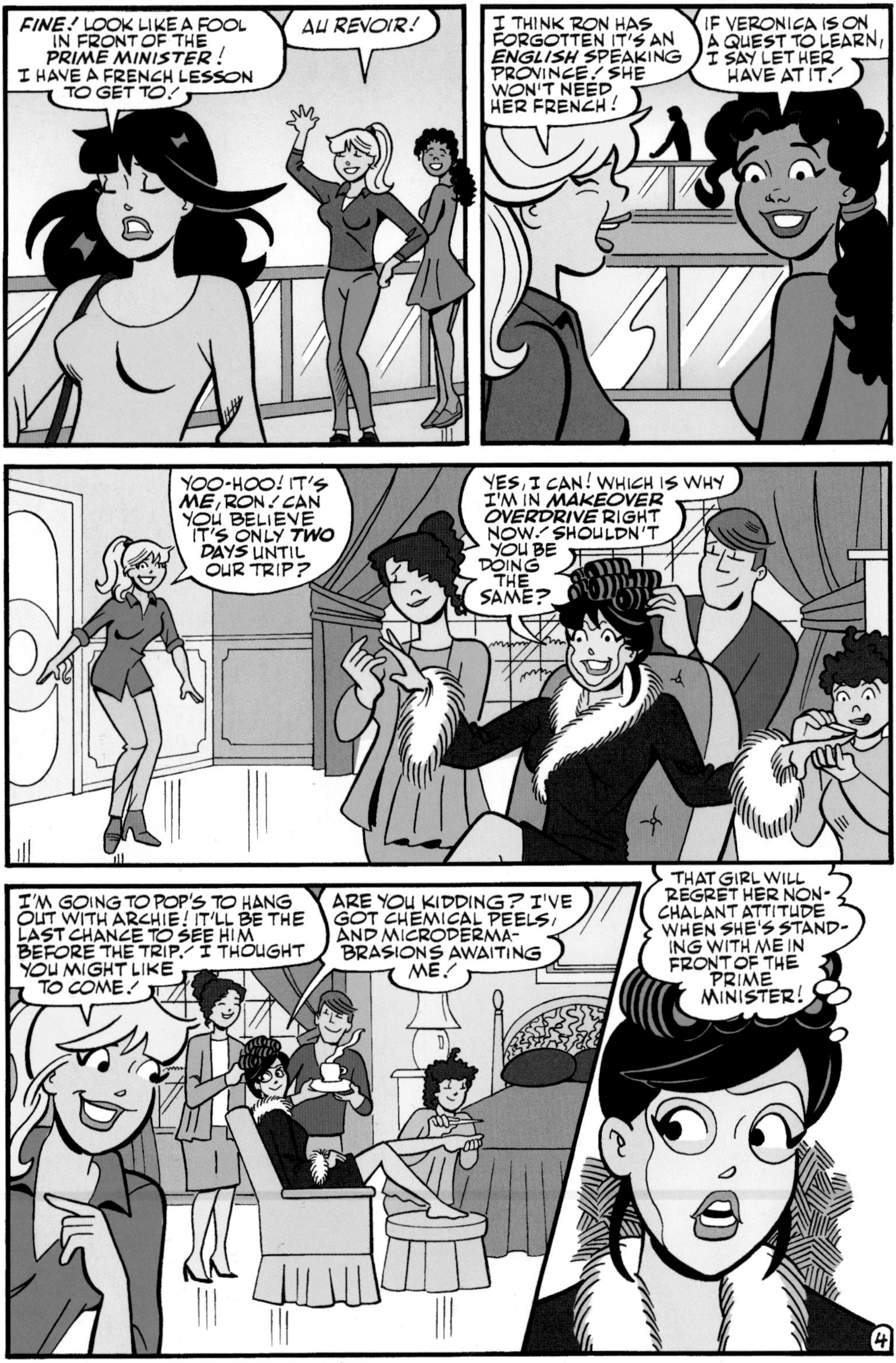
FINE! LOOK LIKE A FOOL IN FRONT OF THE PRIME MINISTER! I HAVE A FRENCH LESSON TO GET TO!
AU REVOIR!
I THINK RON HAS FORGOTTEN IT'S AN ENGLISH SPEAKING PROVINCE! SHE WON'T NEED HER FRENCH!
IF VERONICA IS ON A QUEST TO LEARN, I SAY LET HER HAVE AT IT!
YOO-HOO! IT'S ME, RON! CAN YOU BELIEVE IT'S ONLY TWO DAYS UNTIL OUR TRIP?
YES, I CAN! WHICH IS WHY I'M IN MAKEOVER OVERDRIVE RIGHT NOW! SHOULDN'T YOU BE DOING THE SAME?
I'M GOING TO POP'S TO HANG OUT WITH ARCHIE! IT'LL BE THE LAST CHANCE TO SEE HIM BEFORE THE TRIP! I THOUGHT YOU MIGHT LIKE TO COME!
ARE YOU KIDDING? I'VE GOT CHEMICAL PEELS, AND MICRODERMA-BRASIONS AWAITING ME!
THAT GIRL WILL REGRET HER NON-CHALANT ATTITUDE WHEN SHE'S STAND-ING WITH ME IN FRONT OF THE PRIME MINISTER!
4

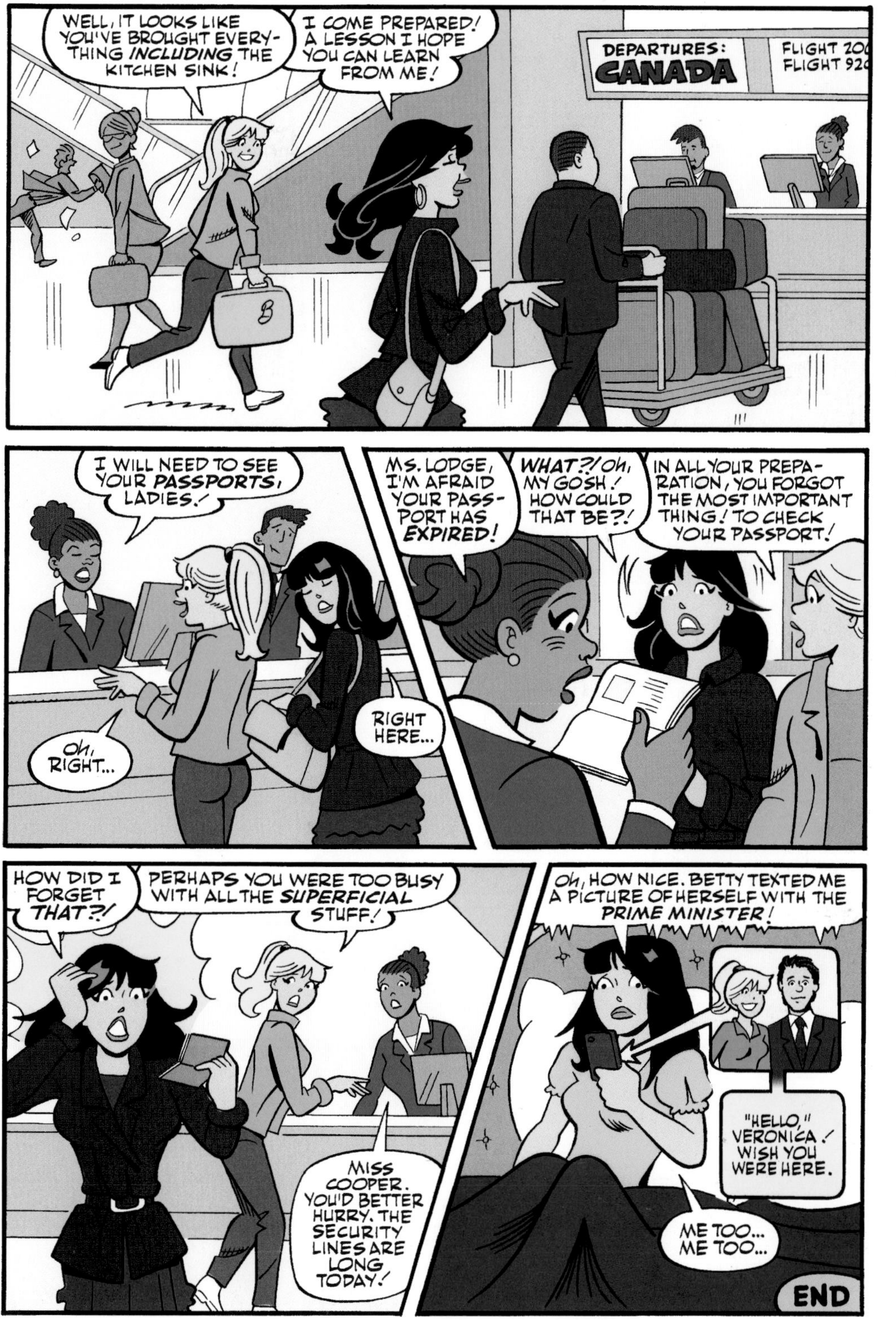
WELL, IT LOOKS LIKE YOU'VE BROUGHT EVERY-THING INCLUDING THE KITCHEN SINK!
I COME PREPARED! A LESSON I HOPE YOU CAN LEARN FROM ME!
DEPARTURES: CANADA
FLIGHT 20
FLIGHT 92
I WILL NEED TO SEE YOUR PASSPORTS, LADIES.!
OH, RIGHT...
RIGHT HERE...
MS. LODGE, I'M AFRAID YOUR PASS-PORT HAS EXPIRED!
WHAT?! OH, MY GOSH! HOW COULD THAT BE?!
IN ALL YOUR PREPA-RATION, YOU FORGOT THE MOST IMPORTANT THING! TO CHECK YOUR PASSPORT!
HOW DID I FORGET THAT?!
PERHAPS YOU WERE TOO BUSY WITH ALL THE SUPERFICIAL STUFF!
MISS COOPER. YOU'D BETTER HURRY. THE SECURITY LINES ARE LONG TODAY!
OH, HOW NICE. BETTY TEXTED ME A PICTURE OF HERSELF WITH THE PRIME MINISTER!
"HELLO," VERONICA! WISH YOU WERE HERE.
ME TOO... ME TOO...
END

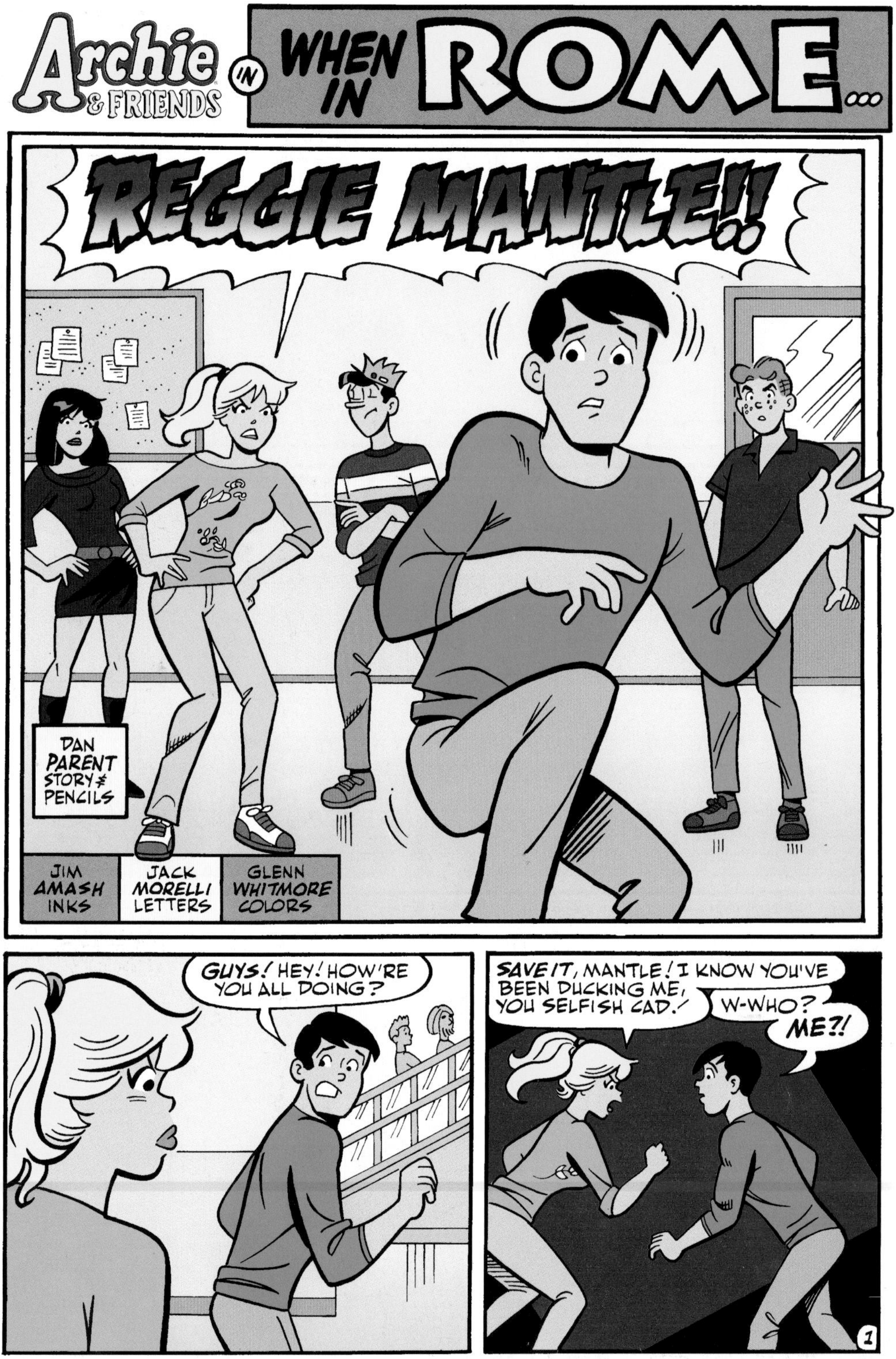
Archie & FRIENDS IN
WHEN IN ROME...
REGGIE MANTLE!!
DAN PARENT STORY & PENCILS
JIM AMASH INKS
JACK MORELLI LETTERS
GLENN WHITMORE COLORS
GUYS! HEY! HOW'RE YOU ALL DOING?
SAVE IT, MANTLE! I KNOW YOU'VE BEEN DUCKING ME, YOU SELFISH CAD!
W-WHO? ME?!
1

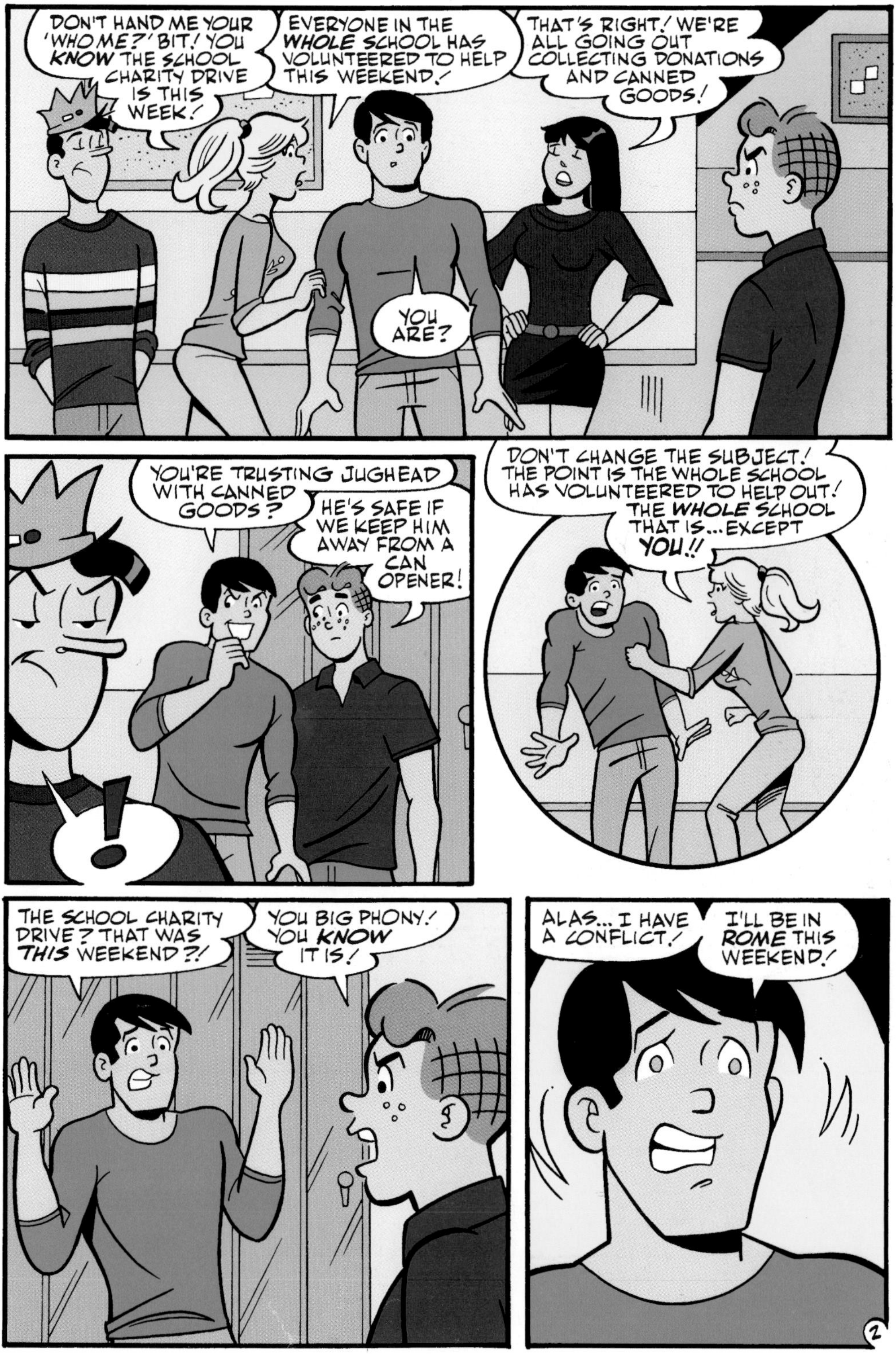
DON'T HAND ME YOUR 'WHO ME?' BIT! YOU KNOW THE SCHOOL CHARITY DRIVE IS THIS WEEK!
EVERYONE IN THE WHOLE SCHOOL HAS VOLUNTEERED TO HELP THIS WEEKEND!
THAT'S RIGHT! WE'RE ALL GOING OUT COLLECTING DONATIONS AND CANNED GOODS!
YOU ARE?
YOU'RE TRUSTING JUGHEAD WITH CANNED GOODS?
HE'S SAFE IF WE KEEP HIM AWAY FROM A CAN OPENER!
!
DON'T CHANGE THE SUBJECT! THE POINT IS THE WHOLE SCHOOL HAS VOLUNTEERED TO HELP OUT! THE WHOLE SCHOOL THAT IS...EXCEPT YOU!!
THE SCHOOL CHARITY DRIVE? THAT WAS THIS WEEKEND?!
YOU BIG PHONY! YOU KNOW IT IS!
ALAS... I HAVE A CONFLICT!
I'LL BE IN ROME THIS WEEKEND!
2

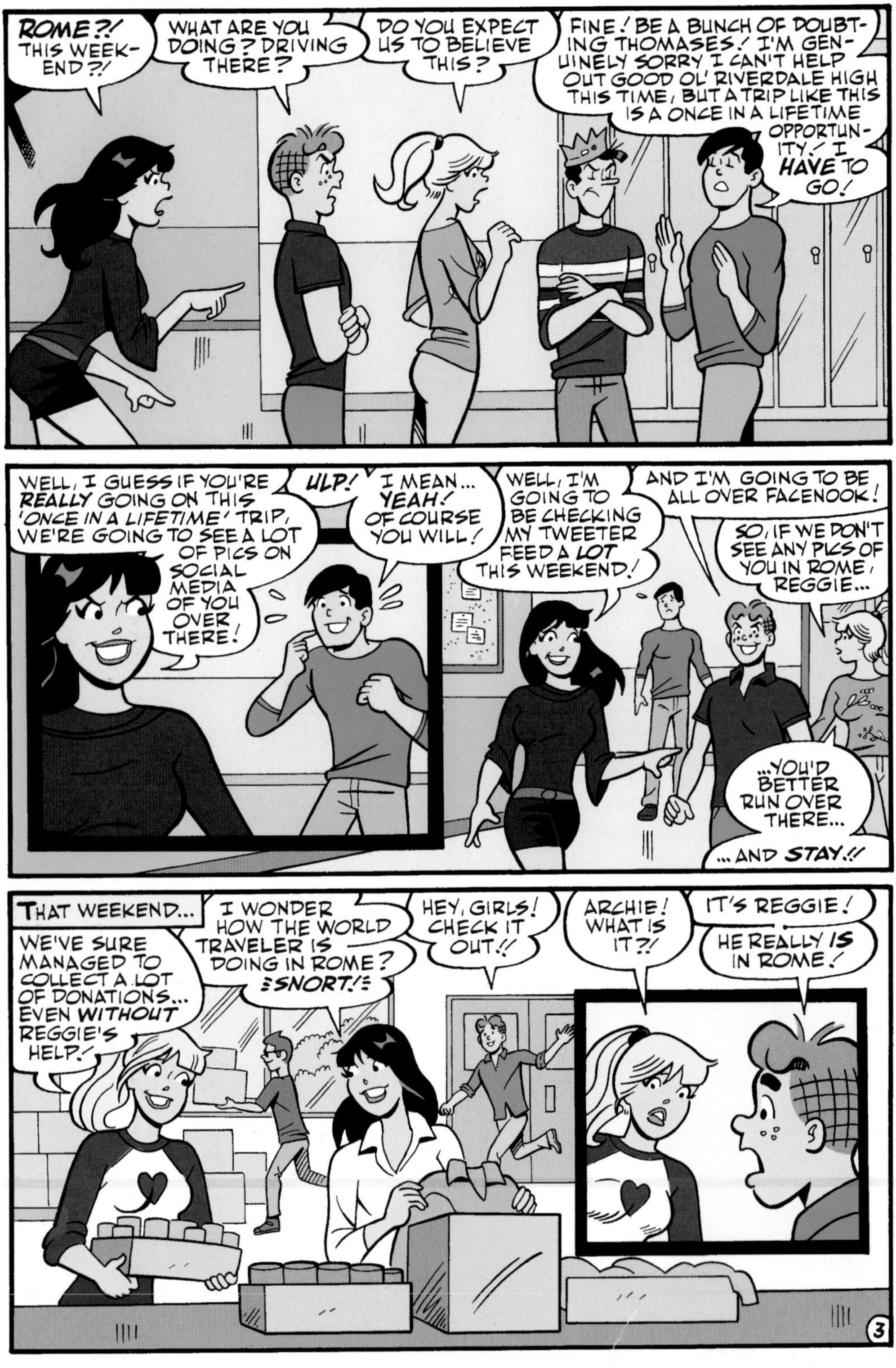
ROME?! THIS WEEKEND?!
WHAT ARE YOU DOING? DRIVING THERE?
DO YOU EXPECT US TO BELIEVE THIS?
FINE! BE A BUNCH OF DOUBTING THOMASES! I'M GENUINELY SORRY I CAN'T HELP OUT GOOD OL' RIVERDALE HIGH THIS TIME, BUT A TRIP LIKE THIS IS A ONCE IN A LIFETIME OPPORTUNITY! I HAVE TO GO!
WELL, I GUESS IF YOU'RE REALLY GOING ON THIS 'ONCE IN A LIFETIME' TRIP, WE'RE GOING TO SEE A LOT OF PICS ON SOCIAL MEDIA OF YOU OVER THERE!
ULP!
I MEAN... YEAH! OF COURSE YOU WILL!
WELL, I'M GOING TO BE CHECKING MY TWEETER FEED A LOT THIS WEEKEND!
AND I'M GOING TO BE ALL OVER FACENOOK!
SO, IF WE DON'T SEE ANY PICS OF YOU IN ROME, REGGIE...
...YOU'D BETTER RUN OVER THERE...
...AND STAY!!
THAT WEEKEND...
WE'VE SURE MANAGED TO COLLECT A LOT OF DONATIONS... EVEN WITHOUT REGGIE'S HELP!
I WONDER HOW THE WORLD TRAVELER IS DOING IN ROME? SNORT!
HEY, GIRLS! CHECK IT OUT!!
ARCHIE! WHAT IS IT?!
IT'S REGGIE!
HE REALLY IS IN ROME!
3

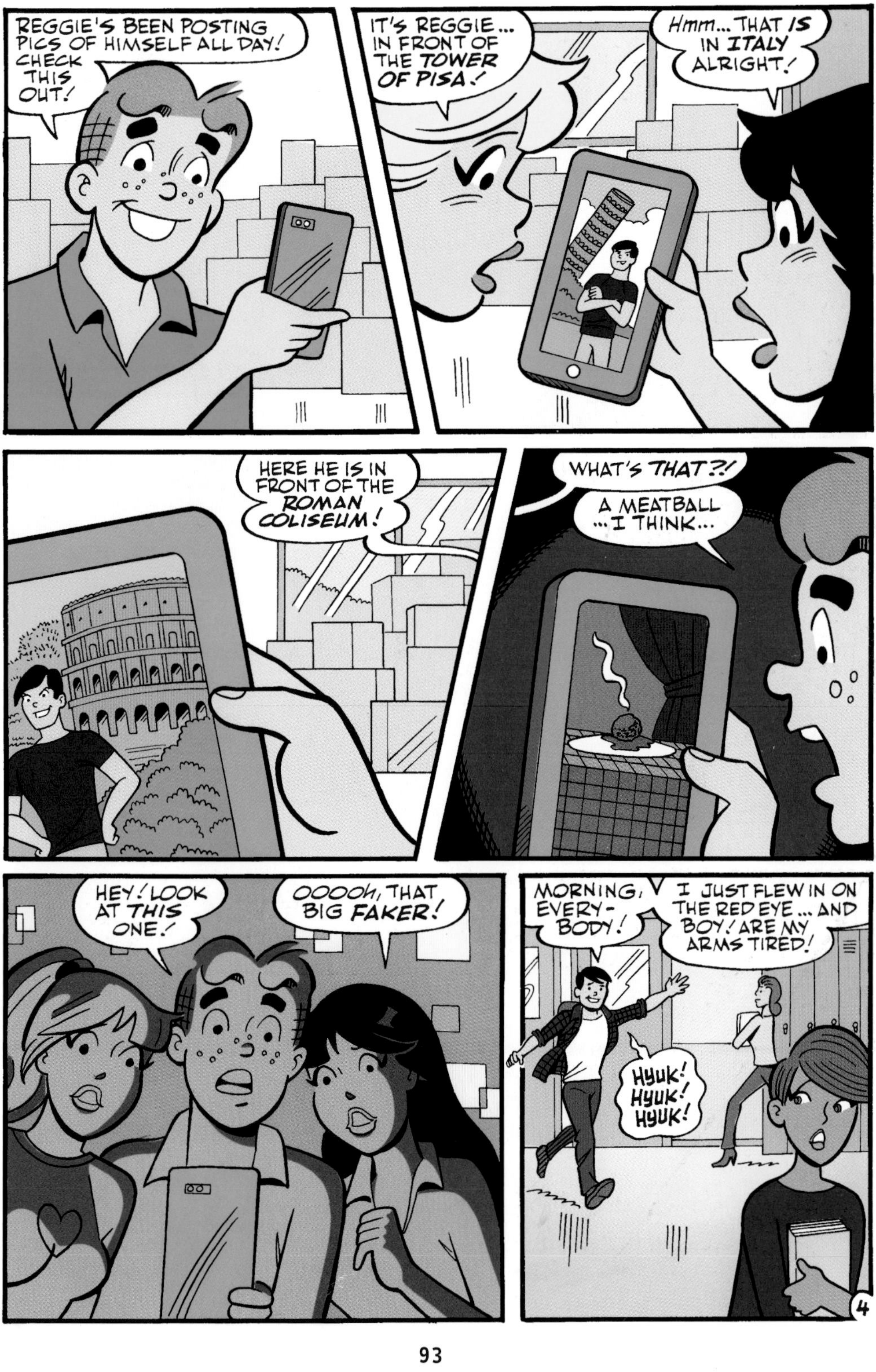
REGGIE'S BEEN POSTING PICS OF HIMSELF ALL DAY! CHECK THIS OUT!
IT'S REGGIE... IN FRONT OF THE TOWER OF PISA!
Hmm... THAT IS IN ITALY ALRIGHT!
HERE HE IS IN FRONT OF THE ROMAN COLISEUM!
WHAT'S THAT?!
A MEATBALL ...I THINK...
HEY! LOOK AT THIS ONE!
OOOOh, THAT BIG FAKER!
MORNING, EVERY-BODY!
I JUST FLEW IN ON THE RED EYE ... AND BOY! ARE MY ARMS TIRED!
HYUK! HYUK! HYUK!
4

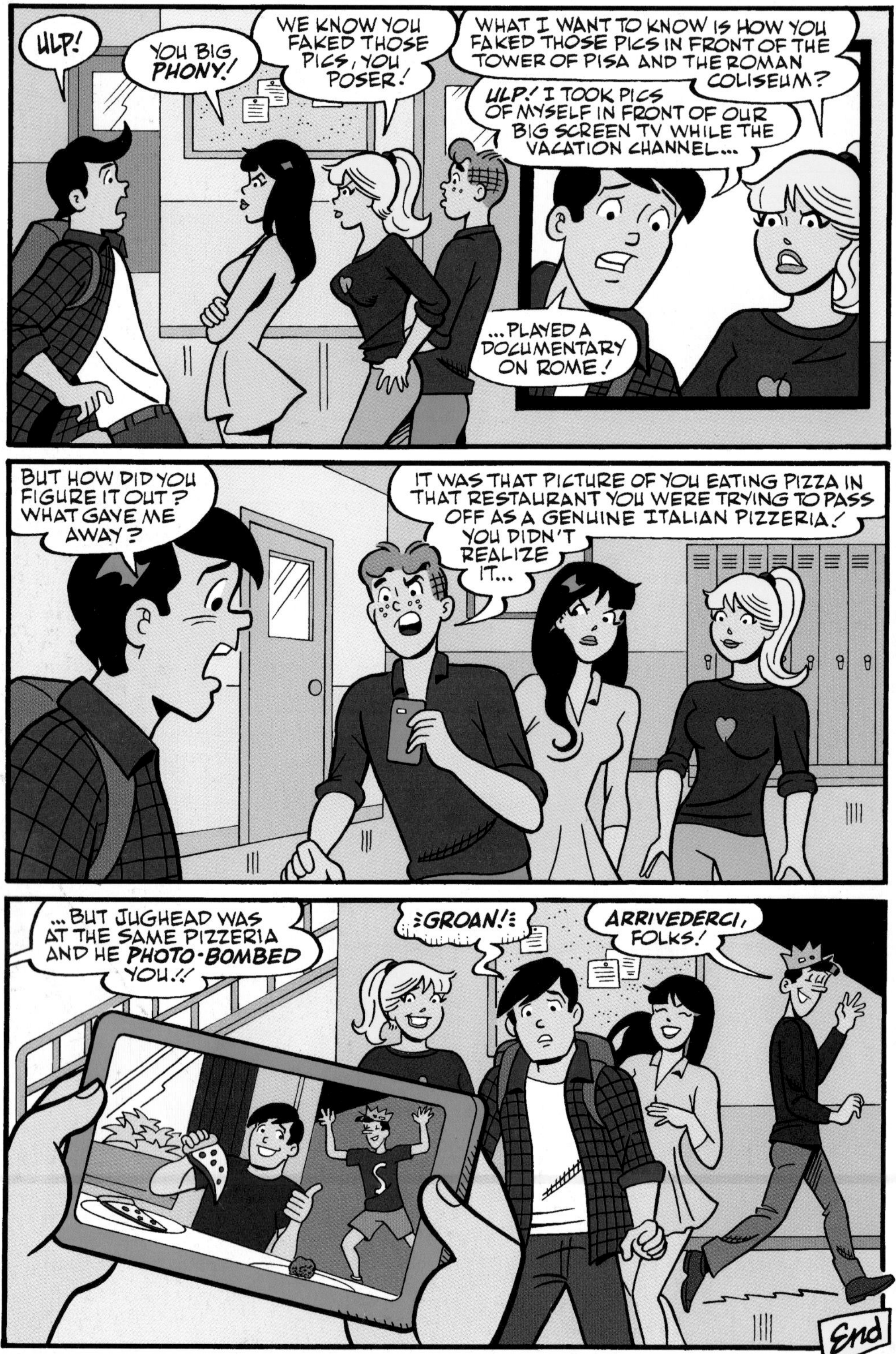
ULP!
YOU BIG PHONY!
WE KNOW YOU FAKED THOSE PICS, YOU POSER!
WHAT I WANT TO KNOW IS HOW YOU FAKED THOSE PICS IN FRONT OF THE TOWER OF PISA AND THE ROMAN COLISEUM?
ULP! I TOOK PICS OF MYSELF IN FRONT OF OUR BIG SCREEN TV WHILE THE VACATION CHANNEL...
...PLAYED A DOCUMENTARY ON ROME!
BUT HOW DID YOU FIGURE IT OUT? WHAT GAVE ME AWAY?
IT WAS THAT PICTURE OF YOU EATING PIZZA IN THAT RESTAURANT YOU WERE TRYING TO PASS OFF AS A GENUINE ITALIAN PIZZERIA!
YOU DIDN'T REALIZE IT...
...BUT JUGHEAD WAS AT THE SAME PIZZERIA AND HE PHOTO-BOMBED YOU!!
GROAN!
ARRIVEDERCI, FOLKS!
End

Archie & FRIENDS
WINTER WONDERLAND

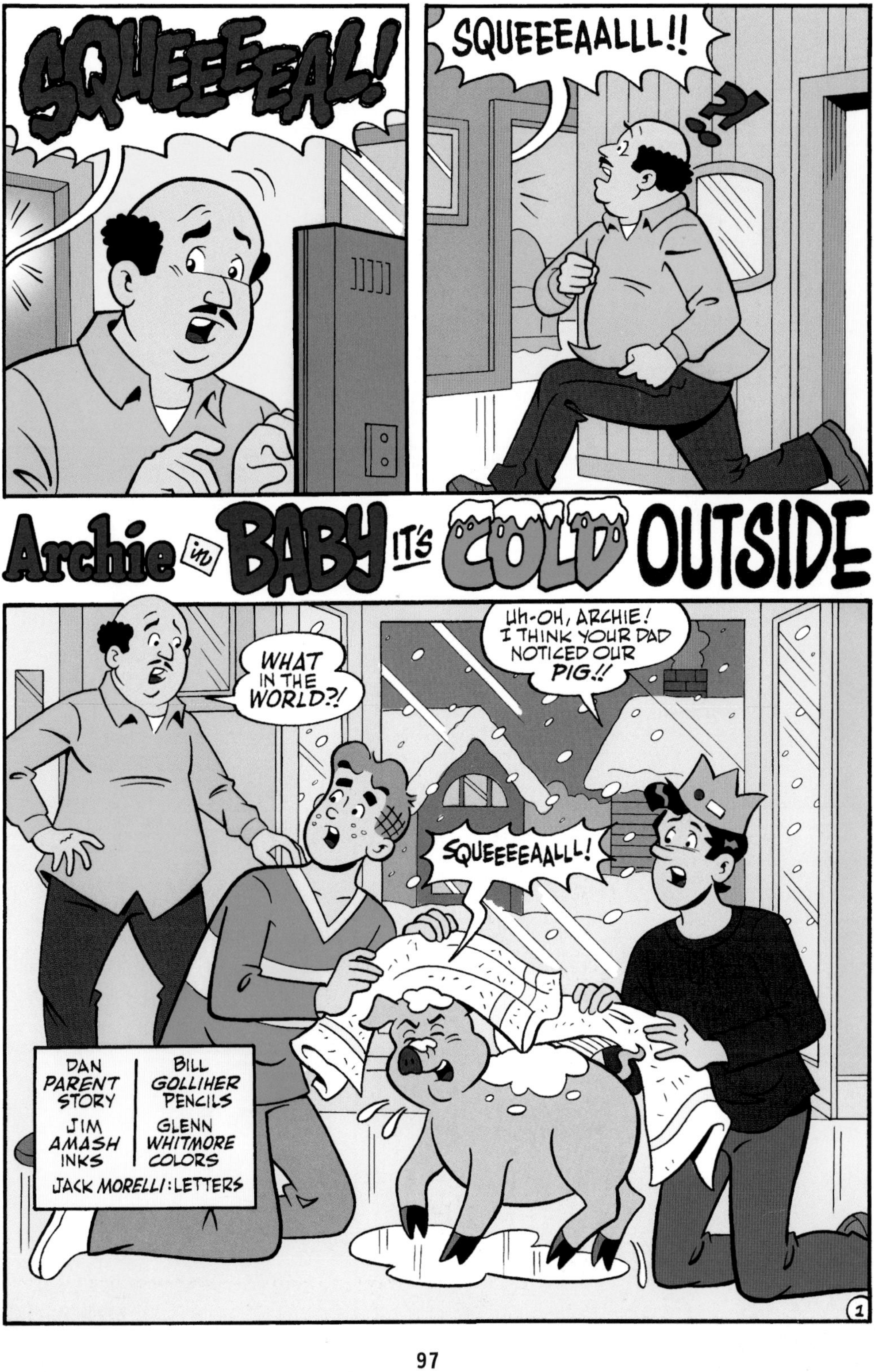
SQUEEEEAL!
SQUEEEAALLL!!
?!
Archie in BABY IT'S COLD OUTSIDE
WHAT IN THE WORLD?!
UH-OH, ARCHIE! I THINK YOUR DAD NOTICED OUR PIG!!
SQUEEEEAALLL!
DAN PARENT STORY
BILL GOLLIHER PENCILS
JIM AMASH INKS
GLENN WHITMORE COLORS
JACK MORELLI : LETTERS
1

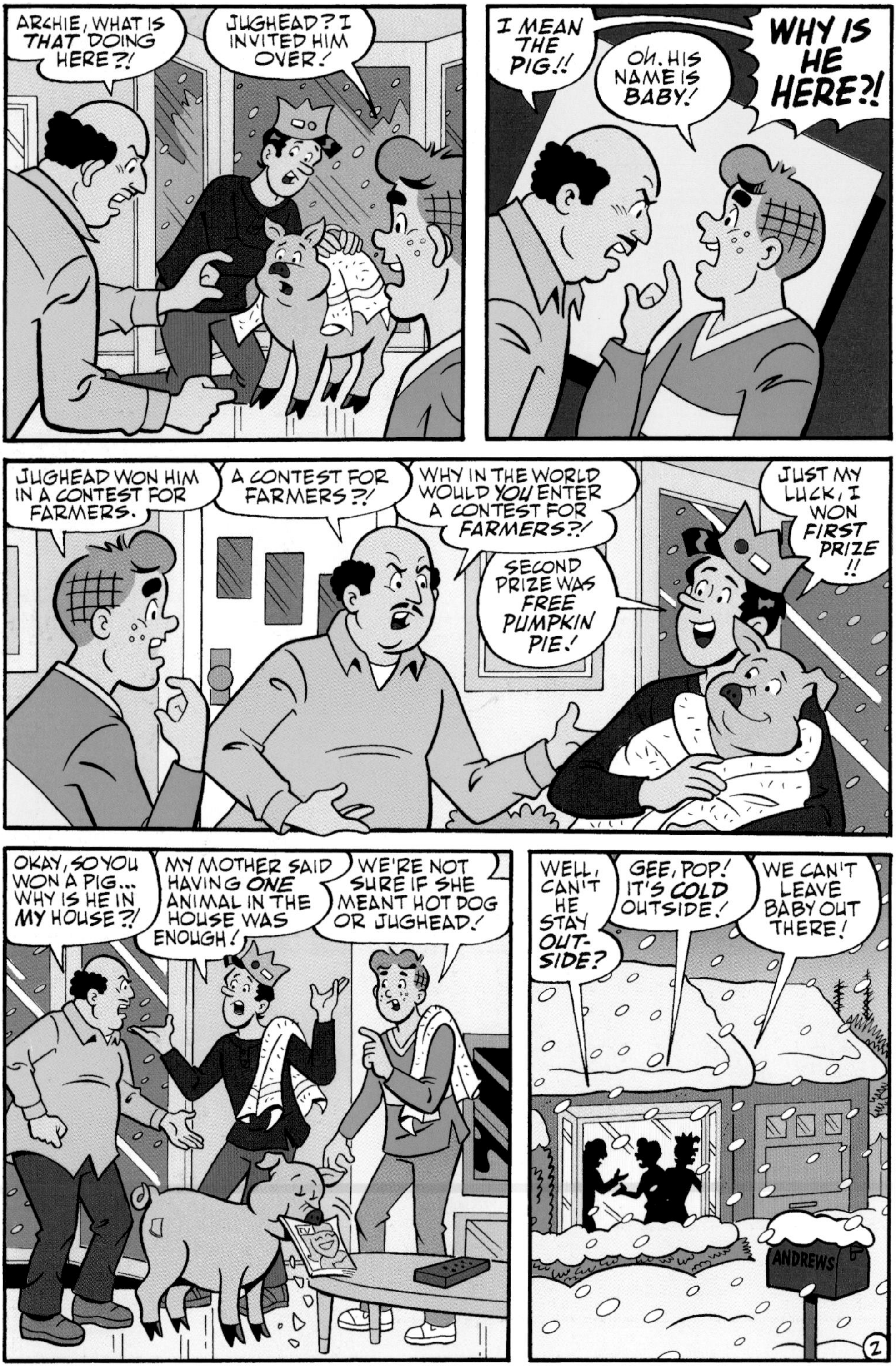
ARCHIE, WHAT IS THAT DOING HERE?!
JUGHEAD? I INVITED HIM OVER!
I MEAN THE PIG!!
OH. HIS NAME IS BABY!
WHY IS HE HERE?!
JUGHEAD WON HIM IN A CONTEST FOR FARMERS.
A CONTEST FOR FARMERS?!
WHY IN THE WORLD WOULD YOU ENTER A CONTEST FOR FARMERS?!
SECOND PRIZE WAS FREE PUMPKIN PIE!
JUST MY LUCK, I WON FIRST PRIZE!!
OKAY, SO YOU WON A PIG... WHY IS HE IN MY HOUSE?!
MY MOTHER SAID HAVING ONE ANIMAL IN THE HOUSE WAS ENOUGH!
WE'RE NOT SURE IF SHE MEANT HOT DOG OR JUGHEAD!
WELL, CAN'T HE STAY OUT-SIDE?
GEE, POP! IT'S COLD OUTSIDE!
WE CAN'T LEAVE BABY OUT THERE!
ANDREWS
2

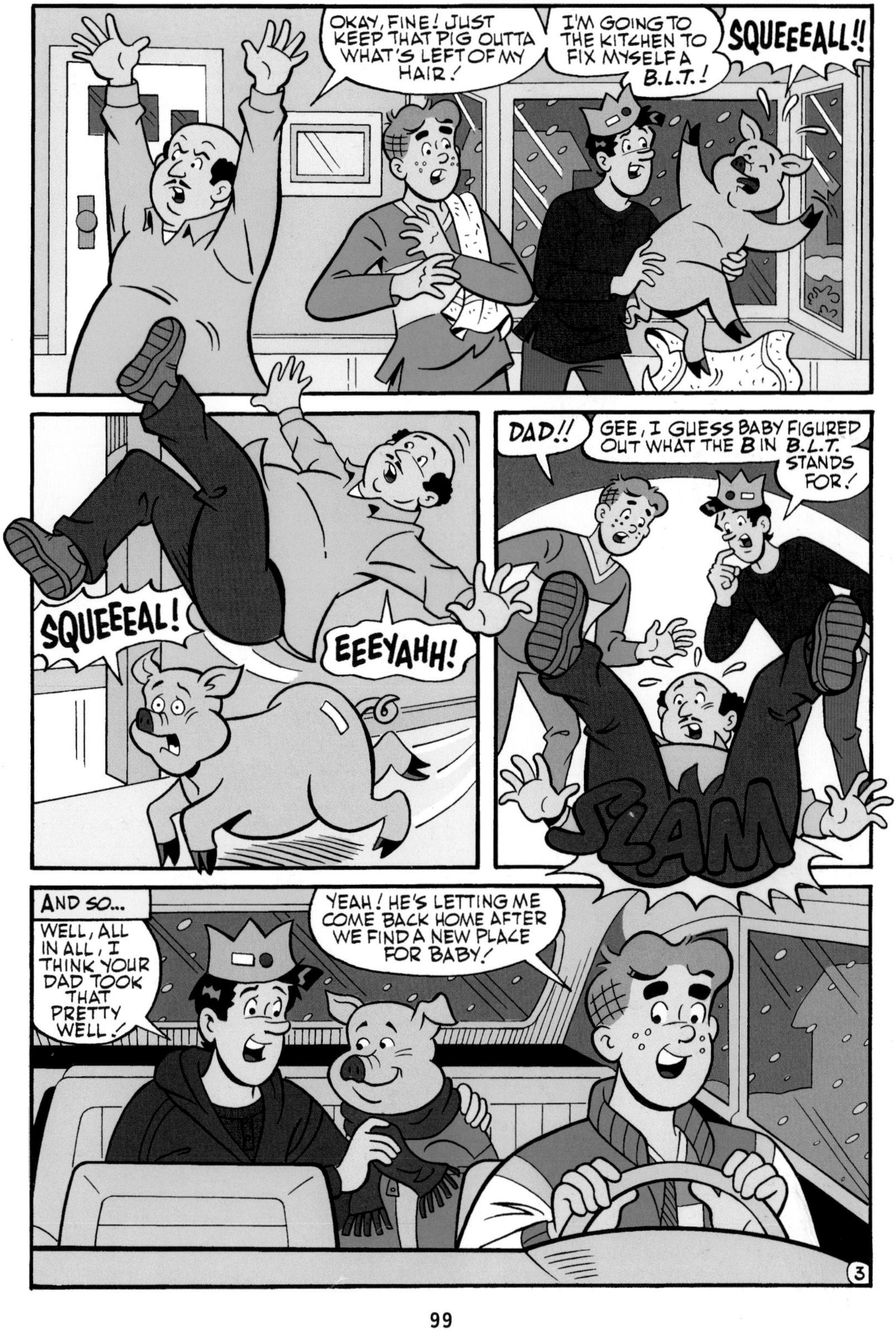
OKAY, FINE! JUST KEEP THAT PIG OUTTA WHAT'S LEFT OF MY HAIR!
I'M GOING TO THE KITCHEN TO FIX MYSELF A B.L.T.!
SQUEEEALL!!
SQUEEEAL!
EEEYAHH!
DAD!!
GEE, I GUESS BABY FIGURED OUT WHAT THE B IN B.L.T. STANDS FOR!
SLAM
AND SO...
WELL, ALL IN ALL, I THINK YOUR DAD TOOK THAT PRETTY WELL!
YEAH! HE'S LETTING ME COME BACK HOME AFTER WE FIND A NEW PLACE FOR BABY!
3

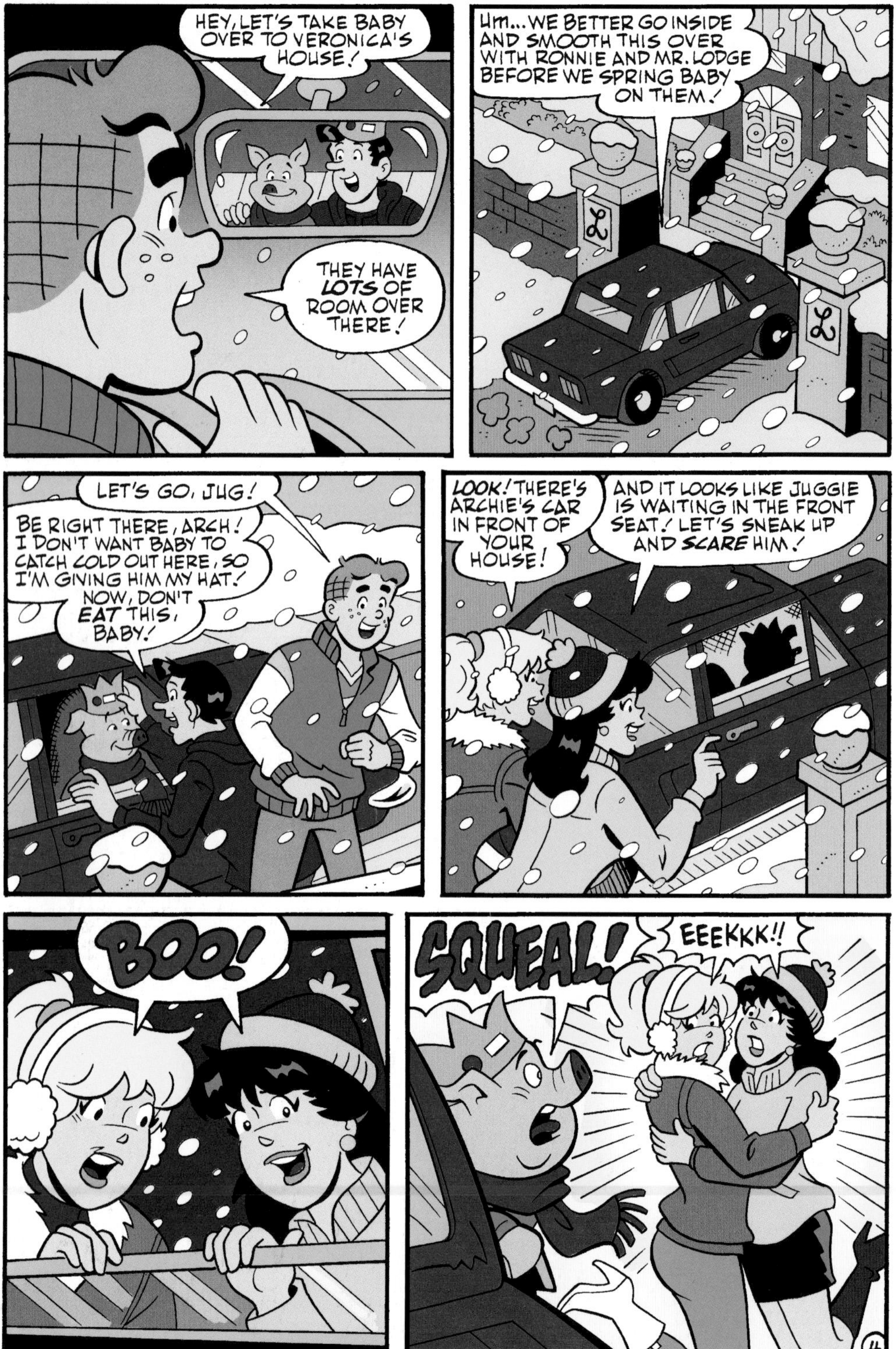
HEY, LET'S TAKE BABY OVER TO VERONICA'S HOUSE!
THEY HAVE LOTS OF ROOM OVER THERE!
UM... WE BETTER GO INSIDE AND SMOOTH THIS OVER WITH RONNIE AND MR. LODGE BEFORE WE SPRING BABY ON THEM!
LET'S GO, JUG!
BE RIGHT THERE, ARCH! I DON'T WANT BABY TO CATCH COLD OUT HERE, SO I'M GIVING HIM MY HAT! NOW, DON'T EAT THIS, BABY!
LOOK! THERE'S ARCHIE'S CAR IN FRONT OF YOUR HOUSE!
AND IT LOOKS LIKE JUGGIE IS WAITING IN THE FRONT SEAT! LET'S SNEAK UP AND SCARE HIM!
BOO!
SQUEAL!
EEEKKK!!
4

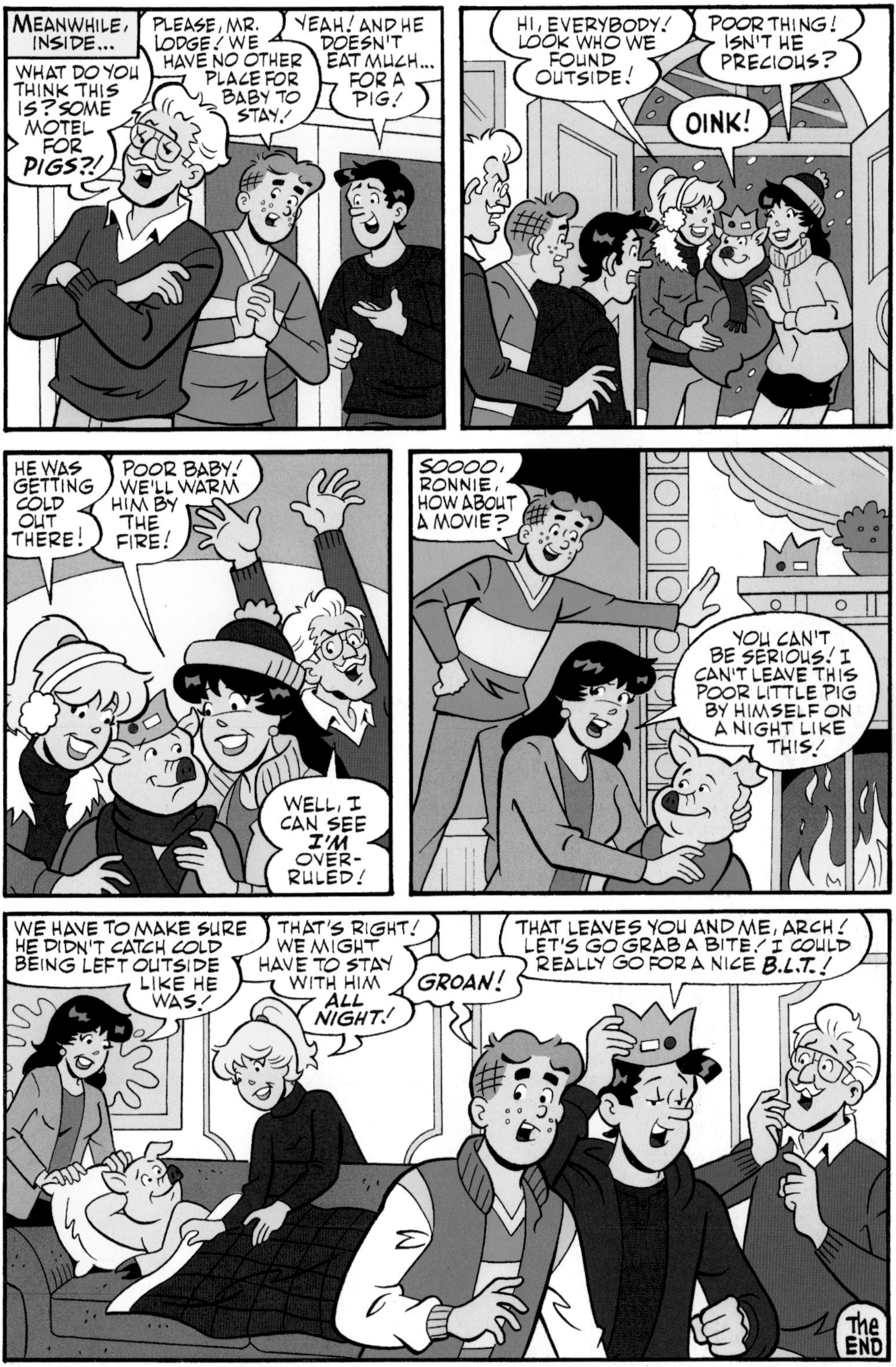
MEANWHILE, INSIDE...
WHAT DO YOU THINK THIS IS? SOME MOTEL FOR PIGS?!
PLEASE, MR. LODGE! WE HAVE NO OTHER PLACE FOR BABY TO STAY!
YEAH! AND HE DOESN'T EAT MUCH... FOR A PIG!
HI, EVERYBODY! LOOK WHO WE FOUND OUTSIDE!
POOR THING! ISN'T HE PRECIOUS?
OINK!
HE WAS GETTING COLD OUT THERE!
POOR BABY! WE'LL WARM HIM BY THE FIRE!
WELL, I CAN SEE I'M OVER-RULED!
SOOOO, RONNIE, HOW ABOUT A MOVIE?
YOU CAN'T BE SERIOUS! I CAN'T LEAVE THIS POOR LITTLE PIG BY HIMSELF ON A NIGHT LIKE THIS!
WE HAVE TO MAKE SURE HE DIDN'T CATCH COLD BEING LEFT OUTSIDE LIKE HE WAS!
THAT'S RIGHT! WE MIGHT HAVE TO STAY WITH HIM ALL NIGHT!
GROAN!
THAT LEAVES YOU AND ME, ARCH! LET'S GO GRAB A BITE! I COULD REALLY GO FOR A NICE B.L.T.!
The END

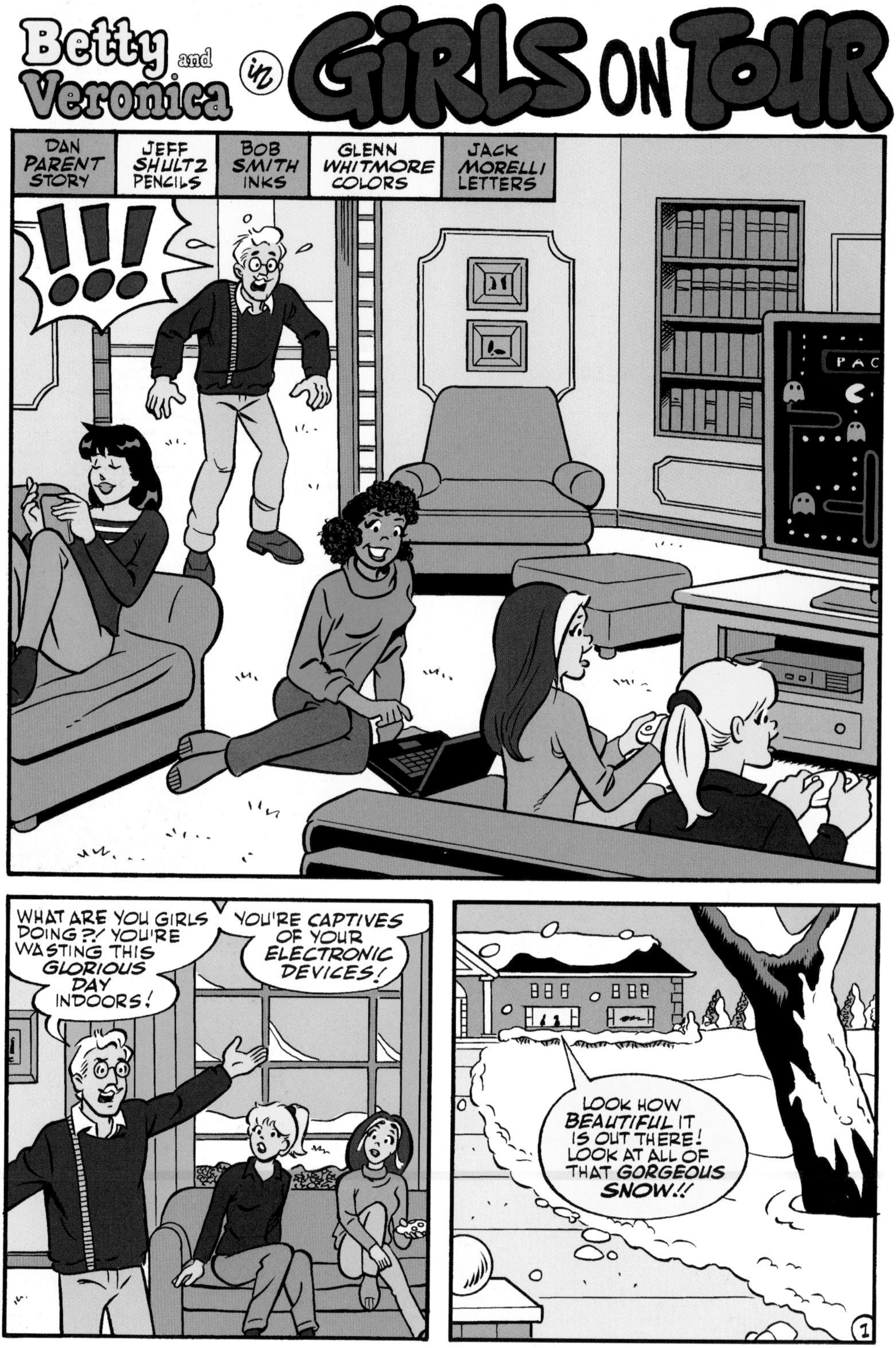
Betty and Veronica in GIRLS ON TOUR
DAN PARENT STORY
JEFF SHULTZ PENCILS
BOB SMITH INKS
GLENN WHITMORE COLORS
JACK MORELLI LETTERS
!!!
PAC
WHAT ARE YOU GIRLS DOING?! YOU'RE WASTING THIS GLORIOUS DAY INDOORS!
YOU'RE CAPTIVES OF YOUR ELECTRONIC DEVICES!
LOOK HOW BEAUTIFUL IT IS OUT THERE! LOOK AT ALL OF THAT GORGEOUS SNOW!!
1

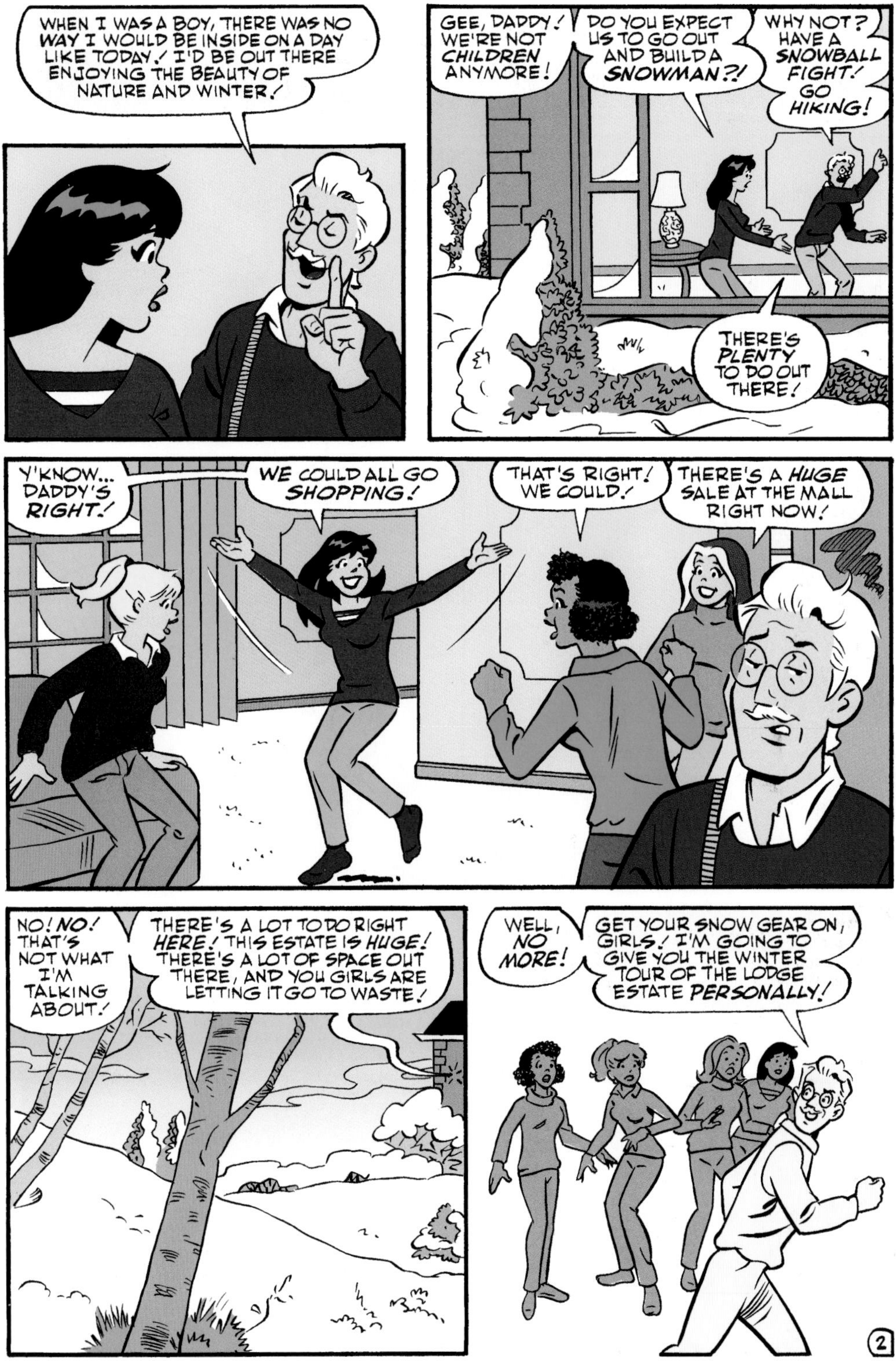
WHEN I WAS A BOY, THERE WAS NO WAY I WOULD BE INSIDE ON A DAY LIKE TODAY! I'D BE OUT THERE ENJOYING THE BEAUTY OF NATURE AND WINTER!
GEE, DADDY! WE'RE NOT CHILDREN ANYMORE!
DO YOU EXPECT US TO GO OUT AND BUILD A SNOWMAN?!
WHY NOT? HAVE A SNOWBALL FIGHT! GO HIKING!
THERE'S PLENTY TO DO OUT THERE!
Y'KNOW... DADDY'S RIGHT!
WE COULD ALL GO SHOPPING!
THAT'S RIGHT! WE COULD!
THERE'S A HUGE SALE AT THE MALL RIGHT NOW!
NO! NO! THAT'S NOT WHAT I'M TALKING ABOUT!
THERE'S A LOT TO DO RIGHT HERE! THIS ESTATE IS HUGE! THERE'S A LOT OF SPACE OUT THERE, AND YOU GIRLS ARE LETTING IT GO TO WASTE!
WELL, NO MORE!
GET YOUR SNOW GEAR ON, GIRLS! I'M GOING TO GIVE YOU THE WINTER TOUR OF THE LODGE ESTATE PERSONALLY!
2

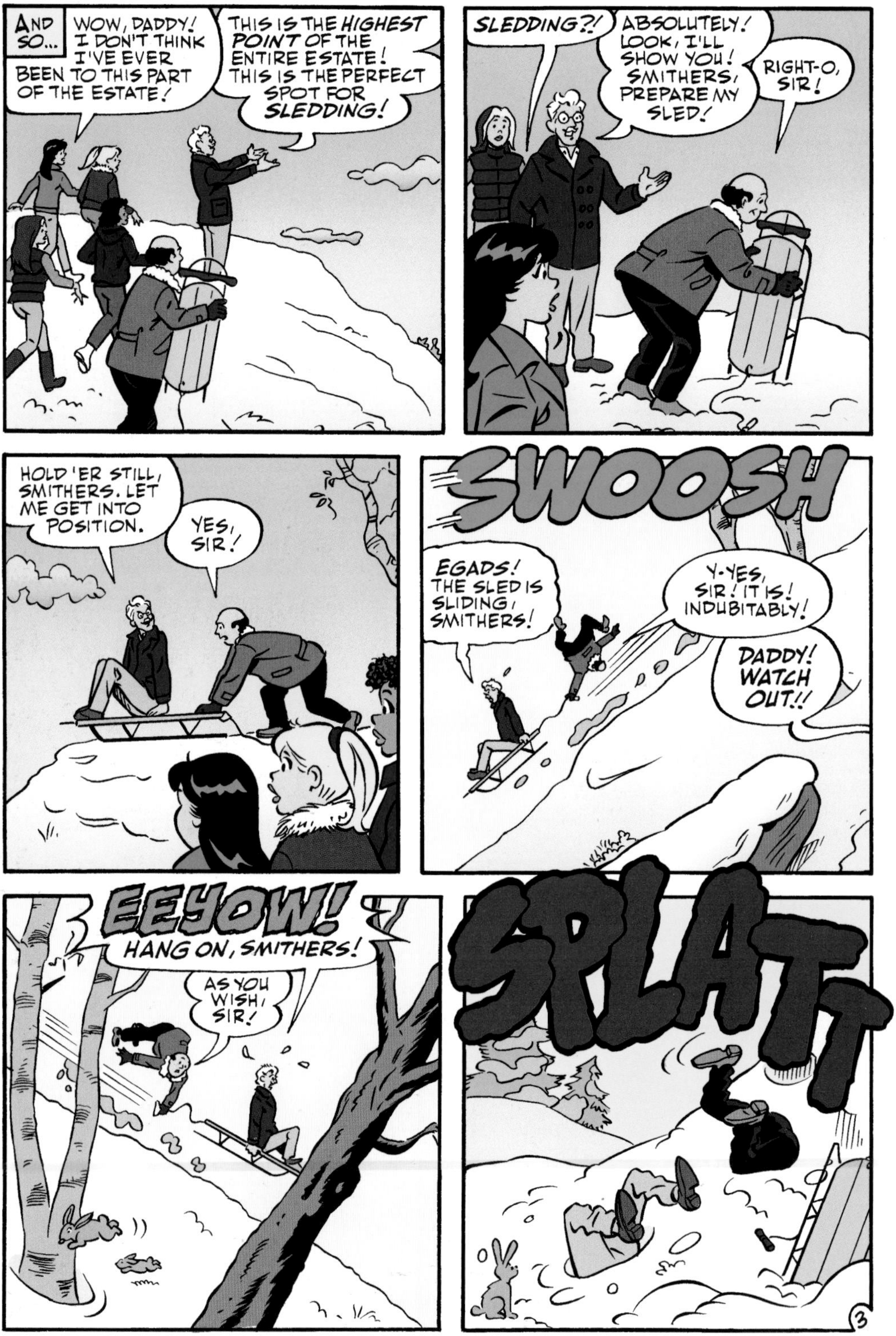
AND SO...
WOW, DADDY! I DON'T THINK I'VE EVER BEEN TO THIS PART OF THE ESTATE!
THIS IS THE HIGHEST POINT OF THE ENTIRE ESTATE! THIS IS THE PERFECT SPOT FOR SLEDDING!
SLEDDING?!
ABSOLUTELY! LOOK, I'LL SHOW YOU! SMITHERS, PREPARE MY SLED!
RIGHT-O, SIR!
HOLD 'ER STILL, SMITHERS. LET ME GET INTO POSITION.
YES, SIR!
SWOOSH
EGADS! THE SLED IS SLIDING, SMITHERS!
Y-YES, SIR! IT IS! INDUBITABLY!
DADDY! WATCH OUT!!
EEYOW! HANG ON, SMITHERS!
AS YOU WISH, SIR!
SPLATT
3

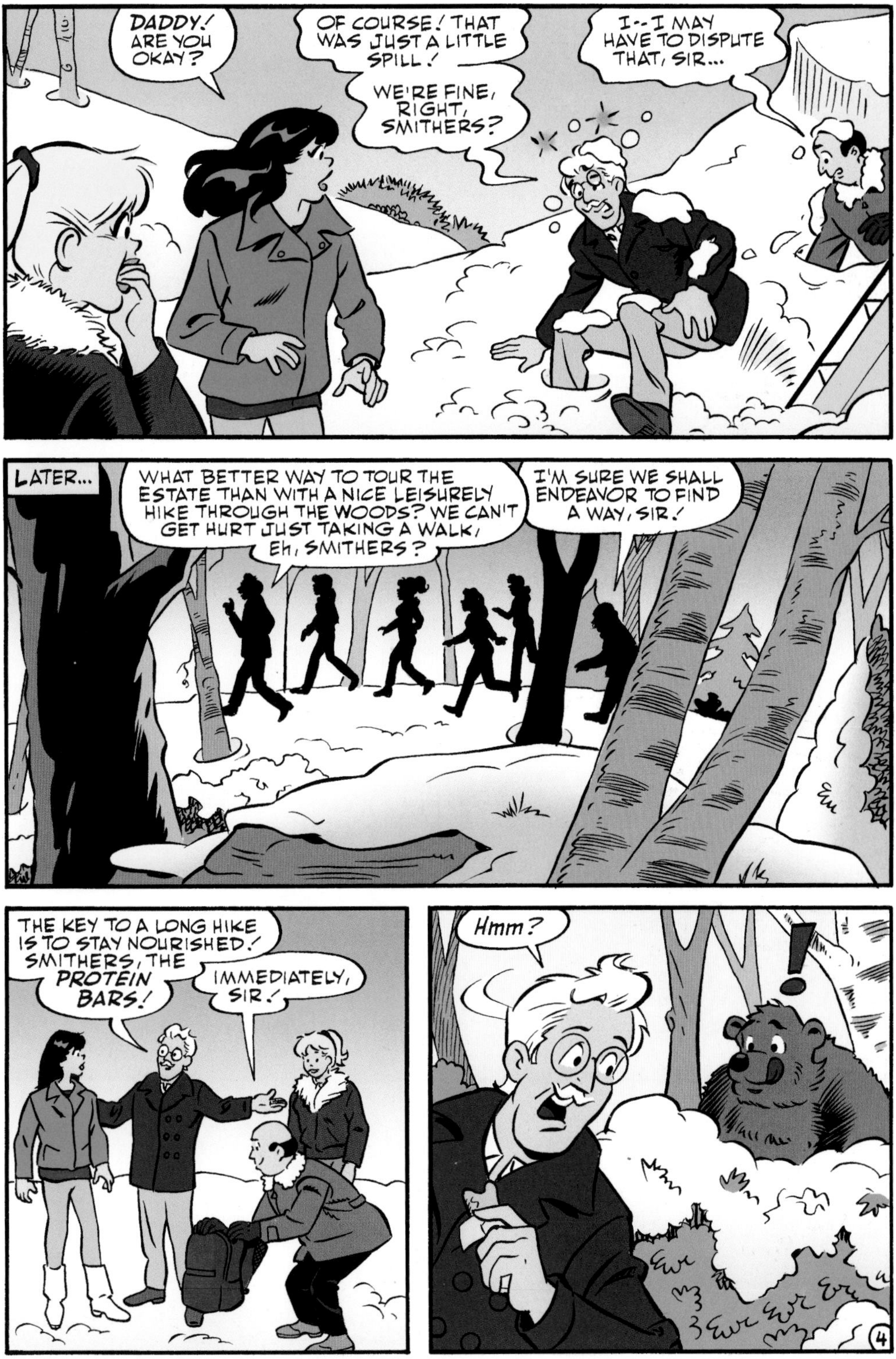
DADDY! ARE YOU OKAY?
OF COURSE! THAT WAS JUST A LITTLE SPILL!
WE'RE FINE, RIGHT, SMITHERS?
I--I MAY HAVE TO DISPUTE THAT, SIR...
LATER...
WHAT BETTER WAY TO TOUR THE ESTATE THAN WITH A NICE LEISURELY HIKE THROUGH THE WOODS? WE CAN'T GET HURT JUST TAKING A WALK, EH, SMITHERS?
I'M SURE WE SHALL ENDEAVOR TO FIND A WAY, SIR!
THE KEY TO A LONG HIKE IS TO STAY NOURISHED! SMITHERS, THE PROTEIN BARS!
IMMEDIATELY, SIR!
Hmm?
!
4

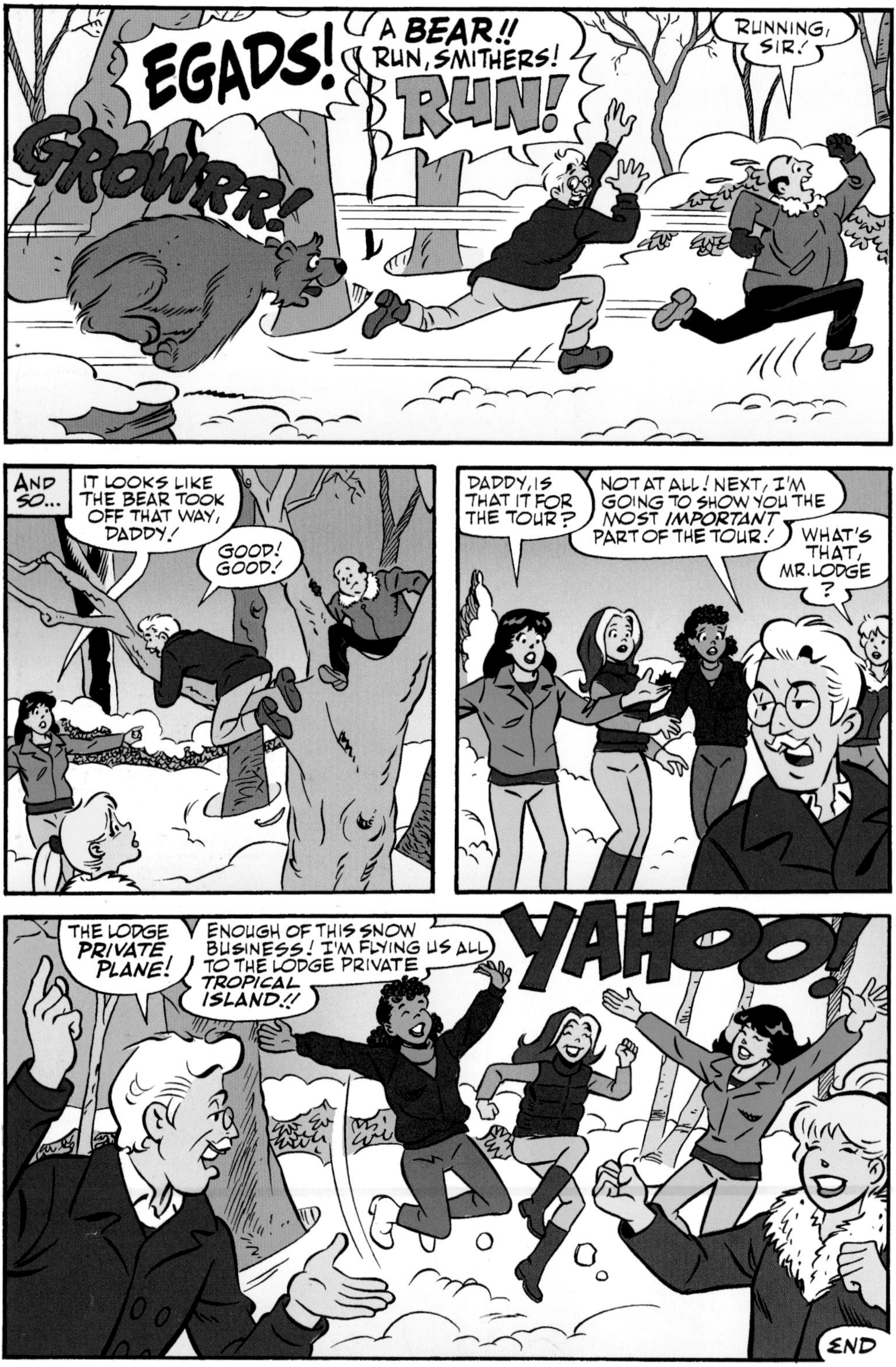

EGADS!
A BEAR!! RUN, SMITHERS! RUN!
RUNNING, SIR!
GROWRRR!
AND SO...
IT LOOKS LIKE THE BEAR TOOK OFF THAT WAY, DADDY!
GOOD! GOOD!
DADDY, IS THAT IT FOR THE TOUR?
NOT AT ALL! NEXT, I'M GOING TO SHOW YOU THE MOST IMPORTANT PART OF THE TOUR!
WHAT'S THAT, MR. LODGE?
THE LODGE PRIVATE PLANE!
ENOUGH OF THIS SNOW BUSINESS! I'M FLYING US ALL TO THE LODGE PRIVATE TROPICAL ISLAND!!
YAHOO!
END

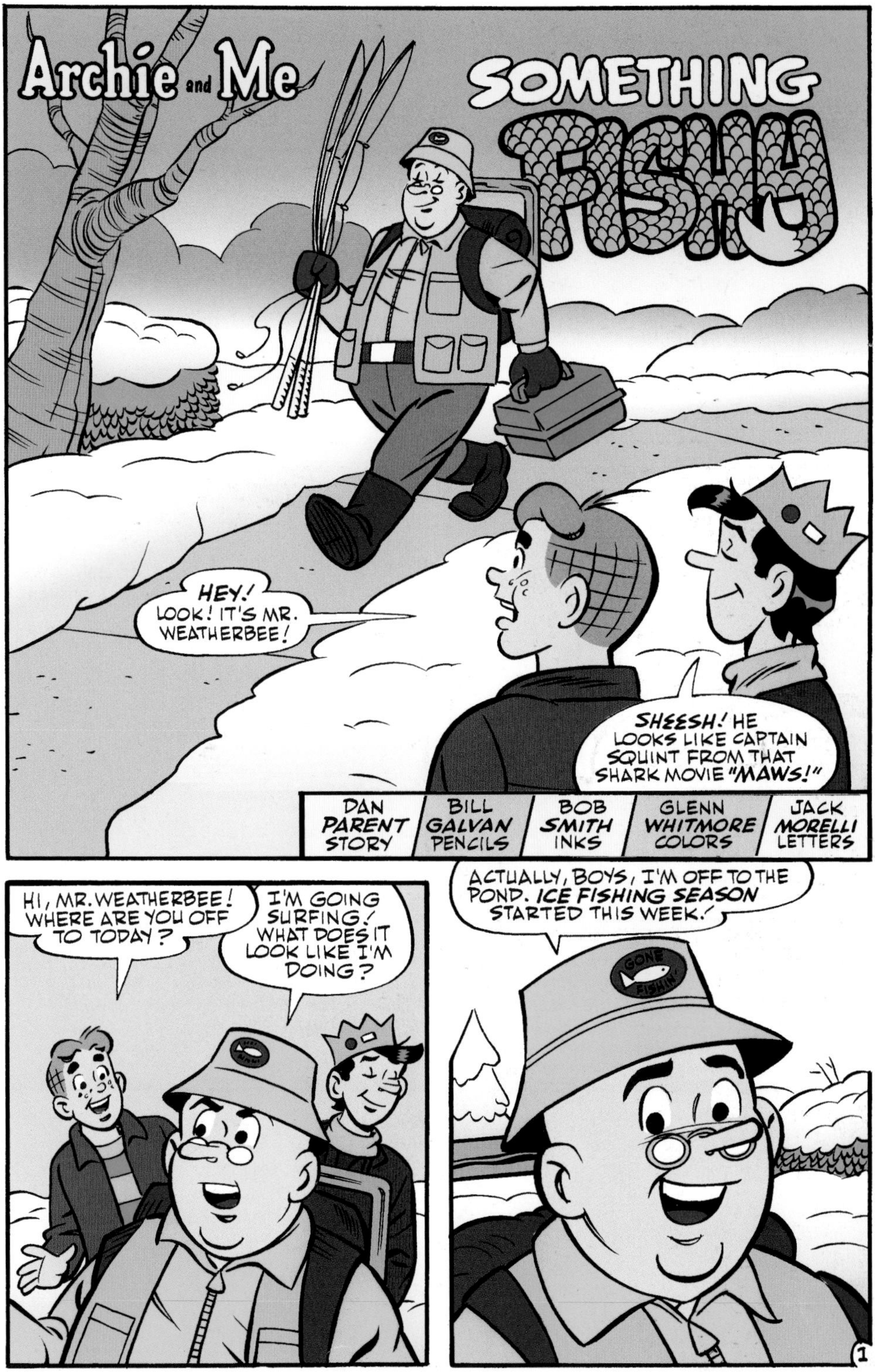
Archie and Me
SOMETHING FISHY
HEY! LOOK! IT'S MR. WEATHERBEE!
SHEESH! HE LOOKS LIKE CAPTAIN SQUINT FROM THAT SHARK MOVIE "MAWS!"
DAN PARENT STORY
BILL GALVAN PENCILS
BOB SMITH INKS
GLENN WHITMORE COLORS
JACK MORELLI LETTERS
HI, MR. WEATHERBEE! WHERE ARE YOU OFF TO TODAY?
I'M GOING SURFING! WHAT DOES IT LOOK LIKE I'M DOING?
ACTUALLY, BOYS, I'M OFF TO THE POND. ICE FISHING SEASON STARTED THIS WEEK!
GONE FISHIN'
1

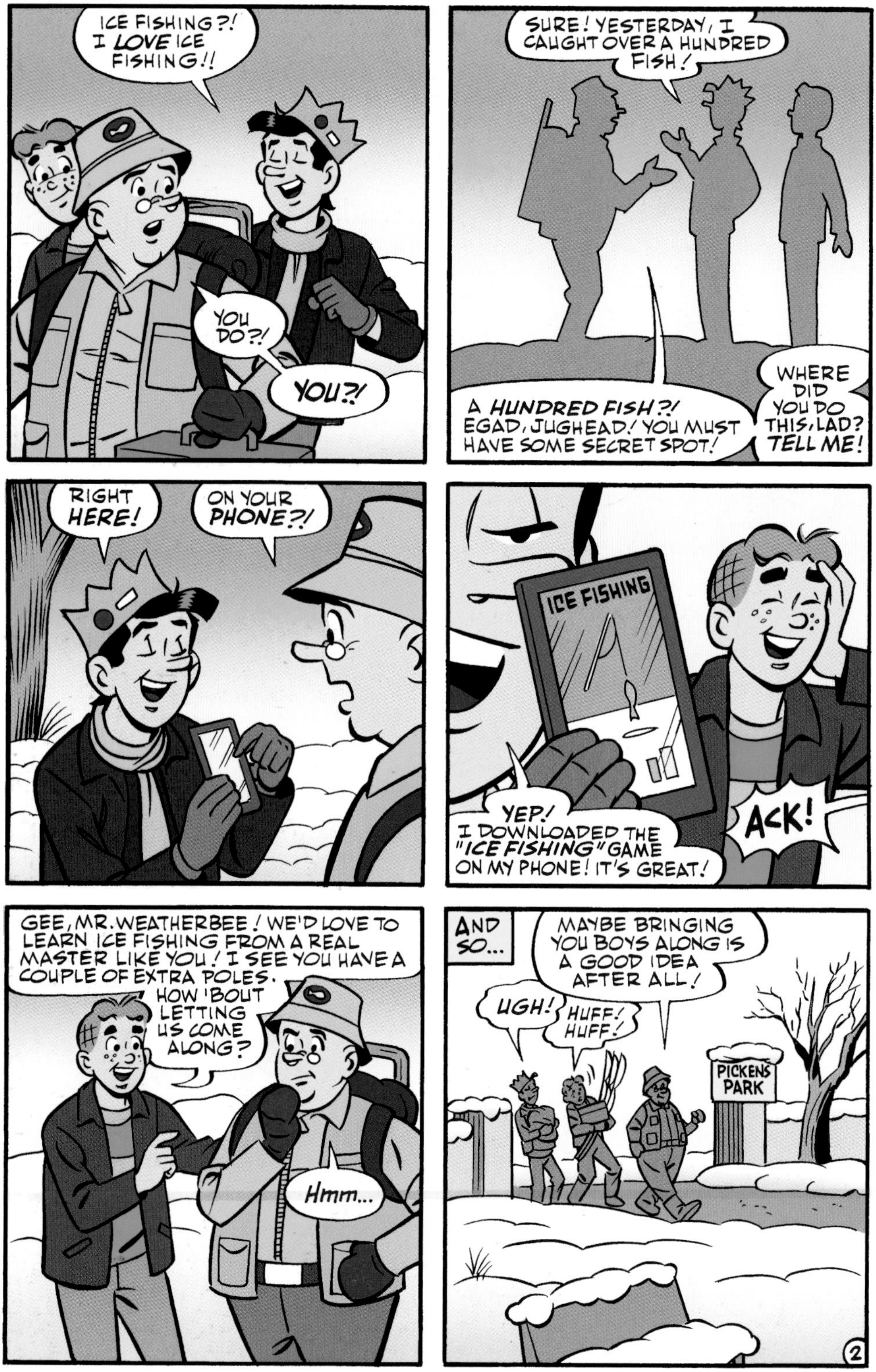
ICE FISHING?! I LOVE ICE FISHING!!
YOU DO?!
YOU?!
SURE! YESTERDAY, I CAUGHT OVER A HUNDRED FISH!
A HUNDRED FISH?! EGAD, JUGHEAD! YOU MUST HAVE SOME SECRET SPOT!
WHERE DID YOU DO THIS, LAD? TELL ME!
RIGHT HERE!
ON YOUR PHONE?!
ICE FISHING
YEP! I DOWNLOADED THE "ICE FISHING" GAME ON MY PHONE! IT'S GREAT!
ACK!
GEE, MR. WEATHERBEE! WE'D LOVE TO LEARN ICE FISHING FROM A REAL MASTER LIKE YOU! I SEE YOU HAVE A COUPLE OF EXTRA POLES.
HOW 'BOUT LETTING US COME ALONG?
Hmm...
AND SO...
MAYBE BRINGING YOU BOYS ALONG IS A GOOD IDEA AFTER ALL!
UGH!
HUFF! HUFF!
PICKENS PARK
2

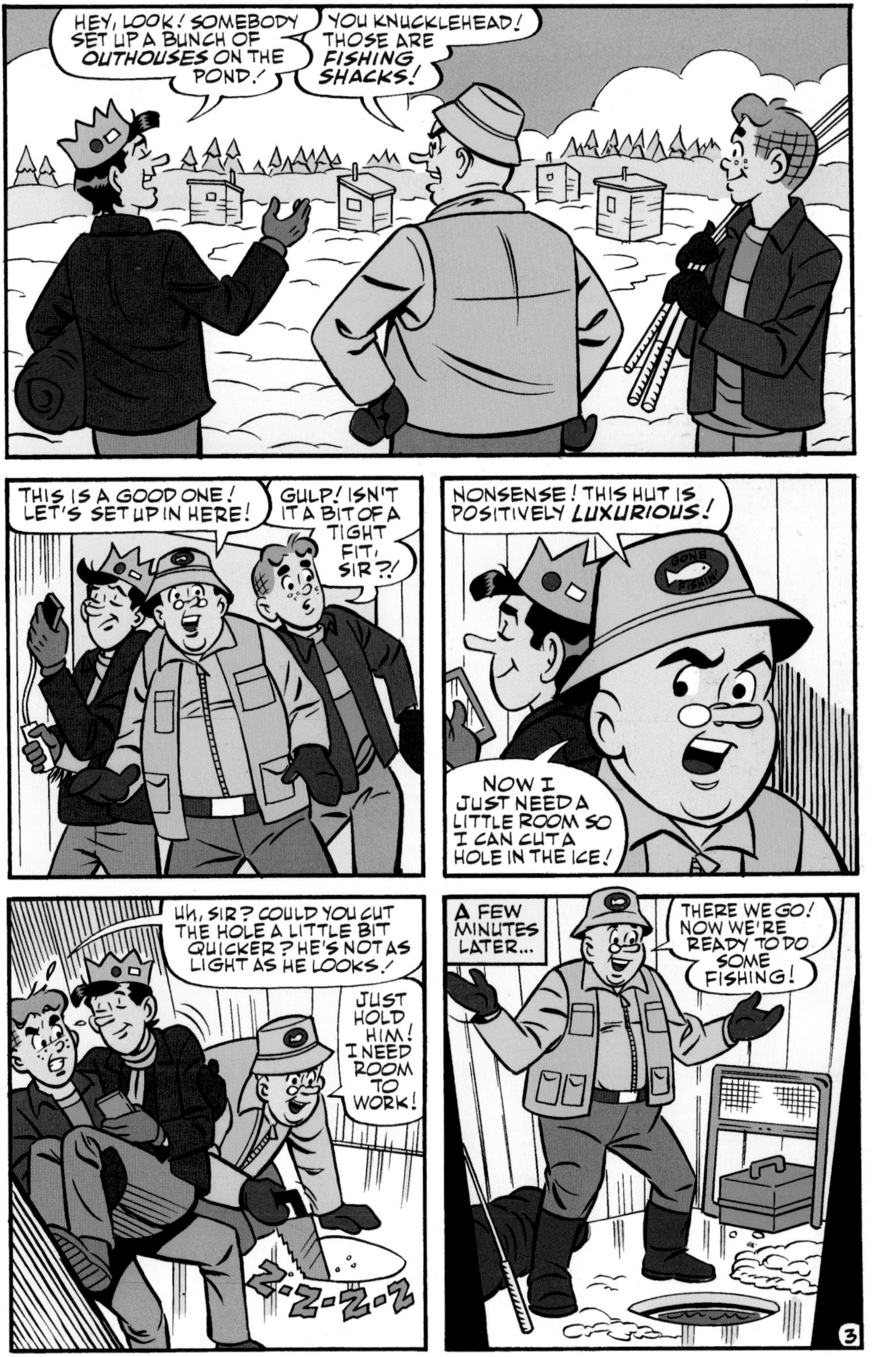
HEY, LOOK! SOMEBODY SET UP A BUNCH OF *OUTHOUSES* ON THE POND!
YOU KNUCKLEHEAD! THOSE ARE *FISHING SHACKS!*
THIS IS A GOOD ONE! LET'S SET UP IN HERE!
GULP! ISN'T IT A BIT OF A TIGHT FIT, SIR?!
NONSENSE! THIS HUT IS POSITIVELY *LUXURIOUS!*
NOW I JUST NEED A LITTLE ROOM SO I CAN CUT A HOLE IN THE ICE!
GONE FISHIN'
UH, SIR? COULD YOU CUT THE HOLE A LITTLE BIT QUICKER? HE'S NOT AS LIGHT AS HE LOOKS!
JUST HOLD HIM! I NEED ROOM TO WORK!
Z-Z-Z-Z
A FEW MINUTES LATER...
THERE WE GO! NOW WE'RE READY TO DO SOME FISHING!
3

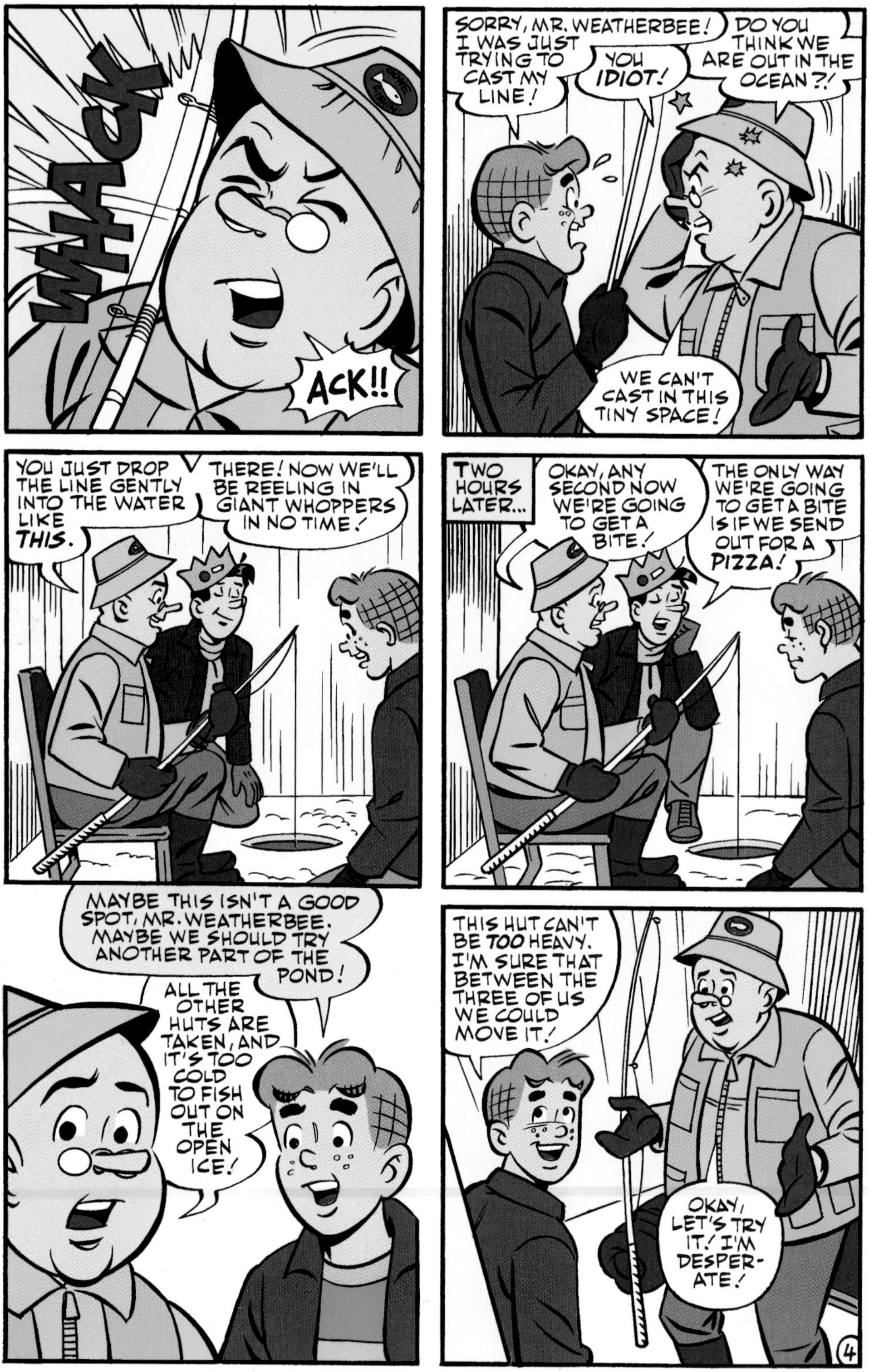
WHACK
ACK!!
SORRY, MR. WEATHERBEE! I WAS JUST TRYING TO CAST MY LINE!
YOU IDIOT!
DO YOU THINK WE ARE OUT IN THE OCEAN?!
WE CAN'T CAST IN THIS TINY SPACE!
YOU JUST DROP THE LINE GENTLY INTO THE WATER LIKE THIS.
THERE! NOW WE'LL BE REELING IN GIANT WHOPPERS IN NO TIME!
TWO HOURS LATER...
OKAY, ANY SECOND NOW WE'RE GOING TO GET A BITE!
THE ONLY WAY WE'RE GOING TO GET A BITE IS IF WE SEND OUT FOR A PIZZA!
MAYBE THIS ISN'T A GOOD SPOT, MR. WEATHERBEE. MAYBE WE SHOULD TRY ANOTHER PART OF THE POND!
ALL THE OTHER HUTS ARE TAKEN, AND IT'S TOO COLD TO FISH OUT ON THE OPEN ICE!
THIS HUT CAN'T BE TOO HEAVY. I'M SURE THAT BETWEEN THE THREE OF US WE COULD MOVE IT!
OKAY, LET'S TRY IT! I'M DESPERATE!
4

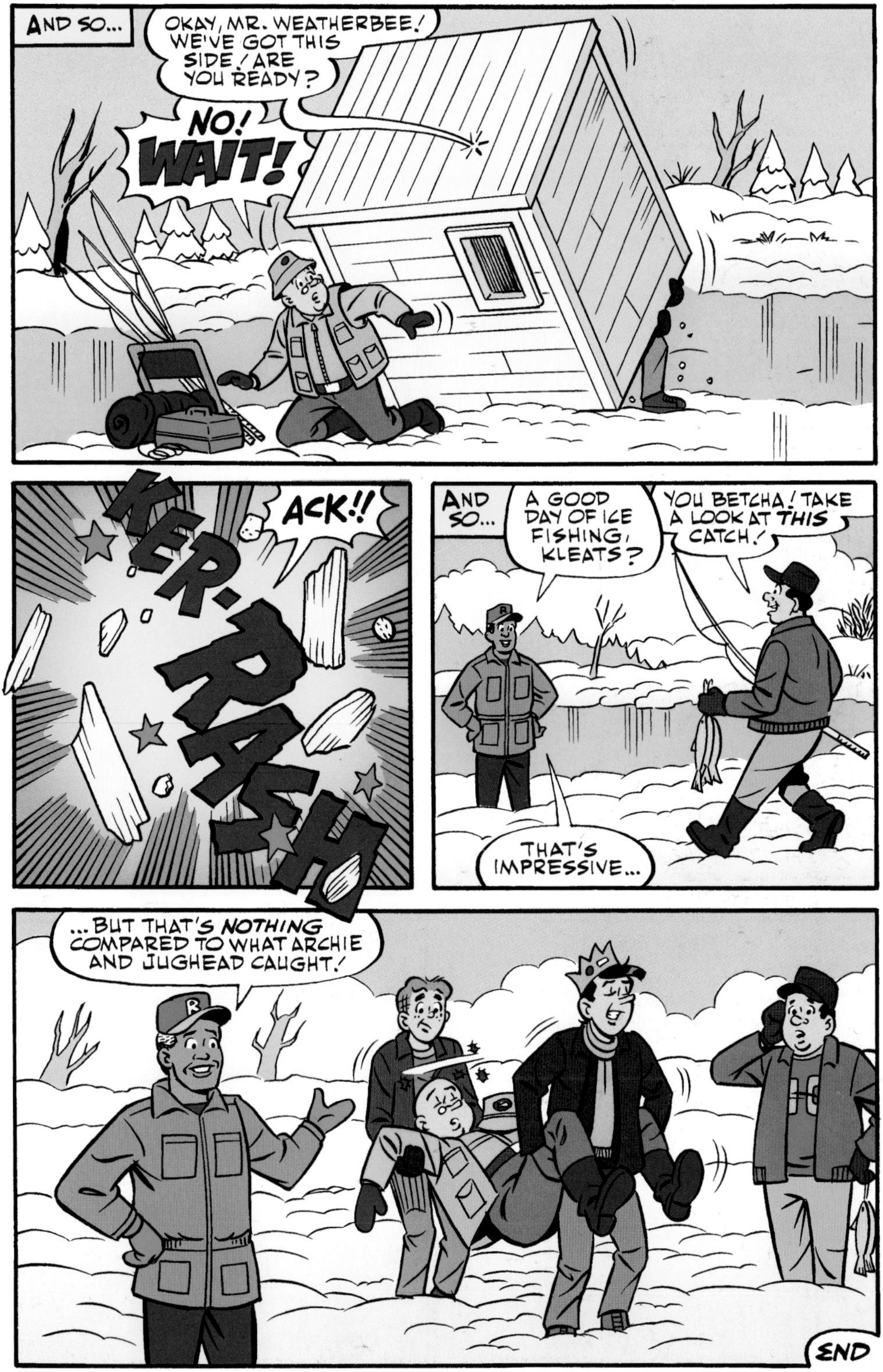
AND SO...
OKAY, MR. WEATHERBEE! WE'VE GOT THIS SIDE! ARE YOU READY?
NO! WAIT!
KER-RASH
ACK!!
AND SO...
A GOOD DAY OF ICE FISHING, KLEATS?
YOU BETCHA! TAKE A LOOK AT THIS CATCH!
THAT'S IMPRESSIVE...
...BUT THAT'S NOTHING COMPARED TO WHAT ARCHIE AND JUGHEAD CAUGHT!
END

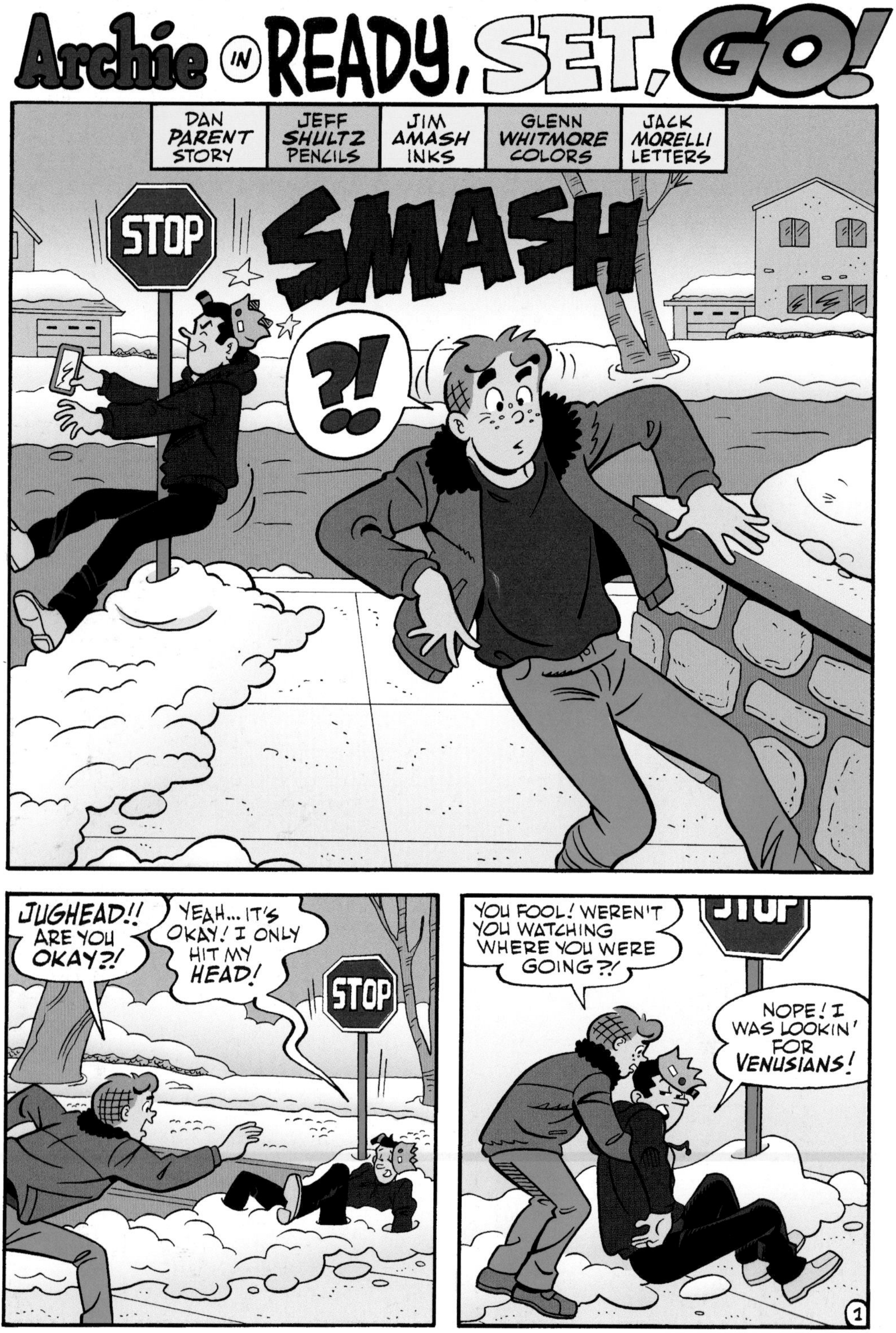
Archie in READY, SET, GO!
DAN PARENT STORY
JEFF SHULTZ PENCILS
JIM AMASH INKS
GLENN WHITMORE COLORS
JACK MORELLI LETTERS
STOP
SMASH
?!
JUGHEAD!! ARE YOU OKAY?!
YEAH... IT'S OKAY! I ONLY HIT MY HEAD!
STOP
YOU FOOL! WEREN'T YOU WATCHING WHERE YOU WERE GOING?!
NOPE! I WAS LOOKIN' FOR VENUSIANS!
1

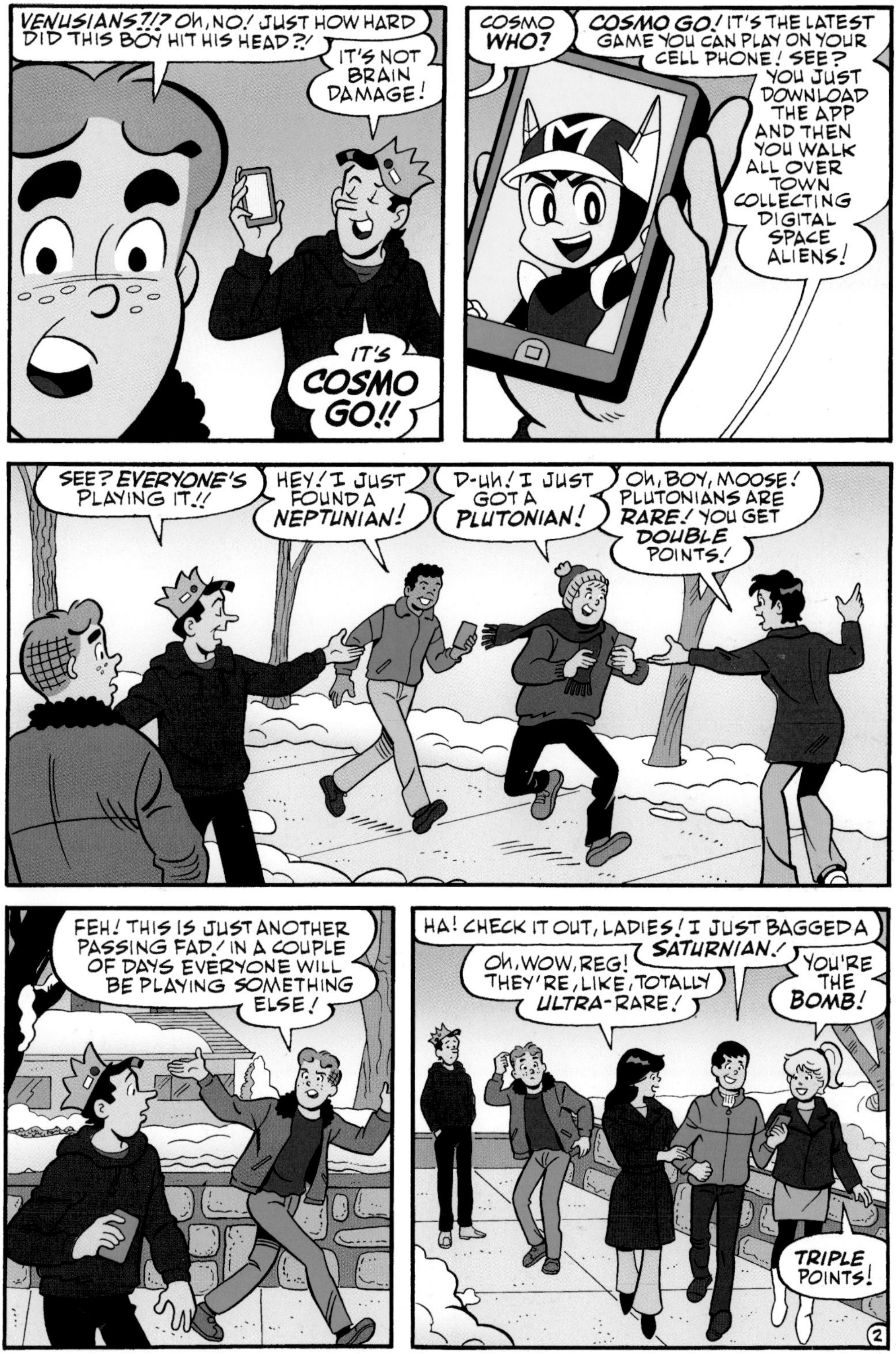
VENUSIANS?!? OH, NO! JUST HOW HARD DID THIS BOY HIT HIS HEAD?!
IT'S NOT BRAIN DAMAGE!
IT'S COSMO GO!!
COSMO WHO?
COSMO GO! IT'S THE LATEST GAME YOU CAN PLAY ON YOUR CELL PHONE! SEE? YOU JUST DOWNLOAD THE APP AND THEN YOU WALK ALL OVER TOWN COLLECTING DIGITAL SPACE ALIENS!
SEE? EVERYONE'S PLAYING IT!!
HEY! I JUST FOUND A NEPTUNIAN!
D-UH! I JUST GOT A PLUTONIAN!
OH, BOY, MOOSE! PLUTONIANS ARE RARE! YOU GET DOUBLE POINTS!
FEH! THIS IS JUST ANOTHER PASSING FAD! IN A COUPLE OF DAYS EVERYONE WILL BE PLAYING SOMETHING ELSE!
HA! CHECK IT OUT, LADIES! I JUST BAGGED A SATURNIAN!
OH, WOW, REG! THEY'RE, LIKE, TOTALLY ULTRA-RARE!
YOU'RE THE BOMB!
TRIPLE POINTS!
2

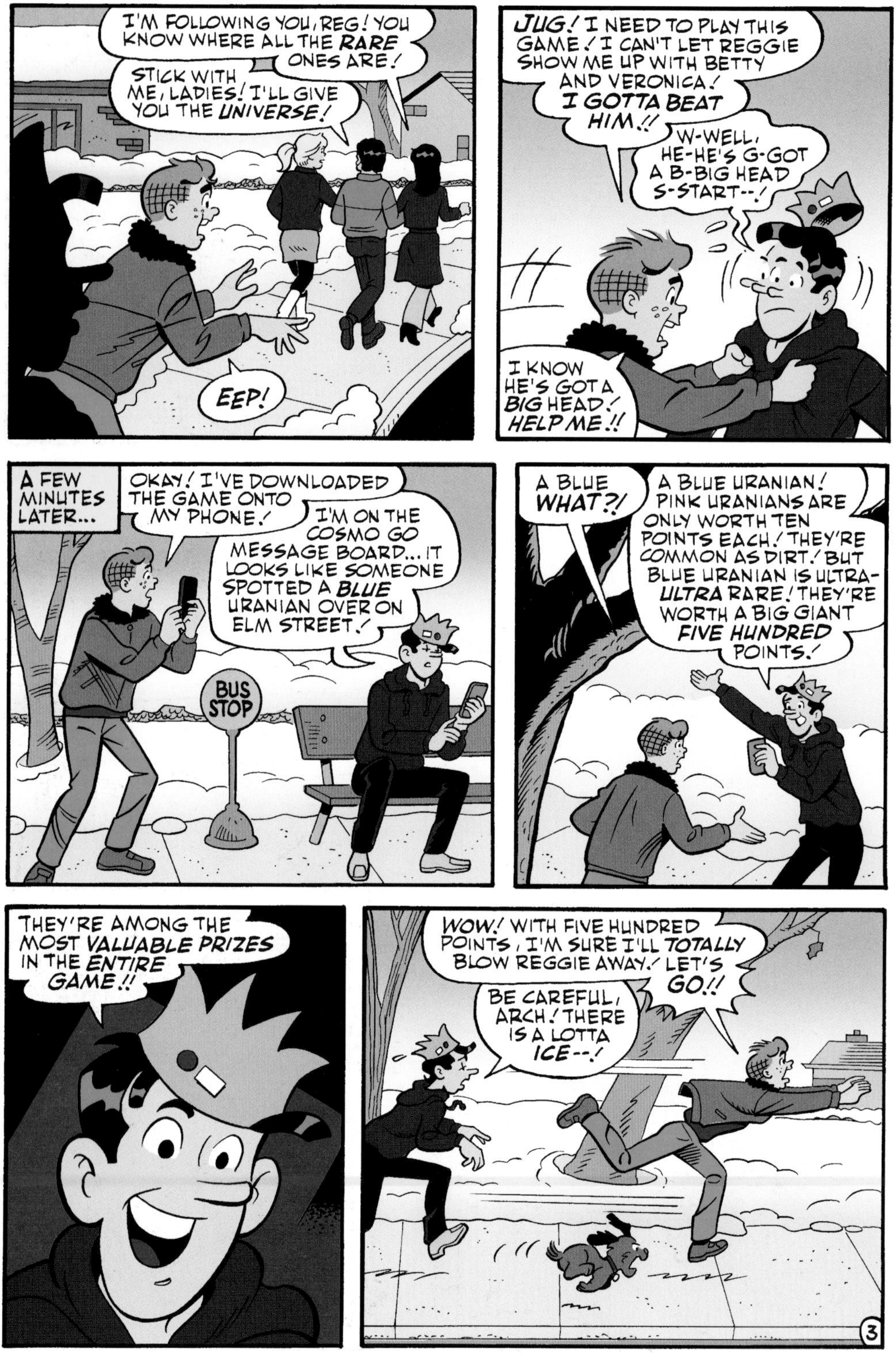
I'M FOLLOWING YOU, REG! YOU KNOW WHERE ALL THE RARE ONES ARE!
STICK WITH ME, LADIES! I'LL GIVE YOU THE UNIVERSE!
EEP!
JUG! I NEED TO PLAY THIS GAME! I CAN'T LET REGGIE SHOW ME UP WITH BETTY AND VERONICA! I GOTTA BEAT HIM!!
W-WELL, HE-HE'S G-GOT A B-BIG HEAD S-START--!
I KNOW HE'S GOT A BIG HEAD! HELP ME!!
A FEW MINUTES LATER...
OKAY! I'VE DOWNLOADED THE GAME ONTO MY PHONE!
I'M ON THE COSMO GO MESSAGE BOARD... IT LOOKS LIKE SOMEONE SPOTTED A BLUE URANIAN OVER ON ELM STREET!
BUS STOP
A BLUE WHAT?!
A BLUE URANIAN! PINK URANIANS ARE ONLY WORTH TEN POINTS EACH! THEY'RE COMMON AS DIRT! BUT BLUE URANIAN IS ULTRA-ULTRA RARE! THEY'RE WORTH A BIG GIANT FIVE HUNDRED POINTS!
THEY'RE AMONG THE MOST VALUABLE PRIZES IN THE ENTIRE GAME!!
WOW! WITH FIVE HUNDRED POINTS, I'M SURE I'LL TOTALLY BLOW REGGIE AWAY! LET'S GO!!
BE CAREFUL, ARCH! THERE IS A LOTTA ICE--!
3

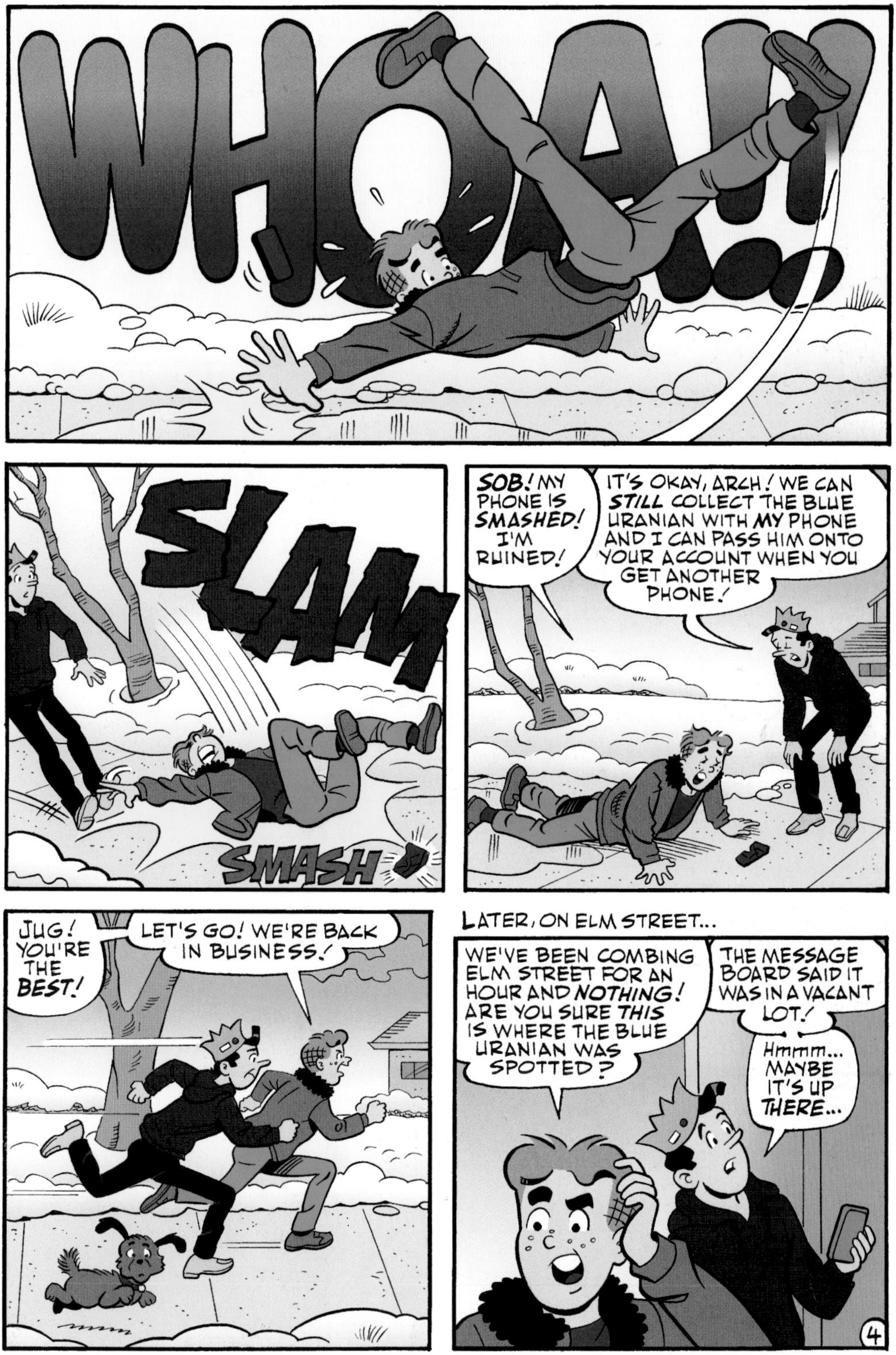
WHOA!!...
SLAM
SMASH
SOB! MY PHONE IS SMASHED! I'M RUINED!
IT'S OKAY, ARCH! WE CAN STILL COLLECT THE BLUE URANIAN WITH MY PHONE AND I CAN PASS HIM ONTO YOUR ACCOUNT WHEN YOU GET ANOTHER PHONE!
JUG! YOU'RE THE BEST!
LET'S GO! WE'RE BACK IN BUSINESS!
LATER, ON ELM STREET...
WE'VE BEEN COMBING ELM STREET FOR AN HOUR AND NOTHING! ARE YOU SURE THIS IS WHERE THE BLUE URANIAN WAS SPOTTED?
THE MESSAGE BOARD SAID IT WAS IN A VACANT LOT!
Hmmm... MAYBE IT'S UP THERE...
4

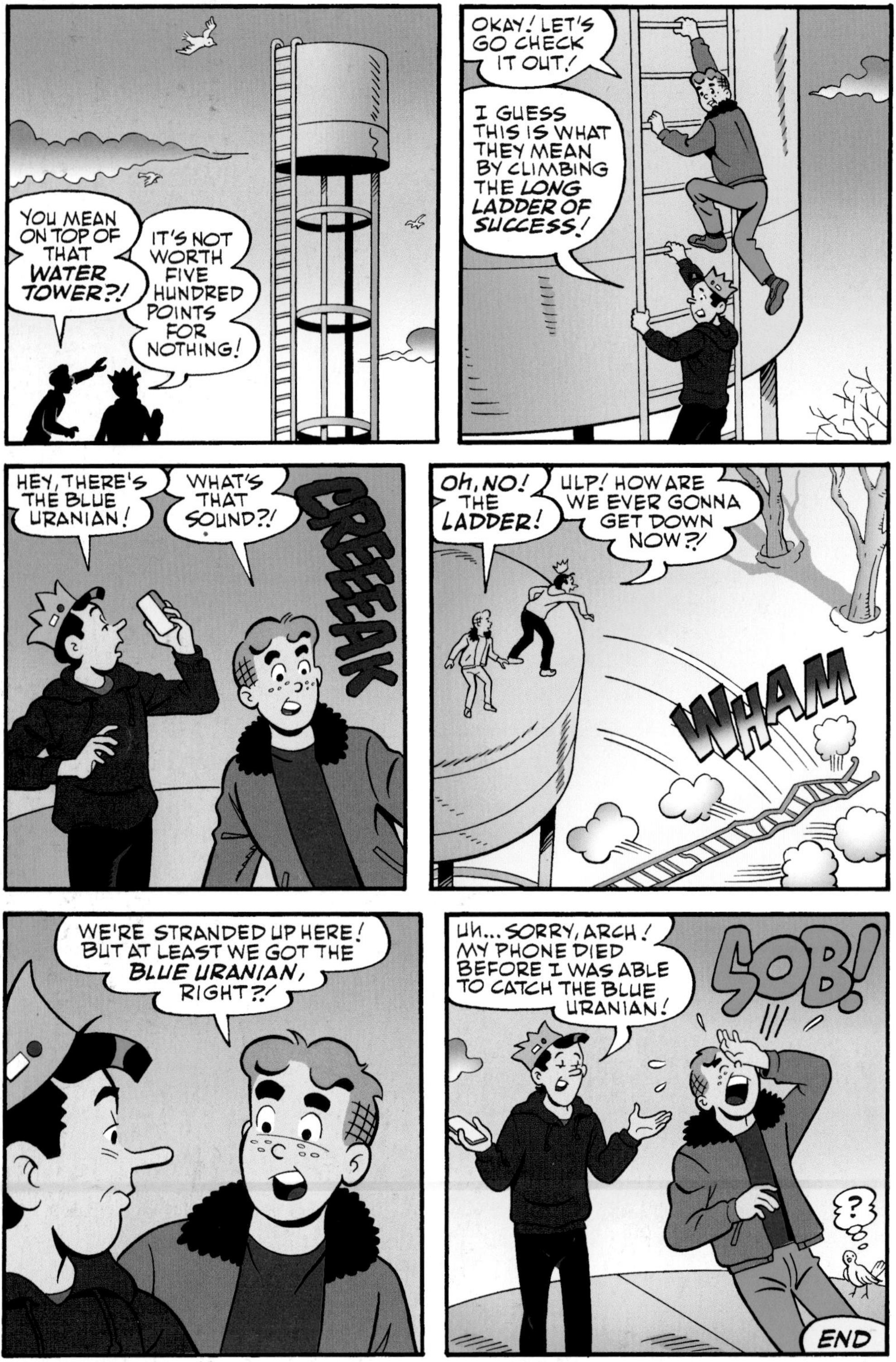
YOU MEAN ON TOP OF THAT WATER TOWER?!
IT'S NOT WORTH FIVE HUNDRED POINTS FOR NOTHING!
OKAY! LET'S GO CHECK IT OUT!
I GUESS THIS IS WHAT THEY MEAN BY CLIMBING THE LONG LADDER OF SUCCESS!
HEY, THERE'S THE BLUE URANIAN!
WHAT'S THAT SOUND?!
CREEEAK
OH, NO! THE LADDER!
ULP! HOW ARE WE EVER GONNA GET DOWN NOW?!
WHAM
WE'RE STRANDED UP HERE! BUT AT LEAST WE GOT THE BLUE URANIAN, RIGHT?!
UH... SORRY, ARCH! MY PHONE DIED BEFORE I WAS ABLE TO CATCH THE BLUE URANIAN!
SOB!
?
END

Archie & FRIENDS
COVER SKETCHES

Artists Jeff Shultz and Rosario "Tito" Peña worked together to produce the amazing covers for the *Archie and Friends* series. Shultz would send in his detailed pencil sketches and Tito would brighten them up with his expert coloring. Here you can see all the covers at both stages.

MUSIC JAM

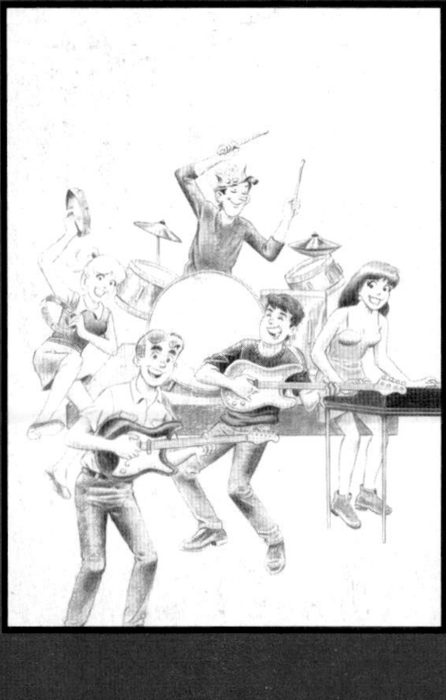

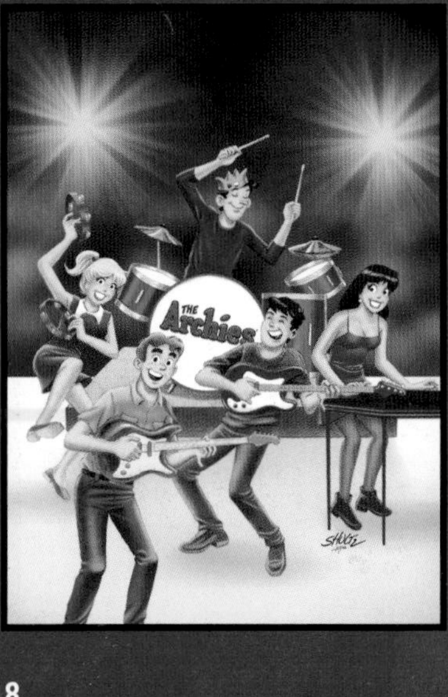
THE
Archies

BEACH PARTY

BACK TO SCHOOL

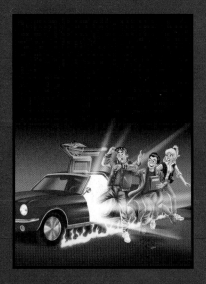

TRAVEL

WINTER WONDERLAND